SCARS:
The Archangels Saga Part I
By Joseph A. Haiflich

I0525523

This is for everyone who doesn't want to look back on their life in twenty years and say to themselves, "I wonder what would have happened..."

1

Ba'an stopped in front of the door to the High Commander's war room and tried to mentally prepare himself to stand in front of what has quite possibly become the single most successful and intimidating Gora of all time. Ba'an was about to be in the same room with a being that has been singly responsible for some of the most successful colonization and harvesting missions of any being in the Eiligor Empire. He has been responsible for supplying the organisms for almost fifty million Goraan annexations over the last five years. Ever since ascending to the rank of High Commander of the Second Fleet, he has rolled on like an unstoppable juggernaut, championing the cause of Imperial expansion. This new planet would not stand a chance against him. Ba'an slowly positioned himself in front of the door's sensors and spoke.

"Ba'an Vichen," he said in a shaky voice. "Your new secretary as designated from Imperial Command reporting as ordered, sir."

The Goraan were creatures that resembled large slugs. After living with this form for many centuries, they discovered that their own bodies were insufficient for continued existence. To compensate for this, they evolved a means to burrow their slug-like forms underneath another creature's skin. They would crawl up the creature's spine where they chewed out and replaced part of its brain. They called the process "annexing." The bodies they annexed were just shells. As far they were concerned, they were simply taking required property.

Ba'an had just moved his slug-like body slowly up the spine of his shell and chewed out its brain a few days ago. He was still fatigued by the annexing. Despite this, however, he had already been ordered to begin his new task as the secretary to the High Commander of the Goraan Second Colonization and Resource

Harvesting Combat Fleet. Ba'an's shell resembled a white octopus with legs.

"Enter," growled a deep, intimidating voice.

The door slid silently open. Ba'an entered the room as quietly as possible and stood near the entrance. Until now, he had only seen the inside of the High Commander's war room in holographic images. To the left side was a large door that was the entrance to the High Commander's personal quarters. Around the room were various other Goras of many different shapes and sizes going about menial tasks. The Goraan Empire had taken many races and planets since they started traveling the stars thousands of years ago. Despite the fact that all of these races posed some kind of resistance to the Empire, not one of them managed to defeat the Goraan effort to conquer them. Some came close, but in the end, all had fallen before the might of Eiligor. A few managed to escape but in doing so gave up their home worlds and lost most of their species to the Goraan. None had ever defeated the Imperial Fleets.

"Host," The High Commander growled. "Power On."

The High Commander hunched over the holographic view table flanked by his second-in-command who was also his best, and only friend. Four infantry Command units were seated around the table as well. As the High Commander hunched over the war table, the spines on his back protruded through his battle gear and jutted upward to slash at the air. They seemed to be nothing less than a jagged scaly, blue mountain range as he did this. Some of them had to be at least three feet in length. They were all colored red at the tips which made them appear even more grotesque. It was like they were on fire.

The computer startup hologram appeared above the table. The logo appeared to be a simple square flag waiving in a breeze. The flag was sectioned into four equal squares colored red, green, blue and yellow. It appeared every time the computer was started up.

"Thank you for choosing *Windows Ultima*: Invasion Force Edition," said the computer's feminine voice. "I look forward to serving you, High Commander."

"Host," said the High Commander. "Bring up the topographical representation of the planet designated, 'Erf,' along with its neighboring moon and the current location of the second fleet."

"Of course, High Commander," responded the computer.

An almost completely accurate hologram of this "Erf" planet appeared from the holo-projectors to hover above the table. It also showed the planet's moon and the fleet with all the moving vessels and fighters in between the twelve main battleships.

"Our current situation is as follows," said the High Commander to his second in command and the infantry commanders. "This is the planet 'Erf.' We have been assigned to discuss possible options regarding the planet's continued existence. On a personal note, from the reports that I have read I really have no respect for the dominate creatures of this planet. I am simply amazed by the fact that they have not managed to kill themselves off by now. We are here to consider options for pacification. These options include, but are not limited to: breeding, slave race, annexations, cellular reharvestation and death. The floor is open."

"If I may, High Commander Esham'aut, I believe it is pronounced 'Earth'," said the feathered Gora.

"What is that you say, Commander Doshan?" asked Esham'aut.

"The planet's name is pronounced 'Earth', sir," said Commander Doshan.

Doshan and Esham'aut had known each other since they were larvae. It was rumored that they committed their first genocide together. Doshan was High Commander Esham'aut's second in command. He was also in command of one of the fleet's twelve battleships. Commander Doshan was the only Gora ever allowed to correct Esham'aut. To anyone else, correcting the High Commander privately meant a severe beating. If done in public, it meant death.

"Earth, you say, old friend?" chuckled Esham'aut. "I would call it target practice."

Doshan chuckled slightly at Esham'aut's joke.

"Well, do you have anything useful to say?" Esham'aut asked as he cut off the laughter.

Commander Doshan motioned as he spoke, "My staff has been conducting research on the planet and its occupants. I have submitted my report through proper channels, but allow me to highlight some of the more interesting parts."

"Excellent," rumbled Esham'aut. "Please continue."

"To begin with, the planet itself is rich in resources for such a small rock. It is definitely worth harvesting the planet," he explained. "The dominate species however, is inferior to every other known species in the universe. They are even smaller and weaker than that little white secretary over there. They call themselves 'Hoo-mans.' They are constantly at war with each other somewhere on the planet's surface."

"I read the report from your science officers, Commander. It mostly entailed personal specifications of the species," explained the High Commander. "I skipped over their form of government after I read the highlights of their meager technological achievements."

"They are rather backward, are they not?" mused Doshan. "What did you expect from this planet? After all, the rest of the universe has been dumping their toxic and chemical waste products on that planet for millions of years. The creatures that formed are nothing more than the by-products of interstellar trash. They are truly nothing more than genetic garbage!" laughed Commander Doshan. "They cannot even function as proper shells. Their bodies are too toxic of an environment for us."

"Well Doshan, I suggest we depopulate the planet and then send the rock back home to the mining yard to be stripped of resources," replied Esham'aut.

"As Executive Officer of the Goraan Second Colonization and Resource Harvesting Combat Fleet, I officially agree," said Commander Doshan.

"Good," said Esham'aut. "I shall send recommendations back to Imperial High Command. Have you given thought toward the depopulation sequence?"

"Not entirely, High Commander. I do suggest, however, that we assign at least six battleships in the second fleet to hold the planet together though," said Doshan thoughtfully.

"My thoughts exactly," agreed the High Commander. "We will place all ships in high orbit around the planet. Once there, ships three through eight will envelope the planet with their magnetic stabilization fields to hold the mass together. After that, our two vessels will fire high intensity thermo-rays into the polar ice masses. This will cause them to melt and flood the oceans, which should envelope most, if not all, of the land mass. After this, ships nine and ten will join us in directing the next phase of heat blasts into the oceans until all the water and atmosphere has evaporated off. Upon completion of the second wave of heat blasts, ships eleven and twelve will fire a full spread of thermo torpedoes that have been set to explode on the planet's surface to burn off the top layer of surface crust. In the last phase, all ships will join the magnetic stabilization field which we will reconfigure to dissipate the heat out from the planet so that the core will freeze and solidify. After all, we can harvest a lot of iron from that core. Then we will section it up and open a gate to the Imperial mining yards. We can then push the dead rock through for the Empire to harvest at its leisure."

"This is a good plan, High Commander," said Doshan.

"Yes," agreed the High Commander. "Are there any other matters of importance to discuss?"

"Our intelligence network reports that there are 'Runners' in the area," said Commander Doshan.

"How?" bellowed Esham'aut. "They have no ships!"

"Apparently a large group of them managed to somehow steal four old battleships, a large number of support vessels, some smaller combat ships and a little over four thousand fighter ships from various fleet recycling yards," explained Doshan offhandedly. "They overrode the decommissioned ships' security measures and made off with them. Not before they took heavy losses, however."

"Good," said Esham'aut. "I have not been given the opportunity to have a decent battle in quite some time. We will make those blasted Runners pay! It serves them right for running away and not dying with honor like the rest of their races."

"Infantry Command!" the High Commander bellowed at the four combat robots that commanded the infantry. "Place all combat robots on high level alert. Staff all troop transports and await my command. We most likely will not need them, but we should be prepared for any case."

"Yes, sir," they snapped to attention while they spoke in unison.

"Good day, Goras. Leave me with my secretary now. I need to send word to Imperial High Command," said Esham'aut.

The four infantry Commanders left through the entrance into the hallway. Commander Doshan made his leave into the High Commander's personal chambers. As High Commander Esham'aut's counselors left the room, he foresaw no possible resistance that the feeble creatures of this planet could possibly present to the mighty Goraan war machine.

"Secretary!" snapped the High Commander. "Secretary, come here and take this down to send back to Eiligor."

"You have a message for the home world, High Commander?" asked the secretary in a shaky voice.

"Secretary, what is that shell you have annexed? I believe I have never seen the like?" asked the Commander.

"I was not as fortuitous as you, great High Commander," explained the secretary wryly. "After I finished my training a few days ago and it was time for me to annex a shell, all that was available was this pathetic creature," he complained. "I am not even sure what it is or where it came from. How pathetic!"

"Secretary, after you are done here, schedule yourself for a severe beating! It is not your place to complain about your lot in life!" he yelled at the secretary. "You think I am lucky to have annexed this creature? There are many luxuries my shell does not have! My body's superior size and strength may be well suited for a combat warrior, but it is very ill suited more subtle tasks. Do I complain, though?" growled the Commander. "No! I do not, because it is not my place to complain! You should feel lucky that a shell was found for you in time and we did not need to slate your cells for reharvestation!"

The floor plates rumbled under the foot falls of the High Commander as he approached his secretary. Ba'an stood in fear. He looked up slightly at the High Commander. For the first time Ba'an realized exactly how much larger the High Commander was than he.

"Stop complaining!" grated the Commander as he back handed the secretary. "You will never be more than someone else's servant if you spend your life complaining!"

"Ye-yes sir," stammered the secretary.

"Now stop all this whining and take this down. Send the following message back to Eiligor High Command:" said the Commander. "I have finished surveying planet 8793.12 orbiting the yellow star in galactic section 3562 mark 8 of the galaxy designated 314.6. The local intelligent species has designated the planet as 'Earth.' The superior beings of this planet are absolutely useless to us. Their genetic chain is too simplistic to support the complex additions required to make them decent shells in order to perpetuate our species. The females may be useful for breeding if we can find a way to make them support our more complex and highly evolved genetic chain. They can actually survive many more birth processes as opposed to only one or two as we have encountered with our Breeders. The males of this planet are, to put it bluntly, completely useless. I cannot see that they could serve any useful purpose to us whatsoever."

"The species overall, is puny, weak, breaks easily, and cannot even be made into descent house pets," he continued. "Their communications consist of primitive vocal processes and some sort of unspoken bodily gestures. In fact, they have not even advanced far enough into their development to achieve a unified language. They spend more time fighting among themselves than any other species I have encountered to date. I can honestly say that this is the first species that I have encountered that can quite possibly be considered to be its own greatest cause of unnatural death. They seem to embody the very worst combination of traits that any species can have. They are primitive, war-like, and technologically inferior. They spend so much time fighting amongst themselves, in fact, that whenever they discover a new piece of technology, they immediately try and see how they can use this new knowledge to kill each other. The only strength they have is their ability to breed. They do so incredibly quickly and multiple times during the course of one creature's life time. They could easily overpower us through population alone if they managed to stop fighting amongst themselves long enough to do so. I do not feel that this will pose a threat, though, because their hatred for each other runs so deep, that I doubt they would ever consider this option."

"As for the planet itself," he went on. "It is equally pathetic for colonization purposes. The planet can only support very specific life forms that can tolerate its peculiarly mixed atmosphere. Aside from that, it is covered for the most part with very impure water. Because of its impurity the water is useless and even potentially dangerous to us. Hoo-mans, however, not only seem to need it to survive, but also seem to take great pleasure in going to large sand covered areas called 'beaches' and playing in the water for recreation. I do not seem to understand this fixation because according to our sampling, their water carries a great amount of germs and other hazards by our standards. The planet does however, have an abnormally large amount resources available to harvest for a planet this small. My final suggestion: mark the creatures of this planet for cleansing. After this, slate the planet itself to be stripped of resources and destroyed in the name of the Empire."

"Sign it from Gr'Nach Esham'aut," he concluded. "High Commander of the Goraan Second Colonization and Resource Harvesting Combat Fleet."

"Did you get all of that, secretary?" asked Esham'aut.

"Yes sir," squeaked the secretary.

"Good," replied the Commander. "Now leave me....and don't forget to schedule your beating. Return here after lunch, in case I need you for some menial task."

***

The High Commander left the war room for his private chambers. He found Doshan sitting on the far side of the ocheck game board. The board was in a checkered pattern of green and yellow squares. On one end sat two rows of yellow pieces and on the other sat two rows of green pieces. The various pieces were of different sizes and shapes, each moved according to specific rules. The entire game set was made from a very fragile crystal and all the pieces were carved to be very intricate and detailed.

"Host," said the Commander, "raise anti-listening field around my personal chambers."

"Yes, High Commander," replied the computer.

"Are we starting to get a bit paranoid, my old friend?" asked Doshan.

"I have heard things through my intelligence network," said Esham'aut sitting down at the head of the green pieces and making the first move. "It appears that some of my own Commanders aided the 'Runners' in their missions to steal ships. They were given quite a bit of wealth to do so, from what I am told."

"Will you bring them up on charges, Esham'aut?" asked Doshan making his first move.

"I have no solid proof to bring before the Imperial Council," explained Esham'aut. "All I have are the words of some rather disreputable Goras. All the stories match, however, which leads me to believe them."

"Which Commanders are suspect?" asked Doshan.

"All save you, old friend," replied Esham'aut.

"Why not just have them killed and be done with it? I am sure you can make up some fictitious acts of treason or something," responded Doshan.

"No, I could not do that, Doshan," said Esham'aut. "These men may have plotted against me, but they also have friends in high places among the Imperial Government."

The game went on for hours. The two players were excellent strategists. They have known each other for years, and were familiar with the play style of their opponent. Finally, Doshan saw an opening and moved his piece to place the green Emperor in defeat.

"Well played, Doshan, I did not even see that on the board," exclaimed Esham'aut.

"When we do not pay attention, accidents will happen," said Doshan quietly, "Perhaps our traitorous Commanders will have some accidents in the near future."

"Perhaps this was an exceptionally good game, Doshan....Yes, I believe that accidents do happen at times," responded Esham'aut with an evil grin.

***

The leader of the Runner fleet was Admiral Mihanna so'Chareck Mihanna. He was a slender Kashin with long black cat-like tail and black cat-like features complete with small retractable claws in his fingertips. He was chosen because he was the best strategist they could find amongst the Runners. The

Kashin were a very emotional race. This was most evident by the look of worry on the Admiral's face while he thought about the upcoming mission. He sat in his council chambers at a round table in the center of the room. The Captains of the other five battle ships and the three Commanders of the infantry were there with him. There were four Kashin amongst the eight of them. The Kashin made up the bulk of the population of Runners.

The Kashin totaled around two million among the Runners numbers. Only two million Kashin were left in the entire universe. Two million were left alive out of the nine billion from their home. Their home planet was now part of the Goraan Empire. All those left behind were either now serving as shells for the Goraan, or their cells were harvested for use. The Kashin knew all too well the might and efficiency of the legendary Goraan Fleets.

"Host," started the Admiral. "Power on."

The computer turned on and the holo-projectors showed the boot hologram above the table. It appeared to be a flag sectioned into four equal squares colored red, green, blue and yellow at the four corners.

"Thank you for using *Windows Ultima*: Runners Edition," said the accompanying cheerful female voice. "How may I serve you, Admiral?"

"Host," said the Admiral. "Bring up a topographical representation of the Earth, its moon and our fleet in relation to them."

Everyone was silent as the map came up from the holo-projectors. There was a definite feeling of impending doom that hovered like a fog in the room. The silence seemed to go on forever as everyone looked at the map until the Admiral spoke.

"Brothers," began Mihanna. "Is there any way we can save this planet at all? I know that the humans are not worth much as a species, but it would be a great moral victory for our side if we could stop them from being annihilated."

"We have investigated this option, Brother Admiral," said an orange Kashin. "But we can see no way of defeating the Imperial Fleet. They out-number us two to one, or maybe more, and their ships are the latest models in the Empire. At best we can hold them off while we evacuate some of the humans."

"I see. Thank you, Captain," responded the Admiral.

"We have been discussing the operation sir, and have formed a plan," said the Captain. "We will keep our cloaks engaged and fly into the Earth's atmosphere. Timing will be crucial as the troop carriers do not yet have functional cloaking abilities. As a result, as soon as they leave the hanger bays, the Goraan will spot them. The most likely response will be for them to send in the fighters and the infantry. We have decided not to send any infantry into the fray. This will clear more cargo space so we can evacuate even more humans in the troop ships as well as the freighters. We will most likely have time for two or maybe three runs before we need to escape the on-setting wave of fighters and the arrival of the main battle ships. We will be able to save about three hundred to five hundred thousand humans from various parts of the planet."

"Any idea how we are going to house them during flight?" asked one of the Captains.

"We will build multi-tiered temporary rooms in all the cargo bays of the main ships," he stated. "The rest we will pack into the troop carriers, cruisers, frigates and destroyers as necessary. We will even cram two or three humans in the fighters if we have to. Let us just get as many as we can. After this we will have to jump back to base before they can get a good lock on us to track our travel to safety. Please put some thought tonight as to how we might cover our escape."

"I certainly hope these humans prove to be worth it," said the orange Captain.

"I have put some study to them, Brother," said another Captain. "They are physically of an equal average size and shape as we Kashin. They possess two arms and legs like Kashin. They even have similar body functions and reproduction as we have. Their DNA chain, however, is very simplistic compared to ours and they are not very technologically advanced."

"Can these creatures be of any use to us, Admiral?" said the fish like Captain.

"That remains to be seen," replied Mihanna with a shrug. "At any rate Brothers, this plan seems to be the best we can do for these humans. Everyone rest tonight, because my ship's intelligence center intercepted a message from Goraan Imperial

Headquarters. They will commence positioning themselves and start depopulation of Earth in twenty four hours. I will inform the advisory council of my findings and our suggestions. In the mean time, we should position ourselves to move accordingly to counter act the Goraan. Rest well, Brothers. You are dismissed."

***

Morgan Mendenhall was sitting in his recreational vehicle with his family. It was parked in a small camp ground near Houston, Texas. Morgan was six feet tall and weighed around two hundred pounds. He had a thick head of curly brown hair and a matching thick brown beard. He had glasses which he only wore when reading. He was in his late twenties and had been married since he was eighteen. He was one of those guys that had the intelligence within him to do anything. He was bright enough to be able find a cure for cancer or discover a limitless energy source if he chose to do so. Instead, however, he traveled around in a recreational vehicle with his small family. He made a living designing and testing roller coasters for theme parks. It was much more fun than cancer research. At times, all the traveling was stressful but he enjoyed the experience overall. It gave him ample time to spend with his wife and daughter, whom they were home schooling.

Keri, his young daughter, was intently watching "Tangled" on her iPad for what possibly amounted to the three hundredth time that week. He and his wife, Alexandria, were relaxing and playing chess, as they often did.

Keri was very petite ten year old girl. She had blonde hair and blue eyes like her mother. It was curly, though like her father's hair. Alexandria was the same age as Morgan. She was tall and slim with a good physique and nice curves. Like her daughter, she had thick blonde hair. Her bluish eyes were large and trusting.

Morgan towered over both his wife and daughter. He had very broad shoulders and thick arms and legs. He could easily pass for a bar room bouncer, which contradicted his intellectual nature. His green eyes were the type that could look right through someone's soul.

"So anyway," Morgan was saying on his cell phone. "I told this guy not to run it that fast and he was just set on not listening to me."

"What kind of stupidity is that?" asked the voice on the other end. "Who ignores the man that actually designed the damn roller coaster? Tell that dumb bastard that while he has his head that far up his ass, he should probably start looking for his park insurance. He'll probably need it. That goes to exceed every bit of stupidness I have ever heard. It reaches an entirely new and heretofore unseen level of complete stupidity."

"Wait, wait," said Morgan as he laughed, "That's not the good part, Flea. While I wasn't on park grounds, he went ahead and started the ride up at the speed he wanted."

Flea was an old friend of Morgan's since childhood.

"Shit!" said Flea. "Was anyone on it? Did anybody get hurt or anything like that? Dude, did you get it on your phone? Tell me you got that! That needs get on you tube! Send me the file!"

Flea was not the most reputable of characters. However, he and Morgan had been close friends for many years.

"No," laughed Morgan. "No one was on it. But it jumped the track and went careening through two of the park's other rides and destroyed them both! Now I have to redesign the other two as well!"

"Cool," said Flea. "I'll have to jet down for the new rides when you're done."

"That's cool," said Morgan. "We'll clear a spot on the floor for you."

Flea and Morgan went on chatting about what was going on in their lives at that point in time until they hung up at the frustrations of a bad cell phone connection. They didn't have the opportunity to get together as much as they did when they were kids, but they still spoke whenever they could. Morgan felt very close to Flea. They were like brothers. Physical differences aside, the two were very much alike. Who was actually the bad influence between the two of them was something that neither of them had ever really figured out. Most people who knew them would say it was Flea.

Morgan and Alexandria were both involved in the game at hand. He straightened his back and cracked the vertebrae in his neck with a jerk of his head. His spine in his neck popped out loud, before he bent his head back down to his task.

"Ugh, gross," complained Alexandria. "That's sick. Don't pop your neck like that. You'll get arthritis when you're old."

With that, she started informing him of what would happen if he continued to crack his neck throughout his life. They went back to playing and chatting, as couples do, while finishing their game.

***

A young man was sitting in front of his television late at night in the mid-sized city of Fort Wayne, Indiana in the United States. It was a cool Monday night at the beginning of summer at ten forty five. He was five feet eight inches tall and weighed one hundred sixty five pounds. He sat on the floor and stared intently at the television screen while he played his Xbox 360. He had short, straight brown hair which he hid under a black cotton baseball hat with the word *Pornstar* written on it. His goatee matched his brown hair. His eyes were also brown and at the moment were completely focused on the television screen as he played *Dead or Alive: Extreme 2*. The entire point of this game was to watch girls in bikinis. There wasn't anything more complex about it. No strategy. No tactics. No firearms. It was all about volleyball, mini-games and bikinis. It wasn't the newest game out, but it was rendered nicely. For what this young man looked like, he could easily pass as any average guy walking down the street anywhere in the world. He had one of those faces that seemed to look familiar to people, but they couldn't remember where it was they saw him. He could pass for anyone and no-one all at the same time.

His name was "Flea." It was a nick-name he picked up somewhere, but had lost the reason why. The name seemed to go with him wherever he went whether he mentioned it or not. He had been called this now for so long that he even referred to himself by this name in his own head. It had become so much a part of him that he rarely responded to his real name unless he was talking to his family. He wasn't exactly large, but he wasn't exactly small. He wasn't in particularly great physical shape, but he wasn't in bad shape either. His average appearance and easy nature belied his intelligence. Flea often tried to hide this fact. He didn't enjoy standing out. The military taught him to always do his best in everything he did simply because it was the right thing to do. Recognition for doing so bothered him and made him feel awkward.

He was in his mid twenties, and had been playing video games since he was a kid. He even had his Xbox with him while he was in Iraq as a Marine. On this particular day, Flea had been playing for about fourteen hours straight. This wasn't the first time, nor would it be the last that he played this many hours at once. When he was a young boy, he used to be able to play for hours on end stopping only for bathroom breaks and food.

As he sat and played he thought about this and remembered many times when he and his best friend growing up would be playing for seemingly days on end. Sometimes they stayed up for several days straight just to keep playing. They played combat simulators, strategy games and fighting games. Almost anything they could get their hands on they were willing to try.

That was many years ago, however, and the only things that have changed since then are the games and technology available to play with. Even his best friend, a man named Morgan whom he had known since he was five years old, remained the same person. Morgan may have a wife and child now and lived in a different place, but he was still relatively the same. He was also still Flea's best friend. If Morgan had changed over the years, Flea had changed at the same time, and probably in the same ways.

At this moment, all that concerned Flea was the game in front him. He pushed all the reminiscent thoughts from his mind and concentrated on the task. The game may not have been very difficult, but he had put a lot of hours into it, and wanted to win the current volleyball match before bed. Failure has never been something he dealt with very well. Some people can be described as having the ability to lose gracefully. He was not one of them. Flea did not believe in second place. He was either winning, or not winning. Not winning sucked and second place was the top rated loser. He looked forward to seeing Morgan at the end of the month. He had been issued a few challenges by some local players and he and Morgan together were almost entirely unbeatable.

Eventually he looked at the clock and realized that time had continued on, as it inevitably does. It reached three thirty in the morning.

"I need to get to bed," he muttered. "I hate going to class."

Flea had class in the morning at one of the local colleges. One of the classes was American history and the other was a philosophy class. He hated them both. They were a necessary evil to attain his degree from IPFW so he could move out of Fort Wayne. He preferred somewhere with a nice beach. Maybe he would go to Florida.

After a while, Flea decided it was time to shut off the Xbox and call it a night. He had to go to class in the morning, despite how much he didn't like it. Philosophy was his first class, which he had an extreme distaste for. At least the girls in class were cute. Sometimes, that made it more tolerable.

2

Ba'an Vichen awoke the next morning to painful sores on his back. He had scheduled his beating as instructed by the High Commander. He was still not pleased with the shell that was selected for him. He supposed he should get used to the body. Now that he was joined the only way out of this damnable shell was death.

He had experienced many new sensations since he gained his shell. Pain was new to him. In a way, he was very intrigued by this feeling of pain. This was the first time he experienced pain. The joining made him tired, but for his part in it, it wasn't actually painful. During the beating he found himself in a state that he could only describe as some type of heightened arousal. He felt some sort of rush as he expected the Inquisitor's whip to strike him one more time. When the Ship's Inquisitor would raise her whip appendages and hesitate for a brief moment, he found that his excitement would grow with the anticipation. He experienced an odd sort of pleasure in being beaten. If he had lips instead of a small black beak he would have smiled as he made the mental decision that he would schedule another beating for a few days after he properly healed. The pain made him feel somehow stronger and more secure. He did not scurry down the passage way toward the High Commander's war room as he had yesterday. This morning, his stubby legs carried him at a more confident and stately pace.

Ba'an approached the war room again and prepared himself for another meeting with the High Commander. He squared himself in front of the door's sensors and straightened his back so he might seem taller. He was slightly aware of the pain from his wounds as the rough fabric of his uniform scratched across his flesh. His knees trembled a bit with pleasure, causing him to stop and refocus his thoughts before he spoke.

"Ba'an Vichen, secretary to the High Commander, reporting for duty," he said.

The door slid silently open. As he entered, the room was empty except for the two guards standing at the High Commander's personal chambers.

"Esham'aut," he thought. *"His name is only Gr'Nach Esham'aut. This is how I will think of him, only as Esham'aut."*

He would never call Esham'aut by his name out loud. However, Ba'an found that the High Commander seemed less intimidating if he was thought of as simply Esham'aut.

He looked around the room and spotted his station on the other side of the round war table. He walked over and sat down at the small seat that someone, most likely not Esham'aut, had put there for him.

"Host," he said. "Power On."

The familiar logo appeared on the screen in front of him as the computer's voice chimed in,

"Thank you for using *Windows Ultima*: Invasion Force Edition, How may I serve you, secretary Vichen?" it replied.

"Show my communiqués for the morning," he replied.

"Yes, Mr. Secretary," replied the computer.

The computer pulled the list of messages that Ba'an received that night. There was only a single message. It was from the Imperial War Council to the personal Secretary of High Commander Gr'Nach Esham'aut of the Goraan Second Colonization and Resource Harvesting Combat Fleet.

"Please open and read the message the Imperial War Council," said Ba'an.

"Yes, Mr. Secretary," replied the computer.

"Goraan Second Colonization and Resource Harvesting Combat Fleet, we received your transmission and have reviewed your statement along with the attached plan in regard to the 'Earth' planet," said the computer as it read the communiqué. "We see no fault in your plan, and can find no purpose for this 'Earth' planet's continued existence. It holds no strategic value and its creatures are not fit for use. Their cells are most likely too simplistic and will not serve us for reharvestation purposes. Feel free to wipe these feeble creatures from existence."

"Be forewarned," continued the computer. "We have confirmed rumors of a fleet of Runners to be in the same area. Feel free to adjust the time line of your plans accordingly. Engage and destroy them with extreme prejudice. It would be a shame for the High Commander of the mighty Goraan Second Colonization and Resource Harvesting Combat Fleet to besmirch his otherwise spotless and exemplary record by allowing these Runners to enjoy continued existence. If the High Commander of the Second Fleet cannot dispatch this feeble mob of mismatched and stolen vessels, it may become an issue for his next advancement. We suggest that the High Commander treat this situation with the utmost importance, or we may be forced to find someone who can. We are positive that the High Commander is aware of how much the presence of this rabble upsets our delicate young Emperor."

"The communiqué is signed from the Secretary to the Goraan Imperial Council of War and Strategic Command," finished the computer.

Ba'an saw the words: *Urgent, inform High Commander immediately* written in the subject line of the transmission. After seeing this and reading the message, Ba'an decided not to run off and inform the High Commander immediately as the subject line instructed.

"Instead," he thought, *"I think I will wait to tell the High Commander. Perhaps by doing this, he may tell me to schedule another delicious beating."*

He found his knees started to tremble again as he thought of experiencing more joyous pain.

***

Mihanna so'Chareck Mihanna awoke that morning to the tranquil sounds of running water and the familiar smell of the woods. He was very lucky to have enough space in his personal quarters to have a proper place of rest. It was complete with a nice tree that had a thick trunk in the center or the room. His personal quarters were designed to simulate the tranquility of the woods on his home world. No matter how much he enjoyed the place he had turned his sleeping quarters into, he was painfully reminded it was only a facsimile by the metallic, grey ceiling. The birds, the sound of the rushing water and even the smells were all generated by computer. No matter how accurate they may have been, they still seemed somehow cheap and manufactured when compared to the real thing. He longed to liberate his planet from the Goraan before it suffered a fate similar to that which was in the Earth planet's near future.

He hopped down from the tree branch he was sleeping in and counted himself lucky. Most of the two million Kashin among the runners did not have a proper tree to sleep in. He went into the adjoining kitchen. The floor was covered with a thick green grass, like the main chamber, that brushed between his toes. He stretched briefly and started preparing breakfast.

"Host," he said. "Power On."

The screen was in the main room in the tree, but he could still communicate with it through the room's sensors.

"Thank you for using *Windows Ultima*: Runners Edition. How may I help you, Admiral?" asked the computer.

"You may start by making breakfast, please," he replied. "Then, read transmissions from the advisory council, if there are any."

"The following three messages were received by the advisory council," responded the computer. "I will read them in the order they were received. Fish for breakfast, Admiral?"

"That will be fine, host," replied Mihanna. "Start breakfast and continue with the transmissions, please."

"First transmission reads as follows," started the computer. "Admiral Mihanna, the advisory council deliberating on the subject of the 'Earth situation' is pleased at your apparent efficiency and knowledge of the circumstances. We have decided that the risk is acceptable. Try and save some of these human creatures. Despite their apparent deficiencies as a species and their overall inferior standing, it would be a great moral victory if we could keep the Goraan from accomplishing all of their goals. It would be cause for much celebration. We look forward to your inevitable success."

"It is signed with the official seal of the Advisory Council for Population Control," finished the computer.

"The what?" asked Mihanna incredulously as he pulled his breakfast from the matter combiner.

"The Advisory Council for Population Control," said the computer. "The seal appears to be many different species holding hands, tentacles or their personal equivalent surrounding the Runners hidden space station."

"It probably took them a week just to decide on a seal," snorted Mihanna as he ate.

"Two weeks, three days, thirteen hours and thirty six minutes," responded the computer.

"Incidentally, is the Council for Population Control still a legal advisory body?" asked Mihanna.

It was a very pertinent question. The Runners "government" formed and disbanded councils more frequently than most creatures changed clothes.

"No, it was disbanded and all decisions made by it were rescinded shortly after 01:30 last night," replied the computer.

"Next message, please," said Mihanna in between bites of shell fish.

"Dear Admiral," began the computer. "Your efforts and expertise as a strategist are sincerely appreciated. We understand how hard you worked to prepare to save the lives of some of these wretched human creatures. However, it has been decided after much deliberation that they are not worth the risk. The potential for loss among the Runners is unacceptable. Perhaps if the humans offered some sort of strategic advantage to help protect the various Runner species we might deem a few of them worth salvaging. However, given the potential danger involved with the second Goraan fleet in the area, and the fact that humans are inherently an inferior species, we are ordering you to stand down the current mission. Do not to attempt to save any humans."

"The transmission," continued the computer, "is signed with the seal of the Advisory Council for Peace. The seal is a picture of a Runner Ship flying over a field of wild flowers."

"The advisory council for what?" he questioned in a loud and astonished voice.

Mihanna was trying not to choke on his breakfast.

"Peace, Admiral," responded the computer.

"We actually have a council that believes we can have peace with the Goraan?" inquired Mihanna. "This is going too far!"

"Is the Council for Peace still in effect or has it been disbanded?" asked Mihanna.

"Please," thought Mihanna, *"say it has been disbanded."*

"It was ordered disbanded and all decisions made by it were rescinded at 02:45 last night," responded the computer.

"This is ridiculous," said Mihanna. "If someone doesn't pull us together soon, we will all end up in some horrid Goraan reharvestation chamber. Read the final transmission, Host."

"Dear Admiral," began the letter. "Please move forward with the mission to save as many humans as possible. The order is signed with the seal of the Advisory Council for War. The seal is a large red 'R' in front of a planet."

"That was short," said the Admiral, "Is the council for war still a legally established body?" asked Mihanna.

"Yes," replied the computer.

Mihanna sighed for a moment after he finished his meal. He thought for a moment as a sly smile spread across his face.

"Hold all communications from Runners Command until after the mission for planet Earth," He grinned. "Reply to any transmission with an automatic courtesy response that reads as follows: As Admiral of the Runner Fleet, I thank you for your concern in the affairs of the military. However, I am presently a very busy individual with the current endeavors of the fleet. Please forgive me if I am not able to promptly return correspondence to your transmission. Take heart that I am sure your orders and concerns are only in the best interest of the fleet and aimed at the well being of all Runners."

"Sign the Automatic transmission: Mihanna so'Chareck Mihanna, Admiral of the Runner Fleet," he finished.

Mihanna returned to the main chamber. There was a mirror behind the tree in the back of the room. The wall slid open as he walked toward the mirror to reveal his closet. He pulled out his uniform and glanced briefly at the insignia of the Admiral of the Runner Fleet.

"Admiral of the Runners," he thought sadly. *"These creatures could not unify long enough to decide what to have for dinner."*

"Stop that!" he said out loud. "These creatures are looking to you to lead their fleet. Let the politicians play their politics."

"Perhaps by saving some of these humans, they will see that they can make a difference and decide to stop arguing," he thought. *"Or perhaps that is too much to hope for."*

***

It was nine o'clock in the morning on the surface of Planet Earth in Houston, Texas. Alexandria and Keri had gotten up early and forced Morgan out of bed so they could ride some of the rides in the park before he began working. The sun was shining, the sky was blue and it seemed like the day was perfect for a good coaster and a warm breeze. It was nice being here. They were allowed in the park before anyone else this morning. They had the whole place to themselves for a while. Despite how gorgeous the day was, Morgan found himself looking up toward the sky and feeling as though something terrible was about to happen. He shook his head to try and rid himself of the bad feeling. He scooped Keri up in his arms and started carrying the little girl on his shoulders.

"Let's go on that one next!" she said excitedly. "It has three loops in it!"

"I know, sweetie," Morgan sounded slightly proud. "That one is one of mine."

***

Shriek! Shriek! Shriek!

Flea briefly opened one eye.

"Ass....clock....morning....stupid," he mutter as he looked at the clock with its alarm going off. "This is sooo wrong."

Shriek! Shriek! Shriek!

Flea's arm struck faster than an angry cobra. It slammed against the face of the clock and sent it flying across the room. It shattered when it hit the wall.

"Goddamn clock," he muttered.

That was the third clock this week. Flea went back to sleep.

***

High Commander Gr'Nach Esham'aut had finished his morning meal to sustain his shell. He faced and annihilated five captured humans in the combat pit this morning in lieu of his regular workout. He felt a bit disappointed as they did not turn out to be quite the workout he had hoped for. He faced them all at once. In armed combat they proved to be less than adequate adversaries. He stood almost three times taller than any of them, and was much, much stronger. They were truly as weak and fragile as all the reports he had read claimed them to be. Perhaps they were more challenging in greater numbers.

It was mid-day. After cleaning up from his workout, he donned his Imperial Battle Gear that bared his insignia of rank. His personal standard was on his chest underneath the Emperor's standard. His purple cape, which was different than a regular officer's red cape, denoted that he was appointed to his position directly by the Emperor. This made him the subject of much jealousy from the other Commanders and many members of the Imperial Senate. Many would love to see him fail in such a simple task as destroying the human-creatures and transporting the dead Earth-planet to the mining field. It could make him forever fall out of the Emperor's good grace. Any chance for advancement would be lost. He finished dressing and entered the war room which adjoined his private chambers.

"One day," he said to himself, "I will be Marshal-General of the entire Goraan Military. Then my enemies will pay."

He couldn't help but wonder what "accidents" his good friend, Doshan had executed through the night. He saw Commander Doshan smile a wicked grin when Esham'aut entered the room and started to speak.

"There was a small accident last night," he said evilly. "It would appear that the Commander of Battleship Seven attached to the Goraan Second Colonization and Resource Harvesting Combat Fleet died as the atmosphere in his personal chambers changed to one that had rather unpleasant effects with his respiratory system. Apparently one of the technicians failed to inform the Commander that there was going to be some maintenance and testing on his quarter's ventilation."

"It is a tragic loss, Commander Doshan," said Esham'aut in mock sympathy.

The High Commander's puny white secretary was seated at his work station as Esham'aut spoke with Doshan. He wondered briefly where the secretary received a chair from.

"Secretary!" Esham'aut bellowed. "Inform the Imperial Senate that I will make a field appointment immediately."

"Doshan," he continued, "find a Gora loyal to me of any rank and standing and tell him that he is appointed to Commander of the Battleship in question on my authority."

"Do you wish to know his name or qualifications High Commander?" asked Doshan.

"It will not be necessary. Use your own judgment. Just tell him that I handsomely reward those loyal to me," replied Esham'aut. "Make arrangements for a dinner or something if he insists on meeting me."

"Secretary!" growled Esham'aut. "Read back last night's communiqués."

The High Commander's secretary read back a communiqué marked: *Urgent, inform High Commander immediately.* After listening to the secretary finish the message, Esham'aut was absolutely fuming. He stood there, clenching his jaw and could feel the muscles in his arm tightening.

"YOU PRESUMPTUOUS LITTLE FOOL!" he screamed.

Esham'aut raised his giant arm and back handed the smaller creature across the head. The secretary landed on his back on the far side of the room.

"When a message is marked: Urgent," Esham'aut was dreadfully quiet. "Then it means COME AND FIND ME THAT INSTANT!"

"If a single Runner ship escapes," he growled. "I will, personally ensure that you spend the rest of your life feeling every bit of pain and agony that your shell can tolerate! Mark my words, puny creature! I will make your disgusting existence miserable! DEATH WILL BE TOO GOOD FOR YOU!!"

He turned to Doshan.

"Rally the fleet Commander Doshan!" he growled. "Staff and launch all available fighters and attack vessels as soon as we are in range of Earth. Meet any Runner ships we encounter with horrible, burning death! We will commence depopulation of the Earth and prepare it for the mining yards immediately upon arrival!"

***

Mid-day came and Mihanna found himself sitting in his council chambers with the Captains of the other Runner battleships. One of the Captains formulated a plan that might cover their escape. If properly executed it could buy the Runners some more time to avoid their certain doom.

"We start our sensor disruption fields and fire a blast directly between our individual ships and the Goraan fleet. We can then open a gate in front of us. After that, we escape through it. This will make it seem as if we exploded," the fish-creature finished.

"Do we not need to be sitting still in order for the field to be effective?" asked Mihanna.

"Normally we would," responded one of the Kashin Captains, "but this time we set the field up as a web using unpiloted drone vessels disguised as troop carriers. We launch them at the last instant. We outfitted them with enough hull reinforcement and shield strength to withstand quite a few hits. Jump gates are not completely accurate to begin with, and these will be even less so."

"This way," continued the fish-creature through his bubbling environmental helmet, "the drone vessels will generate the field for us. If we shut down all but essential flight systems and life support, we will pass through the gates without detection. It will appear as though we have been destroyed."

"How long will it take to set up these drone vessels?" asked Mihanna.

"They have already been prepared," responded one of the Rankorack Captains.

"Good, we move immediately," decreed the Admiral.

***

It was mid-afternoon. It could have been any other normal day in Texas. Morgan and Alexandria had a nice morning with their daughter in the park. Morgan had decided he wanted a day off and spoke to the park manager earlier to let him know this. He and his family were going to have some quality time today. They stopped in the food court for lunch. Keri was playing on some nearby swings.

"What can I get for you?" asked the young man behind the counter of the burger stand.

"Let me have three number four combos with large fires and large Cokes please," stated Morgan in response.

"That'll be eighteen fifty," said the attendant.

Morgan didn't respond. He was ignoring the attendant. Alex saw him staring intently at the sky and moved in to pay for the food.

"Thanks," she said.

Morgan didn't hear what was going on. As he continued to look up toward the sky, the glint started to take shape. He realized it was flying toward them. The closer it came, the easier it was to discern its shape. It was a large golden craft with wings that formed a graceful arc connecting to the ship's main body. It had a wide, long flat nose, and a round solid gold bulb where he imagined the pilot would sit. A large fin swept backward with the wings just behind the cockpit. Protruding behind the cockpit was a long slender tail that ended in a "V" shaped split fin at the end.

"Alex!" he pointed to it, "Check that out! It's some kind of strange fighter."

"Is there some kind of air field around here?" asked Alexandria. "Do you think it's from the government? I thought stealth planes were black. Weird."

Without cause or warning, the golden craft opened fire. It was being chased by a larger dull grey craft with a wide midsection and wings that angled downward above twin engines. The golden craft strafed the ground with blazing blue colored blasts that burned and crackled with heat and intensity. Some of the blasts came almost lethally close to Morgan. Tables from the food court sailed over their heads.

"Run!" he heard Alexandria scream.

They both darted toward Keri. Morgan reached her first followed closely by his wife. He scooped his daughter up in his arms. Grabbing Alexandria's hand, all three bolted toward the parking lot with blue hellfire lighting the sky and setting ablaze whatever it didn't explode.

Another golden craft appeared and began strafing after one of those large, dull grey flying hulks. It was missing its target. The golden ship strafed through the parking lot, launching cars, trucks and asphalt into the air with reckless abandon. The three finally reached their green Suburban, which was luckily still undamaged.

"In the truck!" shouted Morgan desperately. "IN THE TRUCK!"

All three piled into the truck. The engine stuttered a bit before starting. Morgan floored it, stomping on the gas pedal so hard that he was afraid he might push it through the floor boards.

He tore out of the parking lot, pushing his truck to its limits. His tires squealed as he raced to keep ahead of the blasts as the golden crafts continued their fury. He could hear his daughter crying in the back seat as Alex tried to quiet their child. After he left the scene of carnage he looked up in the sky. It was littered with gold crafts. The sunlight glinted off their hulls and caused onlookers to squint while watching the battle. Blazing blue death was arcing through the atmosphere from the golden ships toward both the grey ships and the people on the ground. The grey ships returned fire. They shot some kind of orange energy blast in return. He looked in his rear view mirror and saw the wreckage of the amusement park smoldering in the distance. He pushed his Suburban as he sped away trying to avoid other fleeing vehicles. He turned away as he saw a nearby convention center cave in on itself. Dust, debris, smoke and flames were sent into the sky. The smoke rose like thick black claws trying to squeeze out the light from the sun. He glanced back at his wife and child in the back seat and heard Alex muttering to their daughter.

"Everything will be okay sweetheart," she said. "Shhh, everything will be okay."

As she spoke the words, she couldn't help but look at Morgan. He glanced back at the questioning look in her eyes. She wondered if everything really was going to be "okay."

They reached the camp ground where the R.V. was parked. Morgan felt lucky when he saw the recreational vehicle was still undamaged. He decided to take the thing, pile his family inside and run for cover. It was risky, but he was clinging to a false hope that the larger vehicle might provide some measure of protection against the blue and orange shots of destruction hurling through the sky and down at the Earth.

***

The Kashin pilot of one of the Runner evacuation vessels looked out the starboard side window. He saw an oddly shaped large vehicle careening down the paved road. It was zigzagging to avoid eminent destruction. A golden Goraan space fighter was having a bit of fun using it for target practice. He was a bit impressed with the way the human piloting that vehicle was desperately avoiding being destroyed. Chunks of dirt and pavement were thrown widely into the air every time the Goraan pilot missed.

"How many do we have on board?" he asked the pilot.

"We have room for maybe ten more," responded a voice over the intercom. "I am with them down here in the hold. They are a bit larger than what I thought. They are about the same size we are."

"We should probably get out of here," advised the copilot. "The sky is getting thick with Goraan fighters."

The pilot did not avert his gaze from the vehicle bolting down the road. It looked like a mobile dwelling of some sort. He was overcome by a surge of sympathy for them. For a moment, he felt a little braver.

"Forward guns!" bellowed the pilot. "Open fire on that Goraan fighter chasing that large vehicle! Cargo hold personnel, ready the emergency docking clamps! This will be risky! Songs will be written of our bravery! Move Brothers!"

The pilot swooped down to follow as the Goraan fighter darted forward with tremendous speed. It was trying to avoid being hit from the Kashin craft's forward photon cannons. He tried briefly to get the vehicle on the road to slow down by speaking over the external loud speakers. He stopped when he realized they couldn't understand him. The pilot looked up and saw the Goraan fighter that he chased off arc around to return at him some distance away.

"I will only get one attempt at this," thought the pilot grimly.

He dropped the ship down hard, and luckily it made contact with the intended target. The emergency docking clamps ground into the vehicle on the road.

"Are we going to be able to break from the Earth's gravity with that thing?" asked the copilot.

"I do not plan on taking it with us," responded the pilot.

"Get the humans out of that thing so we can get out of here," he ordered. "Go Brothers! We have no time left!"

***

Morgan was driving down the road sweeping wildly from lane to lane. He was trying to avoid being hit from the blue blasts. He was starting to realize that his chances were better in the truck. The blue shots were joined briefly by some orange shots. Then, the golden craft went bolting out ahead of them faster than he thought possible.

"Shit!" he exclaimed.

Briefly, he thought he heard what sounded like a voice saying something unintelligible.

"What the Hell is that?" he asked worriedly.

"Please, God!" exclaimed Alex. "Please stop this!"

There was a loud "thud" followed by some scraping as part of the roof in the middle of the R.V. buckled and then caved in.

"Oh shit! Oh shit! OH SHIT!" exclaimed Morgan.

He didn't have time to look while driving, but Alexandria and Keri screamed as a large piece of the roof dropped onto the floor. The R.V. was lifted off the road. Morgan, Alexandria and Keri looked up at the newly formed hole in the roof. All they could do was stare in astonished silence as they took their first glance at a non-human life form. It vaguely resembled a cat. It had strongly human-like facial features and pointed ears on top of its head. Thick yellow and orange fur ran down the back of its arm that was reaching out extending its slender hand. It was saying things in an alien language.

"Alex!" said Morgan pointing to the creature. "I think it wants to help us!"

"Are you sure?" croaked Alexandria.

"Do we have a choice?" asked Morgan.

Alex went first because she did not want one of those cat-creatures touching her daughter. Morgan handed Keri up to her and then followed them with help from the cat-person.

The hole sealed up behind them. Morgan looked around and saw many other people on board the craft. They were all just as scared and confused as he was. He looked out the side window and saw the ground getting smaller. He heard what he could only assume were blasters firing. He looked up front where he could see two pilots sitting in control of the vessel. One of those golden fighters was heading right toward them. The craft he was in was exchanging fire with it. He assumed at this point that he must be in one of the dull grey ships. He looked out the various windows and started wondering what happened to his R.V. He felt the ship he was in bank up and to the right. The gold ship banked in the opposite direction to avoid a head on collision. He heard a loud "clank" and the sound of metal briefly scraping. As he heard this he looked out the side window again. His R.V. dropped from the vessel he was in. Its trajectory and speed were just right to send it face first into the golden craft as they turned to climb sharply upward.

"Ah," he thought wryly to himself as he watched the mid-air collision. *"There it is."*

***

Flea left his philosophy class feeling as though he had thoroughly wasted just as much time as he did every Monday, Tuesday and Thursday in that particular class. He walked down the hall, turned at the double doors and went down the stairs. At the bottom of the stairs, he saw the large tree outside the glass exit doors blazing in flames. Rubble was piled up around some of the stone benches that were either turned over and split or shattered entirely. Flea ran outside just in time to hear an ear piercing whistle as something careened by. Whatever it was, it was flying dangerously low. He turned and started to chase after the noise. What he saw when he looked up stopped him dead in his tracks. The sky was riddled with gold and grey ships battling for superiority over Fort Wayne, Indiana. They were spewing orange and blue blasts at each other that seemed to decree their judgment against their enemies. Flea could not move.

"Oh my God," he thought. *"This is how it all ends."*

He heard an ear shattering roar behind him. One of the gold ships was chasing a grey one in his direction. It opened fire and rained down hot blue Armageddon at the grey ship, hitting it twice. It tore up the ground in a strafing maneuver headed in Flea's direction. Flea bolted up the sidewalk and ran toward the parking garage where his truck was located. Vehicles, dirt, pavement and bodies were thrown through the air to drop like a hail storm of carnage all around him. Flea didn't look over his shoulder. He already knew what was behind him. It was death. Flea ran from it as fast as he humanly could. He reached his truck in the parking garage and glanced at the Library off to the right. It was on fire and the sky was thick with its smoke.

Flea was numb. He couldn't feel anything as he got into his truck and buckled his seat belt. He turned the engine over and his red Chevy S-10 came to life. He almost jumped out of his skin when the speakers started to blast at full volume. His radio was turned on to *The Jim Rome Show*.

"This is it, clones!" Jim Rome screamed over the radio. "Don't go out like a bunch of punk-ass losers! Fight to the end! If it's time to die, let's grab some guns and TAKE SOME OF THESE INTERGALACTIC BASTARDS WITH US!!"

At this point, Flea decided that roads were stupid. He drove straight through the campus yard, dodging between the trees. He accelerated hard and his truck's engine was growling violently. He moved with such speed that he felt as if he had strapped himself to an Intercontinental Ballistic Missile. He turned right onto Coliseum Boulevard and his tires screamed when they hit the pavement. He slammed into guard rail in the median of the four lanes, swiping the driver's side of the truck as he turned down the road. Rome had stopped speaking over the radio.

He was trying to pay attention to what he was doing. Flea couldn't help but see the fighter jet that had been made into a monument sitting in front of the Allen County War Memorial Coliseum burst into flames. It fell to the ground with a crash. He looked up and saw the roof and all the glass from Coliseum collapse under fire and destruction.

He flew down the road feeling afraid inside as he saw the city he grew up in being decimated around him. The landscape was nothing but flames and rubble. In the midst of all the chaos he failed to see the oncoming vehicle flying down the wrong side of the road. The situation was quickly turning into a blur of fear and destruction. The truck suddenly lurched off to the left. Flea was sprayed with glass as the passenger side window burst inward. He looked to his right. The window and passenger side mirror were gone. The door was caved in and hanging by its hinges.

Flea continued down Coliseum Boulevard at a death defying speed. He was narrowly avoiding traffic. He zipped through the blue and orange blasts that rained from the sky. He looked out the windshield. To the left he saw "Sears" at Glenbrook Mall turned into a giant fireball as part of the roof caved in. The parking lot was a mess. Bodies and cars were everywhere.

"Oh Shit!" he thought. *"We're being invaded. I need to find a gun shop!"*

A new wave of fear and panic tried to overrun his emotions. He wiped away the sweat that was stinging his eyes. He drove like a machine, not sure exactly of the passage of time. As he reached the intersection at the far end of Coliseum Boulevard, he felt the truck lurch forward. A deafening explosion came from behind. He continued to look out the windshield where he saw the strip club at the intersection. The pavement came into view as he continued looking out the windshield. He felt the back end of the truck lift off the ground. Then, the sky came into his vision. He felt sick and dizzy as his truck flipped dangerously through the air. Suddenly, there was a bone jarring "crunch" as Flea saw a wall appear right in front of him. The front of his truck crinkled up like a piece of tissue paper as he careened through the side of the building. Tables and chairs were thrown out of the way. His truck split through them like Moses parting the Red Sea. Strippers were diving for cover from the debris as the truck took out the main stage. Flea closed his eyes. He prayed to live through all this.

Flea didn't want to open his eyes. After his ears stopped ringing he noticed that the truck's motor was no longer running. The engine noise had been replaced by the sound of loud techno-stripper music from the club. He realized that he just crashed through the front wall of the establishment. He looked up. Inches from his face was the jagged tip of a broken brass stripper pole sticking through what remained of the windshield. He looked around and felt a sense of elation that he was not dead. Flea tried wiggling his fingers and toes to make sure everything still worked. It did. He did a quick "package check" to make sure all his male parts were still intact. They were. He pushed the stripper pole back through the windshield.

"Thank you, Jesus!" he shouted as he raised his arms in the air.

He was covered with a multitude of cuts and wounds from all the glass and crashing. Some of his wounds still had glass sticking out of them. A particularly large piece protruded from the front of his right shoulder. Blood was slowly making his white tee shirt stick to his skin. He removed his black hat and wiped some blood from above his right eye with the back of his hand. Flea briefly thanked God for the invention of seatbelts and then put his hat back on his head. He looked down at the steering wheel and wondered why the airbag didn't deploy.

"What the Hell happened to the airbag?" Flea thought looking around.

With that, the airbag burst through the steering wheel and threatened to give Flea a heart attack.

***

The pilot of the Kashin fuel tanker looked out at the small city that these humans had built and felt sorry for them. He already piloted three successful runs, but still couldn't help feeling sympathy for those he couldn't save. This was already one more run than the flight plan called for. Maybe he could make one last pick up.

He briefly searched the ship's computer for maps of Earth before the mission began and discovered that he was flying over a place called "Indiana." This city was "Fort Wayne." It looked like it might have been a nice place to live. Now, however, rubble and bodies were flying everywhere. They were trying to flee in any manner possible. They were trying everything from their "automobiles," to simply running on foot. He flew over a group of buildings as he desperately tried to avoid being shot down.

"Crew!" he shouted over the intercom. "Keep blazing those cannons! Do not give those detestable Goraan scum a single centimeter! Make them buy it with their blood!"

The crew responded with raging cat-like hisses as they shot at the Goraan space fighters. A Goraan fighter was tailing him as he swerved to narrowly avoid being hit with their blue plasma. He took two hits while he was above a piece of large square pavement where many human automobiles were parked. The ship jolted with the impact, but kept flying onward. He was in a tanker that had been specially converted for this mission. It was a bit sturdier than the standard troop carrier/evacuation ships being used by some of the other pilots. The tail gunners returned fire and the Goraan kept shooting as it dodged wildly. Parked automobiles and chunks of pavement flew high through the air. The Pilot swung wide and noticed a small red vehicle go shooting across the grass. It dodged through the trees at a break neck speed in between the group of buildings he just passed over. It swiped its left side along a rail in the middle of the road. It took off down the street, bent on escape, or destruction at the hands of whomever was in control of it. It was the most reckless thing the pilot had ever witnessed.

"Whoever is in control of that little red thing is going to kill himself!" the pilot thought. *"You should not speed to your death, human, the Goraan will bring it to you soon enough."*

Four or five Goraan fighters were screaming up and down the road that little red vehicle was on. They were tearing up everything on the ground or in the air. The pilot pulled back on the controls to gain some breathing room from their fury. The gunners continued to fire.

"Alright, Brothers," he said over the intercom. "We have an empty cargo hold and a little bit of time left. Let us try and make one last run before we get out of here. Let us get it done and go home!"

The vessel turned to arc downward toward the ground. He caught site of the little red vehicle one more time.

"I cannot believe he is still going," he thought. *"It must be a tenacious little human in that thing!"*

"Get ready, Brothers!" he yelled.

The whole crew hissed as it entered a stretch of air that was thick with Goraan. The pilot's eyes were following the little red vehicle as much as possible while still watching out for the Goraan.

"Maybe I can help that little human," the pilot thought.

Then he saw them. Two Goraan fighters were bearing down on the tiny red thing, strafing everything in site along the ground. The ground exploded beneath the small red vehicle. It flipped through the air right through the side of a building. For some reason, this made the pilot furious.

"Take those two out!" he shouted.

The forward and side gunners responded and rained down superheated orange vengeance at the Goraan fighters taking both of them out. The pilot checked his sensors. The remaining Goraan were fleeing toward space.

"They must be getting ready to kill the planet!" he shouted over the intercom. "The Goraan are leaving! Make this quick!"

He hit full throttle toward the building the red vehicle collided with. He was going so fast, that he almost ran the tanker straight into the ground. At the last minute, however, he hit emergency reverse on the throttles. He pulled back on the controls lifting the nose and landing the ship.

"Get the doors!" he shouted over the intercom.

As the back doors opened, sunlight flooded into the back of the ship. The screams of humans could be heard coming in through the back.

***

Two strippers, one wearing a bright orange thong and the other in red silk, ran over to help Flea from his truck. Pain started to shoot through his body from a number of small wounds as the young women pulled him out the window. The two stood him up and started asking him if he was okay.

"Ahh...," he moaned. "Give me a second."

He bent over with his hands on his knees for a minute. He panted for breath as sweat dripped off his face. He spit some blood and saliva on the floor. As he stood, he looked around the club briefly. The dancers and patrons started to poke their heads up from where they took cover. There was a huge hole in the wall where the bar was once located. Part of the building was starting to catch fire.

"The owner is gonna kill you!" the stripper in the orange thong gasped in astonishment.

For some reason, this comment roused Flea's fury. These people had no idea what he just went through.

"Screw the owner!" responded Flea angrily. "Go look outside!"

She and the others in the club ran out the huge hole that Flea's truck left in the wall. After all, they did want to escape the small fire that was starting. They also, however, were becoming curious from the sounds outside. The few patrons ran to their parked cars after noticing and flew down the street.

"They probably don't want to stick around for the mess," Flea thought.

Up to this point, they were unaware what was happening to Fort Wayne. Inside the establishment, the loud music and good insulation covered up most of what happened outside. Because it was a strip club, there were no windows to see the invading forces through.

They walked outside to see Fort Wayne crumbling around them. Flea went with them. The air was still filled with those gold and grey ships. He tapped the girl in the orange thong on the shoulder. He pointed up to the sky at the strange fighters. He kept silent as she turned her face back toward the sky. Her eyes were wide when she looked back at him after it donned on her what was going on.

"See why I don't give a damn about the owner?" asked Flea harshly.

The fighters were destroying everything. The smoke rose up in thick plumes. The Skyscrapers downtown were just smoldering hulks from this distance. They weren't even half as tall as they used to be. The fire at Glenbrook Mall had gotten so large that when they looked in that direction the entire sky was orange. Whoever these aliens were, they sure seemed to know how to destroy things.

Then, with as little warning as their arrival, the ships started to leave. At least, the gold ones were leaving. Some of the grey ones were leaving as well, but after the gold ships left, the grey ones stopped firing.

"Maybe they are here to help," said one of the girls.

"If they are," responded Flea sarcastically, "they've sure done an awesome job so far."

Almost as soon as Flea finished saying this, one of the grey ships was spotted heading for them at a blinding speed. Just before it would have crashed, it came to almost a complete stop. The nose lifted up in the air. It let down some small retractable landing gear and set down with a dull "thud." Flea and the small crowd of strippers that had formed around him stared in amazement at the creatures that came running out of the craft. One of them was a huge blue thing with massive arms and legs with long spikes on its back. The other two looked like the way humanity might appear if it evolved from house cats. No one, not Flea, or any of the strippers spoke. They all stood there with their collective mouths open as if trying to catch flies. This was the first time any of them ever saw alien races before. The creatures were hopping up and down excitedly and saying things that none of them understood. One of the cat-people was pointing at the ship and motioning for them to get in.

"They want us to come," whispered Flea.

"What should we do?" asked the stripper in the orange thong.

"After what I saw earlier, I think we should go," responded Flea.

"What if they want to experiment on us?" she asked.

Flea just scowled at her.

"What if they try and kill us?" she sounded frightened.

"For some odd reason," Flea sounded tired, "I get the impression that we'll probably die either way."

"So what should we do?" she asked again.

"I don't know about you," Flea said, "but, I think maybe we should go with them."

"Are you sure?" she asked.

The ground rumbled beneath them as the gentleman's club caved in on itself.

"You got a better idea?" asked Flea cocking an eyebrow.

Flea and the club occupants ran and got on board the ship. It tore through the sky like it was being chased by all the wrath of Hell. After it broke through the atmosphere, Flea saw two distinct groups of ships, firing back and forth at each other through one of the windows. One group was gold and beautiful. This was not the group his ship was heading for. The group he was headed for was dull, grey and ugly.

As the ship he was on drew closer to the grey fleet, the firing broke off. He looked down at the Earth. It was enveloped in a strange green field. Two massive ships were blasting the polar ice caps, which promptly melted. The Earth was flooded with water. He could see the massive weather changes from up in space. Lighting streaked across the Earth's atmosphere. Flea was in muted shock at the sight. The two massive golden vessels redirected their fire and were joined by two other huge gold ships. They were now blasting into the oceans. He looked around the vessel. All the occupants were either sobbing or pointing in stunned disbelief toward the Earth. Some of the smaller golden ships started breaking away to chase the grey ones. The two groups started shooting at each other once more. The waters on Earth boiled away as he looked back to the planet. All the green had been scorched off. Flea sat down hard in stunned amazement. He would not remember when the small ship he was on docked with the larger one. He also would not remember the details of their escape before doing so. All he would remember is what he and his fellow humans saw as they looked out the window. He couldn't help but see it. He knew they all saw it, too. The Earth was a dead brown hulk.

3

"Tactical Report!" bellowed Esham'aut standing in the middle of the bridge.

"No trace of the Runner fleet, sir," responded the tactical officer.

"Comms officer!" shouted Esham'aut. "Contact Commander Doshan's battleship."

"Connection established, sir," replied the Gora at the communication grid after making some adjustments at his console.

"Doshan, our sensors read no traces left of the Runner fleet," stated Esham'aut. "Can you confirm our readings?"
"We have taken two independent sensor sweeps of the area, sir," replied Doshan's voice over the bridge speakers. "We have not detected anything. No residual sensor readings or life form signatures were evident either time."

"Excellent," he responded, "Esham'aut out."

Esham'aut walked over to stand behind his Communications Officer.

"Open a wide band communication to all ships in the area," growled Esham'aut.

The Communications Officer worked at his station for a moment and then nodded to Esham'aut.

"Member vessels of the Goraan Second Colonization and Resource Harvesting Combat Fleet, this is your High Commander," Esham'aut began transmitting to his warships. "Well done on a flawless mission. We received few casualties from the now destroyed Runner fleet. The Emperor will hold each and every one of you dear in his heart. Have joy fellow Goras! Now you are all heroes to the Empire. Thanks to you, a painful thorn was removed from under the skin of the Imperial Legions. You all have my personal thanks."

"There," he thought. *"That should satisfy their stupid need for Imperial gratitude."*

"Comm!" he said. "Inform Commander Doshan to meet me in my war room as soon as possible. Helm, continue with the ordered flight plan."

"On to the next mission!" he bellowed. "FOR THE EMPIRE!"

All the personnel on the bridge stood up at attention at the recognized military phrase from their stations.

"FOR THE EMPIRE!" they responded in unison.

The bridge staff slammed their clenched fists to their chests in salute as they shouted. Esham'aut walked from the bridge into the hall. He headed to a nearby docking bay to take a shuttle to the forward end of the craft. It was a large ship, and this would be faster than walking.

The bridge was situated on top of the vessel. It was set into the hull just forward of the rear dorsal fin stabilizer. Esham'aut's war room was near the very bottom in the front of the vessel. In a ship designed to hold fifty thousand personnel, it was quite a task to walk from one end to the other. He usually took the corridors and walked along the personnel conveyers. This could speed one's travel across the huge ship to a small degree. Today, however, he decided to take the much faster shuttle craft. They were normally reserved for moving large pieces of cargo around the ship that could not be move through the halls.

"All that is left," he thought as he walked through the gold and silver trimmed halls, *"is to push the now dead piece of rock that was once the Earth through the gate to the mining yards. Hoo-mans are such trash!"*

Esham'aut walked through the dock and onto the shuttle. He saw the interstellar jumpgate open through the shuttle's window in blackness of space. The giant mining facility was on the other side. In the background beyond the facility, he could see his yellow home world, Eiligor. It was located at the extreme far end of the universe. As the Earth was pushed through the gate, the mining facility opened its receiving doors.

"Pilot," said Esham'aut to the craft's pilot. "Hold position, I want to watch this."

Esham'aut looked on from the shuttle. The Earth had been sectioned into manageable pieces after the battle. Those pieces were slowly pushed through the gate by some of the support ships in his fleet. The much smaller pieces were sent on a trajectory straight toward the facility. The Empire had six such facilities placed strategically across the universe.

The harvesters were nicknamed "World Eaters" and were the size of a small moon. They were called this because they vaguely resembled the heads of some great metal beasts. Their doors would open horizontally from top to bottom. The seam where the doors met was in a zigzagging pattern that looked like giant metal teeth. The effect was heightened by the two slanted windows to the control chamber of the mining facility above the doors that glowed like angry, red eyes.

The chunks of the Earth were met on the other side by four large vessels. They commenced to shoot out beams that sectioned those pieces further as necessary. The doors to the mining chamber closed as the first piece of the Earth floated through. Sparks shot out of the roof and sides of the mining chamber from the vents that were positioned there. Along with the sparks came a slick looking brown mixture that solidified in the coldness of space and floated off. It was comprised of rock, mud and other useless materials that were stripped from the planet's remaining crust during the process. Side panels opened up on either side of the World Eater's head. Large chunks of various metals and elements that made up the Earth came out one by one in a purified form through the openings. Cargo ships darted out of from somewhere on the other side of the gate that Esham'aut could not see. They towed the resources off in various directions to meet the needs of the Empire. He watched this procedure until the remaining pieces of Earth were processed and distributed.

"Good," he growled with a wicked grin. "Along with the Earth, my 'Runner' headache has now been removed. Pilot, carry on!"

The shuttle started moving again and docked at the front of the ship shortly thereafter. He disembarked from the shuttle and walked down the golden passage way to his war room. It was empty. Doshan had not arrived yet.

"Host," he said with a grim expression. "Locate my worthless secretary and order him to come to my war room, immediately."

"Yes, High Commander," the computer responded.

The High Commander waited patiently until his secretary entered the room. He had a large green swollen welt that contrasted sharply against his pasty white flesh from where the High Commander struck him earlier.

"Secretary Ba'an Vichen reporting as ordered," he said with some defiance in his voice.

The sound of his voice and the sight of the secretary made the High Commander's blood start to heat. He walked over to the secretary and backhanded him again. The secretary was sent flying and now had a mark to match the first he had been given.

"You are hereby reassigned to permanent cleaning duty of the cellular reharvestation chambers!" bellowed the High Commander. "Furthermore, beatings will be scheduled for you twice a day from now until the DAY YOU PERISH!"

He picked the smaller creature up by the tendrils just above his small black beak and dragged him toward the door. As the door opened, he threw him out of the war room. Instead of the door shutting afterward, it remained open as Doshan walked through the entrance.

"Going to make a request for a new secretary, High Commander?" he asked as he came through the door.

Esham'aut looked down at his hand and noticed he had a few of the creature's tendrils in his claw. He tossed them through the door at their owner and the door then swished shut.

"No," replied the High Commander. "They seem to be more trouble than they are worth. I can check my own correspondence."

"What a day, old friend!" he said clapping Doshan on the back.

Doshan withered slightly under the weight of his friend's beefy arm.

"I suppose we accomplish our goals," responded Doshan. "But, I have to say, I expected at least something from the hoo-mans."

"That part was a bit disappointing. Although, the fighter pilots did probably have some fun with the Runners' feeble attempt to save some hoo-mans," said Esham'aut. "I was hoping they might try to be a little more challenging. I thought the hoo-mans had Nuclear weapons?" asked Esham'aut.

"They did. They just did not have time to use them. After all, they were very far beneath us in technology," said Doshan.

"Yes," agreed Esham'aut. "That must have been it."

"The battle was rather disappointing," said Doshan, "The Runners were outnumbered and the hoo-mans were severely outclassed. Perhaps if the Runners had more numbers, it may have been a bit more amusing. They barely equaled half our fleet."

"Yes," responded Esham'aut. "But even so, a chance to kill an inferior enemy is better than nothing. I am surprised that they would be willing to risk themselves over creatures as pathetic as hoo-mans."

"I believe they were trying to express their moral superiority," said Doshan sarcastically. "Nonsense!"

"Little good it did them," replied Esham'aut with a laugh.

"In the mean time," said Doshan, "we should plan our next move."

"We follow the Imperial flight plan to our next destination," replied Esham'aut. "Then respond to the situation upon our arrival. For now, we can discuss matters over our evening meal."

"Yes, sir," replied Doshan. "It is always my pleasure to share a meal with you."

"Oh, and let us try and arrange a few more 'accidents' among the other Commanders during our trip before we return to Eiligor," he said grimly.

***

Mihanna sat at the round table in the center of his council chambers with the Captains of the ships in his fleet. He could sense that they were pleased with themselves. He couldn't help but share in their feeling.

"Any battle one can walk away from is a good one," Mihanna thought.

"Well done today Brothers," he said with a small smile, "We did not defeat the Goraan entirely, but we did manage to buy ourselves some well needed time."

"Did the sensor disruption web work?" he asked, "I know my ship was not followed."

"According to our readings, none of us were followed. The web blocked all the scans sufficiently enough to cover our escape before the drones were destroyed," replied the fish-Captain.

"Brothers," said Admiral Mihanna, "Today we managed to fool the Goraan. It will only buy us a small amount of time before they realize what we have done. A few months at most are all we have gained. We need to capitalize on this time. Press the councils of your species to unify together. Our strength will depend on it."

"Admiral," said one of the Kashin Captains, "We should start trying to adjust the humans to their new surroundings."

"Yes," agreed the Admiral, "They may be inferior to the rest of us, but now they are here. We brought them here and now we must deal with them. Start installing their linguistic chips. At least then we can understand their odd human chatter. It may take time for the chips to synchronize with their inferior brain structures and translate their multiple languages. Try to be patient with them. Try to remember the weeks it took the rest of us to get synchronized with our own chips. They are not very advanced, after all. Hopefully, they might turn out to be useful to us."

"How many vessels did we lose on the planet?" asked one of the Captains.

"Thirty six small transport shuttles," responded Admiral Mihanna, "Our losses were not too heavy."

"How many humans did we rescue?" asked the same Captain.

"We did not get as many off the surface as we had hoped," said Mihanna, "They were not cooperating as well as we thought they would with all the confusion of the attack. Out of the entire population on planet Earth before the attack, we managed to rescue around three hundred thousand. We'll have a more exact count after today."

There were some murmurs of approval.

"Brothers," said the Admiral, "you are dismissed. Maintain a communication link during the trip home. We will reconvene upon our arrival. Report any difficulties you may have with helping the humans so we can learn from each other's mistakes during the trip."

Mihanna left the council chambers with his Captains. As they went their separate ways, he decided to go down to the hanger bay and see these human-creatures. Despite how inferior they might be, he was always excited to meet a new species. Perhaps they might show him some gratitude. After all, he and his people had just saved them. He walked through the halls, passing a troop of four legged hospitality robots that were also on their way down to the hanger. The scene he saw upon entering the hanger was not exactly what he expected. The hanger was filled with humans. There was almost no room for them to sit. Most of them were huddled in small groups, crying and seeking comfort. Some of them briefly glanced at him as he walked by. That was all the recognition that they gave him.

He continued making his way through the crowd. Some of the humans were coming out of the back of a converted fuel tanker at the urging of some of his pilots.

"Come on out of there, little human-creature," one was saying.

"We promise not to harm you," said the other.

A rough looking human stopped exiting the craft to see what was going on. It was a bit stockier than the other humans. Admiral Mihanna walked up behind them and stood off to the side so as not to be seen.

"Let us just see how this unfolds," Mihanna thought as he looked on curiously.

"Come on human-creature!" one of the pilots said a bit more forcefully.

"We have to empty the ship for post flight checks and go to debriefing!" the other followed up.

"This is pointless!" said the first. "Let us just go in and get it! We do not have all day!"

The two pilots walked in the back of the vessel through the open door and took a small human that was still inside by the arms. Mihanna could not tell if it was male or female. They all looked the same. It was speaking in one of the many human languages as they tried to force it out the back of the ship. The stockier human did not appear to like this. The human lunged and yanked hard on the tail of the grey Kashin pilot. The pilot was forced to let go of his charge as he sat down hard, writhing in pain. Tail pulling was one of the most painful things one could do to a Kashin. This was made evident by the pilot's mindless yowl.

"I better step in before that human gets hurt," Mihanna thought.

The human positioned itself and threw a punch that connected full in the face of the second pilot that was on hand. The black and white Kashin crumpled to the ground in a furry heap. He was knocked out.

"Oh my!" thought Mihanna worriedly. *"Angry humans can apparently do more damage than I thought."*

"That is it you human scum!" the grey Kashin said as it started to get up.

The human squared off to fight. The grey pilot bared his claws and hissed in response.

"Pilot!" interjected the Admiral now standing at the back of the vessel. "Stand down! NOW!"

The pilot retracted his claws. He was visibly angered by the situation.

"Collect your fellow pilot and carry on elsewhere," said the Admiral.

The grey Kashin collected his knocked out comrade and started to exit the back of the vessel. He turned briefly and hissed. The human raised one of his hands and extended his middle finger and said something Mihanna could not understand.

As the human stood there, it looked Mihanna directly in the eyes. They stared at each other for quite a while. The human was refusing to break eye contact.

"These humans can be very defiant," he thought as he turned to walk away.

***

Ba'an Vichen picked himself up off the floor outside Esham'aut's war room. The tendrils above his beak were in a vast amount of pain. He touched his hand to them as green and white fluids covered his fingers. Three of them were missing. He pulled his hand back from the injury as the three missing tendrils were tossed out the door. They landed on the floor in front of him. His dark green blood contrasted sharply against the gold and silver patterned floor of the ornate hall way. The door swished shut.

"You rotten piece of filth!" he whispered through the blood running down his small beak. "I will get you for this!"

Ba'an walked the halls shakily because of the pain he was in. He made his way to the infirmary for the second time that day.

"You are back," said the technician upon seeing Ba'an again.

Ba'an just stared at him with his black Goraan eyes.

"Well, come over here and let me take a look at you," said the technician.

Ba'an hopped up on the table. And the technician went to work.

"Name and position please," started the technician.

"I told you this earlier," responded Ba'an.

"I know. It is procedure for tracking and log purposes," replied the technician.

"Ba'an Vichen," said Ba'an in quiet fury, "Cleaning technician to the cellular reharvestation chambers."

The technician raised a small device which shined a blue light in Ba'an eye.

"Name and position verified," said a voice from the small device.

There was a long period of silence that settled over the room.

"You do realize that this is a useless position?" replied the technician. "The cellular reharvestation chambers have an automatic cleaning sequence. You serve no purpose."

"Yes," said Ba'an shortly.

A good Gora used everything to its fullest. That was the principal behind everything from the recycling yards to the cellular reharvestation chambers. The entire Empire was based on the principal that everything should be organized and used to the very fullest. If something existed which did not serve a purpose, it was recycled and made into something new. Few things were ever destroyed entirely. Most could be recycled in some way. With this in mind, to be a Gora assigned to a useless task, such as cleaning the cellular reharvestation chambers, was the single greatest shame anyone could endure. It was like announcing to everyone in the Empire how useless you were. He would have felt better if he had been executed. The only thing keeping him going was a need for revenge.

The technician gave Ba'an a half hearted treatment. If you served in a useless position, no one respected you. Ba'an cried out briefly as the technician cauterized his tendrils that had been torn off by Esham'aut.

"What are you doing?" demanded Ba'an. "I have sustained an injury that demands replacement tissues!"

"Yes," replied the technician disdainfully. "But I have decided to save those cells for a Gora that serves a higher purpose than cleaning something that has an automatic cleaning system."

Ba'an glared at him.

"What was your name, again?" asked Ba'an.

"Medical Technician Grumma," responded the technician.

"Thank you for your treatment," replied Ba'an sarcastically.

As Ba'an Vichen left the medical unit, he took some mental notes.

"Medical Technician Grumma," he thought to himself, *"I will have my revenge."*

The door swished shut behind him.

"Then," he continued, *"I will have High Commander Esham'aut."*

He walked down the halls with a grim determination to remain alive and accomplish this task. Many Goras would try to kill him. The hate they would have for a Gora that was useless would drive them to do so. He could not blame them. He would do the same in their position. He only had to remain alive long enough to kill those two.

"I will live," he reassured himself. *"Yes. I will live. They will die, and I will live. I swear it."*

***

Morgan and Alexandria were clutching their daughter in a fierce hug. After the vessel they were on landed, the exited through the hatch in the back. They found themselves inside some sort of docking bay for a larger ship. A giant monitor was on one of the walls inside the bay. Keri, much like most of the other humans packed into the dock with them, was crying. They had just watched the destruction of all life on Earth over the Monitor. Alexandria would have cried too, but she was too shocked to find the tears right now. Morgan was trying to be strong for his family. It was hard, given what he just witnessed, but for the sake of his family, he would try.

"Is this real, honey?" asked Alexandria.

"I don't know anymore," responded Morgan softly. "If it isn't, I hope they stop soon because I don't like this."

"Me, either," whispered Alex.

"I just," he stammered, "I can't..."

"Sweetie," she said calmly. "We should find a place to sit down and think."

They made their way through the tightly packed crowd. Many of the people were injured. Their faces were either blank expressions or tear streaked from crying. Alex led them to a spot against one of the walls that no one was occupying. Some of those cat-people were going through the crowds checking on people and trying to take the injured away. None of the humans struggled against the cat-people. They silently went along with them, too shocked to realize what they were doing. Morgan briefly thought about trying to stop them, but didn't seem to have the energy. After everything that had gone on today, he was exhausted. All he wanted to do was keep his family safe.

Soon, a small cube shaped robot walked over to them on four spindly legs. It came from somewhere inside the crowd. Some of the lights on it lit up and a strange language came from one of its speakers.

"Morgan!" Alex said with slight alarm in her voice.

A panel on the front of the robot slid open and presented some cups and small square objects. Morgan looked to some of the other humans and noticed they were eating and drinking these things. He took some from the robot and started to feed his daughter as he held her.

"Here, princess," he said softly, "It's going to be okay."

Alex was stroking Keri's hair with one hand. Her other hand was around Morgan. Keri took a few bites and fell asleep. As Keri snoozed in her father's arms, three creatures walked up wearing what looked to be space suits. The helmets they were wearing had glass face pieces. Behind the glass he could see the helmet was filled with water. Inside the helmets were creatures which resembled cat-fish. One of them said something he could not understand and reached out toward Morgan. Morgan flinched back away from the creature. The creature decided that it would try to touch Keri instead. Morgan's hand darted out and caught the creature's wrist in an iron grip. The creature tried to pull back, but Morgan wasn't letting go.

"Honey," responded Alexandria softly, "starting a fight isn't a good idea."

Morgan let the creature's wrist go, but continued to glare darkly at it. This time, the creature reached out again toward Morgan, moving very slowly. It had a small black thing on the tip of its finger that resembled a computer chip. Morgan allowed the creature to place the chip on his temple next to his eye. His skin tingled slightly in the spot the chip was placed. The creature produced two more chips and did the same thing to Alex and Keri as she slept. When Morgan put his finger tips to where the chip had been placed, he found that it was gone. There was no evidence that the chip was ever there.

The words that one of the fish creatures was saying slowly became something coherent that Morgan understood. His eyes widened at the experience.

"gurgle…glub glub...portant, and try to remember these humans are very far beneath us," one of the cat-fish people was saying.

"Yes, sir," the other two responded in unison.

"It took species much more advance and genetically superior to these creatures weeks before their linguistics chips could take effect," the first continued. "So until then, you must show them a modicum of patience. As soon as enough of the chips take effect, they will send out an update signal so we can understand them as well."

"I can understand you," said Morgan softly.

"Oh…oh my," blurbled the first fish-person softly. "Already? Remarkable."

"Where are we?" asked Alexandria.

"Ah…," he said turning his fishy gaze on Alexandria, "You can understand us, it would seem."

This appeared to trouble the fish-person.

"You are on my ship," the one facing Alex stated regally. "I am its Captain, Captain Roshom. We managed to rescue some of you from your planet before it was destroyed."

"Destroyed?" exclaimed Morgan. "What we saw on the screen was real?"

"The Goraan, they are another species of intelligent life, destroyed your home world," he explained gently, "By now, it has been sectioned and mined for its various elements and redistributed across the Goraan Empire. You are safe, for now, with us. We are the 'Runners,' the Goraan destroyed my home world, too."

Morgan sat with a blank expression on his face. The Captain confirmed his fears. The Earth was destroyed.

The Captain and his two companions walked off muttering about how impossible it was for the inferior human brain structure to accept the advanced technology of the linguistics chip in a few mere seconds. Morgan and Alex were stunned as the Captain walked away.

"What are we going to do, Morgan?" Alex asked earnestly.

"I don't know Alex," he shook his head. "I just don't know."

Time passed slowly as they sat there. Morgan had been ignoring the huge monitor on the wall since he had seen the destruction of Earth. He stopped to look up at it again as he held his daughter and noticed that it had changed. Now all it was showing was the blackness of space dotted with small white stars.

"Alex, look," he said and pointed briefly to the screen.

She looked up with a somber expression. She was holding up as well as she could. At the sight of the star dotted screen, her eyes got very wide.

"Is that where the Earth was?" she managed to choke the question from her throat.

"I don't know," whispered Morgan. "I just don't know."

"Our home," she whispered and started to sob.

"It'll be okay. At least we're still alive," Morgan said softly.

He tried to comfort his wife, but Morgan could not help but wonder if everything really was going to be okay.

***

Flea's senses were reeling. He had just seen the Earth destroyed, with his home and all his family. He glanced around briefly as the doors in the back of the vessel he was in finally opened up. The scene was not very heartening. He looked past the small group of strippers to see a very packed and crowded hanger bay full of people. He assumed they were taken in the same manner he was. A few of the girls wandered out the back. Flea opted to sit and feel sorry for his situation. He began picking out various pieces of glass and shrapnel that had embedded in his skin during his "death ride" down Coliseum Boulevard.

After a period of time Flea could not discern, two of those cat-people appeared at the back and started to try coaxing them out of the small ship. One was grey furred and the other had black and white fur. Flea and the most of the passengers got up and walked out.

They all left except for one girl that was sitting down in the back. Her legs were pulled up in front of her. She folded her arms across her knees. Her head was resting on her arms so her face couldn't be seen and her body was trembling as she cried. She was wearing an outfit from the club Flea had crashed in to. It was a blue, plaid school girl skirt that was very short. Her white blouse was tied in a knot under her breasts so it bared her pierced belly. She had knee high white stockings on and white tennis shoes with six inch thick soles. Her black hair was done in long pig-tails on top of her head with blue ribbons.

Flea watched as she sat unmoving. The two cat-people entered the vessel. They started to grab her by the arms to try to move her. She was looking away from them and shouting something while she cried. Flea thought it sounded like Japanese. She was struggling very hard against them. He wasn't sure why, but Flea decided to take action. He came up behind the cat-people and yanked hard on the grey one's tail. It yowled out in true catlike fashion and lost its grip on the girl. She bolted back to her position where she was sitting as the other turned around to see what happened. Flea bunched up his fist, cranked back his arm and threw an angry haymaker at their second visitor. The black and white cat-person turned around just in time to catch the punch with his face. It was sent reeling through the door at the back of the vessel and landed in a black and white lump. The other cat-person got up and hissed threateningly. It bared the claws on its hands and backed up. It took a position to lunge at Flea. Flea heard another of the cat-people at the rear of the vessel saying something in their strange language. The grey cat retracted its claws and stood there fuming. Its breath could be heard being pushed in and out forcefully through its nose. It stood up straight. It was slightly taller than Flea. It went over and collected his knocked out companion, and walked away through the hanger. It stopped briefly to hiss at Flea as it left. Flea raised his right hand and extended his middle finger.

"That's what you get, asshole!" growled Flea as he did this.

Standing at the end of the vessel was a lean black cat with silver pins on the collar of his jacket. They stared at each other in an unspoken contest that dragged on for quite a few awkward minutes. The black cat looked away first and disappeared through the crowd. Flea turned to find the girl had resumed her original position.

"Hey," said Flea softly.

She sat and cried.

"What's your name?" he asked quietly.

She didn't respond.

"People call me 'Flea'," he said.

One of the other girls had come back to see what was going on. She joined them in the small craft.

"Her name is Kaida," she said. "She's some Japanese skank the owner brought in a few weeks ago."

In Flea's opinion, some girls often got waspish when they felt threatened by another female. He glared hatefully at the girl who spoke.

"You see the door in the back of this ship?" asked Flea grimly.

"Umm, yes," responded the stripper.

"You need to use it," he said as he stared at her angrily.

"Huh?" she sounded confused.

"Leave!" barked Flea. "NOW!"

The other girl jumped at Flea's response and stomped off. After she left, a young man appeared at the back of the ship. He was wearing loose fitting cargo pants and an orange eighties retro tee shirt with white trim and a big "Atari" logo in the middle of the chest. His hair was light brown with blonde highlights. He was very skinny with ears that seemed to stick out like they were trying to catch some wind. He was wearing glasses with thick black frames over his grey eyes.

"You stoo…," he stammered, "stood up to them."

"Don't be too impressed kid," responded Flea. "We're most likely out numbered. They have better technology, and I have no clue as to where we are. So, I can't say as that was one of my best strategic moments."

"Oh," the boy said.

The boy stood there for a while watching as Flea and Kaida sat in the small vessel. Kaida was apparently not ready to move yet, so Flea just sat there.

"So what's your name, kid?" asked Flea noticing the boy still standing there.

"Thomas Dobson," said the young man.

"Are you coming in or just standing there, Tommy?" said Flea bluntly.

The young man came in and sat down on the other side of Flea away from Kaida.

"So how old are you Tommy?" asked Flea.

"Fif…fifteen," replied the boy.

"You have any family, Tommy?" Flea continued questioning.

"They…I…," Tommy stopped and shook his head for a minute and began sobbing.

Flea put an arm around the boy's shoulder and tried to comfort him as best he could.

"It's been a long, bad day, Tommy," said Flea.

"Yeah," was all Tommy could say.

They sat there for a few more minutes and then Tommy tried to speak again.

"I stole my Dad's car," he said softly. "We had an argument and I told him I hate him and then took the car. I got my permit last week. I wasn't trying to run away. I just wanted to go to the beach."

"Where were you at, Tommy?" asked Flea.

"Florida," said Tommy. "We lived in Florida."

Tommy looked at Flea intensely.

"I don't really hate him," he said earnestly. "I never meant that. I don't hate him. I just wanted to hang out at the beach."

"I know, Tommy," Flea tried to assure him softly. "I'm sure he knows, too."

"I never meant that. We fought and I just wanted to go to the beach," said Tommy. "The last thing I told him was…I hate you. That was the last thing I said to him."

"I know, Tommy. He knows you didn't mean it," said Flea. "Do you have any family here?"

Flea knew the answer before he could say anything from the look in his eyes.

"N-no," said Tommy in response.

"Well, you can stick with me and Kaida," said Flea. "You can run with us until you and your family get hooked back up, okay?"

"Really?" asked Tommy.

"Sure thing, Tommy," replied Flea.

"Sure thing," mimicked Tommy.

He sounded less than enthusiastic about the situation.

Kaida was still sitting with her head down crying. Flea was not very familiar with these types of situations. He felt awkward.

"Sweetie," he said to Kaida. "We should probably start leaving the ship."

Kaida didn't move.

"Kaida," he said softly. "We need to go sweetheart."

No response.

"Everything will work out," he lied.

She looked up into his eyes. Her very large eyes were red from crying. Her make-up was running down her face. She was very scared. Flea started to reach out toward her and she flinched away briefly. She was a very small, young looking girl. Flea was guessing she was Japanese. She looked to be barely over eighteen, if she was even that old. Suddenly, she threw her arms about his neck and started crying quietly again. Despite the make-up running down her face, Flea thought she was very beautiful.

"Kaida," he said softly. "You can come too, if you want. You can hang with me, but, we need to leave now. You can stay with me for a while. Okay?"

He put one arm around her back and the other beneath her small legs and lifted her up. She was very light so it didn't take much effort despite the pain his body was already racked with. She turned her head and looked briefly at Tommy before burying her face back in Flea's shoulder and mumbled something.

"Fam-a-ly," she said with shaky, accented voice.

"Sure," Flea tried to sound confident. "Family."

"This sucks," Flea thought as he carried her away.

4

Ba'an Vichen had risen early to move into his new quarters near the cellular reharvestation chambers. The condition of the new quarters reflected his new station. He lived in the only part of the ship that was not gilded in gold and silver trim. It was a dull metallic grey with sporadic patches of rust. His new room had a hard metal table built low to the ground which served both as his eating table and as his bed. Against the wall was a small sink that he washed at. He didn't have a closet, just a small box that held his clothes that slid under the table when not in use. He no longer had private meals with his own kitchen. He had to eat with the general crew and low ranking military staff. They made him sit by himself. When a Gora was useless, word spread very fast. They often would glare at him as he ate. They hated him.

He touched a tentacle to where his missing tendrils had been cauterized by Medical Technician Grumma. The burnt ends of those tendrils were rough and tender. Every now and then, a thick white substance would ooze out from underneath them. When he wiped the substance away with the back of one of his tentacles, his pasty white flesh tingled.

He walked to the room which held the cellular reharvestation chambers and found the technician.

"Ba'an Vichen," he said with downcast eyes. "Cleaning technician to the cellular reharvestation chambers reporting for duty."

The technician's shell was one of those Kashin species. His shell's fur was completely yellow and he looked very lean and graceful. Like Ba'an, his eyes were pure black. He walked over to Ba'an, balled up a fist and punched Ba'an in the mid section. Ba'an doubled over and crumpled onto the floor in pain.

"Welcome to the 'soup makers.' I hope you enjoy your stay," said the technician gruffly.

Ba'an lay on the floor wheezing and holding his stomach. He may have enjoyed his first experience of pain, but he did not enjoy this one.

"Thank you," he mumbled sarcastically in between gasps.

"You know why we call them 'soup makers,' down here?" asked the technician harshly. "Let me show you!"

The reharvestation chambers were located in the far wall across from the entrance. They were located in a bank that stretched across the wall from one end of the room to the other. Each one had a large glass door with a tray underneath that could slide in and out of the chamber after a body was loaded on to it. Some of the chambers were larger than others to accommodate bigger creatures. The technician was standing across from one of those sliding tables. That particular table was already loaded with a dead body.

"Come here!" growled the technician.

He grabbed Ba'an by his tendrils, which were still sore from similar treatment the day before. The technician lifted him to his feet and led Ba'an over to the body.

"Let me introduce the two of you!" growled the technician driving Ba'an's face into the chest of the dead creature.

Ba'an decided not to struggle. Many Goras would treat him this way before he perished because he held a useless position. Instead of fighting back, Ba'an decided he would add this individual to his mental list of Goras to kill. Ba'an took mental note of the creature's face. In a divine moment driven by hate, Ba'an etched every singular detail of the other creature in his brain. After lifting Ba'an back up, the technician placed his hand on Ba'an's chest and shoved him hard against the wall opposite of the reharvestation chamber. Ba'an hit the wall forcefully and slumped to the ground facing the technician and the dead Gora on the table.

"First," began the technician. "Insert the body."

The technician slid the table into the chamber. He reached up and engaged the two locking clamps. After the second locking clamp was in place, a light inside the chamber turned on to illuminate what was going inside the chamber through the glass door.

The technician walked over to the control panel next to Ba'an. He stopped briefly upon reaching the panel to kick Ba'an in the chest. It seemed almost like an afterthought.

"Next, flood the chamber," continued the technician as he flipped a switch marked with the number three above it.

There were ten different switches. One existed for each corresponding reharvester. Despite the pain he was receiving, Ba'an was interested in the process and looked into the window to try and see what was going on. The other Gora saw this and decided to help him to his feet by yanking him up by his tendrils again.

"Let me help you with that!" growled the technician as he did so.

After pulling Ba'an to his feet, the technician led him over to the window. He released Ba'an' tendrils and pushed him closer to the chamber door. Ba'an saw that the chamber was starting to flood with a clear, thick fluid that had a slightly pinkish cast to it. As the fluid filled the chamber, the body lifted with it and eventually was left floating in the middle of the flooded chamber.

"Then, add the reactant," said the technician from behind flipping the same switch.

A red substance leaked into the chamber slowly from a small port in the back. As it mixed with the pink fluid, small bits of flesh started to float off and dissolve in the new mixture. As Ba'an continued watching, he was aware of the technician who had moved up behind him.

"Please commit this Gora's name to be remembered by all who knew him." said the technician. "He served his Empire in life, and will do so again in death. He was a true servant of the Empire."

After the short benediction, the technician kicked Ba'an's leg out from under him and then returned to the panel.

"Next, agitate the solution," he said flipping the same switch again.

Ba'an picked himself up and continued to look in the window as the technician reached up and flipped the same switch yet again. The solution started to swirl around the body. The technician was standing behind Ba'an once again. His silent movements irritated Ba'an.

"WATCH!" he yelled as he grabbed the back of Ba'an's head and pushed his face to the glass.

Ba'an looked on at the swirling solution as his face was pushed against the glass. As it continued to swirl, more and more of the dead body started to break down. The solution started to drain out a grate as it did so. In the end, nothing was left but a thick red soupy looking mixture. It was a combination of the cellular reharvestation fluid and the cells of the body that had just been reharvested. The cells of a dead body continue to live for a short time after death. If one moved quickly enough, they could be salvaged and reused. The reharvestation fluid broke the tissues of the dead body down into their component cells and left them in tact to be cryogenically stored for later use. The mixture continued to drain out the bottom through the grate until it was empty. There was still a small amount of fluid that had seeped into the cracks and corners of the chamber. This is what Ba'an would have to clean.

The technician dropped Ba'an and hit him in the back one more time before returning again to the control panel.

"Finally, reset the chamber," said the technician flipping that same switch one last time.

As he flipped it, Ba'an looked in the window to see the grate shut in the bottom of the chamber.

"You will be cleaning these chambers after the bodies are reharvested," said the technician blandly.

Ba'an decided that the technician must not be very intelligent if he was assigned to a task that only required him to flip the same switch over and over again.

"I can see how difficult it is to flip that switch four times," said Ba'an dryly. "You must have a vast intellect."

The technician walked quickly over to Ba'an and beat him severely.

"I will hear nothing from you!" he screamed. "At least I have a useful purpose!"

Ba'an's beating continued for a few moments until the technician finally stopped from overexertion.

"I am sorry," Ba'an lied to the technician. "With whom shall I be working?"

"Cellular Reharvestation Technician Scivistan," said the technician with an air of superiority.

In Ba'an's opinion, Scivistan was obviously assigned to this position because someone felt sorry for him. He was really not very bright if the only task he was useful for was flipping the same switch four times to operate these chambers. Most likely, Scivistan knew someone important otherwise he would have been placed in the core of a combat robot. Operating the reharvesters was not a difficult task and could easily be delegated to automated functions.

"You have been added to my list, Scivistan," Ba'an thought. *"The Empire will not miss you when you are dead."*

Ba'an repeated the three names on his list of people to kill in his head. He then entered the chamber with some cleaning supplies and started to clean the inside.

***

Mihanna walked onto the bridge of his ship. He was a bit disturbed from yesterday's activities on the hanger bay. On one hand, he hoped that many of the other humans were like the young individual he witnessed that was fighting his pilots. If they were, the Runners' could benefit from their fighting spirit. However, he was also afraid that they might all be like that individual. If they were an overly belligerent species, they could become hard to deal with. He wasn't sure yet what to make of these creatures. He was, however, starting to believe that despite their simplistic genetics, these humans may be more complex than his scientists reported.

"Communications officer," he said. "Raise wide band comm frequency to the Captains of the other vessels."

"Good morning, Brothers," he said to his Captains. "Have you anything to report? How are the humans doing?"

Some of the Captains bid their Admiral good morning in response.

"I had an incident in my hanger bay," the Admiral went on. "One of the humans knocked out one of my pilots. He then tried to fight one of the others. The two pilots were being a bit rough handling a smallish human. If I had not been there, the situation may have turned foul. Be careful around these humans, they are quite aggressive and in a highly emotional state. The human I encountered turned most…troublesome."

The few non Kashin Captains chuckled.

"Just be careful around them for the time being," he added as the slight laughter faded. "And try to have some patience."

"I noticed something odd about them yesterday," said a voice over the intercom.

"Yes, Captain Roshom," responded the Admiral. "Go on."

"While installing their linguistic chips, I too, noticed their moderately belligerent nature," Roshom began. "We were attempting to install the chip human youngling, and its parent, I believe it was the male parent, grabbed the wrist of my crewmember. Later, the crewman was treated for a sprained and swollen wrist. The human had quite a grip. At least I think it was a male. They all look the same to me."

"He was probably just protecting his young one from something he did not understand, Roshom," responded the Admiral. "There is nothing odd about that."

"That was not the odd part," replied Captain Roshom. "The odd part is what happened after we installed their chips. After placing the linguistics chip to the human's skull, he could understand me almost immediately. We found this to be the case in every human we equipped with a linguistics chip."

"I received similar reports from my own crewmen," responded the Admiral.

The rest of the Captains concurred with the Admiral.

"It really seems quite extraordinary," said Roshom. "But completely against all the trends. Their brains should not have been able to do this so quickly. I will have some of my scientists conduct some research into the matter. It probably happened because it was easier for the chips to form an effective link with their very simplistic brains."

The other Captains chuckled, but the Admiral did not join them in their mirth.

"I would not be so quick to judge. After what I saw yesterday, these humans seem to be fighters," Mihanna said. "They may turn in to quite an advantage later on."

A few murmured in agreement.

"At any rate, Brothers," concluded the Admiral, "Take advantage of how quickly the humans adapted to the chips. Go ahead and begin conducting classes with them to help make them more familiar with their new surroundings. The Goraan are not following us, but keep a channel open to maintain communications regardless. Mihanna, out."

"Admiral," said the communications officer, "we received a transmission from the station last night. I thought I would wait to tell you about until you came to the bridge this morning instead of waking you."

"Go ahead, comm," replied the Admiral.

"They told me to relay a message to you to stand down from rescuing any humans and entering the Earth's space," he said. "They deemed the risk too great."

Admiral Mihanna and his bridge staff could not help but laugh as he turned and walked off the bridge.

***

Morgan was surprised by the breakfast buffet that had been set up by the fish-creatures.

"Looks like they've been doing a little homework on us," said Morgan as he checked out the spread.

"Yeah," agreed Alex, "We got eggs, bacon, toast, pancakes, waffles, sausage….and fiberglass."

"Guess they should do a little more homework," said Morgan to his wife and daughter in an upbeat manner.

Keri cracked a small smile, but her eyes were still very red. Morgan and Alex decided they would try to put on positive faces for the sake of their sad, little daughter.

"We're supposed to have some kind of meeting after breakfast with the ship's Captain. He wants to talk to us humans as a group," said Morgan.

"He'll probably just take the opportunity to explain our current situation to us again," responded Alexandria.

"Or tell us how inferior we are," Morgan added. "I don't think I want to sit through something like that."

***

Flea was feeling only slightly better this morning. He, Kaida and Tommy had taken the opportunity to eat breakfast after a fitful sleep of nightmares. Their sleep was only broken by the sobbing of the other humans occupying the small chambers that were provided for them. He was pretty pleased with breakfast. He hadn't had steak and eggs in a while. Everyone was surprised by the food that morning. As Flea and his companions left the table he painfully got up. His body was still sore from the day before so he decided to try and find some sort of medical facility to get checked out. His ribs were on fire. He probably had at least a few broken bones.

"Excuse me," Flea said to one of the box-like four legged hospitality robots crawling by. "Does this place have a medical ward or something?"

"Perhaps I should lead you there," replied the robot. "Your inferior brain structure may not support remembering my directions in your current highly emotional state."

Flea got up close to what he believed to be the robot's electronic eye.

"Just give me the damn directions," he growled.

The robot gave Flea the directions he would need to go through the ship to the medical department. After receiving them, the three started to leave toward their destination. As an afterthought, Flea stopped and turned to the four legged, cube shaped robot one more time.

"Oh and one last thing," Flea said cheerfully.

"Yes?" responded the robot.

Flea cocked back his leg and kicked it squarely in the center of its cube shaped body. He landed the blow between the robot's two front legs. It flipped over to land on its top. It sat there letting off a high pitched squeal and flailing its legs helplessly which could not touch the ground in its current position. The robot could not seem to turn itself over as its legs flailed in the air.

"Have a nice day," Flea said cheerily as he walked away, now with a noticeable limp.

The three walked into medical and spoke to the Kashin Doctor that was present.

"Good morning, little Brother," said the Doctor with a smile at Flea. "I have been waiting to attend one of you humans. I have been studying about you in our computers. You look like you might need some assistance."

The Doctor was a very large Kashin. He was almost twice the size as the ones Flea encountered earlier and had a thick mass of hair that resembled a lion's mane. He was very intimidating. Most Kashin that Flea had seen up to this point were the same size as humans.

Kaida's eyes widened.

"You study ME?" she asked looking up at him incredulously.

"No, no," chuckled the Doctor with a deep voice. "Not you in particular. We have all the information that was ever gathered on your planet stored in our computers. We had been studying humans for weeks before the Goraan arrived. We downloaded everything you have done and placed it into storage."

"Really?" Kaida asked with her eyes still wide.

"Yes," the Doctor said with a jovial rumbling laugh. "I did not, however, mean to imply that I was studying you in particular, young lady."

"I was in an accident," said Flea shortly with a scowl. "I would appreciate being looked at. If you could, maybe you could give these two an examination, also, to ensure they are in good health."

"Please step behind the screen, little Brother," replied the Doctor. "You don't seem to like us very much."

Flea walked over to what appeared to be a large ten foot tall flat screen. He stood in front of it and waived his hand behind it. It remained blank.

"Host, screen level one, please," said the Doctor.

"Yes Doctor Armalan," replied the computer in a feminine voice.

"Now try again, little Brother," said Armalan.

Flea waived his hand behind the screen. It appeared as if all the skin was now gone.

"Cool," Tommy said looking on.

"Yeah, I guess it is kind of cool," Flea agreed begrudgingly.

"Now, step behind the screen, please, little Brother," said the Doctor. "When you are ready, I mean."

Flea glared at him. Flea was still none too trustful of these cat creatures from his first encounter with them.

"Whatever," growled Flea.

"Is there a reason you don't like me?" asked Armalan. "Have I done something to you?"

"Goddamnit!" responded Flea. "I was just yanked off my planet, which was destroyed not too long ago, in case you didn't notice! Then I was dumped into this damn place where I saw some of you feline bastards trying to do something to Kaida!"

Armalan flinched as if Flea had just slapped him in the face.

"They weren't being very nice so I stopped them! They deserved what they got!" Flea growled angrily.

The large Kashin stared at the smaller human. Flea was not going to allow himself to be intimidated by Armalan's much larger size.

"I'm not afraid to do it again," Flea added glaring right in the larger creature's eyes.

"Yes," responded Armalan quietly. "I can see that you are not. The Admiral brought those two here himself just before he doubled their workloads as punishment for their actions."

Armalan's deep voice had a purring quality to it that was unlike the smaller members of his species. Flea felt slightly soothed by the sound.

"You did quite a rough job on them," Armalan said in a soothing manner. "One had a broken jaw and the other needed to have his tail realigned. Why do you dislike me, though? I did nothing to you."

"Hmm," Flea grunted in response. "Sorry. I'll try to be nicer."

"It is quite alright, little Brother," responded Armalan.

"So, how do I look in this thing?" asked Flea after he stepped behind the screen.

"Flea!" said Kaida with wide eyes. "No skin!"

"Yes, Kaida," he said looking in her direction. "I know."

The Doctor adjusted the screen looking at Flea from various angles and slowly looking deeper and deeper into Flea's body.

"It appears you have broken four ribs, one bone in your right forearm and still have some bits of glass and shrapnel I need to remove, little Brother," spoke Armalan.

"Why do you keep calling me that?" asked Flea.

"Calling you what, little Brother?" asked Armalan.

"Little brother," responded Flea, "Why do you keep calling me 'little brother?' I just think it's odd, that's all."

"Well," began the Doctor smiling with his deep rumbling voice. "It seems we could both learn something, today."

Armalan started explaining to Flea about Kashin culture. After being born a Kashin child is placed in a large "rearing" group. The parents of all the children were responsible for it. These groups made it easier for both parents and children alike, while allowing parents to maintain loving relationships with their young. It also helped to broaden the children's educational experiences. As a result, all the children thought of each other as brothers and sisters. The Kashin had been doing this ever since the beginning of their species, largely due to the large number of multiple births. Most Kashin were born in a litter of at least four young. It made for a very emotional and love filled society.

Armalan also told them a bit about their current situation. Flea learned a bit about the "Runners" that he and his new friends were now a part of. The Doctor told them how the Runners formed and their seeming inability to create a coherent working government. Flea was amazed by everything the Doctor told him. The Doctor, in turn was amazed at the experiences Flea and his two companions shared about growing up on Earth. Flea was most astonished, however, by Kaida's story.

"I was on streets in Tokyo as small girl," she began. "People try to hurt me and be mean."

Her English had somehow improved with the understanding that came with the linguistics chip. She started to break down a little so Flea held her hand as the Doctor applied a pinkish paste to his arm.

"Japan government find me and put me in foster care with mean families," she continued. "I save money and come to America after I old enough to leave. I come on boat and am smuggled to America. Club owner help pay for me to come. I work at club to pay debt."

Her eyes were brimmed with tears. Flea squeezed her hand briefly as she looked at the floor in shame.

"You're with me and Tommy now," Flea added softly. "You have us."

"This sounds like a very harsh life, little Sister," replied the Doctor.

"Flea," she said in quiet reassurance. "Family."

"So do all the Runners think that we humans are inferior?" asked Flea.

"The ones who are not so educated will see your more simplistic genetic and biological structure as proof that you are inferior beings," the Doctor stated. "But the ones who know the truth realize that all this really means is that humans are…easier to make, in a sense…than the rest of us. This could even be turned to an advantage. Please lay on the table little Brother."

Flea lied down on the table. The sides of it folded up to encase his body so only his head could be seen poking out the top.

"For example," said Armalan as the machine started to warm around Flea's body, "Since you have been here, I managed to isolate your DNA and used it to grow some cells, which I have cultivated in the temporal accelerator into a few new organs," he smiled as he looked down at Flea. "I believe they were slightly damaged in your automobile crash. I can replace the old organs with the new and recycle the old cells for later use."

"Uh…yeah," responded Flea sounding nervous. "That sounds gross. Is it really necessary?"

The machine removed Flea's clothing instantly. They seemed to have melted from his skin. What was left of them slid out the through the bottom of the table.

"What are you going to do, anyway?" asked Flea. "Hey! Come on!"

"Fix you," responded the Doctor. "It will only take a moment. Oh, and do not forget to go to the indoctrination this afternoon. The Admiral will be there."

"Uh Doc," started Flea, "Hey Doc! Are you going to let me know what's happening?"

Armalan decided he liked this tiny human. He looked down at him and smiled.

"Doc?" asked Flea.

Armalan continued smiling down at Flea. Kaida was hiding a small smile behind her hand and enjoyed watching Flea squirm a bit. Tommy didn't even have the courtesy to hide his open grin.

"Doc!" Flea was more insistent.

The Doctor winked at Kaida and grinned. He then started a sequence on the machine which put Flea to sleep.

***

Morgan was absolutely astounded by the technology of the fish-creatures' ship. They had the entire vessel flooded with water except the hanger bay where the humans were staying. When the door to the hallway opened, they found themselves facing a shear wall of water on the other side. As they stepped toward the water, they were handed small devices from some hospitality robots. The device caused a bluish air bubble to form around them as they walked through the passages. When they entered the room where they were supposed to have their indoctrination the bubble opened up around them and vanished. They now found themselves standing in another air filled room. Seats were lined up in rows and some of the other humans were already seated talking about the experience of walking through the halls in that bubble.

As he turned and saw the rest of the humans slowly making their way into the room, he noticed for the first time how many of them there really were. Morgan, Alex and Keri took seats near the wall next to the door. They could easily see the raised platform in the center of the room. Standing on it was a fish-creature wearing his environmental suit. Morgan assumed it was the Captain. It was hard to tell if it really was or not. All of those fish creatures looked the same to him. The room filled up and the fish-person at the podium on the platform began to speak. Speakers hiding somewhere in the room carried his voice to everyone.

"Greetings, humans," it began. "I am the ship's security officer. The Captain will be along shortly."

"I thought that was the Captain," Alex whispered to her husband.

"Me too," Morgan replied. "They all look the same to me."

"Fret not, simple humans," he said in an overly grand manner while extending an arm with an open hand to his listeners. "We have discussed your natural inferiority at great length. We will aid you in your feeble attempts to join our cause.

I am sure the Captain is also aware of how inferior you truly are, though I have not spoken with him about it personally."

Morgan's face turned red in rage. He stood on top of his seat to be more easily seen.

"Who the Hell are you to judge us?" he demanded angrily. "I heard your story from the Captain!"

The room was silent as Morgan screamed his accusation.

"You're running, too!" Morgan shouted. "You're no better than us!"

"Excuse, me!" replied the fish with some indignation. "Are you implying that we might be in some way, the same?"

"No," responded Morgan with a small grin. "I don't think you and I could ever be on the same level."

"Captain!" said the astonished security officer. "Did you hear this creature?"

The Captain heard part of the exchange as he entered the room. He rushed to the stage as quickly as he could in his environmental suit.

"Comrades," he said reaching the podium. "Please, be calm."

The Captain said a few words of admonishment to the other fish-creature that did not register on the speakers. No one could hear what was said, but the security officer made a few strangled choking sounds and then stormed off the stage after muttering an apology. He stood silently at the back of the room.

"My apologies, fellow Runners," began the Captain. "That is what you are now…Runners…like us."

The Captain made sure to look directly at the fish-creature standing at the back when he said this.

"My name is Captain Roshom. I command this vessel," he continued. "We Runners are all the species that have attempted, with some small success, to band together for security purposes."

"Why do you need security?" asked a human near the front.

"We are all outlawed by the Goraan Empire," he responded. "They are the ones who destroyed your planet. We managed to rescue a total of three hundred twenty two thousand four hundred thirteen humans before they did so."

"We had six billion people on that planet," said someone slowly.

"Our planet was destroyed, too, we grieve your loss with you," said the Captain with sincerity.

"Who are these 'Goraan' people?" asked another human.

"They are a race of slug-like beings that resemble larger versions of the leeches on your home world," replied the Captain.

"How can a bunch of leeches do all that damage?" the same human asked.

"They do not live as regular leeches," explained the Captain. "They take over another creature's body by crawling up its spine under the skin. Then it chews out the parts of the creature's brain that are unnecessary to it and takes over the body. They have gained a very expansive empire. Up to this point, they have destroyed, harvested or conquered everything in their path."

After that, Morgan stopped listening so intently. He tried to hear the Captain's words. It was difficult to fathom the total loss the human race had just experienced. The Captain told the assembled humans about the Goraan. As Roshom outlined what he knew of the enemy. Morgan didn't listen very well. Roshom discussed the Runners and their attempts to form a unified government, but Morgan hardly heard him. All Morgan could think about clearly was the shear loss of human life at the hands of the Goraan.

"Captain," interjected Morgan. "How many humans are left from our planet again?"

Roshom pulled a small computer-like device from one of his pockets and tapped it a few times to verify his original number.

"Around three hundred thousand. Well under less than one tenth of a percent," Roshom responded softy. "I am truly sorry for your loss."

"How…," Morgan spluttered hoarsely, "How long did we hold them off?"

"Forty two minutes," the Captain replied. "That was all. I am sorry for your loss."

***

Flea awoke to find that he was laying in a small bed still in the medical department. He rubbed his eyes and stretched a moment before adjusting his hat. He looked around the room and saw the face of Armalan. The big lion-like Kashin was sitting in a chair at the edge of the bed. Flea felt a bit groggy and his mouth was very dry. He took a glass of water which one of the others probably had placed on the stand next to the bed for him. Tommy was gone.

Kaida was seated on the foot of the bed watching him intently. She smiled a bit shyly and blushed when Flea looked at her. She had taken a shower and was cleaned up. She had also changed her clothes from the schoolgirl outfit she was wearing earlier. She was now wearing a pair of low cut jeans which were slightly flared at the bottom. Her toes were peeking out from underneath her pant legs to reveal the bright blue polish that had been added to them, which matched her fingernails, and lip stick. The tightly fitted tank top she was wearing was the same color blue as her polished nails. She had a small silver belly button piercing with a blue jewel on it. Her hair was still done in pigtails with blue ribbons to match the rest of the outfit. Her open toed sandals were tan with thick soles. She crossed her legs as she sat on the end of the bed.

"What happened?" asked Flea, "Where are my clothes."

Flea sat up and noticed that he was wearing a new outfit.

"Your old clothes were a bit…fragrant, so I had the computer make you some new ones," Armalan replied. "You slept longer than I anticipated and missed the meeting. Do not worry, I let the service robots bathe you while you slept. I allowed little Sister to add some personal touches as well."

Flea's new clothes were in an Earth style. He was wearing loose fitting jeans that were a light shade of blue with a black fitted tee-shirt. He was also wearing a pair of black leather boots with steel toes. They had leather straps that wrapped around them instead of laces. The soles were thick with good tread on them.

Kaida had also managed to put some piercings in him while he slept. There were two in his right eyebrow, two in his left earlobe, two more at the top of his left ear and two at the top of his right ear. Some day he would have to ask her why she did this, and how she accomplished it without waking him.

"Personal touches?" replied Flea as he looked back and forth between Kaida and Armalan, "Man, this is so wrong on so many different levels."

"I thought it would be fine if she did this," replied the Doctor. "After all, she stayed behind to watch over you. She only cares about you."

Kaida blushed a cheery shade of pink as Flea glowered at her. She was apparently undisturbed by his surly demeanor and the accompanying long silence. Luckily, the slightly uncomfortable situation was broken as Tommy came through the door into the small bed chamber. He was wearing a new pair of grey shorts and a long sleeved black tee shirt with a biohazard symbol on the front.

"Oh man, guys!" he began. "You're not going to believe this!"

"What happened?" asked Flea.

"There was this big meeting in the hanger bay. That black cat that watched you beat down those two pilots was running it!" said Tommy.

"Really?" asked Flea. "What was he doing there?"

"It turns out that he is an Admiral and runs the whole fleet," said Tommy.

"Admiral?" questioned Kaida.

"It's like a General," said Tommy.

"It means that he's in charge, Kaida," responded Flea.

"I know this Flea," she said making a face. "I mean Admiral of what?"

"Let me talk, you guys!" insisted Tommy excitedly. "Anyway, he's in charge of this fleet of ships for a group called the 'Runners.' I guess that the guys that blew up our planet have struck a lot of others, too. They don't seem very organized, though. The Runners, I mean."

"I see," responded Flea.

"You see, Flea," said Armalan. "Most of us in the Runners have not experienced war before. In fact, we borrowed the word 'war' from you humans. You are the first creatures we have encountered that have any sort of large scale combat experience. The only time that many of the rest of us ever fought was for self defense."

"You are not giving me a very good feeling right now, Doc," responded Flea dryly.

"Mihanna is a good strategist, but he lacks the backing of a unified government. It undermines his authority," said the Doctor. "Do you know that he was given four different messages on what to do about planet Earth? Each one was different from the next."

"Again," said Flea reiterated. "You are not giving me a very good feeling, Doc. What type of leader is this Mihanna person? What can we expect?"

"There is a good leader inside him, but he is afraid to seize control of the fleet," replied the Doctor. "He does not want to risk disturbing an already shaky alliance by possibly upsetting the member species involved."

"On Earth," responded Flea. "We used to say, 'You can't make an omelet without cracking a few eggs.' At some point, he is going to have to take charge, even if it means hurting someone's feelings."

"I try to convince him of this when we speak," responded Armalan. "I believe he is better suited for civil leadership instead of military command. He and I talk often. He will be in the hanger bay tomorrow morning to monitor some of his fighter pilots training in the simulators. I could introduce you, if you wish."

"Are you sure you want to do that?" Flea sounded surprised. "After all, he and I already met once and it didn't go well. Besides, I don't normally meet the family on the first date."

No one laughed at Flea's joke.

"I don't understand," said the Doctor.

"Never mind," responded Flea. "It was a joke."

"Not a very funny one," Tommy muttered.

"Ah," said Armalan seriously. "Earth humor. Come, I will show you how to use the computers so you can occupy yourselves this evening."

***

Mihanna had left the hanger bay after the meeting feeling a little bad about the current situation. He spent a few hours walking among the humans. He tried to engage them in conversation to get a feel for these war-like creatures. Despite the prejudices that existed among the other Runners against the humans, they seemed to be quite intelligent. They managed to ask some very pointed questions about the organization of the Runners. They universally agreed the condition of the Runners was deplorable. They asked about the might of the Goraan and available technologies. Many still seemed upset by what had recently happened to them, but they showed a strong resilience and drive to continue. It was strange to hear so many humans asking these questions so soon after being attacked by the Empire. However, it seemed that just as many of them were too emotionally distraught to think of such things. These humans were a very different type of creature than the other species he had encountered thus far. They were straight forward and adapted quickly. Despite all they had been through, they still seemed to have some fight in them. Most of the Runners had lost their willingness to fight after losing their homes. These humans had not. Mihanna was beginning to like these simple creatures. They were not the most highly evolved. However, there was something about them that he could sense inside the humans. There was something in them that made them more than what they seemed. After a while mingling with the humans, Mihanna headed for his cabin.

   "There is much more to these creatures than we anticipated," he thought as he entered his private chamber.

   "Host," he said, "Rain sounds, please. I feel a bit disturbed."

   The sounds of rain were heard coming from the room's hidden speakers. Mihanna walked through the central chamber behind the tree and removed his clothing. He, like other Kashin, did not enjoy wearing clothing. It was very hot and uncomfortable against his thick fur. Kashin only wore clothing in the presence of non-Kashin in order to respect their customs.

   "Host," he said, "Activate room shower."

   Small drops of water began falling from the ceiling to add to the sound from the speakers. Most Kashin had an aversion to water, but Mihanna had begun to find it soothing ever since losing his home world to the Goraan. Oddly, he found that he missed the rain. He wanted to liberate his home so he could run through the rain on the beach. He sat on the floor, which was covered with a thick artificial grass-like substance and leaned back against his tree. He sat for a while in contemplation of the current situation. He almost didn't notice the chime coming from the door's electronic sensor that announced someone was outside.

"Enter, please," he said as he pulled on his robe from one of the trees low branches.

The door slid open silently and revealed Mihanna's old friend, Doctor Armalan. The large Kashin stood outside the doorway and chuckled in his deep, rumbling voice.

"I would come in, little Brother," he said. "But your ceiling seems to be leaking."

"Host, deactivate room shower and silence rain noises," he said with a smile, "It is good to see you, Brother. How was your day?"

"It went very well, little Brother," he replied, "I made some new friends. These humans are interesting creatures."

"Indeed," agreed Mihanna looking up at the Doctor, "They had some very pointed questions during the meeting this morning. Their minds are much quicker than we anticipated."

"Yes," agreed the Doctor. "They are."

"Are you hungry?" asked Mihanna, "I was thinking of trying some of their planet's sea food to see if it as good as our own world's."

As they walked toward the kitchen together Mihanna spoke to Armalan, "Are you looking forward to returning to our home tomorrow?"

"As much as one can look forward to returning to that place," responded Armalan sounding slightly depressed, "It may not be my tree on our planet, but at least I can see my Brothers and Sisters."

"Yes," agreed Mihanna. "At least, we have that."

They entered the kitchen and dining area. Armalan sat his large lion's frame down at the small table.

"Host," Mihanna said, "I would like five lobsters, please."

"How would you like them prepared?" asked the computer.

"In the way that they are served most frequently on Earth," responded Mihanna.

"We do not have fresh lobster available in the ships stores," replied the computer.

"Earth was destroyed, Host, you will have to combine it," replied Mihanna.

Mihanna walked over to a small machine set in the wall. It had a small window in the door, which flashed briefly as the lobster dinners materialized inside. Mihanna opened the door and took out the plates. He sat three of them in front of Armalan, since he was the larger of the two creatures.

"Is my Brother hungry?" Mihanna began the old ritualistic dining formality.

"Yes, Brother, I am," responded Armalan in turn.

"Will my Brother eat with me?" said Mihanna.

"I have no food to add nor gifts to give," replied Armalan.

"I have food for you, Brother. Your presence is gift enough," replied Mihanna, "Will my Brother eat with me?"

"I will eat with you, my Brother," Armalan responded.

They each cut a bite from their plates and handed the first bite to their Brother. With a small bow of the head toward each other, they finished the fasting ritual.

"Is there a reason we practice the old childhood rituals?" asked Armalan with a small grin. "We have not done that since we were very small."

"I draw strength from it, Brother," responded Mihanna. "And for some reason, I feel I am going to need a lot of strength. Our enemies are not unintelligent. They will realize what we have done. We only have a month, maybe two at the most before they find us. We now have these humans to deal with as well. On top of all of this, we are going to have to try at some point, to unify ourselves under a single cause."

"Do you think we can do all this with such a diverse group?" asked Armalan.

"I can only hope, Brother," replied Mihanna before taking a bite. "You mentioned a new friend?"

"Yes I did," responded Armalan stuffing more lobster in his maw. "Oooo, this is delicious by the way."

"Yes, indeed," agreed Mihanna, "Host, place this dish into my personal selections."

The computer beeped in response.

"There were three humans that came into the medical ward today," Armalan began. "One was really quite damaged and I am surprised he was still alive after seeing the extent of his wounds."

"Oh really?" responded Mihanna.

"Yes, apparently he had quite an exciting chase before he was picked up off the planet. He was accompanied by a young female and another young male slightly younger than the female, I think," he continued. "They seemed very nice. They were a bit emotional from their latest experiences, but still very nice."

"Many of the humans I experienced glared at me today," responded Mihanna.

"The human I met started out that way before I gave him treatment, but that could be expected given the situation under which our species met," explained the Doctor. "After I spoke with him a bit, he opened up and started to accept me. I think the problem is that everyone thinks these humans are inferior because our enemies named them to be so. The rest of us just sort of accepted the Goraan's judgment about them without really researching it ourselves."

"The influence of the Empire is rather extensive," Mihanna sounded drained.

"Indeed," agreed Armalan. "I believe you already met this human I treated."

Armalan had a sly grin framing his long fangs.

"Oh really?" asked Mihanna. "Where did I meet him?"

"He sent two of your crewmembers to the medical ward yesterday," continued Armalan.

"No!" Mihanna was shocked. "Not him!"

"Yes," said Armalan chuckling. "Him. I told him he could accompany me to watch you conduct fighter pilot training tomorrow."

"What is his name," asked Mihanna.

"You will have the chance to meet him in more detail tomorrow, little Brother," responded Armalan with a smirk. "His name is Flea."

5

Ba'an awoke, not looking forward to another day of abuse. He would be beaten severely by the reharvestation technician. After that, he had the two automatically recurring beatings that were scheduled as part of his daily activities. He would even get beaten in the mess hall. Everyone else simply looked the other way. His body was covered with bruises, scratches and open wounds. The ship's medical staff was instructed to heal him enough to make sure he would not die, but nothing more. White fluid was leaking from underneath the tendrils above his beak again. Instead of wiping it away, he let it drip on to the floor as he sat on the edge of his bed.

"I will kill them all," he thought grimly to himself. *"I will make them pay."*

He held his head in his tentacles as he leaned forward. He noticed for the first time what was happening to the metallic floor. The white fluid from under his tendrils slowly dripped past his chin. The floor hissed slightly with every drop that touched it. White smoke misted up from where it landed. Ba'an's eyes widened slightly as he studied what was happening more intently.

"I did not know my shell could do this," he thought wickedly. *"Oooh...the possibilities."*

An idea then dawned on him. He placed one of his tentacles on either side of the tendrils that massed above his beak. As he squeezed, he could feel muscles that he was not previously aware of, start to contract and apply pressure on a pair of sacks under his tendrils. White fluid spurted forward. Ba'an hopped up from the bed. He delighted at the thought of what he could do with this new skill.

"Let me see," he said as he stood and picked out a spot on the wall.

Ba'an concentrated on the spot and tried to line himself up to aim at it. With one hard contraction of his new found muscles, the sacks that contained the fluid emptied themselves in a solid white stream. He shot with surprising accuracy. The spot he was aiming for was coated in white fluid. The metallic wall hissed, popped and fizzled as the acid burned a scar on to it. Ba'an chuckled to himself as he surveyed the damage. He lovingly ran a tentacle along the outside of the new mark he just made. He caressed one of the spots where the metal had solidified after running down the wall as it melted.

"*All I need is one chance,*" he thought to himself wickedly. "*Yes, they will pay.*"

He was surprised that his skin didn't burn when he wiped a bit of excess white fluid from above his beak. The wall he hit was probably five feet away, and from the force with which it was struck, he could probably get another nine to ten feet of distance if he tried to apply this technique to his enemies. He made a mental note of this as he pulled out his small box he stored under his bed to dress himself to go to breakfast.

Ba'an walked down the dull grey halls of this part of the ship toward the communal eating area. He was greeted by foul language, name calling and the occasional short and painful physical confrontations of the other Goras that lived and worked in this area of the ship. This part of the ship was not covered in gold, silver and jewels. Because of its physical location in relation to the rest of the ship, this part of the vessel was commonly referred to as "the lower end." It was also used as a derogatory joke in reference to the less intelligent and usually more disreputable Goras that lived down here. Ba'an was now considered a "low-ender." Not only that, but he was the worst kind of "low-ender." He was one that served no useful purpose.

"*I will have my way with all of them,*" he thought.

Ba'an entered the dining area to the greeting of more verbal abuse. He stood in line to receive his food, and every time the line stopped the Gora behind him used it as an excuse to push Ba'an. The other Gora seemed to take quite a bit of enjoyment in this, as did those who were looking on. Finally, Ba'an had had enough.

"Is this necessary?" Ba'an asked the other Gora. "Or do you have a more intelligent way to amuse yourself?"

The other Gora was a large, grey, round creature. He had a wide flat forehead with a mass of short, stubby, fleshy protrusions on top of its cranium. He stared back at Ba'an incredulously.

"You would presume to raise protest with me?" asked the grey one.

"Yes," said Ba'an grimly. "I would."

The other creature raised his arm and backhanded Ba'an out of the serving line. Ba'an stood up off the floor and leaned on one of the tables. As he got up, he noticed the other Goras in the room beginning to rise.

"Not here," Ba'an muttered to himself. "Not now."

Ba'an resigned himself to taking no action at this point, and tried to get back in line. The others in the room shouted derogatory names as he did so and accused him of trying to skip the rest of the line. As Ba'an relented and started to go to the back of the line, everyone else started throwing food at him.

"Settle down!" said the room's monitor. "Stop this, now! I am sure the little piece of slime, is sorry for trying to cut in line."

The room settled down and Ba'an eventually got his food. He wasn't exactly sure what he was eating, and didn't really care. He was focusing on the grey Gora that had hit him. His eyes never left the one that had struck him in line while he ate. As the grey Gora finished his meal, Ba'an got up and carried what was left of his food over to the reclaimer and placed the tray inside to be recycled. It flashed and reclaimed what Ba'an had not eaten. He turned and followed the larger grey creature out of the communal dining area. The grey creature was walking with two other Goras. Ba'an followed them close enough to monitor them, but not close enough to arouse notice. He ducked around a corner as the three stopped.

"Can you believe that stupid little Gora who tried to stand up to me?" Ba'an recognized the grey one's voice.

"I know!" one of the others laughed. "What nerve!"

"We all know how useless he is," said the third. "I heard he works at the reharvestation chambers."

"He should do us all a favor," said the grey Gora, "and reharvest himself."

Ba'an could feel his blood pressure start to rise as he listened in hiding from the three. The skin around his beak tingled as white fluid stared to leak from the sacks under his tendrils. He longed to kill this creature. The urge to destroy was stronger than anything else he had ever experienced.

"See you at lunch?" the grey one asked.

"Yes," responded the other Gora. "Maybe that white creature will be there for our amusement again."

They all laughed at this. Ba'an waited until he could hear footsteps walking down the hall again, and then followed behind.

"Scivistan will be angry with me and beat me for being late," he thought.

Ba'an stopped for a moment.

"So what if he does?" he continued. *"He would probably beat me anyway."*

Soon the two he was following stopped again.

"See you at lunch?" asked the grey one.

"See you at lunch," responded the other with a wave.

Ba'an waited again until it was safe to start following once more. After he judged that it was, he quickened his pace slightly to start catching up with the other Gora. He was being as silent as he knew how. He looked around the passage way to see if they were alone. Spotting no one, he moved even closer to the larger Gora. The lower end lacked the security cameras that were prevalent on the more important decks of the ship. The larger creature stopped when he finally noticed he was being followed. He turned around and looked down at Ba'an.

"Oh," he said with a malicious grin, "I see you have been following me."

"Yes," Ba'an replied shortly.

The other creature walked up and punched Ba'an in the chest sending him sliding across the floor.

"Was there anything else?" asked the larger creature.

Ba'an did not reply. He remained on the floor lying on his back looking at the other creature. The other creature walked over to him and stood over Ba'an looking down at him again.

"I said was there anything else?" demanded the other creature.

Ba'an's response was not what the other creature had expected. White acid spewed from underneath his tendrils and struck the larger creature in the eyes and dripped down his face. The grey one's hands shot up to cover his face. He tried to scream, but all that came out was a low gurgling sound as the fluid dripped down his neck and burned his vocal chords. Ba'an jolted up to a standing position, looked around briefly to ensure they were still alone. Seeing that they were, he threw himself on to the chest of the larger creature. The other creature fell backward and they landed with Ba'an sitting on top of the larger creature's chest. He put his tentacles around the wrists of the grey Gora's hands and forced him to uncover his face. The flesh was gone along with part of the skull. A large gaping hole was where the Gora's face once was. He looked inside the skull and saw the Gora's small slug body squirming as it was still attached to what was left of its shell's brain. Ba'an reached inside the hole he had made and very carefully removed the small slug-like creature. He pulled the little Gora from its now dead shell. It squirmed a bit as it tried to escape, but Ba'an knew it wasn't going anywhere.

"Was there anything else?" Ba'an mocked the creature spitting its last words back at it.

The creature stopped most of its squirming. Only its tail continued to slowly slither back and forth.

"You know," said Ba'an. "If I leave you here, you will probably die before anyone finds you."

He put the Gora down on its dead shell, knowing that it would soon die. Now that it was forcibly separated from its shell it wouldn't last much longer unless Ba'an took it to the medical ward. He stood up and looked down at the small Gora slug.

"Do not worry little one," he said evilly. "I will help you."

He placed his foot on top of the tiny creature and pushed down. It popped as he squished it under his boot. He scraped the bottom of his boot off on the dead shell's chest.

"I should go get cleaned up before reporting for duty," he said as he turned and walked away.

***

The ship Morgan was on was the first to dock with the Runner's base. As it pulled in, Morgan monitored the view screen in the hanger bay. It showed the base as the ship slowly came closer. The main hub of the station was a large sphere with a flat circular plane that cut through the middle. The bottom half of the sphere was metallic grey with long spike-like objects jutting out from it at irregular intervals. The top half of the sphere was a clear dome that had many building like structures underneath it sitting on top of the metallic grey half. Sticking out from the glass dome half of the sphere were a multitude of glass tubes that led to smaller spherical structures that were much like the largest one that the tubes were attached to. Running between all the smaller spheres were even more glass tubes. Morgan thought it made the whole thing resemble a gigantic version of a plastic gerbil cage.

"Great," he said to no one in particular as he viewed the large monitor. "I wonder if that thing comes with a hamster wheel."

"Attention everyone!" said Captain Roshom's voice over the ship's announcing system. "I would personally like to congratulate and thank the crew one last time for their superb effort on behalf of the human's on planet Earth. We successfully rescued a little over three hundred thousand of them to join our cause. Well done!"

"Three hundred thousand out of six billion," muttered Morgan.

"What was that, sweetheart," asked Alexandria.

"Never mind," replied Morgan.

"It was a great moral victory. I also wish to extend the heartiest of welcomes to our human friends as they reach their new home," continued the Captain. "You will each be given a small palm computer when you disembark with brief instructions on how to use it. You will find directions mapped out in the computer, leading you to your new home on the station. There is a sphere which has been assigned specifically to the humans. Thank you everyone, for a trip well worth it, and a successful fight against the Goraan."

"Anyway," Morgan sighed. "Let's go see where our new home is."

"You know, Dad," said Keri. "Maybe it won't be so bad. Maybe it'll have a bunch of cool technology and stuff."

Morgan tried not to seem too excited by the fact that this was the first time his daughter had spoken since they left planet Earth.

"Yeah, sweetheart;" he tried to sound upbeat. "Maybe you're right."

"Maybe we won't have to suffer through mom's cooking anymore!" she said making a face trying hard to be cheerful.

"Hey you two!" interjected Alex playfully. "What did I do to earn that one?"

"Meat loaf surprise," said Keri and Morgan in unison.

"Not funny," scowled Alex.

"If you eat it and you're still alive when you're done," Keri giggled. "It's a big surprise."

Morgan and Alex laughed as they saw their daughter's effort to try and be positive. Her laughter was a nice musical sound to her parents, but Morgan could tell her heart was not in it. He played along anyway.

"Daddy?" asked Keri as her eyes flashed briefly. "Are we going to get back at them?"

"At who, sweetie?" asked Morgan in response.

"The ones who did this to us!" she said emotionally. "The Goraan!"

"We can only wait and see," replied Morgan. "Just give it time."

They made their way through the ship. They walked the water filled halls secure in their air bubbles. Eventually, they reached another open area where the water had been drained and saw a long line of humans. Some of those fish creatures were interspersed to the side of the line explaining the use of the palm computers. The tension between the humans and the fish creatures was visible on their faces. The humans were still upset at the fish-creature's remarks about humans being inferior during yesterday's meeting. Morgan, Alexandria and Keri took their places at the end of the line and were quickly attended to by one of the fish-creatures.

"These are your own personal palm computers," she explained.

"Excuse me," interrupted another fish-creature as it walked over to them. "Are you the humans from the hanger bay that I spoke to after you received your linguistics chips?"

"Yes," Morgan said flatly.

"I don't mean to sound rude, you know," he leaned in and put his hand to the side of the helmet's speaker near his mouth and whispered. "But you all look alike to me."

Keri forced a small smile and tried to be cheery for the creature. The creature quickly stood upright again and gave what the three humans assumed was a grin.

"You all look alike to us, too," Morgan leaned in and whispered his reply.

They all laughed at this. The tension in the line broke up when the others saw the fish-creature and the humans laughing together.

"I am Roshom," the fish creature introduced himself.

"I'm Morgan," Morgan replied politely. "This is my wife, Alexandria and our daughter, Keri."

"I have young ones, too," responded Roshom. "Sometimes they can be quite trying. Well worth it, in the end, though."

"We like to think she is," responded Alex.

The Captain squatted down so he could look Keri in the eye and beckoned her to come closer.

"Come here little one," Roshom said. "I'll show you your computer."

Keri moved toward the Captain and leaned in as he gently reached out and took her palm computer. The entire unit looked like a very thin smartphone.

"You are dismissed," he said to the other fish-creature. "I will help these humans personally."

The other fish-creature turned and walked away.

"First," said Roshom pushing a green button on the side, "you turn it on."

Morgan, Alexandria and Keri looked on in astonishment at what they saw next. After turning on the computer, the "Windows" logo appeared on the screen.

"Thank you for choosing *Windows Ultima*: Human Edition. How may I help you?" the computer asked from a small speaker.

"Oh my god!" exclaimed Morgan, "That's Windows!"

"Yes," responded Roshom. "No one is really sure where or when the Windows operating system came in to existence, or even who invented it. Its origins are shrouded in mystery. Most of the known universe that has achieved interstellar travel usually was either given or traded for the technology from a more advanced species. Our researchers had to dig around quite a bit, but from what we can surmise, it was 'seeded' on planet Earth many centuries ago in the genetic lineage of a 'Bill Gates' human."

"Impossible!" Alex exclaimed in frustration.

"No," Morgan said softly. "It makes sense if you think about it. Ancient human civilizations all over the world have legends and stories about some 'god' that dropped from the sky and bestowed on them advanced technology and mathematical abilities."

"Oh yeah?" Alex challenged him. "Name one!"

"The Aztecs," Morgan smiled. "Quetzalcoatl was their god that came from the sky and gave them math. Would you like me to name another?"

"How do you know that?" Alex asked skeptically.

"History channel," Morgan explained.

"The species that put this information on your planet has since been destroyed by the Goraan," Roshom continued. "They must have been able to predict the Goraan would not be able to use you as shells and wanted to give you an advantage."

"Why did the Goraan decide not to use us?" Morgan asked jovially. "Aren't we good enough for them?"

"I do not mean this as an insult, but you should probably know the truth of your species," Roshom said sincerely. "Humans are the result of evolution mixed with intergalactic chemical waste dumping and high background radiation levels."

"What?" asked Morgan incredulously, "Toxic waste? Radiation? What the Hell are you talking about?"

"You did not know?" asked Roshom sadly. "Your world was used as a dumping ground by more technologically advanced species for hazardous waste materials. Some even dumped radioactive waste. Even after you became more evolved, it was easy for them to do this to you. Your own technologies were not advanced enough to be able to detect them when they did this.

No one among the Runners did this to you. Not even the Goraan used Earth to this means. If it helps, the Goraan have since destroyed the species that did this to your planet. They didn't do it as an act of revenge; however, it was more of a coincidence. I am sorry."

"I see," responded Morgan.

There was a long period of silence.

"Don't be sorry," said Morgan. "It's not your fault that this happened. I don't hold you to blame. I just need to get used to the idea, I guess."

"You were telling us about our smartphones?" said Alex trying to ease the tension.

"Yes," said Roshom. "Smartphones? Oh, the computers. Yes, of course."

Roshom continued to show the three humans how to use their new phones while they waited in line. They had simple touch screen interfaces, just like the smartphones on earth.

"You know," said Roshom, "I am stunned by how quickly you humans learn things. Your brain structure, and again I am not trying to be insulting, is very inferior to our own."

"Maybe it's easy for us with a more simplistic brain structure because it doesn't turn in to a complex biological ordeal when we try to learn new things," Morgan growled slightly. "Or maybe we've seen this stuff before."

"This is an interesting theory," responded Roshom.

"Anyway," said Morgan. "What other things were 'seeded' on Earth?"

"All sorts of things," began Roshom. "All of your concepts about space, time and distance. Units of measure and many scientific theories were planted on Earth. These are just a few things."

"Wait a second," replied Morgan. "That can't be right! Our measurements of time are based on the movement of the sun!"

"That was just a coincidence," Roshom brushed the comment aside.

"Why would they go through all this trouble to help us?" asked Alex. "I mean, if most of the rest of the known universe is so much more technologically advanced than we are, why not choose one of them?"

"Excellent question Alexandria," began Roshom. "You see, the species that planted this information on Earth did so in hopes that it would advance the timeline of human evolution faster than the rest of the universe. This is because they were, at the time, at war with the Goraan. Perhaps they thought it would prove useful later. After all, it was thousands upon thousands of years ago."

"Yes," said Morgan. "But why us?"

"All our archeologists can tell us is that they planted this information on planet Earth after discovering that humans cannot serve as shells for the Goraan," he stated. "The ones who planted the information in your species knew this meant that if the Goraan found out, they would try to destroy you and harvest your planet for resources."

"Which is pretty much what they did," said Morgan.

"Yes," responded Roshom. "But the goal of planting this information on Earth was in the hopes that eventually, the humans would develop into some sort of super-species that could defeat the Goraan. At least, that is the theory."

"Have you told the rest of the Runners this?" asked Alex.

"Sadly," replied Roshom, "the Runners are only unified in name. We do not often share information. The Kashin and Homarell get along very well and share information, but the rest of the Runners are not very unified."

"Who are the Kashin?" asked Morgan.

"A feline based species. They look a bit like how humans might appear if they evolved from cats," responded Roshom.

"And the Homarell," asked Alexandria.

"I am a Homar. Together we are called Homarell," responded Roshom.

"Well," said Morgan. "We're at the front of the line, now what?"

"The transport platform will arrive. When it does, you stand in the yellow squares and tell it where you wish to go. It will take you there," Roshom said. "I added my own domicile's location into your computer in case you have any questions later."

"Thanks," said Morgan, "Maybe we'll come by."

Roshom turned and walked away. They approached the large glass tube the ship was docked with. The transport platform swished up and came to a stop. It was on the ceiling of the tube when it arrived. Slowly, it rolled down the inside wall and repositioned itself on the bottom of the large fifty foot diameter glass tube. When it reached the bottom of glass tube, the three walked on to it with the rest of those that had been waiting. They stood on the platform in the yellow squares as they were told. Morgan stood there until he heard a voice come from a speaker he saw in the floor of the platform.

"Please state your destination," it asked.

"Human Sphere," responded Morgan.

"Thank you," the disembodied voice replied. "Please remain in the yellow squares to ensure you do not fall from the platform after we have disembarked."

The platform slowly took off, gaining speed as it progressed through the glass tube. They could see the stars go by outside as the platform winded its way through the glass tube. There was no way to judge how fast they were going. Other platforms passed them on the other side of the tube going the opposite direction. Occasionally one would go the same direction as they were until it turned. The awestruck group of humans waived to the varied creatures overhead. They were promptly and directly ignored.

"Close your mouth, Keri," said Alex to her daughter noting the girl's look of astonishment. "Your face will freeze like that."

Eventually, the platform came to a stop at a large opening. They could only assume that this was the sphere that had been designated for the humans. As they walked up the path, Morgan and Alexandria started laughing as they saw a sign which confirmed their belief. On the sign, words had been written to designate this sphere as the one the humans were to live it. On the sign, in large bold letters, were written the words "Habitat for Humanity."

***

As Flea was approaching the hanger bay on board the starship, he was lost in thought. Many things had been divulged to him the night before. Apparently, almost all of the Earth's technology and scientific advancements that had taken place for the last few hundred years had been planted there by an alien species. The thought of this disturbed him.

"Hey, Flea?" asked Tommy. "Where are we headed?"

"Armalan invited us to meet the Admiral of this outfit," responded Flea. "I thought we'd take him up on it."

"Flea," said Kaida in a thick Japanese accent. "When we go home?"

"We'll go to our new home, soon, Kaida, and stay away from me with the piercing gun!" he admonished.

When Flea woke up this morning he looked in the mirror at his new piercings again. He would have to figure out how Kaida had done this without waking him up. Apparently, Kaida thought this was fashionable. She set his clothes out for him this morning, which included a fitted purple tee shirt and black jeans. A personal grooming robot cut his hair in a military style buzz. She, however, seemed to have a preference for the color blue. She decided to wear a very blue, very short mini skirt with a black spaghetti top and black boots. Her eyes were a shade of blue that matched her skirt. She had Armalan conduct a bit of surgery that made them the shade of blue she seemed to like the most. It was a very bright and unnatural color for her eyes. She wore matching lipstick and finger nail polish that were same shade as her skirt. Her hair was once again in pig-tails with blue ribbons. Tommy, it would seem, was also attacked by Kaida's sense of "style." He looked like a shorter, skinnier version of Flea, except dressed in red. She did not, however, attack him with the piercing gun.

"Kaida," said Flea. "You do realize that you have made the three of us look like bad comic book characters."

Tommy nodded his agreement.

"Flea!" she said earnestly. "No! We look cute!"

Flea and Tommy laughed and Kaida looked slightly hurt.

"We were only teasing, Kaida," said Tommy.

"He's right Kaida," agreed Flea. "I was just teasing. We look very good. Thank you for doing this."

She looked very pleased with Flea's approval, whether he meant it or not. Kaida had never had a real family that cared about her before. Flea had learned some of her past. It was rough, so he elected to go along with her odd fashion sense to help her feel welcome.

"I make us cute everyday!" she said excitedly as she hopped up and down.

Tommy and Flea laughed at Kaida's excitement.

"Okay," said Flea.

"Okay, okay," agreed Tommy.

"Okay," said Kaida.

They entered the hanger bay and saw what had to be a few hundred sleek looking grey fighter ships. They were bigger than the fighter jets Flea had seen during his days in the Marines. They were much bigger. They were long and sleek. Four wings were on the back of the fighter. They were set at equal, ninety degree angles and swept back toward the rear of the fighter. At the intersection of the four wings was a large thruster engine. Eight more engines were set in the corner of the angles. Each wing had three small missile pods in the center of it, and each pod had four missiles. The main body of the fighter was a long, sleek, perfectly round tube. The cylindrical body slowly narrowed to a point, which appeared to be made of yellow glass. This was where the pilot would sit. Two guns were located above the cockpit, with two more underneath.

"Awesome," Flea yawned. "We're being protected by heavily armed, intergalactic lawn darts."

Flea could see the Kashin pilots with their helmets on and their visors down inside the cockpits. They were laying flat with their hands on two control sticks in front of them. The pilots seemed to be responding to some kind of training program while they were there.

"Flea," said Kaida pointing ahead. "Look."

She was pointing at a giant monitor on the far end of the hanger bay. There were some Kashin standing around watching the monitor and taking notes on some computer tablets. Flea and the other two were given smartphones last night by Armalan. Flea used his to download some music that the Runners had taken and stored from Earth before it was destroyed. At least he didn't have to worry about paying for it. It was downloading video games, movies, specifications for various consumer objects, and a few books that he had always wanted to read from the same resource. They became available thanks to the weeks the Runners had spent monitoring the humans and downloading everything they could. It would appear that the internet still worked.

"It looks like a giant video game," commented Tommy. "Can we go see what they're doing?"

"Sure thing, guys," said Flea curiously. "Let's go."

They walked across the expansive hanger bay and approached the large screen where a Kashin took notes. They stopped and looked at the humans with disdain as they approached.

"Can we help you?" asked one of the Kashin slowly.

"Nope," said Flea as he studied the tactics of the fighter pilots. "We're cool."

"Are you cold? The Admiral told us to try and be accommodating until you leave," a second Kashin that spoke stressed this last word for the benefit of the three humans.

"No," said Flea dryly. "I am not cold, thank you."

"Then why did you say you are cool?" asked the first one.

"Never mind," responded Flea. "Some things the language chip just doesn't translate. When I say 'I'm cool,' it means I'm fine."

"Then why not just say that you are fine," the second one asked angrily as both Kashin turned their backs on the humans.

"He just did," said Tommy with a scowl at the Kashins' backs.

Flea watched the pilot's tactics intently. They had good instincts, but no tactics. They had no structure, everyone was by themselves, and no one seemed to be watching out for each other. If someone was hit by an enemy, it seemed to spark some sort of personal challenge that needed to be answered.

"If they could control their emotions," said Flea softly to the other two humans, "and stop flying off on personal vendettas, they would be a lot more effective."

"Do you think you could do better, human?" asked a yellow Kashin wearing a pilot's helmet from behind him.

"I don't know how to fly your fighters," responded Flea bluntly. "I bet I could if you showed me how, though."

"Oh, please," responded the yellow Kashin disdainfully. "With your inferior human brain structure and overdeveloped rage centers, you would probably kill yourself before you shot any enemies down!"

"Are you kidding?" countered Flea. "You stupid assholes didn't even know what war was until you were attacked by the Goraan! In fact, last night I learned you didn't even have a word in your language for 'war.' You had to steal it from us! I could beat you into the ground! I could make you hurt so bad you'd piss blood for a week!"

The Kashin were not accustomed to the blustering and trash talking that was done by many humans. The yellow Kashin was astonished and enraged by this human standing here talking to him in this manner. The Kashin stood there making choking sounds.

"What's the matter?" asked Flea as he sneered and cocked his head at the yellow pilot. "You got a hair ball stuck in your throat? I hope you Goddamn choke on it!"

He brandished the middle of his right hand in the yellow Kashin's face. Flea didn't realize the gesture was lost on the Kashin, but it still felt good to do it.

The Kashin pilot walked over to the nearest fighter and pounded on the bottom of the glass cockpit. He gestured to the pilot to exit the craft and the pilot wriggled out through the back and slid down the exit hatch just behind the cockpit glass.

"This human seems to think he can fly one of our fighters," explained the yellow pilot angrily.

Flea could not see it before because of the flight suit and helmet, but with his helmet off, the second Kashin was a slightly auburn color.

"Oh really?" responded the auburn pilot. "Are we going to show him how wrong he is?"

"Actually," said Flea smugly "I suggest you watch and take some notes."

"Excuse me?" asked the auburn pilot.

"Did I stutter," Flea glared at the pilot.

Kaida stood next to Flea nodding her head with a grim expression on her face.

"Take notes," she said over Flea's shoulder.

Flea and the two Kashin walked over to the fighter. The two Kashin harshly explained to Flea how to get in the fighter and start the simulator program. They gave him a brief rundown of the controls and then stepped back. A small crowd of Kashin pilots had gotten word of what was going on and had gathered to surround Kaida and Tommy as they all watched the monitor.

"Which one is Flea?" asked Tommy.

"That one," said one of the Kashin taking notes as he pointed to a section of the monitor.

All the pilots were running a giant combat simulation program. Flea was now part of that program.

"Which one is Flea?" asked Kaida looking worried.

She could not find him.

"Here," said the Kashin. "I'll make it easy. Host, mark the human pilot in red."

"No!" insisted Kaida. "In purple!"

"Fine," the Kashin taking notes sounded slightly annoyed with her. "Host, mark the human in purple."

They saw a small purple ship light up on the monitor. First, it was standing still, and then it started to move. It swooped wide to the left and then crashed into another pilot. All the Kashin started to laugh.

"Laugh it up, furry bitches!" they heard Flea's voice over the monitor's speakers, "I'm still getting used to the controls! How many enemies has your best pilot shot down before getting killed?"

"Twenty three," responded the Kashin monitor into a small microphone in his head set.

"Thanks," Flea replied.

The little purple ship reappeared on the monitor. This time it started moving immediately. It moved out forward toward the enemies.

"I need two wingmen with me," said Flea calling for back up.

"Huh?" a Kashin pilot responded on the communication system.

"What are you trying to say, human?" asked another.

There was a long pause.

"Never mind," sighed Flea. "I'll do this one alone. We'll talk tactics later."

The purple fighter on the monitor swooped out wide and dodged a strafe of incoming blasts. The blasting fighter came up behind him. Flea made his fighter come to a dead stop. The enemy fighter shot past him. Flea pulled up and fired the fighter's engines at full blast. He locked on and opened fire, shooting down his first simulated enemy.

"I think I got it, now," said Flea's voice over the speakers.

He flew on with a heart filled with rage. He let out all his hate, anger, and disgust at the way these creatures thought about humans into his simulated enemies. As he passed the previous best mark of twenty three kills, he kept flying on. He let out all the bad emotions that had been welling up over the past few days. The Kashin watched on in dead silence at what Flea was doing. Tommy and Kaida were screaming with excitement and shouting encouragements to Flea as he fought on.

The Kashin were shocked by the stream of obscenities they could hear coming from Flea over the speaker. He was shouting so loud from the cockpit of the craft that his voice could be heard throughout the hanger bay. Flea had drawn a small crowd around the fighter he was in. They could see him cursing inside the cockpit with an angry snarl and gritted teeth.

As Flea looked out into the perfectly simulated, holographic space and saw no more simulated enemies, everything went silent.

"This can't be!" said one of the Kashin taking notes at the monitor. "We actually finished the simulation!"

"Where?" asked Flea. "More!"

"Human pilot, this is simulation control," said one of the Kashin watching at the monitor. "What do you mean by 'where?' I don't understand."

"More enemies!" Flea responded. "I want more!"

"Host," said the controller. "Begin simulation. Set at level two."

Half way through the simulation all of the Kashin were dead. They managed to take out just less than half of the enemy before getting taken out. This left Flea to kill the remaining twenty nine himself. He weaved through the enemy fire with the ease of a fish moving through a calm stream. He felt a strange rage overtake him as he fought. It consumed him inside.

A very long time passed as Flea flew like a madman. Finally, the simulation was over. Flea killed the remaining simulated Goraan fighters. Kaida and Tommy were cheering wildly. The simulation ended and Flea was still alive.

"I'm coming out, now," said Flea quietly. "I'm done."

As he slid out through the bottom of the fighter and walked over to the assembled crowd, all the Kashin were silent. They looked at Flea in disbelief. Tommy gave him a high five as Flea walked over. Kaida rushed over, hopping up and down and throwing herself at Flea to give him a big hug.

"Flea!" she said excitedly. "Awesome!"

"That never happened before," said the Kashin running the simulation. "Not only did we finish level one, which we never did before, but we even finished simulation level two."

The Kashin monitor was astonished at what he had witnessed.

"Oh yeah," Flea sounded cocky. "That just happened!"

"I can't believe the human did that," the auburn pilot whispered. "It was brutal, yet eloquent at the same time. I have never seen such controlled rage before."

"Thanks," Flea said.

"You were like death with wings," said the Kashin running the simulation to Flea.

"You got lucky and that's all," said the yellow Kashin Flea exchanged words with earlier.

"Lucky or not," responded Flea harshly, "I'm the one still alive. You know Earth cats used to lick themselves to get clean, right?"

The yellow Kashin, along with many of the other pilots surrounding the three humans hissed at the insult.

"Perhaps I should teach you some manners!" hissed the yellow Kashin.

"You want a piece of me?" yelled Flea as he pounded his own chest. "I'm right here, bitch!"

As Flea started to lunge toward the Kashin, Kaida stepped in between them.

"Stop!" she shouted as she pointed to the fighters. "Fight Flea! In there."

"Fine!" said the yellow Kashin.

"Fine!" responded Flea. "You're going to lose, you know that, right?"

"Just get in the fighter," responded the Kashin.

"How about a wager?" asked Flea.

"I saw something about you humans and gambling," he responded. "You take unnecessary risks."

"Not confident with your skills?" Flea cocked an eyebrow. "I'll even give you the advantage. You and eleven of your fellow Kashin pilots versus me, Kaida and Tommy. Just give me ten minutes to discuss some strategy and teach them the controls."

"What do you have in mind for this wager?" asked the Kashin.

"If you win, the three of us will personally wash all the fighters this evening," Flea replied. "If we win you and all the other Kashin pilots can show me if you Kashin are as limber as the cats on Earth."

"What do you mean?" asked the yellow Kashin.

"You can show me if you can get down and lick your own asses like the cats on Earth used to," he said with a malicious grin.

"That is insulting!" protested the yellow Kashin pilot. "It is insulting and degrading!"

"Do you accept or are you a scaredy cat?" Tommy added.

"We accept," responded the Kashin pilot with the nodding silent agreement of the other pilots.

He turned to the monitor and asked the Kashin standing there, "Who has the top eleven scores?"

One of the Kashin taking notes called out eleven names.

"You eleven!" he responded. "To your fighters!"

"Flea?" asked Kaida a bit afraid. "What now?"

"You were good, Flea," said Tommy. "But I don't know how to fly one of those things."

"You will soon, guys," Flea said confidently. "Just listen up and stick with me. We can take these guys. Trust me."

***

As Mihanna walked the halls to the ship's hanger bay, he and Armalan were chatting about the current situation.

"So tell me of this 'Flea' human," said Mihanna as they approached the hanger. "He does not have a normal human name that appears in our data banks, Brother. He is named after a disease spreading insect."

"I know, little Brother," responded Armalan. "Humans sometimes take or are given names by other humans, called 'nicknames.' These 'nicknames' are supposed to be endearing from what I have read."

"Ah," said Mihanna. "I cannot see what is so endearing about a flea. Spreading disease does not sound like an endearing quality to me, Brother."

"Nor to me, little Brother," chuckled Armalan. "Perhaps someday if he is comfortable with us, we can ask him to explain this name."

"Yes," agreed Mihanna. "It is very strange."

They entered the hanger and were walking in the direction of the monitors.

"That is odd," said the Admiral. "All of the fighters at this end are empty."

Armalan suddenly started to roar with laughter. He clutched his midsection as he laughed and pointed to the end of the hanger bay where the monitor was located. All the Kashin in the hanger bay had gathered on that end.

Standing there facing them were three humans. One was the young man he recognized from their mutual staring contest shortly after the humans came on board. He had many small bits of metal adorning his face and ears now, too. The female was the one he had witnessed two pilots trying to forcefully remove from the back of the converted fuel tanker they used for the rescue mission. She appeared to be fond of the color blue which was made clear by her outfit, and also had many bits of metal piercing through her ears, parts of her face and eyebrow. He did not recognize the third human. He had learned to tell the difference between males and females. The third was a young male with light brown hair and a red shirt.

The appearance of the three humans, however, was not what had stunned Mihanna and stopped him in his tracks. Their bright colors were not what had caused Armalan to burst into laughter. The source of Mihanna's shock, which was slowly turning into amusement, and Armalan's roar of laughter was directly in front of these humans. All the Kashin pilots had gathered to sit on the floor in front of the humans. They all had one leg raised in the air as they sat on the floor. Each one of the Kashin pilots appeared to be desperately trying to fold themselves in half. Their tongues were stuck out as if they were trying to lick their own backsides.

As vulgar as the entire scene appeared, Mihanna could not help but finally start laughing, "Is one of those humans Flea?"

"He is the purple one!" exclaimed Armalan in between fits of raking laughter.

"What has he done to my pilots?" chuckled Mihanna.

"I'm not sure," responded Armalan as his laughter died down. "But at least it is amusing!"

Armalan looked upward at the scene again his laughter roared a new.

"Okay you guys," said Flea hearing Armalan's thunderous laughter, "That's enough."

"Hey, Doc," shouted Flea with a grin, "I guess Kashin aren't as limber as I thought!"

"This is your fault, little Brother?" asked Armalan with a shout across the hanger.

"Sort of," responded Flea as the three humans approached Armalan and Mihanna. "Kaida and Tommy are to blame, too. They helped."

"I got killed," said Tommy dejectedly.

"You kill two first," said Kaida trying to cheer him up.

"It's cool, Tommy," said Flea with a grin. "Don't worry about it."

"You must be Flea," said Mihanna extending his hand as he learned humans tended to do during introductions. "I am pleased to meet you."

Flea and Mihanna shook hands warmly. Mihanna was not used to this Earth handshaking custom. He hoped he got it right.

"Please wait here," Mihanna said. "I would like to speak with you more, but I need to see how training has gone so far."

"We'll be here," responded Flea.

Mihanna trotted off to talk to the simulation controllers. Armalan was making small talk with Tommy and Kaida. Flea watched Mihanna's expressions as he talked to the simulation controllers to get an account of what went on this morning. Mihanna's eyes kept getting wider as he spoke with them. He would look back and forth with an astonished expression between Flea and the Kashin taking notes. Eventually, Mihanna returned from the short debriefing.

"Brother," said Mihanna. "They told me of the performance of you and these other two humans. Where did you all learn to fly like this?"

"Xbox," they replied in unison.

"Will you join me and my fighters?" Mihanna asked directly.

"No," said Flea. "They have too many prejudices against humans. It would never work out. However, if a human staffed carrier ever joins the fleet, I would gladly fly one of its fighters along with Tommy and Kaida. Right now, though, I have a difficult time trying to find the motivation to fight for beings that don't respect me."

"I understand," said Mihanna disappointed. "Will you still be my Brother?"

"If you can keep your prejudice put away and give me an honest chance," responded Flea.

Mihanna smiled warmly, "Wonderful! All the other humans have been reported to be departed from their ships. You are the last three to go to the new human sphere. If you wish, I will show you the way."

"We can have our mid-day meal together, little Brother," added Armalan.

"I'd like that," said Flea as they started to walk to the docking station. "Thanks, guys."

6

Over the last two weeks, Doshan had arranged for the "removal" of the remaining Battleship Commanders in the second fleet. He was really very good. They all appeared to be little more than unrelated accidents. This strengthened Esham'aut's position tenfold. No one would be reporting anything, aside from whether or not the current mission was completed, back to Imperial High Command. This would place Esham'aut in a true position of contention should there ever be a succession war if anything happened to the Emperor since he had no heirs. Despite this knowledge, Doshan could sense his friend was troubled. He and Esham'aut were in the unique position as young larvae to be forced to share a nutrient tank during their growth and gestation periods. They were raised on a remote outpost with few Imperial resources available to it. One of them was born too soon. The station's Elders were presented with the option of either reharvesting one of them or trying to save them both by placing them in the same tank. As a result from the Elders decision, he and Esham'aut were put in the same tank. Because they had to share nutrients and space, neither larva became very large. Of the two of them, Esham'aut was always the more ambitious. However, Doshan was with him everywhere he went. They were very close. Thanks to Esham'aut's ruthless ambition and Doshan's sneaky tactics, they had risen far beyond what was expected of them.

One of the things that Doshan had come to realize about his long time friend was how difficult it was to unbalance Esham'aut's emotions. This is what was surprising to Doshan as he looked at his old companion. Something was visibly bothering Esham'aut.

"Is there something wrong, old friend?" asked Doshan.

"Do you remember when we were in the tank together?" began Esham'aut. "We were in the room with all the other larvae and the Elders used to tell us stories between lessons sometimes."

"Yes," responded Doshan. "I remember that well. I really quite liked Elder Camman. He is one of the few Goras that I have encountered that I would not consider incompetent. Whatever happened to him?"

"He has since been reharvested. He serves the Empire even in death," replied Esham'aut softly. "Do you remember the story he told us about the Choden'gal?"

"Don't tell me that the mighty High Commander of the Goraan Second Fleet is afraid of children's stories!" chuckled Doshan.

"If you were anyone else," responded Esham'aut coldly. "I would have shot you for that remark."

"I apologize," responded Doshan. "Refresh my memory about this 'Choden'gal' story."

"It begins many eons ago," began Esham'aut. "When the Empire was young and so was its Emperor. The Emperor was a very inept leader, and all saw that he was useless. Because the Emperor could not decide what to do, the Imperial High Command had given all the Goras a task to perform for the further advancement of the Empire. One Gora, aside from the Emperor however, could not perform his task and was useless. His name was Choden'gal. Imperial High Command heard of Choden'gal and reported him to the Emperor. The Emperor, not realizing that he himself was useless, decreed that all useless Goras will be executed and their bodies used to feed the beasts which served the Empire. In this way, the Empire could get some use from an otherwise useless Gora."

"It sounds like a good decision to me," said Doshan.

"Yes, indeed," agreed Esham'aut. "Anyway, Choden'gal somehow escaped his fate and was enraged that the Empire did not see him as useful. As a result, he decided to make a use for himself. Choden'gal decided that he would serve the Empire by stripping it of the burden of supporting useless Goras. To this end, Choden'gal began to slay all the useless Goras, including the Emperor. He would chew off their faces and rip the Goras from inside their skulls. Then, he would squish them under his boot. In so doing, Choden'gal found he could serve a higher and more useful purpose of saving the Empire from supporting inept Goras."

"I remember, now. When we were young larvae the elders used to tell that story to scare us in to becoming useful members of the Empire," said Doshan. "They would tell us to be useful or the Choden'gal would come for us. What does an old legend have to do with us?"

"What goes on in the lower-end in your ship, Doshan?" asked Esham'aut quietly.

"The lower-end is a very disreputable place on any ship, mine included," Doshan replied. "It is filled with Goras of lower intelligence. They have been assigned to do the menial work not fit for a more refined and educated member of the Empire. They are really quite unsavory."

"Do you have murders there?" asked Esham'aut.

"What ship's 'lower end' is complete without a few murders?" Doshan chuckled. "Where are you going with this Esham'aut?"

"I have been having murders in my ship's lower end. Very special murders," Esham'aut replied. "My ship's security officer reports that when the bodies are found, their faces have been removed. The Goras inside the skulls were torn from inside. All that was left of these Goras was a small greenish stain somewhere around the dead shell where it had been squished."

"What?" exclaimed Doshan.

"You heard me," responded Esham'aut. "It's been horrible for ship's morale."

"What are you going to do about it?" asked Doshan.

"I am not sure, yet," responded Esham'aut. "I have, however, ordered a formal inquisition from the Ship's Inquisitor. Perhaps she can find something."

"How is the crew down in the lower end responding to the situation?" inquired Doshan.

"They continue about their tasks for the most part," started Esham'aut. "But some reports to me have said that the crew in the lower end is afraid to walk through the passageways. I could just let it go. After all, most of those killed are just low-enders."

"Most?" asked Doshan.

"One of them was a medical technician," responded Esham'aut. "He was down there delivering expired Goras for reharvestation. His name was Grumma. He was an officer. I will have to have him replaced."

"So how many have died in this fashion so far?" asked Doshan.

"Twenty three," responded Esham'aut grimly.

***

"Who is the Choden'gal?" shouted the Ship's Inquisitor as she squeezed Ba'an's cheeks together while holding his face.

"I said," she screamed with small flecks of spittle striking Ba'an's cheek. "WHO...IS...THE...CHODEN...GAL?"

She backhanded him across his white cheek which made a small cut where she struck him.

"You are too dense to know anything about the Choden'gal. Is this not so, pet?" she asked coyly.

"As my Mistress says," he responded mechanically. "I am too dense."

"However," he thought to himself, *"I am not too dense to kill you for this. I will add you to my list."*

She licked the blood from his cheek and then turned to strut away sensuously. Ba'an could do nothing to stop her in his present situation. He was strapped into a rack that forced him to raise his arms above his head. The shackles around his tentacles cut into his flesh and blood slowly trickled down his arms to drip on the floor.

The Ship's Inquisitor was a very powerful young female despite her small frame. She was much smaller than Ba'an. Her flesh was a deep red color which was offset by the black, wet-leather pants she wore with a matching half shirt that bared her well defined arms and muscular abdomen. Her long, bright orange hair was tied into a top knot on top of her head that hung down to her waist. The long finger nails on her five fingered hands were lacquered a bright orange color to match her hair and lip paint. She was very slender, yet curvaceous.

Her most distinguishing feature, however, was not her curves. It was the eight foot long whip-like appendages that were part of her arms. They attached just under her wrists. She kept them coiled up her forearms when she wasn't using them to beat someone. All members of the inquisitor race had these whips. It was a racial trait. Ba'an could see the tiny gold, pointed needles that she affixed to the ends of them. They provide both a protective tip and a means of adding an additional bit of pain while using them to beat her subject.

"There is a more important matter I have to discuss with you," she said as she strutted over to him. "You see, you are my pet."

Ba'an shivered as she continued to walk around behind him.

"And what I want to know is who exactly has been beating you?" she purred into his ear hole.

"I do not know what you are talking about," replied Ba'an.

"I don't know what you are talking about...what?" she screamed as she stepped away from him and uncoiled her whips. "Is this how you address me?"

"I do not know what you are talking about, Mistress," he replied quickly.

She struck out and quickly added three new gashes to the multitude that already existed on his back.

"I don't know what you are talking about," she screamed at him as she continued the whipping, "Mistress who?"

Ba'an winced in pain as he felt small bits of white flesh torn from his back by the tiny needles that tipped her whips. He could feel his green blood oozing down his spine.

"I do not know what you are talking about, Mistress Toren," he responded instinctively.

"I will tell you what I am talking about you fool," she screamed in a bloody rage as she continued her relentless beating which put even more gashes in Ba'an's skin. "When I beat you, my marks go horizontally, like so!"

"These other marks which keep appearing," she screamed as she whipped him furiously, "go vertically! THESE ARE NOT MY MARKS!"

She continued to beat him mercilessly. Ba'an could feel the blood go underneath the waist of his pants and run down his legs. His pants were starting to stick to the back of his thighs. After a while he heard the chime that marked the end of his beating and she stopped.

"Now pet," she said as she walked back up behind him and placed her chin on his shoulder again. "I know that you were asked here today before your morning meal."

She began stroking the top of his head.

"And this is your second beating for the day, just before your noon meal," she added. "But this doesn't excuse you from your evening beating."

"The one this morning was ordered for all the 'low-enders' as I try to discern who this Choden'gal styled killer is on behalf of the High Commander Gr'Nach Esham'aut," she said Esham'aut's name with disgust. "So I expect to see you back here later."

She applied a pink salve to his back which burned slightly. Ba'an was used to the healing treatment she administered after a beating. She may have enjoyed her work, but she always tried to heal her subjects as best she could after a session. Ba'an was curious as to why she didn't seem to like Esham'aut.

The pink salve healed the wounds, but always left grey scars on his flesh. When she was finished, she walked around in front of him. She walked over to a table against the wall and picked up a long, wickedly curved, serrated blade.

"In order to deter anyone else that might mistakenly think you are their pet instead of mine," she said as she slowly swayed toward him as she walked. "I will leave a message."

Ba'an screamed as she dragged the awful blade across his bare chest. When she was finished, Ba'an was slick with sweat as she applied more of the salve. She wiped all the pink healing ointment from his body and then walked around him once, as she always did, to make sure he had no open wounds. She stopped in front of him to admire her handy work. She held up a mirror so that Ba'an could see what she had done to his chest.

"There," she giggled rather childishly. "What do you think, pet?"

In Ba'an's chest, which she had previously not marked in any way, were a series of long, thick grey scars. The scars spelled out two words that Ba'an had to concentrate to try and read. They appeared backward in the mirror. They were arranged on his chest to spell out the words: TOREN'S PET. She walked over to the table were his shirt was located and made some cuts into his shirt. She then picked it up and walked over to him and unshackled him from the rack.

"Here," she said with a small smile as she handed him his shirt.

Ba'an put the shirt on, and found that she had cut a large square in the front of it to reveal what she had written.

"So everyone can see you are mine," she said musically. "And make sure you cut the rest of your shirts in this manner as well."

"Yes Mistress," he responded.

She then slapped him hard across his left cheek, and lightly kissed where she had just slapped.

"You are my favorite pet," she whispered to him. "I could beat you all day if I wished."

She dragged her tongue slowly across the spot she had just kissed, "You could never be the Choden'gal, my pet. You are too dense."

She stepped away from him for a moment and stared at the scars she put in his chest. She nodded once in approval at her marks.

"Go eat your meal pet," she said. "You are dismissed."

Ba'an left the Inquisitor's room feeling ashamed as he walked through the gold and silver gilded halls. The pain was enjoyable at times, but not the feeling of shame. He couldn't really explain why, but he often had that feeling after a session with Toren. Having her mark on his chest for everyone to see made him feel especially ashamed. He decided to skip his mid-day meal after some of the Goras he passed in the hall started to laugh and point as he went by them. Instead, he would spend the mid-day break in his meager room.

He passed more Goras who sneered and laughed at him as he made his way out of the lavish section of the ship down to the dull grey area of the lower end. Everyone knew who the Inquisitor was and could easily make her name out on his bare chest. As he made the turn toward his quarters, there was a Gora that was approaching him. He was a short, squat orange creature with a breathing apparatus that was carried on his back. Tubes went from the apparatus into a small mask that covered the creatures nose. Ba'an could smell sulfur as the creature approached and saw that the tubes were filled with a yellow gas. The yellow, sulfur smelling gas was expended out the creature's mouth when it exhaled. It was munching on a piece of hard, green fruit as Ba'an approached.

"It seems the trollop has marked you," he said laughing as he pointed at Ba'an's chest. "She sure has it for you!"

Ba'an glared at him as he felt the now familiar rage toiling inside his brain. He stared at the orange creature with hate in his black eyes.

"Oooo," said the orange creature. "Does she beat you real good when you stare at her like that?"

Ba'an's tentacles started to curl and uncurl at the ends. His head started to twitch toward the left on his neck. He forced the air angrily from his lungs.

"What is wrong little one?" asked the orange Gora condescendingly. "Did she beat you in the head a few too many times?"

The tendrils above Ba'an's beak where his acid sacks were located started to itch and leak the now familiar white fluid. They began to do this lately the more he used his acid. The skin above his beak started to tingle, as his flesh normally did, when the white acid came in contact with it.

"Maybe she needs a visit from me," he said gruffly. "She probably just needs a real mate to satisfy her needs."

That was the last Ba'an could handle from this creature. He stole a move from his Mistress and whipped one of his tentacles at the orange creature's face. It found its mark and he latched onto the orange creature's skin with the suction cups located on the bottom of the appendage. As he jerked his tentacle back, it returned to him with a chunk of orange flesh.

"You piece of useless filth!" bellowed the orange creature as it dove at him.

The orange creature wrapped his arms around Ba'an's mid section and the two were wrestling on the floor in an instant. The orange creature came up on top. It was bigger and stronger than Ba'an. Ba'an, however, had been in this position before. The creature wrapped his thick fingers around Ba'an's neck and started to squeeze. Before Ba'an struck, he struggled briefly to make sure no one was in the hall with them. He did not want anyone to know of his special ability. He could not risk getting caught.

Seeing the hall was empty, Ba'an decided it was time to make the kill. He took his aim, and spewed forth liquid white fury into the creature's eyes and face. The creature released his grip from Ba'an's throat to clutch at his melting face. He tried to make a noise, but all that came out was a liquid gurgling sound.

"Keep trying to scream," Ba'an whispered with a distant smile. "They always try to scream. It amuses me."

He crawled out from under the orange Gora and then kicked him in the chest to help him fall backward to the ground. Ba'an moved to straddle the creature until it finally stopped trying to struggle against what was happening. The stench of sulfur was strong in the air. The yellow gas was pouring out of the two burnt tubes that were once attached to the Gora's now melted nose holes. Ba'an forced the larger Gora's hands away from his face. He looked down at the orange creature to see a now familiar sight. There was a large hole were the majority of the creature's face was once located that ran down to include a large portion of the creature's neck.

"That's odd," said Ba'an as he hunched closer to the ruined creature. "How did this get missed?"

He was peering into one of the creature's eyes that had somehow escaped the destruction. It seemed to be looking around.

"I wonder if you can still see me?" he said softly as he gazed into the eye.

A few more low choking sounds came from the creature's throat.

"Stop that," said Ba'an as he stomped forcefully on the orange Gora's mid section.

Ba'an sat down on the creature's chest and looked into the orange Gora's skull. The tiny slug like Gora creature was huddled in the back of his enemy's head. Ba'an reached inside with a tentacle and tore the tiny Gory from its spot on its shell's brain. He lifted it out gingerly and sat it on the ground.

"I have an idea. If you can make it up the hall and turn the corner," Ba'an pointed to the corner almost thirty feet away. "I will help you to the medical technician and maybe you will survive."

Ba'an started to laugh sadistically. The tiny creature started to squirm down the hall at a mind numbingly slow pace. It left a small slime trail as it moved.

"At this rate, it will take you all day," said Ba'an after it had left a trail less than half a foot long.

"I don't have time for this," growled Ba'an impatiently.

He lifted his foot and squished the Gora under the sole of his boot. It made a small popping sound as Ba'an crushed it. Ba'an looked around and made sure no one saw him. He then wiped his boot off on the dead shell's chest and walked back to his room.

Ba'an entered his room and looked around a bit.

"Everything seems in order," he said to no one in particular. "I thought they might start to suspect me and search my room by now."

He walked over to the wall where his acid had initially scared it when he discovered its use. Next to the melted spot was a series of long melted marks on the wall. Ba'an turned over his tentacles to reveal his suction cups. He dripped some of his white acid into one of the large ones half way up the appendage. He dipped a tentacle gingerly into the small pool that was in the cup. After getting what he judged was a sufficient amount on the end of his tentacle, he pressed it to the wall and ran it down vertically next to the other marks. He then sat down on the floor with his legs underneath him. He reached under his bed to pull out a long, thin, flat flexible rod. He turned to face the wall with the marks on it, and looked at the fresh mark he just put there.

He stared at the marks as he lifted the rod up over his head. He brought it down quickly on his left shoulder. It bent at his shoulder and whipped down his back. Ba'an felt the wound open vertically down his back as he beat himself mercilessly. The blood started to ooze forth from the freshly opened cut. He beat himself over and over again as he stared at the marks on the wall. Finally, he stopped beating himself and just sat there for a time staring at the marks. One mark was made for each kill.

"Twenty four," he muttered darkly.

***

The Human Sphere in the Runner base was more than what the humans needed. It was designed to comfortably house seven hundred fifty thousand humans. Because only three hundred thousand were rescued, many of the houses were unoccupied. Many of the humans were also banding together to form new family units under the new circumstances. All of the humans seemed to have made the unspoken agreement that they would live in the dwellings nearest the transport tube that led to the sphere. All of them huddled in the homes around it, except for one human. He chose to live apart, and took his two companions with him.

Flea made his home away from the rest of the humans. He chose to live on the extreme opposite end of the sphere with Tommy and Kaida. This gave Flea the distinct advantage of combining multiple small dwellings to make one larger one with a large yard in front and back with many trees growing from the dirt that the computer had fabricated. The soil was given nutrients to feed the grass and plants that grew in it from a generator buried underneath it. The plants were fed simulated sunlight on a regular basis from the artificial lighting that turned on and off to correspond with a regular day's cycle. Oddly, the Doctor Armalan had been spending a lot of time in the human sphere as well. He, along with Admiral Mihanna and Mihanna's fourteen foster kittens, spent most of their waking time there. One of the kittens, a little purple female named Armina, usually took great pleasure in shadowing Flea around all day.

Flea was not exactly sure why these Kashin had taken such a liking to him, Kaida and Tommy. He had grown to like them over the last few weeks, though, and was glad they were around. The laughter the young kittens brought with them helped ease the pain of everything he and the others had lost. They had been taking their meals together, but today, Mihanna, and the rest of the kittens were strangely absent from the mid-day meal.

"Host," said Armalan, "Kashin red baiter fish. Six portions, please"

Flea, Kaida and Tommy were sitting at the table they had placed on the roof of the dwelling's second story balcony. They had been taking their meals under the glass dome so they could see the stars. As Flea looked up, he could see a light shining off the flat roof of the third story part of the dwelling. Flea had moved his bed outside onto the top of the third floor and set up a clothing station and computer terminal as well. He also had a few lamps up there, which was probably where the light was coming from. He must have left one on this morning.

"You will like this," said Armalan. "It is a delicacy from our home. What are you looking at, little Brother?"

"I left a light on," responded Flea. "That's all."

"I have been meaning to ask you," followed up Armalan. "Why do you make your bed up there? It seems awfully strange."

"So I can see the stars," said Flea. "And watch for the Goraan."

"What will you do if you see them?" asked Armalan quietly.

"Probably die," he responded with grim humor. "But at least I'll see them coming."

Kaida was sitting at the table next to Flea. She squirmed a bit closer to Flea after he said this and placed a hand on his shoulder. Flea patted her hand and smiled at her with the corner of his mouth.

"Sorry guys," he said. "I didn't mean to bring down the mood. So where are Mihanna and the kittens?"

"Brother Mihanna and his foster kittens are visiting another family of humans on the other side of the sphere," responded Armalan as he set down the plates, putting two servings in front of his own place. "Apparently, these humans are trying to get a combat vessel and some fighters allocated to the humans so they can join the fight against our enemies. Perhaps you will fly with them, little Brother? I personally have no stomach for fighting. I am a healer. Brother Mihanna, however, was most impressed by your performance in the hanger bay against his pilots."

"Is that why you two keep visiting with us?" asked Flea. "To get us to fight?"

Armalan looked hurt when Flea said this, "Surely you think more of us, little Brother?"

"Of course I do," said Flea shamefully. "I apologize. On Earth, some humans might employ a tactic like this to trick someone into doing something they don't want to do."

"I know," responded Armalan. "And so does Mihanna. We keep visiting for what you might consider to be anthropological reasons. We like you, but we are also trying to get to know about humans. It has nothing to do with getting you inside a fighter. That is why he hasn't said anything about it since the hanger bay incident. He will not mention it, or try to press you into it. It is not how you treat your Brother. If you do change your mind you, though, you will let him know, right?"

"I will," responded Flea with a chuckle. "And besides, maybe if my fellow humans are willing to fight, I might join them."

"Indeed, little Brother?" asked Armalan.

"Maybe," Flea replied. "So why did Mihanna take the kittens with him? I like having them around."

"These humans that he is going to visit," started Armalan.

"You mean the ones on the far end of the sphere," interrupted Tommy.

"Yes," responded Armalan.

"You mean the end of the sphere that isn't this end?" Tommy interrupted again urgently.

"Yes," replied Armalan a bit more forcefully.

"So that would be the end of the sphere on the extreme other side of where we are located?" Tommy growled.

"Okay Tommy," interjected Flea. "I get it. You don't like living so far away from the other humans. Get over it. It's quiet down here and we can do whatever we want without worrying about the neighbors. You want to move out?"

"No," Tommy sighed. "I'm fine down here."

"Good," replied Flea. "You can always move out if you want."

"If I may continue," said Armalan with his deep rumbling voice. "He took the kittens with him because the human registration list told him the family he was going to visit had a daughter. He thought it might be nice if she and the kittens played. Mihanna has a large group of kittens going along with him because the two humans confided to Mihanna that their daughter hasn't made any friends since coming here."

"Maybe the kids will be friends," said Flea.

"That would be nice," responded Armalan with a smile. "I always loved to listen to young ones laughing."

***

Armina was a ten year old female Kashin kitten. Her fur was very thick and a lustrous shade of dark purple. Her Mother's fur was the same shade before she was killed by the Goraan. She had large yellow eyes with vertical cat-like pupils. Her whiskers were also abnormally long, a trait she inherited from her now dead father. Like other kittens her age, she was not yet fully developed physically and as a result her hands and feet looked a bit like overly large kitten paws. Sometimes, this made it hard to hold on to things, but she did her very best. Her father used to help her hold on to things before he was killed.

She hadn't had much experience with humans except for Flea, Tommy and Kaida. She, like many other orphaned Kashin, had been moving from foster group to foster group since her rearing group and parents were killed by the Goraan. She had lived with many new parents and hoped to find one she might ask to be her guardian. Mihanna was the first one, though, to ever take her around humans.

She liked to play tricks on Flea because he had a good sense of humor. He never yelled at her when she pounced on his head after hiding somewhere out of sight. Sometimes, she felt like Flea probably saw her, but if he did, he never let on. He was lots of fun. Armina heard Flea, Mihanna and the big Doctor call each other "Brother" lots of times. This meant that Mihanna must trust Flea quite a bit.

She didn't know why, but Mihanna had been taking her and the rest of the kittens to Flea's house a lot. Armina thought this was really good, because Flea and the other humans spent a lot of time playing with her when they weren't talking about grown up stuff with Mihanna. Sometimes Flea was sad, though. Then, Armina would give him hugs and he would smile.

Kaida talked funny, but she and Armina still spent lots of time together making new clothes with the computer. Armina never had an older Sister before, and thought that Kaida was a good one. They had lots of hugs together. Tommy was different, though. He and Armina would laugh and wrestle together. Tommy was very gentle when they wrestled, and probably let Armina win a lot. They also liked to play video games together that had been downloaded from Earth. Armina wasn't as good as

Tommy because her paws made it hard to hold the controller, but she still liked to play with him.

Armina possessed many of the same qualities that were common among Kashin kittens. She had a short attention span, was overly energetic and loved to run and play. Many of the games she and the other Kashin kittens played revolved around trying to chase and catch each others' tails. Right now, Armina and the rest of Mihanna's foster kittens were on their way to go visit with some humans. Mihanna told them earlier that they had a little girl the same age as the rest of them. She had decided to make the little girl a present so they could play together. Maybe, they would be friends.

"Do human kittens have tails like us, Mihanna?" she asked.

"Does Flea have a tail, little one?" he looked down and smiled gently as he asked this.

"Ummm…" she began. "No, I didn't see one. Does he have one that he's been hiding in the back of his pants, Mihanna? That would seem awfully uncomfortable."

"No, Armina," he chuckled. "He does not have a tail hiding in the back of his pants."

"So the human kitten doesn't have a tail?" she persisted.

"No, little one," he replied. "She does not."

"Good," said Armina. "She will like my present, then. I thought really hard about it before I made it with the computer. It will be a fun thing for a human kitten."

"Children, little one," said Mihanna. "Humans don't call their young ones 'kittens.' They call their young ones 'children' instead."

"Oh…shildren?" she asked trying out the new word.

"CH-CH-children," said Mihanna demonstrating the word for her. "As in the word, 'chance.' See? You have done very well so far learning the humans' English. I am not sure why the linguistics chips have difficulty with them yet. Perhaps it's all their different languages."

"Children," she said satisfied. "Is it like taking a chance for humans to have children, Mihanna?"

"It is a chance for anyone to have young ones, Armina," he responded loudly so all the Kashin kittens could hear and added a playful wink over his shoulder.

All the kittens giggled in response. Armina was only one of fourteen kittens going to see the humans. She was glad that there were no older kittens going because they tried to dominate the games they played. She was also glad that there were not any younger kittens because they could not keep up. Thank goodness they didn't bring any males, either, because they might play too rough. She continued to mostly bounce in excitement along beside Mihanna until they finally stopped in front of a human dwelling. It was a long walk from Flea's house.

"Alright, little ones," said Mihanna after they stopped. "I am going to go inside and speak with some adult humans that have been lodging a petition to see me since my return. They have a young one in there that does not have any friends here, so please make her feel included in your games. Do not force her, just let her come and play naturally on her own. Understand?"

The kittens all nodded and voiced their understanding.

"Wait!" bounced Armina. "I have a present, remember?"

"Oh yes," chuckled Mihanna. "Armina you come with me. The rest of you wait here and play in the yard. Armina will try to bring her out, okay? Please remember to play nice, little ones."

He took Armina's paw in his hand and they walked toward the door. He stopped and knocked three times. She struggle to get a grip on the small box she carried under her other arm with her paw.

"Why did hit the door, Mihanna?" she asked.

"It is a human custom, Armina. They knock on the door as a form of announcement," he responded.

"Flea doesn't make us do that," she said.

"Flea is very informal, kitten," he replied with a smile.

"I don't like doors" she said thinking about her paws. "I can't turn the knob sometimes. I think trees are better."

"I know, little one," replied Mihanna gently. "Your paws will change as you get older."

She smiled up at him as the door opened up. Mihanna was a good foster guardian, but she wasn't going to stay with him. Maybe she would ask if she could stay with Flea and Kaida.

"Hello," Mihanna said, "I am Admiral Mihanna so'Chareck Mihanna, Commanding Officer of the Runner Fleet. This is, Armina."

"I'm Morgan Mendenhall," replied the tall human. "Please, come in."

"Oh you're very pretty," said Morgan with a smile as he squatted down so the kitten could see him. "Yes, very lovely."

"You have a fury face," giggled Armina as she noticed his beard.

This caused the human to laugh, "Yes, I suppose I do."

"Mihanna says that you have a human kitten?" she asked.

"A child, she means," corrected Mihanna gently.

"Yes I have a daughter. How old are you?" asked Morgan.

"Ten," she replied.

"Then you two are the same age," said the human female that was standing off to one side. "I'm Alex, Morgan's wife. I requested the meeting with you, Admiral."

"Yes, of course," he responded. "Will your daughter be coming down?"

"Keri!" shouted Alex up the stairs near the door, "Come down here, there is someone I want you to meet."

A little yellow haired girl came walking down the stairs. She was wearing a red top and black shorts and white running shoes. The yellow haired girl looked up and smiled a small smile of acknowledgement toward the two Kashin. Armina could tell she was sad, even though she smiled.

"Umm...," began Armina. "I am Armina esh'Camman Soharim. Would you like to play?"

"What does all that mean?" asked Keri.

"It means that I am Armina, daughter of Camman, of the Soharim clan. What is your name?" asked Armina.

"Keri," replied the girl with a small smile.

"Here! I brought you a present! I thought it up all on my own, and the computer helped me make it!" she said excitedly.

Armina was smiling broadly and extending the box she had brought with her to Keri.

"It is for you and it is a present and I made it!" she said proudly holding out the silver box. "Open it!"

Keri flipped back the box's hinged lid. She pulled out something that looked like sparkly red metallic cat ears attached to a hair clip with black trim.

"What's this?" asked Keri.

"KITTEN EARS!" shouted Armina excitedly with a big smile. "Now you can have Kashin hearing and Kitten Ears! It is Kitten Eeeaarrrs! Put them on! Put them on! Put them on!"

Armina was hopping up and down with excitement. Keri started to smile at the kitten's energetic manner. It wasn't a sad smile. It was a real smile. Armina looked around and saw the human grownups looking very pleased. The human adult female looked like she might cry as she smiled, but was trying very hard not to. Keri put the ears on and it automatically adjusted to fit her head to remain in place. Armina reached out and flipped down two small probes that went behind Keri's ears. The little human girl's eyes got very wide.

"What was that?" she asked looking around astonished.

"Did you hear something?" asked Armina playfully.

"Yes," shouted Keri as she bolted over to the couch.

Keri lifted the cushion and saw a small bug crawling underneath it.

"I heard it, Daddy! I heard it!" she shouted in elation.

"I know, princess," replied Morgan.

"Wait there is more," said Armina Hopping up and down with a grin.

Keri's eyes were sparkling, "More?"

"Yes! Look in the box and see," Armina said.

Keri looked in the box and pulled out the remaining object. Her eyes got very wide as she looked at it. Attached to a few straps was a long, segmented, sparkly red tail with black trim.

"Is this a tail?" asked Keri with large eyes and an open smile.

"Yes! Yes!" responded Armina pouncing about in excitement, "Kitten tail! Kitten tail! Kitten tail! Put it on!"

"Like this?" asked Keri as she put her legs in the two smaller straps and unbelted the large one, wrapping it around her waist. It fit similar to a pair of shorts. The tail moved itself into place at the bottom of her spine

"Yes!" Armina giggled. "Now you are a kitten like me! Hurray!"

"Cool!" shouted Keri.

"Try to swish it! It swishes! It links up to the ears on your head. They hook into your brain signals and now it is like you have a real tail! At least that is what the computer told me. Does it work? Try to swish it!"

The tail hung off the strap on Keri's waist to appear as if it were an extension of Keri's spine. At first it hung limply.

"Grrrrrrr," Keri said as she shut her eyes tight and concentrated harder.

After a moment, the red and black tail twitched slightly and Keri's eyes shot open.

"I CAN FEEL IT!" she said hopping up and down, "In my brain, I can feel it!"

"Tails are good for balance!" Armina giggled.

Keri turned around excitedly looking over her shoulder as she swished her tail back and forth.

"Oh thank you Armina," she cried throwing her arms around the Kashin girl, "Thank you so much! They destroyed my home, you know?"

"I know," Armina said softly embracing the little blonde girl.

"Now I have a friend," Keri choked out a whisper.

"We can be Sisters," said Armina as her eyes welled up with tears.

"Sisters," Keri sniffled. "Thank you."

A long moment passed as the two girls embraced.

"You two should go play," Morgan started to usher them out the front door.

Armina took Keri's hand and half led, half dragged her toward the door, "Come on, I will teach you to play cat-tails! Let's go!"

"Okay!" said Keri excitedly.

"Maybe we can go back to my house and play," she added looking over her shoulder.

"Don't be out too late," replied Alex.

"That was very well done, Armina," Mihanna whispered to the kitten as they walked out the door.

Mihanna watched with amusement as Armina and the human child went scampering outside to play.

"You have a good daughter," Alex said.

"She is a good young one," he said simply. "But she is only my foster daughter. Her family passed on at the hands of the Goraan."

"I am sorry to hear that," said Morgan softly.

"Keri needed a friend. Thank you," added Morgan seriously.

"You are welcome," replied Mihanna. "So, what is this meeting about? I have been receiving some very persistent messages from you, Alex."

"Well," she began, "we tried taking our grievances through regular channels, but we humans have yet to elect an official delegation to the council. They have been less than helpful."

"I understand and agree with your feeling about the council," replied Mihanna. "They are not very effective. The members seem to be more interested in making sure the respective species they represent have more authority than the other species represented. They constantly vie for power and authority."

"I see," said Alex.

"As a result," he continued. "They spend more time arguing among themselves than they do making any policies."

"How did you get your position, then?" she asked.

"During a moment of clarity," he started. "The council decided to have a contest of sorts to find the best strategists amongst the Runners and place them in charge of a military force for common defense. The others who progressed far enough in the contest serve as my advisors on strategy and tactics."

"That was a sound decision," said Morgan. "Was it effective?"

"In the beginning it was," he replied. "But after a while, the different council members began telling their respective units among the military to stop taking orders from me. They were to only follow my orders if it was ratified by the common council and personally agreed to by the units' respective species. As a result, my job has been getting increasingly more difficult."

"That's a bad situation to be in charge of," responded Morgan.

"I will be the first to admit that I need to be playing less politics. It is no way to run a fighting force," he agreed.

"At any rate," interjected Alex. "I have been speaking with some of the other humans, and many of us agree that we want the opportunity to fight."

"Fight the Goraan?" asked Mihanna incredulously. "Do you realize how strong they are?"

"Yes, we do," she said in a very matter of fact tone. "If we run, though, we only put off the day to our extinction. If we fight, then at least we can have a chance to live if we win."

"What are you getting at?" asked Mihanna slowly.

"We need a battleship," said Alex. "The few council members that would even acknowledge us said we should talk to you."

"And some fighters," added Morgan.

"Do you really think the humans can learn to operate a complex, intergalactic battleship?" Mihanna was skeptical. "I am sure that you are all very intelligent, but the theory and operation of a vessel like that requires many lifetimes worth of scientific achievement."

"It can't be too hard," Morgan said defiantly. "We sent monkeys into space! If a monkey can operate one, so can I!"

"We can learn it and we will," Alex glanced at her husband to calm him. "All we need is a chance. We'll stand by your side and screw the politicians."

"I do not have anything on the scale of a Kashin Battleship," Mihanna began. "But I could probably reallocate some stolen Goraan units. We have some old fighters and an outdated Goraan battle carrier that we have been salvaging parts from over the past three or four months."

"It's better than nothing," responded Alex glancing at Morgan.

"I don't know, Alex," said Morgan. "If they've been stripped for parts it could take time to make them worth something again."

"I will do this," Mihanna interrupted, "but, only if you can convince me that the humans will fight."

"We can get them to fight," Morgan said confidently. "Just give us a chance."

"One more thing," Mihanna added offhandedly. You command the vessel, Alexandria Mendenhall."

"I don't know anything about being in command of a warship!" replied Alex with wide eyes.

"You know enough to realize that you need to fight," responded Mihanna. "And so far, you have shown me that you are willing to try."

"Is that really enough to put me in charge?" she sounded a bit frightened.

Her husband was chuckling behind her back.

"Many times have I seen shear desire to succeed overcome years of training," Mihanna said solemnly.

"Isn't there anyone else?" she sounded trapped.

"I have checked the profiles of all the humans we rescued," he responded. "Very few have any combat experience. There are a few former military, but none that ever commanded anything on this scale."

"I see," she said.

"I was very surprised," responded Mihanna. "For such a war-like planet, I thought we might rescue at least a few with military command experience, but this was not the case."

"Is there anything else?" asked Alex.

"Take command of the ship yourself," he stated again. "Show me the humans' willingness to fight, and I will reassign whatever resources I can to you."

"Come with us to the Communal Sphere," responded Alex. "I sent out a text message to all evacuated humans that we would have a meeting there to discuss possibilities of retaliation."

"Oh really?" responded Mihanna.

"Yes," replied Alexandria fiercely. "Come with me and I will show you the humans' fighting spirit!"

7

Keri and Armina ran outside to play. Keri was very excited to finally make some new friends. Armina was very new and intriguing to her. The Fish-Captain said he had young ones, but Keri didn't want to go over there. She was afraid that something would happen to the weird air bubble that wrapped around her when she traveled in the water. She thought it was cool at first, but then she started to think it might pop or something when she was inside it. Keri knew she could swim, but she also knew she couldn't breathe under water. Now, she just wanted to play with the Armina and the other kittens. She was very excited when she went outside and saw a large group of Kashin kittens of various colors running and playing and climbing trees. Keri looked a little dejectedly at her own hands, not very suited for tree climbing when compared to a Kashin's. The kittens seemed to be throwing themselves up the trees at very dangerous speeds.

"You need paws and claws to climb trees and walls," giggled Armina as she made her musical rhyme.

"Yeah," pouted Keri.

"Got a computer, Keri?" asked Armina.

"Inside," said Keri perking up a little. "Why? Are you planning something?"

Armina perked up a bit at Keri's curiosity.

"Yes, I always have a plan," she smiled and stuck out her tongue.

"Wait though," cautioned Keri. "We can't go inside while our parents do grown up stuff."

Keri decided to stick her tongue out at Armina to return the gesture.

"That's okay," said Armina making another face. "Does this area of the sphere have a common building in it?"

"A what?" asked Keri.

The other kittens were now noticing the two standing there making faces at each other. Keri and Armina were both competitive in nature and had degraded in to a friendly exchange of making faces, trying to see who could make the best one. As the group of kittens watched, they could not help but join the impromptu competition. This in turn, turned the entire front lawn of Keri's house into a place that had been overrun by overly energetic, face making kittens. Finally, the group broke down and everyone started to laugh as they seemed to notice each other making faces. Keri was having fun with her new friend.

"Everyone!" Armina said in between fits of laughter, "This is my new Sister, Keri. Keri this is everyone!"

"That's how you introduce me?" asked Keri giggling, "By just saying that this is everyone?"

Armina giggled and started introducing everyone. After the introductions were over, the other kittens pounced away to play at what they were doing before.

"That's a lot of new friends," said Keri.

"I know," replied Armina. "Is that good?"

"It's good," nodded Keri. "Didn't you say you had a plan?"

"A plan for what?" asked Armina with a slightly worried expression, "Sometimes I lose track of things."

"A plan for paws," reminded Keri gently.

"I already have paws," she said looking confused at her paws.

"No," said Keri. "For me. Paws for me so I can climb better."

"Oh yes," said Armina. "And we need the computer in the common building around here so we do not have to go inside."

"Right," said Keri. "I know the way. Mom and Dad took me a few days ago. It's not far."

"Yes," said Armina. "But let's take the others. We should not go anyplace alone."

"Okay," said Keri.

"KITTENS!" shouted Armina pumping her arms in the air. "FOLLOW ME!"

Armina bolted down the walkway that was in front of Keri's house. Keri noted that in her excitement, the kitten went in a direction that was the exact opposite way of the common building. Armina was closely followed by a fluffy and colorful blur of giggling tails, fur and paws which belonged to the other kittens that ran behind her in a small flurry.

"Wait, you guys!" shouted Keri as she took off after them. "You're going the wrong way!"

After a brief giggling run she finally caught up to Armina and halted the kittens.

"Sorry, Sister," Armina sounded a bit ashamed. "I was just excited to help you and started running."

"That's okay," said Keri as she noticed Armina's disappointment in herself. "We can still make it there, but this time, follow me."

"I will," promised Armina with a smile.

"You just can't take off like that," said Keri. "I know you have a plan, but you have to think things through before you go running off."

"I will try," replied Armina. "Will you help me, sometimes?"

"I'll always help you," promised Keri. "You keep calling me sister. That's what sisters do for each other, right?"

"That is right," responded Armina hopping up and down, "Sisters! Sisters! Sisters, forever!"

"Come on, kittens!" said Keri. "The common building is THIS way!"

Keri was pointing in the opposite direction from which they were running, "And please, let's walk this time, you guys. I'm still getting used to my new tail."

They all giggled and started walking the direction indicated. Keri was in the lead of the group with Armina walking beside her.

"Do they always follow you like that?" asked Keri.

"Who?" replied Armina.

"The other kittens," asked Keri. "Do they always follow you?"

"No," responded Armina. "They are foster kittens like me. We are just together until we find guardians. I used to have a primary rearing group, though. We were what you humans might call a "litter." Kashin kittens live together, even though they might have different parents, for the first twelve years of their lives. Females live with females of the same age and males live with males. That is why there are no males with me."

Keri just noticed for the first time that no male Kashin kittens were present.

"My Daddy used to say that I was the dominate one of my rearing group and this is why they would often follow me," Armina continued. "I don't know what he meant by that, but he also would say that I would be a good leader for my people some day. So I guess he meant something good. We still listen to our parents and follow our parent's rules, but we grow up with each other. That is why Kashin call each other 'Brother' and 'Sister.' After we turn twelve years old, we do not need the security of the rearing group as much."

"Am I part of your group?" asked Keri hopefully.

"Of course!" said Armina, "We are Sisters, remember? You can be my primary Sister! That means we share everything and help each other all we can and never be apart! We'll start our own rearing group!"

"Does your Dad have a primary Brother?" asked Keri.

"He had three, once," said Armina sadly, "They were my uncles. They were killed by the Goraan."

"All my friends and family were killed, too," said Keri. "except for my Mom and Dad. Since you don't have a Mom or Dad anymore, I can share mine. They may not be the same as yours, but they try real hard and do a good job."

"Thank you anyway, Sister" said Armina. "But I will find a guardian that is right for me."

"Okay," replied Keri. "But we can still play, right?"

"Of course!" said Armina enthusiastically.

The two girls stopped, which brought the entire group to a halt, and shared a hug. As they let go of each other, they looked up and saw the sign which designated the common building for this sector of the Human Sphere. The common building was a large structure that some of the humans had painted yellow. Armina liked all the colors that the humans seemed to put on everything. When she left this morning, Kaida was busy painting the large domicile that she, Flea and Tommy shared a brilliant shade of blue.

"Now what?" asked Keri as they walked toward the yellow building.

"Now we get some paws," said Armina. "Come on! We'll use the kiosk inside."

They started to trot up the walkway and entered the large building. Keri looked around and noticed that the building was empty. As far as Keri knew, all the other humans had left the communal sphere to go see her parents speak.

The small group of children entered the common building through some glass doors. It was decorated with some couches, a few screens on the walls and a small computer kiosk in the corner with something that resembled a wall mounted microwave next to it. Keri recognized it as a matter combiner. The technology the Runners had was really amazing. They had matter combiners that could make everything from food to clothes and even toys. The matter combiner could take an existing block of material, pull off a small piece and rearrange the matter inside to produce anything as long as it wasn't too large. Keri learned about it when she watched her dad replace the "matter plug" in the back of the machine at home.

"Okay," said Armina. "Put your hands in there."

"Now what?" asked Keri as she put her hands in the chamber.

"Now we take some measurements," Armina replied. "Host, this is Armina esh'Camman Soharim. Take measurements of these human hands."

"Command verified," said the computer's female voice.

Blue lasers started to run across Keri's hands. They didn't hurt her. They were kind of like those laser pointers she used to buy at the gas stations on Earth. They formed a very tight grid all over Keri's hands.

"Measurements complete," responded the computer.

"Good," said Armina. "Now Host, I want you to make some Kashin paws. They will need to be gloves with retractable claws that fit on those hands. Pull up my commands from when I made the tail and ears that worked interactively with a human, that way, when the human wears them, they act just like real paws, complete with feeling and actions."

"Tail and Ears file located. Would you like to make them red and black to match the previous artificial constructions?" asked the computer.

"Yes," said both girls at the same time.

"Host, this is Keri Mendenhall," added Keri. "I need matching face paint."

There was a flash in the chamber accompanied by a quiet buzz. Armina opened the door and Keri reached in pulling out the two small jars of metallic red and black, sparkly face paint as Armina reached in and pulled out a pair of gloves.

"Wait a sec," said Keri taking the cap off the jar of face paint. Keri painted kitty whiskers on her face near her nose and giggled.

"See?" Keri asked. "Whiskers!"

"Cute," said Armina. "Now put these on."

She handed Keri the gloves. Keri reached a hand inside one of the gloves. After it was on it automatically shrank to fit snuggly around her wrist and hands.

"Cool," she said putting on the other one. "Just like the ears and belt."

"Can we put on some paint, too?" asked one of the other kittens.

"Sure," said Keri.

Armina instructed the computer to produce more face paint of various colors. Keri, Armina and the kittens went to work giggling and busily applying large amounts of paint to their faces, hands, arms and legs. Keri liked her new friends. Armina liked her new primary Sister. All the kittens were laughing and having fun. It was a good day for little girls.

***

"Are you alright?" asked Morgan as he looked towards his wife with some concern.

"Why aren't you doing this again?" Alex asked worriedly.

"Because you lost the coin toss, remember?" Morgan replied seriously. "Besides, you're in command of the ship if we get it. You need to do this. Are you ready?"

"I think so," she said. "I planned out what to say, but I haven't given any speeches since college. It's been a while since then."

"Yeah," chided Morgan. "A long while, huh?"

Alexandria scowled at him slightly.

"I hope you think the couch is comfortable," she said ominously.

Morgan laughed slightly at her response. They were wearing black when they left the domicile with Mihanna along with them.

"By human custom that I have studied," said Mihanna. "Black is a mourning color. Why do you wear it?"

"It reflects the graveness of our current situation," responded Morgan.

"It could also be said," added Alex softly, "that we are in mourning for our planet and her people that were lost."

They were standing behind a raised platform in the center of the Communal Sphere. Out in front of the platform were all the humans that had been rescued off Earth. Or so they thought.

"Host," said Morgan talking to his smartphone. "Are all the humans present?"

"No," replied the computer. "Four have not elected to come to today's proceedings."

"All but four," said Morgan. "One of them is Keri with the kittens. Not a bad turn out."

"Many of the Kashin have come, too," said Mihanna. "I confess that I have some inside connection among the humans and had prior knowledge of what you were going to do. I put word out to the Kashin."

"That explains what they are doing here. Of course, now I have to speak in front of a larger crowd. Thanks," Alex said dryly.

"You'll do great, sweetheart," said Morgan. "The two of us will go up with you. Are you ready?"

"Host," said Alex. "How many total Runners are out there waiting to hear me speak?"

"Two million seven hundred thirty six thousand nine hundred eighteen," replied the computer. "Do you wish to have your voice amplified?"

"After I get to the designated spot," replied Alexandria.

"Well," said Morgan, "let's go before you change your mind."

They walked up the white steps on the back of the raised platform. The platform itself was a large white marble affair with a black marble podium at the front. In front of the platform was a sea of creatures. The humans didn't even make up the majority of them. Most of them were Kashin, but there were some other races present that Morgan and Alexandria didn't recognize. Alex's heart raced as it dawned on her that she had never been in the presence of this many people, and now she was expected to speak to them. Everything that she had planned to say emptied from her reeling brain as a wave of fear set in. She peered out at the hungry beast of a crowd in front of her, thinking that they would surly eat her alive.

With all of her confidence shot, she stopped in the middle of the large platform before she reached the podium. All of a sudden, she felt like a little girl looking up at the jar of cookies she couldn't quite reach on top of the kitchen counter. Her goal just seemed too far away. She looked back for a moment, and found some strength in the face of her husband. He nodded slightly to her and silently mouthed the words, "I love you." He looked like some great fury monster behind his beard. In that gentle monster, however, she found a small amount of strength. She didn't know what she was going to say now, but she turned and started walking back toward the podium. Some vomit reached the top of her throat and she swallowed it back before it became worse. Despite her fear, she knew that someone had to do something. The roar of the crowd died down as she slowly made it to the podium.

"My name," she jumped a bit as she noticed how much the computer amplified her voice, "is Alexandria Mendenhall. Two weeks ago, I was at an amusement park in Texas. I was with my husband and daughter, who luckily, are still with me. We were there for my husband's job as an enemy shot through of the sky. It was like nothing we had ever seen before. They are greater in strength, technology and numbers than our entire planet put together. They brought us to the brink of extinction."

The crowd slowly started to stir as Alex said this. The humans were shuffling around and looking at each other as she spoke. Being told about the direness of the situation seemed to bother them.

"There is less than a fraction of a percent of the entire human population left. My husband, my daughter, myself" she said seriously, "and all of you. We are all that is left. I would like to say that our situation has gotten better, but it hasn't."

She placed her hands on the sides of the podium and leaned forward toward the crowd. The humans were starting to nod and mutter their agreement. Some of the other species in the crowd were angered by this statement. Most of the Kashin however, were agreeing with the humans.

"We have been ripped from our homes to escape a force of destruction unlike any we have ever seen!" she said slamming her fist on the podium. "We were thrown across space into a situation we know nothing about!" she said slamming again. "We have been forced to side with an ally who seems to not just ignore us, but is insulted by our very presence!" she said pounding again to drive those last six words home. "And now, we cannot even fight back!"

The humans stirred even more. Alex looked out and felt her resolve strength as she noted the crowd's response. Rage burned inside her. People were listening.

"Our rescuers say we have nothing to fear," she growled, "and yet if that were true, then why do we call ourselves 'Runners?' Is it our choice to run?"

She heard a few humans shout a responsive "No."

"NO!" she shouted. "IT IS NOT!"

The humans in the crowd started to get louder when she said this.

"OUR ENEMIES CALL US RUNNERS!" she continued yelling. "This is not something we call ourselves. THEY call us this as a derogatory term! I never chose to run, but that's what they call us! And what do we do with this? Are we are so weak? Are we so willing to just lie down and die as we accept that name and its fate for ourselves!"

The roar of the crowd was even greater. She looked briefly over her shoulder and saw her stern looking husband nod in encouragement. Mihanna stood there looking stunned, as if he didn't believe this could be happening. Alex turned back to the crowd.

"Do you know what I say?" she asked.

Some in the crowd started to ask her what she would say.

"Would you like to know what I say?" she asked even louder.

A few more in the crowd responded by asking what she would say. The crowd had grown larger as she spoke.

Someone shouted, "What would you say?"

"I say that I AM NOT A RUNNER!" she shouted.

The crowd went crazy. The roar was so great, that the few left in the Communal Sphere were looking out the windows to see what was going on. The sound was so loud that it almost threatened to push Alex from the podium.

"I AM NOT A RUNNER!" she shouted again. "I AM A FIGHTER!"

The roar grew and started to shake the glass windows of the buildings around her.

"I AM A FIGHTER!" she shouted again feeding off the crowd and pumping her fists in the air. "I AM A FIGHTER!"

The crowd had reached a frenzied state. She only hoped it would be maintained. Mihanna had told her that the Runners were having trouble unifying. Many among their numbers, which was much smaller than their enemy's, didn't want to fight. Many were content with running. Some even wanted peace. She knew asking this next question was a great risk. If no one responded, then there was no hope. She braced herself on the podium as she prepared to ask a question for her final statement.

"WHO WILL FIGHT THEM WITH ME?" she yelled.

The crowd went silent. Even the humans, who were previously yelling even louder than the rest looked around as no one spoke. Their enemy had them outnumbered by so much, that most were scared to even think about fighting. She gathered her resolve and prepared to ask again.

"WHO," she yelled, "WILL STAND WITH ME AND FIGHT?"

The crowd was dead silent. Alex felt sick again.

***

"So how do the paws work?" asked Keri as she looked down at the red metallic paws that matched her new ears and tail.

"Kind of like your tail," replied Armina.

Keri and the rest of the kittens were covered with paint on every part of their bodies that didn't have clothing or fur on it.

"You think about it and it just works," said Armina

Keri continued looking at her paws for a moment, and then they started to wiggle as she gained control of them. Shortly after she started to wiggle her new kitty paws, she managed to pop the small two inch long retractable claws that came from the finger tips.

"Cool!" she gasped. "Mom is sooooo going to hate this!"

"You know, Flea uses that word a lot, too," Armina said. "So does Tommy and Kaida. What is it humans have about the temperature?"

"When I say something is 'cool,' it means that I like it," said Keri.

Keri was silent for a moment as it dawned on her what Armina had just said. She mentioned someone named Flea. Keri had known a person on Earth named Flea. She knew him her whole life. He was her Dad's close friend for many years. Flea grew up with her Dad. Most of the people on Earth died, but not many people called themselves "Flea." No one else that she knew ever called themselves "Flea". If it was the same "Flea," it meant that Keri, Dad and Mom had family left from Earth. This was very important.

"Sister," said Keri very seriously. "Did you just say something about a man named 'Flea?' This could be important."

"Yes," said Armina. "Me, Mihanna and Doctor Armalan started visiting Flea, Kaida and Tommy about two weeks ago here in the Human Sphere. I have not known him very long, but I can sense something strong and good in Flea. He is really nice to me. We play a lot."

"Can you tell me about Flea?" asked Keri quickly.

"Of course! I was thinking about asking him to be my guardian. Now that I am an orphan, I would like him and Kaida to be my family," she said hopefully. "It has been a long time since I had a family of my very own. He does not know it, but I think we need each other."

"Sister," said Keri earnestly. "I am sure he is a nice person, but please, just tell me about him, okay? What does he look like?"

"Sorry," said Armina. "I got off track again. Well, he is kind and likes to joke around a lot. He is about this tall," she said raising her paw above her head and hopping to reach Flea's height, "and has brown hair and brown eyes. He has brown fur on his face around his mouth, like your Dad, but not as much. Kaida put some metal piercings in him one time while he slept. I think it is funny that he did not wake up for that. He left them in to please Kaida."

"Anything else?" asked Keri intently.

"Well," continued Armina, "he likes to play with me and does not get mad when I pounce on him. Sometimes I can tell he is still sad from losing his planet. He misses his home. That is when I pounce on him and make him feel better! Then he laughs at me and we wrestle. He is very gentle with me, though. Oh, and he sometimes he swears a lot."

This sounded very familiar. Flea used to do things like that when she and her Dad would go over to visit him when they were in Indiana. Keri knew there was only one last question she needed to ask.

"Did he tell you about his home, Sister?" asked Keri as she leaned forward hanging on Armina's every word. "Where is he from?"

Tears were welling up in her eyes as she asked. She could only hope that someone she knew on Earth, someone she knew her whole entire life, was still alive.

"Are you okay, Sister?" asked Armina worriedly.

"Please, Armina," implored Keri. "Think hard. This is important. Do you know where Flea is from?"

"Earth," replied Armina looking confused.

"Where on Earth?" insisted Keri.

"Oh," said Armina. "You mean like one of the places on Earth?"

Keri nodded her head and placed her paw clad hands on both sides of Armina's face. Keri was now crying.

"Indiana," said Armina confidently. "I think he said Fort Wayne, Indiana. He showed it to me on the computer when I asked him about it."

"Take me!" Keri choked out as she cried. "Take me to Flea's house!"

"I will do that," said Armina more than slightly worried for her Sister. "Are you alright?"

"Just take me there!" said Keri earnestly.

"This way," said Armina as she started going toward the personnel conveyor.

"Run," said Keri. "Please, we need to hurry! Show me!"

They started to trot up the conveyor with the other kittens in tow. The other kittens thought this was some kind of game.

"Don't skip!" shouted Keri angrily. "This is serious! I know Flea! Run! Please, RUN!"

They all swarmed up the personnel conveyor toward Flea's house as fast as their little legs could carry them.

***

After lunch, Armalan had gone to check on some experiments he was running in his laboratory near his own home. He told the humans he would be back a bit later. He was absolutely thrilled at how easily human body organs could be reproduced synthetically. This was probably because of the more simplistic human DNA chain. He was hoping he could use this to his advantage and somehow figure out how to make synthetic organs that could be used in other species. He was working on some sort of all purpose, generic multi-species heart muscle. This meant that Flea, Tommy and Kaida were left to their own devices at the house. As a result, the three of them were outside, painting the house at Kaida's insistence. Part of the house was still a dull grey, but the areas where they had already managed to paint were a brilliant blue color. Kaida had obviously chosen the color to match her wardrobe. Music from Earth was playing from the speakers they had strategically placed in various hidden locations around the yard as they worked.

"Exactly why," complained Tommy, "are you making me do this, again, Flea? Can't we just get the stupid robots to do it?"

"This is a chance for us to bond as a family, Tommy," explained Flea. "So shut up and bond, damn it."

"Yeah, Tommy," giggled Kaida. "Family is together. Now we bond."

Kaida's English had improved slightly since joining Flea and Tommy. She was becoming very close to Flea. They laughed at the small joke and Tommy began splattering Flea with paint.

"Bond with this!" he said grinning as he emptied a bucket of paint at Flea.

The paint splatters covered the left half of Flea's body and made his shirt stick to his torso. Kaida pointed and laughed. Flea pulled off his shirt, which made him look slightly less blue. That was remedied, however, as Kaida snuck up behind Flea while he was throwing paint at Tommy and dumped blue paint over his head. The situation deteriorated into a three sided paint war and ended when all three were blue from head to toe. At some point, Armalan had quietly snuck into the yard and was watching curiously as the three laughed and continued to pointlessly throw paint at each other.

"Do humans often adorn each other with unnatural colors?" he asked as we walked out into the middle of them.

The three looked at each other as they realized the opportunity that had been presented.

"Is something wrong?" asked Armalan as the three looked at him mischievously.

"Oh dear," murmured Armalan as he realized he was in exactly the wrong place to be.

Without word, the three humans started laughing and screaming playfully as they covered the great lion-type Kashin with blue paint. All three emptied their full paint buckets in his direction. Armalan's majestic golden fur was soon covered with blue paint that hung limply from his body in blue dreadlock-like clumps. The situation degraded even further as Armalan joined in the gleeful battle by grabbing two or three paint buckets in each of his huge hands and commenced to empty them at the smaller humans as he roared with laughter. Soon, all four collapsed in the front yard, out of paint, breath and energy. They smiled at each other as they continued laughing from their recent little war.

"I like the way you humans play," said Armalan with a rumbling laugh. "It is very messy and spur of the moment. That is probably why Armina has taken to you so quickly. You know, Flea, you are not nearly as angry as when we first met. I think the kitten as aided in that. I am glad I had the opportunity to meet you."

"Me too," replied Flea simply.

"Flea!" Kaida said from behind Flea. "I help you clean now."

As Flea turned to look at Kaida and see what she was talking about, she laughed and dumped a bucket of water she had snuck off and retrieved over his head. Kaida bolted off out of reach before Flea could retaliate. Without warning, Tommy entered the fray, throwing more water at Flea and Armalan.

"I see no choice, noble Brother," said Flea with mock sincerity. "We must take to arms and thoroughly route these upstarts from the glorious field of battle!"

"Yes, my valiant Brother warrior," agreed Armalan as he thickly laid on the gallantry. "These young rapscallions must truly be taught a lesson in respect!"

The four entered a complex war of alliance and betrayal through the act of thrown water until they were mostly clean. At the very least, they were streaked with blue in fewer places. The yard became a mess, which matched the condition of the house, which caught the brunt of the missed exchanges.

"Now, will you call on the maintenance robots?" asked Tommy as the four called a truce and met in middle of the front yard to parley.

"I believe the young one shows some wisdom, little Brother," agreed Armalan.

"Kaida," said Flea giving her the last word. "Should we call the robots, or use this opportunity to clean up the place ourselves and bond as a family?"

"Ummmmm…" she started looking up at the dome and bighting her lip, "Robots."

They laughed a bit more and started to pick up some of the buckets in the yard. Flea went inside to get his phone and call the maintenance robots to come repair any damage and clean up the yard. They would finish the house later.

"Flea!" Kaida heard a voice screaming from up the street as they worked.

She looked up and saw a pack of Kashin kittens running up the personnel conveyor as fast as they could. She recognized Armina and started waiving to her.

"Armina!" shouted Kaida as they ran up.

"Kaida, guess what?" interrupted Armina. "This is Keri!"

She introduced the blonde girl that was wearing some curious metallic red, sparkly Kashin apparel.

"Hello Keri," Kaida said bowing to the girl.

"No wait, Kaida, listen!" insisted Armina. "This is Keri and sh…"

"Where's Flea?" demanded the young girl hoarsely with tears running down her cheeks. "I know him. It has to be him! Where's Flea?"

"What?" asked Armalan gently with his deep comforting voice. "You say you know him, child?"

"Please," insisted Keri tearfully. "It has to be him."

"Keri?" said Flea shocked as he came back out the front door.

Keri looked over and saw the man she knew as Flea standing in the front door of the house. He was still streaked with blue paint. She smiled with all the emotion in her small heart as she looked up at him.

"Keri!" said Flea running to her and picking her up in a tight embrace. "Oh, baby girl!"

"You're not dead!" cried Keri. "Everyone is dead, but here you are! You're not dead!"

"I know, sweetie," said Flea softly as tears welled up in his eyes. "I know."

"They're all gone," said Keri. "But not you!"

She buried her face in his bare shoulder and cried. Flea had his arms wrapped around her in a fierce hug.

Keri smiled through her tears, "Not you!"

"You know me, sweetheart," replied Flea softly. "It takes more than an alien invasion to put me down."

The other two humans looked on with stunned expressions. So many people were killed on Earth, that most of the humans who survived did not know each other. The chances that someone would know another person from before the destruction were astronomical. Flea and Keri stood their clinging to each other for a very long time. Flea looked up and finally noticed the other three standing there smiling as they watched and shared in the moment.

"Oh, I almost forgot. Come here you guys," Flea motioned to the others.

"Keri," he began. "This is Kaida, Tommy and Armalan. I met them during the evacuation. We are staying here together. I see you met Armina."

"Yes," Armina chimed in. "We are Sisters now, Flea. Maybe now, you will not be so sad sometimes."

"Yes, kitten," said Flea choking back tears, "Things are starting to look up."

"Keri and I had lots of fun, and now she is like a Kashin," said Armina excitedly, "And I see you painted each other! Me and Keri and the kittens painted each other, too!"

Flea looked at Armina, Keri and the rest of the kittens noticing that they had painted a myriad of hearts, shining suns, rainbows, birds, flowers and all sorts of happy, childish, girly things all over every inch of uncovered skin. They were a very happy looking, comical bunch of painted, pouncing kittens. Flea wanted to ask Keri about her parents, but was afraid of what the answer might be.

"Can we paint you, too?" asked Armina with large eyes.

"Of course," said Flea lost in the moment.

The children happily went to work painting on Flea and the other three. They had a particularly good time painting Armalan, who had the most surface to cover. As Flea sat and watched, he finally worked up the courage to ask about Morgan and Alexandria.

"Keri," he said softly. "What happened to your parents?"

"They're in the Communal Sphere giving a speech!" she replied excitedly. "We can surprise them when they're done! I know they'll LOVE to see you!"

The wheels in Flea's head started to slowly grind as he processed what Keri had just said. Not only were two of his closest friends alive, but they were off giving a speech. The gears in Flea's head started to turn and put things together.

"A speech?" Flea arched an eyebrow.

"Yes," Keri replied earnestly. "They'll love seeing you!"

Morgan and Alex weren't the types to go around giving speeches.

"They're giving a speech?" asked Flea. "A speech about what?"

"I don't know," said Keri. "They said it was grown up stuff."

"Fighting," replied Kaida. "They give speech for fighting."

"Kaida, what do you know about this?" asked Flea.

"You never check messages!" accused Kaida. "I send you email two days ago about meeting in Communal Sphere! You never check! I not get any email back from you!"

"We live together in the same house! Why would you email me when you could just speak to me?" Flea exclaimed. "I don't check my email! I never get anything important! Earth is destroyed and the only email I get is STILL about growing a larger penis!"

"I know," agreed Tommy. "Even this 'higher technology' internet is just used for porn, penis size, and dating!"

"What do you know about porn, young man?" accused Flea. "Look, just never mind about that! Stop getting me off track. What were you saying about a speech, Keri?"

"I told you," she said. "They're down there giving a speech in the Communal Sphere. Mommy is probably really nervous right now."

"Host," said Flea as he pulled his smartphone from his back pocket. "Play the speech going on in the Communal Sphere."

Flea looked at the small screen and saw a picture of Alex and Morgan walking across the marble platform in the Communal Sphere. Alex looked scared to death. She turned around and briefly looked at Morgan. Seeing his long time, close personal friends in trouble, something in Flea snapped. He shoved the phone into in his back pocket. He jerked his head up to look Armalan directly in the eyes.

"You know how to get there, Armalan?" he asked intently.

"Yes, little Brother," replied Armalan noticing the determination in Flea's eyes. "What are you going to do?"

"I'm going to pick a fight," said Flea with grim determination.

"With who?" asked Armalan.

"The Goraan," replied Flea with a growl as his eyes continued to burn.

"How?" responded Armalan breathlessly caught up in Flea's emotions.

"I don't know," Flea shook his head. "But I know it starts down there."

Flea turned and looked at everyone.

"LET'S GO!" he shouted.

They all ran off the front lawn, leaving the mess where it was. As Flea ran on the personal conveyor, it made him appear to move faster than possible. He and his group made for an interesting fight. He was covered with various happy shapes that had been painted on his face and bare torso. To make the sight even more comical, he was surrounded by a large group of similarly painted kittens, two humans and one very large Kashin. It was if they had been rained on by a color storm. As they ran, they noticed the Human Sphere was totally empty. Everyone but them was at the meeting. They reached the portal tube, and found the transport platform waiting for someone to hop on and state their destination. The small group piled on quickly.

"Communal Sphere," said Flea before the computer wasted his time asking his destination.

The platform whisked away and a few moments later, they reached their destination. Everyone piled off and started to run up the personnel conveyor of the Communal Sphere. Armalan was in the back of the group shouting directions. Noticing that Keri and some of the kittens were having trouble keeping up, Flea and the other larger adults had picked some of them up and were carrying them as best they could to help them along as they ran. As they turned one corner, the group came to a screeching halt. In front of them on the conveyor, was a large group of snakelike creatures hissing at each other and making small talk.

"Can you believe those sssimple humansss down there?" hissed one.

"I know," replied the other. "We could never defeat the Goraan even with our technology."

"Yesss," agreed another swaying back and forth. "And all the Runnersss know how much better we are than sssimple humansss."

The large group of snake people either didn't notice, or didn't care about Flea and the kittens trying to shove their way through.

"Excuse me," said Flea shouldering his way past a few of them.

"Pardon me," Kaida said to another few trying to make a hole.

He pulled out his smartphone and checked it long enough to see Alex was actually giving a speech.

"We have to get down there," he explained to one of them. "Please, move."

The crowd looked with some disdain at the human and his pack.

"You realize thisss isss pointlesssss, do you not?" asked one of them.

"Someday," growled Flea, "I'll come back here and beat some manners into you. Right now, I'm kind of busy."

The lizard drew back from Flea and hissed.

"Hey DOC!" Flea shouted over his shoulder. "Would you do something about this, please?"

Armalan stood up straight and filled his lungs with air.

"GRRRRROOOOOOAAAAAR," he let out a wordless, blood curdling growl that threatened to split the ears of anyone in range.

The lizard creatures quickly darted from Flea and his companions' path, cowering in fear at either side of the conveyor.

"Thanks!" shouted Flea as they took off running again.

"My pleasure!" shouted Armalan in response as they ran.

Finally, after turning a few more corners, Flea and his small group came to a halt. In front of them was a massive sea of humans, Kashin and other Runner species fanned out in front of a large, raised marble platform. On top of the platform was Alexandria Mendenhall. She had married his best friend. Slightly back and to her right was the familiar presence of his friend, Morgan. He was watching intently as Alex spoke. Mihanna was standing back to Alex's left, showing the support of the Kashin for the humans. The two humans were dressed somberly in black. Flea felt a mixture of relief and joy, at seeing his closest friends still alive. Alex was showing an uncommon amount of strength up there, and Flea was proud of how well she was holding herself together. He was reminded at that moment how silly he must look covered with paint.

"Oh well," he thought. *"It's too late now."*

He listened intently as they stood watching from their place about twenty yards behind the wildly cheering crowd. Flea could tell the speech was coming to an end.

"WHO WILL FIGHT WITH ME?" Alex yelled questioning the crowd.

The crowd, which was wildly screaming moments ago, had become strangely silent. They wanted to fight. Flea could tell this. Many of them, however, were afraid to stand against such an impossible enemy. Flea could tell this as he listened to the hushed murmuring that was going on. They were scared. The Goraan were bigger, stronger and had more resources available. Winning this fight seemed all but hopeless to the Runners that were just previously so intent on the speaker's words. Flea had to say something. He had to help the few people left that he cared about.

"WHO WILL STAND WITH ME AND FIGHT?" she yelled again.

The silence of the crowd was like a blanket threatening to suffocate them all with inaction. Now was the time. Someone had to do something. The determination Flea had felt in the Kashin fighter program crept back inside him. This crowd needed a fire. Flea had a match.

***

Alex felt like she was going to vomit. The crowd, which moments ago was so intent on doing something about their situation, was now murmuring quietly at what she had just asked them. If someone didn't speak up soon, she would lose them, and all hope would be gone.

"Next time," she thought wryly to herself, *"don't give an interactive speech."*

She stood there, hoping someone would say something. Finally, she heard a muffled voice from the back of the crowd. She couldn't make out what it said and was straining to see the face beyond the lights in front of her.

"What was that?" she tried not to lose her composure. "Host! Amplify!"

"I said," replied a familiar voice, "I will stand and fight."

Some of the hovering cameras that were around Alex took off over the crowd. They had been projecting her on the many view screens and holo-projectors on the roofs and sides of the buildings.

"I WILL STAND AND FIGHT!" yelled the voice louder.

Alex and Morgan worked hard as they tried to hide their astonishment when they looked at the large screen behind the crowd and saw the familiar face that accompanied the voice. It was Flea. Morgan reached up and squeezed Alex's elbow while the cameras were not focusing on her to help give her some support. Now was not the time to break down. No matter how emotional the two were feeling upon seeing their lost friend.

Flea was standing at the edge of the crowd, looking very serious. He wasn't angry or raging. He looked purposeful. This was apparent on his face. As Morgan and Alex watched him, they couldn't help but smile. Contrasting the look of single minded determination on his face, was a large pink heart on one cheek, and a blazing sun with a smiling face on the other. His forehead had light blue fluffy clouds on it. His bare chest and arms where painted in a similar manner, as was his entire entourage. It gave him the appearance of innocence. It gave his appearance childishness which sharply contrasted his expression. He stepped purposefully toward the crowd. The crowd responded by taking a step back.

"I will stand and fight!" said Flea placing his hand on top of Armina's head and glancing down toward her with a small smile. "For all of those who cannot fight for themselves, I will stand and fight."

The crowd was starting to stir again.

He snapped his face back toward them, "For all of those who cannot stand for themselves, I will stand and fight. For all of those who cannot speak for themselves, I will shout at our enemies in a voice of raging thunder! I scream to them: I WILL STAND AND FIGHT!"

The crowd was responding wildly as Flea spoke to them.

"No matter the outcome," Flea continued more softly. "I will stand and fight."

The crowd was cheering as if they had been starved of inspiration. It was like they were waking up from a nightmare.

"I heard them scream for us!" thought Alex. *"But this is crazy!"*

Flea started walking toward the crowd. As he reached them, they parted around him and his small group leaving a circle around them. Flea was holding the hands of Keri and Armina as he walked toward the stage.

"Our enemies call us Runners and we have shamefully taken the name for ourselves. Stand and fight and we will make them name 'Runner,' a name our enemies will fear! You know, running may not be dying, but it sure as Hell isn't living, either! I will stand and fight! I will fill my lungs with air and scream defiance at our enemies!" he was yelling again. "And should I fall, I will spit curses at them with my very last breath!"

The crowd was going nuts. They continued to part and close around them again as Flea and his group finally reached the stage. He tried futilely to climb the side of the tall platform until he was helped by some of the larger creatures that were in the crowd of humans, Kashin and other Runners. Flea and his group were now standing on top of the platform. They were a motley looking group. They were a pack of colorfully painted, determined children with Flea at their head. A large painted Kashin, which resembled a great man-lion, lifted Flea onto his furry shoulders. Flea raised his clenched fists above his head.

"I WILL STAND AND FIGHT!" he yelled.

Somewhere in the crowd a chant had begun.

FIGHT! FIGHT! FIGHT!

Flea climbed down from his perch and started to approach Morgan and Alex. He muttered softly to his smartphone to end amplifying their voices over the speakers. Morgan and Alex started walking in turn, toward Flea. The three reached each other, and without word, embraced in a group hug. For some reason, this drove the crowd even crazier.

"You're alive," said Flea softly choking back tears. "I missed you guys."

"Me too," choked Morgan.

Alex tried to speak, but found she could only mouth the words, "Me too," to agree with her husband.

It finally seemed to dawn on Flea the situation going on around him. His eyes got big as the three continued to huddle together.

"What have we done?" asked Flea.

"Hopefully," replied Morgan, "something good, bro. Hopefully, something good."

The crowd took up the chant again, returning from their mindless screaming. Armalan was roaring at the top of his lungs from the side of the stage and pumping his fists in the air. The kittens and Keri had joined him and were hissing intimidatingly as they pumped their clenched paws up and down above their heads.

FIGHT! FIGHT! FIGHT!

Flea, Morgan and Alex released the hug and walked to the edge of the stage holding hands. When they reached the edge, they threw their interlocked hands up into the air. The crowd was a wild mob of screaming and chanting. Now, it was time to fight.

8

Ba'an was growing weary of Scivistan. He already had to endure two beatings a day from Mistress Toren, whom had written her name as a permanent scar on his bare chest. Now, he also had to endure the way Scivistan treated him in his workplace. Every day it was the same thing. Report to work and then get a beating. Go to lunch, endure the shameful stares, and then get some more beatings. After that, back to work and yet even more beatings. Go to dinner and continue with more beatings. Being beaten seemed to be the focus of Ba'an's meager existence. All he seemed to have were beatings and the need for revenge. He clicked his beak as he thought of his revenge list. It had been growing. Killing made him feel complete. It was like the window in his blackened heart remained closed, except when he killed. When killing, the window opened. It let in the stagnant and putrid air of his soul. It felt good to him to open the window. He took a deep breath through his nose holes as if he were filling his lungs with the foulness that corrupted him. Scivistan came up behind Ba'an as he cleaned the exterior of one of the reharvestation chambers.

"Having trouble breathing?" he yelled the question as he punched Ba'an in the lower back.

Ba'an felt the sharp pain rack is inner organs.

"That help?" Scivistan growled as he hit him again.

Without thinking, Ba'an whirled around and lashed out with one of his white tentacles and slapped the other creature in the face. Scivistan's shell was Kashin and when Ba'an did this it caused him to yowl and hiss in a feline manner. Scivistan jumped back and the two creatures faced off against each other in a slowly moving circle. This was a lethal dance.

"Are you sure you want to do this?" hissed Scivistan. "You useless piece of filth!"

Ba'an did not speak. Instead he lashed out his tentacles mimicking Mistress Toren. Three rapid, successive strikes flew at Ba'an's enemy. Scivistan was quick as he leapt upward and twisted about to dodge the first two strikes. Ba'an's third found its mark and wrapped around Scivistan's ankle. The squat octopus creature pulled the nimble Scivistan from the air.

Ba'an screamed as Scivistan buried his claws into the tentacle that was wrapped around his ankle, but refused to release his grip. Instead, he jerked his tentacle backward, and threw Scivistan against the operating panel for the reharvestation chambers. Ba'an was barely aware that this caused some of the chambers to turn on. He could hear them begin to fill with fluid. He turned around to survey the damage and saw Scivistan twitching slightly on the floor. Smoke was rising from the panel. Ba'an tightened his grip around Scivistan's ankle and slowly dragged him across the floor. Scivistan lay motionless in front of Ba'an. The injured technician was breathing heavily and twitching. Ba'an let go of him and straddled the Gora's chest to stand above him.

"Hel...," choked Scivistan. "Help me."

Ba'an was fighting the urge not to kill Scivistan. The abuse he endured at the hands of this creature infuriated him. He could almost feel the window to his black heart open to let in the foulness that he loved so dear. He wanted to kill this pathetic creature. It was a difficult not to do so.

"You want my help?" whispered Ba'an.

Scivistan nodded and spit up globs of blood with a raking cough. Ba'an noticed one of the levers from the reharvestation chamber's control panel sticking through Scivistan's chest. Scivistan was feebly reaching out toward Ba'an with a trembling hand.

"P...Please," Scivistan said hoarsely.

Ba'an moved to stand at Scivistan's side. He then got down on his knees and supported himself with his tentacles. He moved closer to Scivistan and put his face right in the face of the other creature. Scivistan's face was so close to Ba'an's that Ba'an could smell the blood on the other's breath. Ba'an reached out and gingerly moved the other creature's face toward the wall. Ba'an turned his face toward the same wall.

"Watch," he said softly to Scivistan.

Ba'an let loose a stream of white acid from under the tendrils above his beak. The acid struck the wall and smeared down the surface toward the floor, leaving a trail of melted metal in its wake.

"I could kill you," said Ba'an in a soft menacing voice. "I could have killed you whenever I wanted. Your life was never yours. It was always mine."

Ba'an turned his head and Scivistan's face so they were looking at each other again.

"You hear me?" he whispered hoarsely. "It was always mine."

Ba'an could sense the other creature's fear. He could also see the creature's life fading. He needed to act quickly. He stood up and started dragging the other creature toward the door.

"I will take you to be healed," said Ba'an. "You belong to me, now."

He stopped briefly and looked down at the other creature.

"Do you understand this?" he asked.

Scivistan nodded weakly.

"You belong to me!" Ba'an growled.

Ba'an dragged Scivistan out the door toward the medical ward. On their arrival, Ba'an quickly changed his demeanor to one more appropriate.

"Help us!" he implored to the new Medical Technician. "I fear we may lose this noble servant to the Empire."

Ba'an had recently kept good on the promise he made to himself to kill Grumma, the old Medical Technician. This new one bore the same type of shell that Ba'an possessed. Usually, Goras with the same type of shell tried to help each other as much as possible.

"Quickly," said the technician in a feminine voice. "Place him on the table!"

The technician acted as quickly as possible. She put Scivistan to sleep while she worked on him. She moved with efficiency and accuracy. She knew exactly what to do. Noticing the scars on Ba'an's chest, she avoided trying to converse with him too much. After she was done, the room grew quiet.

"I hear that you had fallen from the High Commander's good graces," she said looking at the floor. "They whisper about you in the passageways."

"It would seem," Ba'an thought dryly, *"that my reputation precedes me."*

"Yes," said Ba'an softly. "I have changed from the day I joined with my shell. I can only try to do the best that I can, now."

The silence dragged on for a few more moments until Scivistan finally stirred and woke up.

"You were very lucky," said the Medical Technician to Scivistan. "If it were not for the actions of this young Gora here, you probably would have died."

"I know," said Scivistan softly. "I am very...grateful."

"One can only do his part to help maintain the Empire," said Ba'an with false sincerity.

"You seem to have been on the receiving end of the Inquisitor's fury, young Gora," said the Technician noting Ba'an's scars. "Would you like me to remove those?"

"No," said Ba'an thickly laying on the false modesty. "I admit that I had fallen out of favor due to my own uselessness. These scars help to serve as a reminder to me so that I might conduct myself in ways that better serve the Empire."

"It is very noble to learn from one's mistakes," she said sounding very pleased.

"One can only try," Ba'an said continuing the ruse. "Technician Scivistan is going to teach me to operate and maintain the reharvestation chambers so that I might be able to fill a useful position."

"I am?" questioned Scivistan.

Ba'an glared at him briefly and filled the other Gora with fear.

"Oh yes," Scivistan quickly covered his mistake. "I remember now, I must have forgotten with the trauma of the accident."

"Yes," said Ba'an. "I am hoping to recover myself in the eyes of the Empire. Perhaps one day, I will again be a closely relied upon member of the crew, serving the High Commander directly."

"That is a very noble goal indeed," the Technician sounded impressed with Ba'an. "If you need, I could do what I can to help you to this end."

"Yes," said Ba'an softly. "It would be a…noble…thing to once again stand alongside the High Commander."

***

Morgan and Alex moved their living quarters the far side of the Human Sphere to live with Flea and the rest of his group. During the move, Mihanna had kept his word and arranged for the humans to have an old Goraan battle carrier and some fighters that had been used to salvage parts from for the rest of the fleet. Also as the group was moving in and renovating the house to accommodate three more people, the Runner council had appointed three humans to act as the human delegation to the council. Flea was mildly upset over hearing this from Mihanna as he and Mihanna accompanied by Morgan were on their way back to the Communal Sphere.

"I'm not saying that humanity won't appreciate the council's appointment of human delegates," Flea said earnestly. "But you have to understand, Mihanna, I just think that the humans will react better to the council if we are given the time and opportunity to hold a vote for our own representation. We like to elect our own people."

As Flea spoke, he was also trying to shift into a more comfortable position. Armina, who followed along without asking, was trying to crawl up his back and sit on his shoulders.

"I understand this, Brother," replied Mihanna. "But it took a bit of convincing on my part to allow any humans on the council at all. I thought that I should act before the council changed their minds."

"The council members can't still change their minds, can they?" asked Morgan.

"Technically they can. I do not believe they will, though," explained Mihanna. "The council has ratified the decision and endorsed, albeit marginally, the addition of humans to the Runners' numbers. They will not take it back now. The political ramifications could be devastating for any delegate that voted out another species. If one species gets voted out, who is to say that another species, maybe their own, will not be next?"

"I don't get it," said Flea as Armina squirmed around under his arm and began crawling up his chest.

"It's like nuclear missiles, Flea," explained Morgan. "Everyone knew that everyone else had them. What kept them from being used, though, was the threat of what might happen if one were launched."

"Okay," said Flea shaking his head. "If you say so. Politics was never something I was any good at. So who are the human delegates?"

"I do not know," replied Mihanna. "I was just happy that the council actually listened to me for a change. You know, over four million Runners ended up in the Communal Sphere listening to us before you two had finished yesterday?"

"That's a big number," said Flea struggling with the kitten. "Do you think it made a difference?"

"It made some impact," replied Mihanna. "The council acknowledges that at least half the Runners want to fight, now."

"Four out of eight million isn't bad. That still leaves the other half, though," commented Morgan.

"I know," said Mihanna. "Hopefully they will come around. The human delegates are meeting at your domicile with the Kashin and Homarell to discuss some options."

"Homarell?" asked Flea as Armina turned around on his shoulders to face forward.

"Catfish looking people," explained Morgan.

"Ah," said Flea. "cool."

"Alex is hosting them as part of her official capacity," said Mihanna.

"Official capacity?" asked Flea with a small grin. "What official capacity does she have?"

"She's the Captain of the human battle carrier," said Morgan.

"Oh really," said Flea as he laughed at the news. "How many times did you practice saying, 'Captain Alexandria,' in the mirror before you could do it with a straight face, Morg?"

"Shut up," chuckled Morgan.

"Are you quite comfortable?" Flea growled with false annoyance at Armina.

"Just a second," she replied shifting a few more times. "There! Now I'm ready!"

She giggled as she positioned her tail under his nose like a mustache. Mihanna raised an eyebrow at the kitten which caused her to giggle even more. Morgan was trying hard not to laugh out loud at Flea's current feline dilemma.

"You know," began Mihanna, trying to move the focus off the kitten. "Alexandria really has some interesting ideas. She wants to integrate the fleet and military into one sphere and desegregate the crews."

"That seems like a sound strategic idea," agreed Flea as Armina moved her tail to hang between his eyes. Flea gave Armina a withering upward glance. "Troops won't fight and die together if they can't live and play together."

"To that end," said Mihanna, "the Kashin, Homarell and Humans have started an exchange and integration program."

"We don't have any personnel as yet, to exchange," said Morgan.

"No, but you soon will," said Mihanna. "In the mean time, the Kashin and Homarell have transferred some personnel to you to help staff your ship. Then you will start trading personnel with us and the Homarell. I have also assigned some pilots to your fighter unit, Brother Flea."

"That's all fine and everything," said Flea, "but I'm having try outs for my unit. We only have a limited number of fighters, so I can only afford to take the best. Tell your pilots if they want to fly in the human unit, to come down here and try out for it."

"Is that why we are here, Brothers?" asked Mihanna.

"Yeah," responded Morgan. "Flea and I sent instructions to the maintenance robots to set up some trainers down here for try outs. I'll be here doing that while Flea goes and checks out the ship and our fighters."

They approached the area that was used the day before to gather and speak to the masses. In front of the stage was a small table with a holo-projector behind it. It projected the word "Registration" above the table in large red letters. On the stage, the training simulators were set up. If the robots had followed instructions, they should have twenty five of them on stage. In front of the registration table, were a large number of humans waiting to register. To Flea and his group's surprise, they even had some Kashin there that had shown up without receiving Mihanna's message.

"How many fighters do we get?" asked Flea. "I know they've been stripped for parts, kind of like our carrier, but how many do we get?"

"Hold on," said Mihanna pulling out his computer and pressing a few buttons, "It says here I can give you forty six. They have been stripped for parts, so you might end up with less than that. We will stock the rest of your carrier's capacity with Kashin and Homarell units to fill it out."

"Thanks," said Flea. "Morg, hold a points contest. We take the top seventy five and whittle it down from there."

"You got it, Flea," said Morg.

"Forty six, huh," said Flea glancing up toward Armina. "Not much to work with, eh, kitten?"

"Nope," she replied flicking his nose with her tail from her perch.

"Nope," agreed Flea. "Not much to work with."

***

Alex was seated in the sitting room of the domicile she and her family moved in to last night. They had decided to move in with Flea and his small group in order to have more people around them they care about. Kaida, Armalan and Keri were outside finishing putting paint on the exterior while she was inside meeting with some delegates to the Runners Council. Everyone received one delegate for every one hundred thousand members of their race. This is why the humans were allocated three delegates. Only half of the Kashin delegates showed up, though. Along with them, were the five Homarell delegates and the three human delegates that were chosen by the council to represent the interests of humanity. The alien delegates in her presence did not bother her nearly as much as the human ones. To her surprise, the council had chosen people whom they believed held sway over the human population amongst the Runners. They were chosen because the council thought that they must be very popular amongst humans. The council believed this because out of the humans still alive, these three appeared in television and radio waves originating from Earth's former location the most. The remaining survivors of the human population were to be represented by the people left alive that had appeared the most in the mass media.

"For every step we move forward," Alex thought wryly, *"we seem to take another step back."*

She tried to hide her disappointment over who was chosen to represent the humans from the three human delegates.

"Or in this case," she thought surveying the three human delegates, *"we took three steps back. I only hope they don't embarrass us."*

***

Flea, Armina and Mihanna were on a shuttle craft on their way out to the location the old Goraan battle carrier was located in the scrap yard. The Runners had been stripping these vessels for parts whenever they ran out of resources for the matter combiners. If given the proper resources, the matter combiners could produce everything from clothes, small parts and even food. If they ran out of power or resources, however, they were useless. Then the Runners would be forced to start salvaging.

"Let me ask you something," Flea said. "With all the technology we have at our disposal why not just use the matter combiner to make a bunch of new ships and fighters?"

"In order to do that we first must have the resources available to fuse an object together," explained Mihanna. "Then we have to have a matter combiner large enough to produce what we want. We can't build the equipment powerful enough to supply energy to a matter combiner to make large objects like a fighter. We can make some of the smaller parts for one, but that is it. This is why we have to harvest and salvage parts the way we do. To build a matter combiner large enough to produce a fighter or a battleship would take a generator and support equipment of impossible proportions. Even if it could be made, it would be very dangerous to whatever crew had to operate it."

"What about the matter combiners we use in our homes?" asked Flea.

"The size of the generator and support equipment needed to run a combiner decreases drastically in comparison to its size," explained Mihanna. "The one in your home could be run off equipment you could easily store in a closet."

"I see," said Flea. "I guess that rules out the 'instant fleet' plan I had been thinking about."

Flea had done some research and discovered that this was also one of the driving forces behind the Runners' enemy, the Goraan. The Goraan empire had expanded to a level where it was constantly in need of more resources. This is why the Goraan were constantly trying to expand and conquer more territory. Flea thought of this as he held Armina's paw. The three of them passed all the dead hulking ships in the salvage yard and he wondered if the Goraan had to salvage old ships the way he was about to do.

Flea looked out the front window of the shuttle as it approached a very large, dull grey vessel.

"That is it," said Mihanna. "This will be the humans' battle carrier, Brother."

It was very large, but not nearly as large as the Kashin ship he arrived in. The top and sides were all flat and rectangular. As the shuttle arced its path to fly towards the front end and over the nose, Flea noticed the opening in the front.

"Is that the hanger?" asked Flea pointing to the opening.

"Yes," replied Mihanna.

The top of the vessel was also flat and rectangular. In the middle of the top, at the back near the engines, was a large cylindrical tube. Some of the lights were on inside the tube to indicate that someone was probably inside.

"And that?" asked Flea pointing to the tube.

"That is the bridge, Brother," Mihanna said.

Flea felt slightly disappointed when he looked at the vessel.

"Pilot," said Flea, "hold position for a moment."

Flea pulled out his smartphone and started to mess with it.

"What's wrong?" asked Mihanna.

Flea stopped what he was doing on his phone and looked at Mihanna.

"You mean to tell me that after centuries upon centuries of scientific advancement and achievements, that the best you people could come up with is something that looks like an intergalactic shoe box?" he accused. "This has to be a joke!"

"What's a shoe box?" asked Armina.

Flea explained what a shoe box was to Armina and Mihanna.

Mihanna had been studying human sarcasm a bit since he began interacting with his new Brothers.

"I am sorry," he said sarcastically. "Why don't I just take you to where the humans have docked their own ships?"

Flea glared at him sideways.

"Oh wait, that is right!" he said snapping his fingers. "You do not have any!"

Flea gave Mihanna a sour look and then smiled briefly.

"Sorry," Flea apologized.

"It is fine," Mihanna said.

"*Star Trek* looked so much cooler than this," Flea muttered.

"What was that?" Mihanna asked sourly.

"Nothing," Flea replied. "Thanks, by the way, for going through the trouble of getting us this ship. I'm sure it'll work out with some modifications. I'm going to call Alex."

Flea turned back to his computer and finished contacting her.

"You're welcome Brother, and we will help you with anything you need," replied Mihanna.

Flea nodded at Mihanna.

"Captain Alex Mendenhall," said Alex's voice on Flea's phone. "This better be important."

"I see someone is growing into her new title," chided Flea.

"Shut up," she chuckled. "I hate you."

"No you don't," responded Flea. "Call Morg and add him to our conversation. I have something you guys will want to see."

"Is it important?" she replied. "I'm meeting with some delegates. Flea, you will not believe the people they appointed to us as representatives. They should have let us vote."

"I know," agreed Flea.

"You know who they got?" she asked excitedly.

"Don't care. Politics are dumb." interrupted Flea. "Tell me later. For now, call Morg. I'm at the ship. I thought you guys would want to see."

"Okay," she said. "Hold on."

A few moments later Flea heard Morgan's voice on his phone as the screen split in half to show Alex on the right and

Morgan on the left. Armina crawled up Flea's back and straddled his shoulders again so she could see, too.

"Hello?" Morgan answered the call. "Oh hey guys! What's up?"

"I'm up, see?" interjected Armina as she waved to Morgan and Alex through camera above the screen.

"We see, that," chuckled Alex. "I'm glad to see you're taking care of Flea."

Morgan laughed as Armina nodded in approval of Alex's comment and crossed her furry arms on top of Flea's head.

"I'm at the battle carrier," said Flea seriously. "What about you?"

"Been watching potential pilots since you left," replied Morgan. "Got some good ones, too. Honey, how about you?"

"Dealing with politicians all morning. They aren't that bad, though," she chuckled. "Flea, just show us the ship. I need to get back soon."

"Okay," said Flea holding up the computer so the camera above the screen could show the ship. "See it?"

There was a long pause as he tried to capture the whole vessel.

"Guys?" Flea said in an inquiring tone.

Silence.

"Hello?" said Flea.

"Hey, Mihanna," whispered Flea to the Kashin. "Do these phones ever lose connection? Do we ever go through, like, a 'bad cell area' or something?"

"A what?" whispered Mihanna in return.

More silence.

"It looks like a giant shoe box," Morgan's voice finally said over the computer.

"Did Payless give us a buy one get one free deal on that?" asked Alex. "I hope it's in my size, since I'm the Captain."

"*Star Trek* looked so much cooler than that," Morgan added.

Flea looked rather smugly at Mihanna.

"Told you so," he said.

"Could you humans please be grateful?" the Admiral growled. "I went through a lot of trouble for this!"

"Sorry," the three humans said in unison.

"I'm going to get back to the meeting," said Alex.

"Yeah and I have to finish up the pilot try outs," said Morgan.

"See you guys tonight," responded Flea.

"See ya tonight," chimed in Armina.

The kitten was starting to sound more and more human-ish from spending time with Flea.

"Pilot," said Flea. "Carry on."

The shuttle craft silently resumed its path around the battle carrier. Flea could feel a bit of anticipation as the shuttle moved onward to the far side of the vessel where his forty six little fighters were located. Armina climbed down to hold Flea's hand again. It was as if she could sense his feelings. As they crested around the carrier he finally saw them. They were a bunch of pathetic looking tiny grey hulks that slightly resembled the sting rays he once swam with while he was stationed in Florida for training. Many of them had large holes in them, and they all had a bit of rust on them.

"How old did you say these things were?" Flea asked Mihanna with a sideways glance. "Some of them had to have been salvaged from planet wreckage."

"How would you know this, Brother?" Mihanna inquired.

"Rust," Flea replied. "Some of the fighters have rust on them. Rust needs moisture and oxygen. Space has neither. How long did you say these have been here?"

There was a long period of silence.

"I did not say, Brother," Mihanna replied quietly.

Flea started noticing some oddities about the fighters.

"Hey!" he said accusingly. "Where are the windows?"

"You see the bulge in the metal near the two dorsal fins?" asked Mihanna.

"Yeah," responded Flea.

"That is where the cockpit is," explained Mihanna. "Instead of windows the Goraan use solid metal to increase hull strength."

"How do the pilots see?" asked Flea.

"A series of small holo-cameras on the outside of the vessel sent a signal to some holo-projectors inside the cockpit," explained Mihanna. "This would make it appear to the pilot as if he were floating in space in just his control console and chair. They did this to increase visibility."

"How does the pilot eject?" asked Flea.

"He does not," responded Mihanna. "Goraan pilots are expected to die in their fighters. Their cells are reharvested along with the wreckage for greater resource value."

"That's just stupid," said Flea condescendingly. "It's barbaric. Besides, training new pilots and getting them experienced spends more resources than anything gained this way. Stupid, stupid , stupid."

"Stupid," agreed Armina.

Flea smiled briefly and winked at Armina as he turned to the Admiral.

"Mihanna, Could you get me in touch with whoever is supposed to start working on our fighters?" Flea asked. "Have the fighters brought inside the carrier. We'll work on them in the hanger bay."

"Of course, Brother," responded Mihanna. "Is there anything else?"

"Not at the moment," replied Flea. "I have some ideas I need to discuss with Alex and Morgan for the battle carrier, but not until later. In the mean time, let's just get those fighters inside."

"Is that all, Brother?" asked Mihanna arching an eyebrow.

"For now," responded Flea. "Let's hope it's enough."

＊

Morgan had been sitting at his position monitoring the scores all day. Except for the few moments he ate and talked to his wife and Flea earlier, this occupied most of his day. He was pretty impressed with some of the pilots. Most of them, if Flea was right about the simplicity of the controls he was designing for the fighters, could probably do pretty well. He had never flown anything himself, but according to Flea, he would make a pretty good pilot because of all the video games he played. The control system was very similar.

He was almost done for the day. He was highlighting the top seventy five scores on the screen of his smartphone in a different color so they were easier to keep track of. There were twenty three Kashin pilots amongst them. They flew with a lot of passion on their own, but when placed in a group, they had difficulty flying together. Apparently, when Morgan asked them, they seem to have difficulty forming a plan because no one wants to discount the ideas of their Kashin Brothers and Sisters. As a result, it took them a while to make a decision. Flea would have to make sure not to group the Kashin together. Maybe they would work better as a team with a human willing to take charge in it. He would have to test that theory this week as they selected the final seventy five they were going to pull the main group from.

"Does this group have a name?" asked a burly man interrupting Morgan's thoughts.

"What's that?" asked Morgan.

"A name," he repeated impatiently. "Does this fighter group have a name?"

Many of the humans began to curiously gather around the two at the exchange. Morgan didn't respond.

"All the good fighter groups have a name," he repeated. "Like the 'Black Knights' or the 'Hell Cats' or something."

"What's your name?" asked Morgan.

The other man told Morgan his name.

"So," he said impatiently, "Does this group have a name or not?"

"We do," said Morgan defensively.

"Well," said the man gruffly, "what is it?"

"The Archangels," responded Morgan making a name up on the spot.

"What the Hell?" he said condescendingly. "Do you think you're some kind of 'Holy Order' or something?"

"Yeah," replied Morgan. "And right now it's my Holy duty to inform you that I just disqualified you from the list for being an asshole."

"Excuse me?" said the man with astonishment.

"Did I stutter?" asked Morgan roughly. "You're out!"

"Bullshit!" the man exclaimed."

"No bullshit," Morgan said sternly. "You are out."

The other man looked angrily at Morgan.

"Besides," Morgan gushed with a smile. "If this is a Holy order then that means it wasn't my decision. You can blame God. I just follow orders."

Some of the other potential pilots that overheard the exchange started to chuckle. Morgan hoped the rest of the day would go better.

***

Flea was glad to return home from the carrier. He found Keri playing on the front lawn. Three young women consisting of one blonde, one brunette and an Asian were chatting with Alexandria, Morgan and Armalan.

"Can I go play?" Armina asked Flea excitedly.

"Uh," said Flea not sure why she was asking him in particular. "Sure thing, kitten."

Armina ran up giggling to join Keri. Kaida was trying hard, as she attempted to look at the very young women talking with Morgan and Alex, not to be noticed. Flea had been watching her paint the same spot on the house now ever since it came into view. Every now and then, she would glance in their direction. She looked rather comical in her black overalls with the blue tube top and pigtails with matching blue streaks as she put all her effort into her sly bit of spying. Flea and Mihanna were arguing about the use of outlawed weapons as they walked up to the house.

"So now with the new battle carrier," the young blonde was saying, "we'll have the chance to get some revenge?"

"Oh yes," responded Alex enthusiastically. "Not only will it house a fighter group on board, but we also plan to have it armed to the teeth."

"Also," Morgan added, "we'll be able, hopefully, to protect our children as we help the rest of the Runners."

"Yes," responded a young Asian female. "I no think Runners very unified. They need find one leader. One voice."

The Asian girl speaking couldn't be more than twenty years old. Flea approached the group talking on the lawn.

"Can I help you?" he asked looking at the group of very young women.

"No thank you," the blonde said with a polite smile. "We're just here speaking with Captain Mendenhall."

"Huh?" responded Flea rather dumbfounded.

"Ryoko, Daniela and I were chosen by the council as the human delegates. They picked us because out of the remaining humans, we appear most in human media," said the young blonde girl.

Flea thought the blonde who was speaking looked vaguely familiar. At least, she sounded familiar.

"Ryoko?" asked Flea.

"Ryoko Abe," responded the Asian girl with a thick Japanese accent. "I am singer and actress in Japan."

She bowed slightly as Flea shook her hand.

"So then you are Daniela?" Flea asked the other woman.

"Yes," she responded with an Australian accent and tossing her dark brown hair. "Daniela Knight. I was a television actress in Australia."

She was wearing a tight black dress that fell a few inches above her mid-thigh with a black long sleeved jacket and matching black high heels. Her dark brown hair was pulled back in a ponytail. Ryoko and the blonde female standing next to her were dressed in a similar fashion. They looked very official. Flea could not fathom why these attractive young ladies were on his lawn, but when they smiled their greetings and introductions at him, he really didn't care. The young blonde woman without an accent looked familiar but Flea couldn't tell from where.

"I am very pleased to meet all of you," said Flea to them with his best smile.

He practiced that smile in the mirror on occasion. It showed all the work the braces he had as a teenager had done to fix his teeth when he was in high school. He had quite an attractive smile.

"You're such a ham," interjected Alex with a sideways glance at Flea. "Behave yourself."

"If you ignore him," added Morgan, "he'll probably go away."

"I see you are well liked around here," chuckled Daniela.

"I better be," grinned Flea. "I live here. It's my house."

"Our house," corrected Morgan with an elbow to Flea's rib cage.

"Sorry," said Flea in mock pain. "Our house."

They all chuckled at Morgan and Flea's friendly exchange.

"Aren't you going to introduce me?" asked Flea.

"Sorry, delegates," said Morgan introducing his friend. "This is Flea. He's going to lead the fighter group on our carrier."

"What kind of name is Flea?" asked the blonde girl.

"The kind of name you can only get by being as cool as me," he replied with a wink.

The delegates chuckled and Ryoko actually blushed.

"Be nice I said!" interjected Alex as she elbowed Flea in the ribs to repeat Morgan's maneuver.

"Oww!" said Flea.

Alex glared at him for a moment. Morgan may have been playing with his elbow, but Alex probably had left a bruise.

"Sorry," he apologized. "I had a bad day. Our carrier and fighters need a lot of work."

"I'm delegate Masters," the last delegate introduced herself. "Is there anything we can do to help?"

"Masters?" Flea asked with his mouth open. "You mean Christina Masters?"

"That's right," she responded with a smile.

"The pop-star girl?" Flea replied with a stunned look. "The one who won all those awards last month? The same one that had a series of…er…interesting photos to go along with her number one singles?"

"That's me," she giggled.

"I didn't recognize you like that," he said with a goofy looking grin. "I'm used to seeing pictures of you wearing a mini-skirt, a bra and a thong. That one with the thong and cowgirl chaps was nice, too."

"I know, right?" she blushed. "We are all trying to have a more professional look. We can't be politicians without looking like politicians."

"I hate politics," Flea shook his head.

"So do we," Christina said. "But someone has to do it."

"Politics is like putting on a show," said Daniela cheerfully. "It's just a different stage than we're used to. Maybe we're just what's needed."

Maybe things weren't as bad as Flea thought.

"If you will excuse me ladies," he said with a slight nod in their direction. "I would like to clean up a bit. Thank you."

Flea left Alex and the delegates and walked toward the house, and as he went inside, Armina trailed in behind him.

"Flea?" asked Armina. "Can I ask you something?"

"Sure, kitten," said Flea. "What's on your mind?"

"Flea?" sniffled Armina.

"Yes, kitten," said Flea softly as he squatted down to look in her big yellow eyes.

"Well," she sniffed. "You see…"

There was a slightly long pause as the kitten tried to speak.

"It is just that I am an orphan," she said as her voice choked a bit. "And I like being here. It feels like home. I have not had a home in a while and I miss having a family."

"You want to stay here with me?" asked Flea softly.

"You mean it?" she asked perking up a bit with. "You will be my guardian?"

Flea had a great degree of difficulty telling someone in need "no," especially a child. This was evident by the way he had taken in Tommy and Kaida. He may have had a rough exterior, but it was mostly smoke and mirrors. Inside, Flea was compelled to help people in trouble. No matter how hard he fought against it, he could never beat what was in his nature. He hated to admit it, especially to himself, but Flea was at heart, a protector.

"What in the Hell am I getting myself in to," he thought silently.

"Of course I'll take care of you," he said to her as tears welled up in her eyes.

"I can stay with you here and you won't leave me?" she asked getting excited and throwing her arms around Flea's neck.

"Yes," said Flea softly.

"Promise?" she asked intently.

"Promise," replied Flea.

Maybe things really weren't as bad as he thought.

***

The Imperial Palace on the Goraan home world of Eiligor was a sprawling, ornate affair. The young new Emperor was intent on making the Empire into a massive and beautiful thing. The home world, especially the Imperial Palace, was no exception. The walls were covered from floor to ceiling with platinum and gold which were thickly encrusted with rare and precious gems. The floor was a checkerboard pattern of gold and platinum tiles. In the center of the Imperial throne room, where the Emperor was located, the tiles were cut and arranged in various shades of gold, silver and platinum to form the Imperial Seal. On the floor, with their foreheads pressed to the gold and platinum tiles, were the Emperor's two hundred wives clad in sheer white silk. Their nude forms could easily be seen underneath silk wraps. Behind them, also with foreheads pressed to the floor, were the Emperor's four hundred concubines clad in sheer grey silk that also revealed their nude forms underneath. The Imperial wives and concubines were Goras with a myriad of different shells. All were considered by Imperial standards, to be among the most beautiful females in the Empire. They may not be able to be used for breeding, but this stock of females was unparallel in its beauty.

The young Emperor lounged lazily on his throne at the head of the room facing his wives and concubines. The Emperor rested one leg impudently over an arm of his chair. He believed his own shell the most beautiful of all. He was bound and determined to make everything about his Empire beautiful. Being beautiful was a very important thing to him. He had a long slender and athletic body. His skin and muscle tissue was perfectly transparent as were his bones so that all you could see was his shape. His arms and legs were long, and also transparent. His internal organs, however, glowed slightly with a warm golden light that could be seen through his clear flesh. Even what was left of the shell's brain glowed slightly. The tiny Gora slug that was the Emperor could be seen pulsating inside the skull. A servant stepped in front of the large double doors on the far side of the throne room without facing the Emperor and struck a large octagonal gong with an octagonal hole cut out in the center. It rang out clearly through the room.

"The Emperor hears the call of one whom wishes to speak in his presence," said the Emperor in an almost feminine voice. "Who calls upon the Emperor's service?"

"The Imperial Spymaster and the Imperial Combat Statistician, Oh Glorious One," said the servant reverently.

"What business does the Spymaster and Combat Statistician wish to impose upon the Emperor's busy day of contemplation and self enlightenment?" asked the Emperor.

"They claim to have urgent matters of Imperial security to discuss with you, most Divine," gushed the servant.

"Send them before the Emperor," intoned the Emperor.

The two Goras silently went before the Emperor. Without word, they crossed the room and then pressed their foreheads to the ground in front of the throne. The Emperor allowed them to wait there for quite an extended period of time. Finally the Emperor looked in front of the throne and acted as if he hadn't noticed them kneeling before him until that moment.

"Oh," he said. "Please, gentle servants, do excuse me. I failed to notice you there."

They responded with silence. They didn't even move. To do so without permission was the most paramount of insults. It resulted in death.

"You may speak, servants," said the Emperor.

"Thank you, Supreme Leader," said one of them without rising. "I am humbled by the experience of basking in your gloriousness."

"Of course you are," said the Emperor condescendingly. "What urgent business brings you before the Emperor?"

"Runners," said the second without rising. "We believe they are still alive, most Enlightened."

"There will always be those whom run from the expansion of our mighty Empire," responded the Emperor. "What threat do these new Runners pose?"

"These are not new Runners, my Glorious Emperor," said the first again. "We believe that these are the Runners Esham'aut was supposed to dispose of."

"Rise and stand before me," said the Emperor gravely. "You do realize that Esham'aut is one of my old teachers and was personally appointed by me, don't you?"

"Yes, Imperial Majesty," responded the first after the two stood up.

"He sent word personally that told of the destruction of the Runner fleet," continued the Emperor. "I trust his word unconditionally."

"We understand this, Divine One," said the second. "However, there are some disturbing facts that do not add up."

"Servant!" shouted the Emperor. "Send for my personal assistant. Tell him to bring a communications orb. Esham'aut's fleet should be within regular communications range by now if he has kept with his flight plan."

"Tell me," the Emperor turned to the two before him. "What evidence do you bring to me against one of my most trusted servants?"

"We reviewed the logs and recordings of the battle at planet designate 8793.12., also known as Earth by its local populous," said the first again. "The wreckage after the battle does not add up in mass to equal the Runner Fleet that was involved there, Glorious One."

"What do you mean?" inquired the Emperor. "Esham'aut said there was no evidence of Runner Fleet left."

"Be that as it may," responded the second. "We sent recycling ships to go claim the wreckage. The amount of mass that composed the wreckage does not equal the mass of the Runner Fleet that was present in the battle. We believe that a vast majority of the Runner Fleet managed to escape behind some ruse, Supreme One."

"I see," said the Emperor slightly perturbed.

"Esham'aut should be brought before us and placed charges of incompetence, Imperial Majesty" said the second forcefully.

"I concur, my Emperor," agreed the first slightly less forcefully.

"I see," said the Emperor slightly more perturbed.

A loud gong rang out across the room.

"Who seeks council with the Emperor?" asked the Emperor angrily.

"The Emperor's assistant wishes to seek council…" began the servant.

"Send him in," shouted Emperor interrupting the servant.

"Do not kneel, assistant," said the Emperor. "Just approach the throne."

The assistant was the same type of creature as the Emperor. This was arranged because he was the Emperor's younger brother. As such, he was also a Prince of the Empire. He was carrying a small, clear orb as large as a slug in his left hand. It had one flat side and a small touchpad attached to it.

"These two," said the Emperor before his brother could speak, "presume to tell me whom I should or should not bring up in charges, brother."

"I see," responded the Prince coldly.

The Prince knew where this was going.

"Execute them," said the Emperor.

The Emperor's brother pulled out a long curved sword with a serrated back from the sheath hanging from his belt with his right hand. With one well practiced arcing sweep of his arm, the head of both the Spymaster and Strategic Tactician rolled onto the floor in front of their bodies. Blood gushed upward from the headless necks, raining down on their executioner. The bodies stood briefly before crumpling to the floor. After this, the Prince went over to the heads and chopped each one in half along their lengths to kill the Gora inside. The bodies and their decapitated heads oozed blood across the ornate floor around the Prince's boots. The warring colors of the golden floor with the puddles of orange and purple blood intermixing from the two bodies made for an eye wrenching mixture.

"Please appoint a new Spymaster and Combat Statistician when we finish today's business," said the Emperor gently.

"Anything else?" asked the Emperor's brother with a smile as he gingerly stepped around the growing puddle.

"Not for these two," chuckled the Emperor. "To think the nerve they must have!"

"Had, Emperor," corrected the Prince. "The nerve they had."

"Yes," chuckled the Emperor. "Yes, of course."

"Well," continued the Prince, "our old teacher did tell us that insolence should be dealt with harshly."

"Speaking of which," said the Emperor. "We need to contact him. Despite their insolence, these two brought up and interesting point."

"Really Egjoran?" asked the Prince. "What might that be?"

"I will tell you, Iforian," said Emperor Egjoran. "They came here to bother me about Runners that Esham'aut said he defeated."

"Well," said Prince Iforian, "perhaps we should contact Esham'aut and discuss this," he added slyly with a chuckle. "He will probably scold you for having these two killed."

"Yes," chuckled Egjoran. "But he will also scold you for doing it."

"I just follow orders like a good servant of my brother, the Emperor," said Iforian with mock innocence.

"Yes," said Egjoran dryly. "Of course."

Iforian wiped his blade on one of the fallen bodies and then sheathed it. He placed the clear communications orb, which never fell from his left hand, on the ground. It sat on its flat side as Iforian began to contact Esham'aut's ship directly using the touchpad. He then moved to stand next to his brother. A few seconds passed before the holographic vision of the Second Fleet's flag ship communications duty officer appeared.

"You're Imperial Majesty," he stammered as he quickly rose from his seat. "It is truly an honor and privilege to receive a personal message, oh Great and Divine Ruler. How may I service you?"

"Begin by telling the High Commander that I am calling him," began Egjoran. "Then schedule a beating for yourself. You represent the Empire, and I AM THE EMPIRE! A weak greeting gives those who receive it a weak impression of the Empire, and therefore a weak impression of me."

"Of course you're Imperial Majesty," said the communications officer dejectedly.

"You don't want someone calling your Emperor weak, do you?" asked Egjoran.

The communications officer started to speak.

"Of course you don't," he said answering his own question. "Now, put me through to the High Commander."

"Yes, Enlightened One," he responded.

A few minutes went by until the two brothers were faced with the familiar old face of the teacher from their youths. The last time they saw him, he was teaching them their personal diplomacy and political strategies course. This was only one of many classes he taught to them before being asked to join the Military and lead the second Fleet a few years ago.

"Good day Imperial family. It is always a pleasure to see my two most successful students," greeted Esham'aut. "I see you have made a lesson of a few members of your staff this morning," he said raising an eyebrow, "What exactly was their crime if I may ask?"

"They presumed to tell me whom I should bring up on charges, High Commander," explained the Emperor. "I felt it necessary to explain to them differently."

"And who did they say you should bring up on charges?" asked Esham'aut.

"You, High Commander," smiled Iforian with blood drying on his face.

"On a personal note," said the High Commander with a small smile, "I am glad that you are so fiercely loyal to me. However, on a professional note, you should have left them alive. After all, I even left that last idiot secretary you sent me alive just in case I can use him later."

"I only meant to demonstrate who is in charge," said the Emperor defensively.

"I know, noble student," chuckled Esham'aut. "All we can do is live and learn. So what exactly is this call about? Just feeling the need to convey your warm feelings toward me?"

"Partly," smiled the Emperor. "But also to convey some disturbing findings."

"Exactly what are you talking about, Emperor?" asked Esham'aut.

"These two brought to our attention that the Runners you destroyed may still be alive," replied the Emperor.

"Oh really?" asked Esham'aut. "Our sensor sweeps detected nothing after the battle."

"They may have figured out some trick to cover their escape," said the Emperor. "The mass that our recyclers picked up after the battle does not match what would constitute a fleet of their size. What do you suggest?"

"I have about two to three weeks left on my current flight schedule," replied Esham'aut. "If I abandon it the Empire stands to lose quite a bit in potential resources."

"We can't have that," said the Emperor. "At the rate we use our resources we could end up with a revolt on our hands. All the slaves would rebel as soon as we could no longer charge our weapons. Our reserve supplies could last us for about eight to ten months, but after that we would be doomed."

"I suggest you call the fifth or sixth fleet out of dock," Esham'aut said. "Their crewmembers will not be too pleased, but give them some flowery speech about serving the best interest of the Empire. With one or both of them out harvesting resources, we can afford to let the Second fleet hunt these Runners down after we finish our flight schedule."

"Excellent plan, High Commander," approved the Emperor. "In the mean time, I will have some of our fighters use the jumpgate stations to explore space. Perhaps they will happen across them. At least then, we will have an idea of where they are. How long will it take you to back track to the location of the battle and start investigating?"

"Perhaps a month or two more depending on how the rest of the current mission goes," responded Esham'aut.

"We can give the pitiful Runners a month or two more," said the Emperor darkly. "But then we must dispose of them. We cannot let anyone believe that they can successfully resist the will of the Empire."

9

Flea opened his eyes and woke up earlier than expected. His alarm hadn't gone off yet. Normally, the alarm would go off and Flea would hit the snooze button three or four times, but not today. Armina was still asleep in the tree she had added to the roof near Flea's bed. Flea's bed was pushed against a small shack which led to some stairs to the interior of the house. On the wall that was behind the foot of Flea's bed, Armina had painted a finger painting, or in her case a paw painting, of her and Flea fixing up some of the fighters with a few maintenance robots. She was waiving and they both were smiling and holding hands in the painting. Her picture of Flea had six fingers on his right hand.

Armina didn't really do any productive work over the last week as they repaired the fighters that were still salvageable, but she had fun trying. Flea didn't want to send her away while he worked on the fighters. It made her happy to try and help him. Keri gave Morgan a similar experience while he finished the fighter pilot competitions. Flea could hear Armina purring from the high branches of the tree as she slept. Flea looked up and saw the small kitten smiling and batting her paws in the air at something in her dreams. Her tail swished about and Flea thought she was mumbling some instructions on how to repair the fighters. He quietly got up and went soundlessly through the door into their home to make his way to the kitchen. He ghosted his way through the house past Morgan and Alex's room. He passed by Keri's room and the door was still cracked. She began leaving the hall light on since the destruction of Earth and her arrival at Runners' headquarters.

"Host, two portions of swordfish steaks and steamed vegetables," Flea said softly to the combiner. "One small glass of warm milk and one bottle of Mountain Dew on a tray, please. And this time, don't get funny with the bottle, Host."

"Of course, sir," responded the computer.

"Yeah, whatever," said Flea remembering the computer's last version of a bottle of Mountain Dew. "That last bottle had to have been almost two feet tall."

"That was done at Morgan Mendenhall's request," replied the computer. "Normally, that is not the container fused for use."

"I'll have to get him back for that," mumbled Flea.

It seemed like an odd breakfast, but Flea had found that the feline based life form that he had adopted enjoyed eating seafood for breakfast, lunch and dinner. In Flea's opinion this wasn't exactly bad, because he was also a fan of seafood. He even tried some kind of greenish octopus Armina had given him from her home world.

"Hey," said Morgan coming up behind Flea. "Where's mine?"

"The computer just made an interesting confession to me, Morg," said Flea with a yawn. "You do know that these things don't have the ability to lie don't you?"

"I have no idea what you're talking about," he said with a sleepy smile.

"I'll bet," Flea replied dryly. "You want some of this, too?"

Flea waived the tray in front of his friend's nose. He knew how much Morgan disliked most seafood.

"I'll get my own, thanks," Morgan responded with a slightly disgusted expression.

"Where's Alex?" asked Flea. "We should probably introduce the ship's Captain to the pilots today."

"Still sleeping," yawned Morgan. "She can sleep through almost anything. How are you doing this morning? Nervous?"

"Yeah," responded Flea. "A little. It's been a while since I was in the military."

"I know," said Morgan simply.

"Or even been in charge of anything," said Flea. "Civilian jobs aren't the same."

"It's a different environment," agreed Morgan. "I was never in the military, but I'm sure it'll come back to you."

"You coming?" asked Flea. "Armina and I were about to have breakfast. She's normally up before me, but not today. She should be waking up any time now."

"Let me grab some breakfast and I'll get Keri," replied Morgan. "She wanted to be with me before I went off today. I told her she couldn't come, so she is going with her Mom. What are you going to do with the kitten?"

"I'm not sure yet," responded Flea. "I haven't seen any kitty day care centers pop up around here, so I'll probably just end up taking her with me."

"Are you sure that's wise?" asked Morgan raising an eyebrow.

"How should I know?" Flea said shrugging his shoulders. "I've never been responsible for any damn kids before. You're a Dad. What am I supposed to do?"

"If I could only count the number of times I've asked that question," chuckled Morgan. "All you can do is what you feel is right. Worry about the rest later."

"Cool," said Flea turning to leave the room and go back upstairs.

"Think of it like this," added Morgan half smiling. "With no more Doctor Phil you'll never be on a 'dead beat dad' episode."

Flea stopped to turn around and give Morgan a wry expression. Morgan chuckled a bit as Flea turned to look at him.

"Jackass," Flea muttered as he left the dining area.

For some reason, this made Morgan laugh hysterically. Flea just kept walking.

He went back to the roof where he and Armina slept. He sat cross legged under the tree where she slept, and waited. The kitten's metabolism was much higher than a human child's so she ate full adult sized portions even though she weighed less than most human children her age. Flea knew the scent of the fish would rouse her from sleep. Armina finally stretched and opened her eyes. She never climbed out of the tree to get down in the morning. Instead, she dropped off the branch she was sleeping in. Then she would twist in mid air, like a cat, and land on all fours. She landed a few inches to Flea's right, making almost no sound at all. She crawled over and put her head in his lap and he began scratching her back. Armina stretched her paws out in front of her and clawed at the air as she purred happily at the attention she was receiving. Morgan came through the door a few minutes later with a tray in one hand and Alex and Keri trailing sleepily behind.

"Is this where you have been eating breakfast the last week, sis?" yawned Keri.

"Yeah," Armina replied purring sleepily. "I like to eat under my tree."

The five sat under the tree chatting amiably about what they had planned for the day. Kaida and Tommy joined them later with their own breakfasts. They continued chatting until Keri and Alex finally got up and went to get ready to leave. Kaida and Tommy went after them leaving Morgan, Flea and the kitten. Morgan looked at Flea as if he was asking what Flea was going to do with Armina this morning when they left. Flea still didn't know.

"Sweetie," said Flea to the Kitten. "Go wash up and get changed, okay?"

"Okay," she replied. "What should I wear?"

"It doesn't matter," smiled Flea.

"Okay," she responded excitedly, "I'll get a flight suit like yours!"

"Alright," replied Flea.

Armina trotted off to the far side of the roof behind the small shack that had the door leading into the house.

"You know what you're going to do with her?" asked Morgan.

"I can't let her go with us," replied Flea. "A military unit is no place for a little girl."

Morgan smiled.

"You'll cave," he said chuckling. "She'll look at you with her big, yellow, kitten eyes and tell you how excited she is…"

"Shut up, Morgan," interrupted Flea.

"She will," said Morgan defensively. "And then you'll cave in, and let her go."

"Shut up, Morg," Flea repeated himself.

"You will completely cave," Morgan said with certainty. "I know you will."

"Listen, Morgan," Flea started to explain. "…Ah, never mind."

Morgan was chuckling as he left the room. He was muttering something about Flea not being as tough as he acted.

Flea walked over to the shower he had installed on the roof next to the shack. Another shower similar to this one was on the opposite side where Armina was cleaning up. Flea took his shower and started pulling on his flight suit. Kaida had tried to get him to wear a purple one, but Flea told her and Tommy that the flight suits would be a uniform olive green.

He got dressed and left the shower stall to return to his bed where he sat and waited for Armina. The fur on top of her head grew in the same manner and rate as human hair. It was very long and lustrous. She had taken to putting it in pig-tails to mimic Kaida. She was very fond of the Japanese girl. Finally, as expected, she pounced on Flea from behind where she had crept up silently onto a low tree branch. Flea knew she was there, but always pretended to be surprised by her anyway. The two laughed and wrestled a bit until Flea finally stood her up in front of him.

"Kitten," he said gently as he sat on the bed, "We have to talk."

"Is it about today?" she asked excitedly hopping up and down.

She was very energetic after she was fully awake.

"Yes," replied Flea. "Listen…"

"I'm so excited," she said happily. "I've been looking forward to this all week!"

"A military combat unit is no place for a little girl," Flea thought.

"I know," said Flea.

"There could be things going on there that a child should not see or hear," Flea thought. *"It could be dangerous."*

"Look," she said twirling about happily. "I had a flight suit made just like yours!"

"I see," said Flea with a small grin.

"The environment provided by a combat unit is not conducive to the proper upbringing of a child," Flea reprimanded himself.

"And now I get to see the fighters!" she said excitedly. "Remember all the work we did? I made the painting, remember?"

"I remember," said Flea chuckling.

"A combat vessel," Flea admonished himself, *"is a dangerous place for a little girl."*

"And now we get to go see them!" she pounced in his lap. "Right?"

"That's right," Flea sighed with a sad smile. "Just try not to get in the way too much, okay? And don't get upset if I start yelling or acting weird. I only know one way to do this."

He knew it was wrong to take her with him. He caved.

"Okay," she said happily.

"Promise?" asked Flea. "It's very important."

"I promise," she replied solemnly.

Flea left the roof top with Armina on his shoulders, as she often was now. She sat on his shoulders with her feet under his arms and her ankles hooked under his armpits. Unlike human children, Flea didn't need to hold her while she was up there because of her increased balance. Flea noticed that Kaida had already left the house, and saw Tommy admiring himself in his flight suit with a mirror.

"Tommy," said Flea. "You going to leave soon or primp in the mirror all day?"

"What?" said Tommy turning around looking surprised to find someone watching him. "Oh yeah, sorry."

"Let me give you some advice, Tommy," said Flea. "In the military, if you're on time, you're late. NEVER be late. If you want to be on time, show up fifteen minutes early."

"Really?" asked Tommy looking a bit worried.

"Yes, really," responded Flea gruffly.

"You look different, Flea," said Tommy turning to go. "Kind of angry."

Flea glanced at himself in Tommy's mirror. He saw himself scowling.

"I know," Flea said to Tommy. "Get used to it. It's time to go to work. Put some speed on it."

"Yeah, sure," said Tommy.

"The correct response is," Flea said with a scowl, "...yes, sir."

Tommy looked at him for a moment and responded, "Yes, sir."

"Very good," said Flea flatly.

"Oh," Tommy added. "One more thing?"

"Go on," said Flea.

"What do I do if anyone asks how old I am?" asked Tommy. "I'm only fifteen, remember?"

"Lie," responded Flea.

"You want me to lie?" asked Tommy a bit surprised.

"Yes," said Flea. "The Earth is gone, now. What are they going to do? Ask for your driver's license?"

"Are you sure?" asked Tommy a bit skeptical.

"Look," said Flea. "I let you in the preliminary group along with Kaida, because the two of you expressed to me that you wanted to be there. I told Morgan to let you in after what you did on the Kashin battleship before we left the dock. If you want to stay, then lie if anyone asks. Lie like a cheap Persian rug, Tommy."

"Okay," he still sounded unsure.

"You and Kaida are here without trying out," continued Flea. "That means I am cutting you guys a break. You didn't have to try out to get this far. I expect the two of you to give me all your effort and do whatever it takes to make it on the team...even lie. Slack off or disappoint me one bit as your commander, and I'll send your ass packing. I'll do it in a heartbeat."

"Yes, sir," responded Tommy loudly.

"Now get down there," said Flea.

Tommy turned and ran out the room. Flea could hear him stomping as he ran all the way outside to go to the carrier.

"He's right," Flea heard Morgan's voice behind him. "You do look angry."

"Yeah," said Flea. "I know. I thought you left? Did you get my message with the tips and instructions?"

"Yeah," responded Morgan. "I was about to head down there. I'll introduce myself as the Executive Officer and second in command. Then I'll let them get to know a little about me. Answer any questions and then you should show up."

Flea nodded as Morgan outlined the text Flea had sent him.

"Did you get my reply? It outlines a little about our potential pilots," Morgan asked.

"I'll get to it," said Flea. "Armina and I will pass the time by stopping in at Alex's office. We should let her know our plans today, since it's her ship."

"She'd appreciate that," said Morgan.

"Let's get going," Flea said to Armina.

He looked up at her and she smiled a happy and excited smile down at him.

"God forgive me for what I do," Flea said the silent prayer in his head. *"I hope she turns out okay."*

"See you guys down there," said Morgan.

"Sure thing," Flea said.

"Oh," Morgan added, "I see you caved."

Morgan grinned at Flea.

Flea scowled at him, "Just get down there."

"What's he mean by that, Flea?" asked Armina curiously from her perch.

"Never mind, kitten," said Flea gently. "Never mind."

***

"No!" said Mihanna vehemently. "I will not permit this!"

"Let's you and me get something straight, pal!" said Alex threateningly. "You gave us this ship and for that, I am grateful. However," she growled, "this is MY ship! You said you'd give it to us if I commanded it, and I accepted your offer. That makes this ship mine!"

"I will not allow you to arm this vessel with outlawed weapons!" replied Mihanna raising his voice.

"Outlawed by who?" accused Alex. "A bunch of creatures hiding and running scared from their enemy like rats from the barn cat? I will not run! I am going to use any means necessary to win! Victory at all costs!"

They stared at each other, each breathing heavily for a moment.

"Sorry," said Alex lowering her voice as she noticed her friend's distress. "I just want to win. For the sake of my daughter, I have to."

She glanced in Keri's direction. Her daughter was playing in the adjoining arboretum to Alex's office. The maintenance team went through quite a bit to install that.

"I must succeed," Alex said quietly.

"I understand," said Mihanna. "But you must realize how very dangerous some of these weapons are. Not just to our enemies, but to us as well. In some cases, they are even dangerous to the very fabric of space itself."

"What's up guys?" asked Flea entering the room with Armina on his shoulders.

"Don't you look cute in your flight suit?" said Alex looking at Armina with a smile. "Morgan called ahead and said you'd be joining Flea today."

"Yeah!" she said excitedly. "We're going to have lots of fun and maybe even take out one of the fighters later!"

"That sounds very nice, sweetie," she said to Armina. "Maybe after training you can come by and get Keri? She might like a ride in one of those, too."

"Sure," said Flea. "She can ride with her Dad. We can chase each other around in the fighters or something. She'd like that."

"Why are you two scowling?" asked Mihanna sounding disturbed. "Is something wrong, Armina?"

Mihanna was a bit apprehensive to turn the Kashin kitten's upbringing over to a human, but Armina was being very insistent.

"I'm trying to be intimidating. It's to help establish chain of comments," Armina responded flatly.

"Command," Flea corrected the kitten. "It's to help establish chain of command."

"Yeah," Armina agreed. "That's what I meant to say. Chain of command."

Mihanna looked at Flea for a moment and shook his head.

"What was all the yelling about?" asked Flea. "We heard you guys all the way down the hall."

"There are some weapons that Mihanna does not want us to use," responded Alex.

"Like what?" asked Flea.

"The A-bomb," responded Alexandria.

"Atomic bomb?" asked Flea.

"No," responded Alex. "We can use those and any other weapons we developed on Earth. He doesn't want us using Antimatter bombs and devices."

"What are those?" asked Flea.

"They have a core divided into two chambers," she explained. "In one is some very dense matter. The other contains its exact antimatter opposite. When they are introduced to each other, the energy released is enough to leave a hole the size of China."

"Is 'size of China' a recognized unit of scientific measurement?" asked Flea with a straight face. "Or just your best estimate."

"Best conservative estimate," replied Alex just as seriously.

"Can you put some of those on our fighters?" asked Flea.

"Smaller versions," she replied. "They only make holes as big as Michigan and you only have enough space to carry one at a time with your other armaments."

"Do it," said Flea.

"Those weapons turn entire areas into inhospitable wrecks!" interjected Mihanna loudly. "Millions of cubic kilometers are destroyed! Escaping the blast radius is almost impossible in ANY vessel! You will put us all at risk!"

"I did my research! I know what they can do!" Alex yelled. "I'll use anything I can!"

"Are you ready to be responsible for that?" Mihanna shouted. "Are you ready to be able to accept it if one of those things kills us all?"

"Look! This ship is mine, now!" Alex shouted. "And Flea's fighters are his! We will never disobey strategic orders, but we will arm ourselves and make our policies as WE SEE FIT!"

"You will kill us all," said Mihanna darkly.

"We will only use them as a last resort," Alex promised. "Only when all other strategic options are exhausted."

"I swear it," said Flea solemnly.

"So do I," agreed Alex, "but, I will not deny us the advantage that these weapons give."

"Not even the Goraan will use antimatter weapons," said Mihanna.

"The Goraan are bigger and stronger than us. We can only win by doing the things our enemy is not willing to do," said Flea. "If they won't use them for some reason, then we will."

"It will destroy everything it touches, even the precious resources the Goraan need to support their empire," said Mihanna.

"Good," said Flea. "Maybe I'll drop one on them just to make a point."

"Good idea," said Alex viciously.

Mihanna shook his head in disappointment as he realized he wasn't going to change the minds of his two friends.

"You don't realize what needs to be done," said Alex sternly. "I know how relentlessly the Goraan pursue any who escape them. That means they are coming for you, me, Flea and all of us. They are coming for my daughter."

She stepped closer and looked up at the Kashin Admiral's face with a dark and foreboding glare.

"I will make them wade through rivers of their own blood, and climb over mountains of their own corpses before I let them have my baby," she threatened fiercely.

"No," continued Mihanna. "It is you who do not realize what could happen if you use them. The last time an antimatter weapon was used it formed a localized void of oblivion after detonating near a black hole. It changes the physics of space! There was nothing on the other side of the void. It was like looking into a vast, empty nothingness. It sucked in everything! It continued to eat away at its surroundings until it was lodged shut by an entire planet! Everything on that planet died!"

Flea and Alex were silent.

"If you go to that planet," shouted Mihanna, "all you will see is half a sphere stuck there in one place! The far side is an empty hole! Nothing there! Gone! We call it the 'half world,' now! Do you not understand? We call it this because half of it is missing! It is just gone! We do not know where it went!"

"Good!" shouted Alex in response. "Now I know how strong it is!"

Flea was just standing there with a blank expression. He had never seen this side of Alex before.

"Now you know how strong it is?" He shouted. "If one of these weapons the size of which you are putting on your carrier were to have something go wrong, it could easily suck in an entire planet!"

"Good!" shouted Flea. "Maybe it will suck the Goraan in with it!"

Mihanna stared at the two humans angrily. Then he shook his head and went fuming out of the room.

"How many others of these outlawed weapons are you using?" asked Flea.

"Quite a few," responded Alex as she began to calm down, "We have weapons that distort time, chemical and biological agents, nuclear weapons, nerve agents, antimatter weapons, high density solid state energy conversion weapons…"

"How many can we incorporate into my fighters?" asked Flea interrupting her.

"I just recently commissioned a scientific and strategic war research and development department on my ship that is expanding on the Runners' technology. Their combined intelligence is enormous. They should be able to come up with something," she said.

"Great," said Flea optimistically.

"They are trying to advance on our allies work, and are even developing new weapons on their own," she said enthusiastically. "I'll have them see if they can reproduce these on a smaller scale for you."

"Thanks," said Flea as he turned to walk out. "One more thing. If you get a chance, come down and introduce yourself to the potential pilots. They should know who commands the ship they're on."

"I'll see what I can do," she said sitting down hard in the chair behind her desk. "I'm very busy."

She looked distraught. Her exchange with Mihanna was bothering her.

"Don't take what Mihanna said too hard," Flea added gently. "He doesn't understand where we come from. You know, I looked on the computer and it said Earth was the most war torn planet in the known universe?"

"Really?" asked Alex. "Why am I not surprised?"

"I'm just mentioning it to put things in perspective," explained Flea. "The rest of the Runners don't have such a turbulent past. Quite a few of them haven't even experienced war before. It's a new thing for them."

Flea turned to leave and started to walk out of the room.

"Flea!" called Alex. "I won't lose. I will do whatever I must to protect my husband and daughter."

"I know," Flea said gently.

Alex's voice was shaking, "They're all I have left."

"You have us, too," said Armina gravely.

"Yes," Alex smiled warmly. "I have you guys, too."

"And we'll help you fight!" said Armina cheerfully.

"Oh, one more thing," Alex said to Flea handing him a black case with a small purple bow on it. "Our delegation sent this over for you. It's a gift. They gave one to me and Morgan, too."

"Cool," responded Flea, "What is it?"

"Guns," responded Alexandria seriously. "Very nasty guns."

"Outlawed?" asked Flea sarcastically.

"Probably," responded Alex. "Everything else we do seems to be."

Flea opened the case. Inside was a black gun belt with two holsters on either side. Flea pulled it out of the box and strapped it on. They were slung low on his hips. He tied the two small chords around each of his thighs. Still inside the box, two silver and gold guns still remained outlined by a piece of dark grey packing foam. For hand guns, they were extremely large.

"Hey! I only got one. They gave you and Morgan two," Alex said with a mock pouty expression.

"What are they?" asked Flea. "This is some serious hardware. They're like hand guns on steroids."

"They don't look like mine," responded Alex. "Mine is supposed to destroy matter or something like that. It's some kind of a disintegrator. Morgan's guns are different, too. They're some kind of pulsing energy weapons. They act like small energy machine guns."

"Have you shot them yet?" asked Flea.

"No, we thought we'd hold off until all three of us could go out on some shuttle craft and shoot at some training targets together, or something like that," she replied.

"Cool," said Flea. "Hey, here's a manual."

Flea pulled a small book out of the case's lid.

As he pulled out the manual, a small black leather headband was hiding behind it.

"Emotional wave transference and amplification energy pistol?" asked Alex looking over Flea's shoulder with bulging eyes.

Flea leafed through the booklet briefly. He stopped at a page and briefly read through it and looked at the accompanying diagram. Flea pulled the headband out and put it on. It was made up of a black leather strap an inch and a half wide with sensors on the inside. His brown hair stuck up above the headband. He looked at the diagram again briefly and then flipped down a pair of arched pieces of black metal that were shaped to fit behind the tops of his ears. Two purple eye pieces tinted everything as he looked through them. Then he extended a pair of slender two inch long glass like antennas from above each of the ear pieces.

"The antennas glow purple," said Armina with wide eyes. "Cool! What does it do?"

"Well," said Flea. "The best I can figure from the manual is that it channels the bio-waves of my negative emotions through the transmitter above my ear. Then, it sends them to the guns and sort of blasts them at my enemies somehow."

"Really?" asked Alex with a doubtful expression.

"Hey," said Flea, "I don't know how it works, but it sounds cool to me."

"What are the eye pieces for?" Armina asked.

Flea leafed again through the manual, stopping when he found the section on the eye pieces.

"Targeting I think," responded Flea.

"Morgan and I have some similar to yours," Alex said. "My targeting goggles are yellow and his are green. Ours look more like a cool pair of shades, though."

Flea reached up and flipped a small switch on the back of the headband as indicated in the manual. The first thing he noticed was the targeting display in his now glowing eyepieces.

If he focused on an object for a few seconds, it became outlined in a brighter shade of purple. As he looked in the case, the two guns started to vibrate menacingly.

Flea lifted them out one at time and gripped them tightly. They were slightly warm, which contradicted their cold metallic look. The handles were done in pearl with gold trim. He looked down the barrels. The diameter of the barrels was large and angry. The main body of the gun was silver with gold trim. Large vents were on both sides of the barrel near the handles angling upward, away from his hands. A small purple light blinked on the top of the guns near the back above the handles. They were synchronized with the antennas that were now blinking above his ears. When he wielded the guns in front of him, a small pair of cross hairs that were a different shade of purple appeared in his view. When he pointed the guns in a manner that positioned the cross hairs over a target he was focusing on, the cross hairs and target would start to flicker. A small purple arrow would then appear showing the point of impact.

"I like it," Flea growled. "I definitely like it."

He looked back down at his new guns. For some reason, the more he looked at his new guns, the angrier he got. They vibrated in his hands causing his palms to sting.

"Cool," said Flea with a scowl as he looked at his guns. "Hate Blasters."

On both sides of the barrels of both weapons, Flea's name was inlaid with gold wire in Gothic style letters.

"Captain Gabriel Michael Sherman?" asked Armina reading the barrels. "Who is that? Is that your real name? I didn't think Flea was your real name. Is Gabriel your real name?"

"What's that?" asked Flea who hadn't heard Armina.

"Captain Gabriel Michael Sherman," Repeated Armina. "Who is that? Is that you?"

Flea gave Alexandria a withering look.

"That's Flea's real name," she said with a small smile. "He doesn't like it. That's why we call him Flea."

"I'll still call you Flea," said Armina cheerily.

Flea smiled at her, which ended up looking a bit twisted because of the rage that was building up while holding his guns. He turned them over briefly once more and opened his palm to look at the handles. Flea noticed the word: *ArchAngel* was inlaid with more gold wire in Gothic style letters. It was on both sides of the guns running down the handles.

Flea holstered the guns and the pain slowly crept away from his hands. He remembered what it felt like. The anger faded a little more slowly. He could sense that even though his rage faded after holstering the guns, it still burned slightly inside him. He didn't like the way they made him feel. He felt sick. He decided not to mention this.

"Hey," he said. "A note is on the back."

"To Captain Gabriel," he read the note out loud. "This is to help you in your endeavors. Use them to protect your loved ones. Use them to defend your fellow humans. Use them to exact a measure of vengeance for us all. Good luck."

"That was nice," said Alex.

"They signed it: *Love Christina, Ryoko, and Daniela.* That was sweet of them," he said with a disturbing grin.

Flea didn't read the rest of the note to them. This was a personal choice he made on the spot. He didn't want Armina and Alex to worry about him. The rest of it read:

P.S. - Be careful how you use these. All weapons have a price.

***

Ba'an enjoyed the shadows. Because of his pasty white skin, it was difficult for him to hide effectively unless he went very deep in to the shadows. He seemed to be taking quite a bit of pleasure in the act of "lurking." Presently, he was lurking in the ceiling behind the pitiful Scivistan. He was watching, unbeknownst to Scivistan, from the shadows to ensure his new "friend" carried himself in accordance with the plan that Ba'an had laid out for him.

They made their way with Ba'an lagging behind from the lower end up to the more ornate part of the ship. The flesh in his arms was starting to hurt from using his suction cups to cling to the ceiling. The residual pain from his morning session with Mistress Toren didn't help the circumstances, either. Hopefully, Scivistan could lure his target out and he could follow them back to the lower end. If all went well, Ba'an would receive his first promotion by the end of this week. Of course, it would be

Scivistan who gave it to him, but he could kill that loathsome creature later and take his job. Every step Ba'an was promoted, took him one step closer to his ultimate goal. Esham'aut would die.

All of this however, would have to wait until he reached a position in which he could get close to Esham'aut. In his prior position, he could have easily had access to the detestable Gora. In this new one though, it would be much more difficult. To make matters worse, as a member of the empire, he could only move up in position if the individual whose position he would be filling either moved up or died first. There were only a few exceptions to this rule. For example, Ba'an thought he was safe in his former position, since he was appointed by an act of the Emperor. However, Esham'aut was also appointed by an act of the Emperor, and had more authority than Ba'an. As a result, Esham'aut happened to be one of the few Gora's that had the ability to forcibly remove or demote another member of the Empire. Ba'an would make him regret ever exercising that ability. For the moment, though, he was simply focused on removing the ship's first shift Assistant Cellular Reharvestation Technician's Supervisor. If he did this, then Scivistan would be one of the six candidates for the position. If Ba'an removed one or two of the other five Goras that would be up for the job, then that imbecile Scivistan would surely advance. When he did, Ba'an would make sure the idiot took him along for the ride.

"I will kill so much, that eventually that moron Scivistan will be Ship's Resources Supervisor if I have to," he thought grimly.

Ba'an looked on as Scivistan approached the door to his supervisor's office. Scivistan positioned himself in front of the door's electronic sensor.

"Cellular Reharvestation Technician Scivistan requesting to see shift supervisor, Gormak," he said.

The door slid silently open. Scivistan remained in the hallway as instructed earlier by Ba'an. Ba'an didn't trust Scivistan in any way shape or form. However, letting Scivistan live provided Ba'an with both some cover and an alibi should anyone start raising suspicions. This did not excuse him from the list, though. Scivistan would still die, eventually.

"Good morning, Scivistan, is there some problem? I told you never to bother me unless there is a problem. After all, one of my intelligence and standing could do irreparable damage to his reputation if he was seen fraternizing with one of the low-enders that worked for him," responded Gormak.

"Of course, sir," replied Scivistan. "But it is an emergency! I do not know what to do!"

"What is wrong this time?" asked the impatient supervisor. "Did you get your tail stuck in the hinges of one of the chamber doors again and need to file a complaint?"

"No, no," said Scivistan hastily. "It is that stupid Ba'an."

"Go on," replied Gormak.

"He was cleaning chamber number two, when the door slammed shut and I accidentally reharvested him!" Scivistan was being very overly dramatic.

"If he screws this up," Ba'an thought to himself angrily, *"I will rip out his eyes and tear his stupid Gora body off his shell's brain with my beak!"*

"What?" exclaimed Gormak. "Do you know the amount of reports I will have to file? Despite the fact the he was totally useless, he was STILL a member of the Empire, you idiot! Now, you have thrown off my entire day!"

"I am sorry, sir," whined Scivistan. "Truly. I am sorry."

Gormak was a reddish color with a texture to his skin that resembled some sort of rock. When he lashed out and broke Scivistan's jaw, Ba'an could hear stone crumble off the supervisor's fist. Scivistan was sent reeling across the hall and came sliding to a stop when the top of his skull hit the far wall. Ba'an muffled a small chuckle. Watching Scivistan get hurt was mildly amusing.

"Get up!" demanded the supervisor. "Take me down to chamber number two, you idiot!"

Ba'an crawled silently along the ceiling at a safe distance from the two as they made their way to the reharvestation room. The door to chamber number two was left open to help collaborate what Scivistan told Gormak. Gormak walked over to chamber number two and looked inside.

"What is going on here?" he demanded. "The chamber is perfectly dry inside! It has not been run all day!"

"Stupid Scivistan!" Ba'an thought enraged, *"He forgot to run the chamber! I told him to do this! The fool!"*

Scivistan was standing there with a blank expression on his face.

"Don't you even think about betraying me, you spineless worm!" Ba'an thought.

Scivistan nudged his head upward and glanced toward Ba'an's position. Gormak looked up. Ba'an had been spotted.

"What is this?" exclaimed Gormak.

"He made me do it, sir!" Scivistan struggled to whine with his sore jaw, "I did not want to! I was going to die! You do not know what he's capable of! He was going to kill me!"

Ba'an remained frozen.

"This is not part of the plan," he thought grimly.

"That is it!" growled Gormak, "I do not know what is going on here, but mark my words! I am going to tell the Resources Supervisor, right now."

Gormak started to leave the room.

"This is my only chance," thought Ba'an.

Ba'an pushed hard off the ceiling and launched himself at Gormak. He landed on the other creatures head and wrapped his tentacles around Gormak's face. Gormak let go a muffled cry. He reached up and tried to remove Ba'an and dug his thick reddish fingers into Ba'an's flesh. Ba'an could feel his blood burst outward from Gormak's powerful grip. Ba'an cried out a shrill squeal from his small black beak.

"Kill him Gormak!" cried Scivistan. "He's the Choden'gal!"

Gormak was a tall creature. As Ba'an was wrapped around his head, he looked up and lashed one of his tentacles around one of the lights hanging from the ceiling. With a quick yank, he pulled it down on top of Scivistan. Scivistan crumpled to the floor under the light. He wasn't moving very much, but his tail was still twitching. Perhaps he wasn't dead underneath it.

Gormak leaned over and ran head first into the wall causing Ba'an to wrench free his grip around his head. Gormak coughed as he gasped for air.

"What…is all this?" he coughed out the question.

Now was the time. Ba'an could feel the rage inside himself. He filled his soul with hate and vile putrescence. Everything was black and horrible. He became a creature of nightmares. He flared his tentacles out to his side making himself appear larger than he really was. A high pitched, terrible blood chilling scream escaped his beak. It was the type of sound one could feel grate against their bones. Gormak had never heard such a scream before and was frozen in his tracks. Scivistan was starting to rise from under the fallen light. Scivistan heard Ba'an's scream and knew what was going to come next. He looked at Ba'an and wet himself.

"Cho...," stammered Gormak who was visibly shaken.

"Choden'gal!" whispered Scivistan in terror.

Ba'an let fly his white acid from under the tendrils above his beak. His aim was improving through experience, so when Gormak tried to dodge left, Ba'an compensated and found his target. Gormak's hands went to his ruined face and he crumpled to the ground in front of the open chamber two.

Ba'an slowly walked over to Gormak as he lay on the ground clutching his face. Scivistan couldn't move.

"What is this, you ask?" asked Ba'an grimly. "It is revenge. I AM REVENGE!"

Ba'an straddled Gormak's legs and looked down at him.

"I am rage!" he said darkly.

"I...AM...VIOLENCE," Ba'an yelled.

"You are pathetic!" yelled Gormak as he let go of his face to reveal it was unharmed.

Ba'an looked down at him and his eyes bulged.

"That is not how it is supposed to go!" Ba'an stammered. "This is not supposed to happen this way!"

Gormak forcefully raised his leg in a kick that lifted Ba'an bodily from the ground and sent him across the room. Ba'an crashed into the wall hard.

Gormak started to rise up off the floor.

"That was the most pathetic attempt on my life that I have ever experienced," Gormak said darkly as he wiped acid from his face. "You squealing, little slime! You have no idea what you are dealing with!"

"I will have to do this one the hard way," Ba'an thought as he rose to square off against Gormak.

Gormak lunged. Ba'an whipped out one of his tentacles to mimic his Mistress again. Scivistan squealed as he discovered that he, not Gormak, was Ba'an's target. Ba'an wrapped his tentacle around Scivistan's tail and jerked hard. Scivistan was pulled over to block Gormak's lunge and the two hit the wall as Ba'an propelled himself into the ceiling out of harm's way. Gormak and Scivistan landed under one of the suspended lights. They hung from the ceiling on old, rusted, rickety hangers that were pathetically slender. Ba'an hurled himself at the light with all available force.

"Where did you go, scum?" bellowed Gormak as he rose and threw Scivistan into the closed glass door of Reharvestation Chamber number one. Scivistan slid to the ground. The glass door had cracked in a spider web pattern.

Gormak looked up just in time to see the answer to his question.

"Here!" shouted Ba'an as he landed on top of Gormak's face. The light shattered in half across the creature's jaw and Gormak crumpled to the floor again. Ba'an staggered from the wreckage. He would have to see the ship's medical technician before his next beating.

"Fool!" Ba'an growled as he lifted one of the lights slim support rails and bludgeoned Gormak over the head.

Ba'an surveyed the damage for a moment. He walked over the stunned Scivistan who lay weakly on the floor crying in a fetal position.

"Insolate coward!" yelled Ba'an as he kicked Scivistan in the side.

"Please," whined Scivistan. "I am so sorry! I was scared!"

Ba'an kicked him, "Scared? You should be glad I let you live! I still need you! If you betray me again, I will spend the rest of my days tormenting your meager existence!"

Ba'an kicked Scivistan again to punctuate what he was saying.

"Uhgnn," Gormak was moaning from his spot on the floor.

Ba'an tightened his grip on the slender metal rod and walked over to Gormak. He gripped the end of the rod and stood as far away from Gormak as possible so as not to repeat the same mistake.

"Am I still pathetic?" he asked swinging the rod down on Gormak's body.

"Am I still a squealing slime?" he asked striking Gormak with every word.

Gormak was lying still and moaning.

Ba'an reached out and touched Gormak gingerly to test if he would move. His reddish rock like head was now swollen and purple. Ba'an turned and saw the open door to chamber two. He drug Gormak over by his ankles and struggled as he lifted him inside.

"He is not dead," protested Scivistan as he looked on in terror.

Ba'an lashed out with one of his tentacles and gripped Scivistan's tail. He jerked Scivistan over and as he did so, inserted half his tail in the chamber with Gormak and slammed the door shut.

"Never question me!" shouted Ba'an at Scivistan as he screamed.

Ba'an hit Scivistan across the back with the rod he used to beat down Gormak. Scivistan doubled over on the floor with his rear in the air as half his tail was stuck in the reharvestation chamber. Ba'an engaged the door lock mechanism and walked over to the operating panel.

"Wait," screamed Gormak. He had regained his senses and was pounding on the inside of the thick glass.

"Please," implored Scivistan as he struggled on the floor. "Don't do this!"

Ba'an completed the sequence at the control panel that began reharvestation. Scivistan shot upright and tried to remove his tail. He was holding it with both hands and pulling hard to try and remove it from the chamber. Ba'an walked over to the chamber and looked in the door. He swung the rod one last time and caused Scivistan to hit the ground on all fours. Ba'an straddled his back and sat down on him, gripping his tail to keep Scivistan from trying to remove it again. The cat-like creature screamed and hissed as his tail was reharvested along with the still living Gormak.

"You have no idea what you are dealing with," Ba'an threw Gormak's words back at him as turned into a gurgling pinkish soup of reharvested cells and fluids.

Ba'an sat down hard as Scivistan slumped the rest of the way to the ground at the end of the process. His truncated tail slid from the still closed door. It left a long bloody smear as it slid limply to the ground. Ba'an got up and knelt in front of Scivistan and clutched his face with his tentacles.

"Call the maintenance crews and tell them we had an accident. Tell them the lights fell from the ceiling," he said gravely.

Scivistan nodded weakly as tears rolled down his cheeks.

"Go to medical and tell the technician one of the lights fell on you," he added. "I will be along in a few minutes. Get your jaw fixed."

Scivistan again nodded weakly.

"If you ever betray me again," Ba'an said fiercely to Scivistan. "Your life will mean less than that pathetic soup I just turned Gormak in to. Understand?"

Scivistan shut his eyes tight and nodded again.

"You will never escape me," Ba'an whispered darkly. "After all, I am the Choden'gal."

10

Delegate Cormon was one of the water dwelling Homarell. He and the other Homarell politicians were meeting in Cormon's personal dwelling in the Homarell Sphere. The sphere for the Homarell was flooded with water so they didn't have to wear their biological suits. A human was sitting next to him in a small air bubble. He was a young man with short brown hair that covered his forehead with matching brown eyes.

"I know we normally defer our political power to support the Kashin," Cormon began serenely. "But for some reason, they have decided to give these humans too much free reign."

"I agree," replied one of the delegates fluttering water with his whiskers. "I understand we have a long standing, positive, and mutually beneficial alliance with the Kashin even before the Goraan came. However, their seeming fixation they have with these humans as a result of the Admiral's overt support for them will threaten to kill us all!"

"Fellow water dwellers!" interjected Captain Roshom floating to the top of the room. "I have had the opportunity to meet some of these humans, and despite their flaws, they are very endearing and emotional creatures."

"So were the Goraan at first," responded Cormon rising to meet him. "Then they destroyed our home world."

"I believe that in some ways, yes. These humans are similar to the Goraan," replied Roshom as he calmed down and returned to his seat. "Inside them burns the urge to fight. They wish it more than any of the rest of us, despite the short amount of time they have been here. Perhaps they can help us to have a chance against the Goraan."

"You are a fool, Captain!" said another delegate. "These humans are rash creatures. They act on emotion and without reason. All they want is revenge!"

"And would you not also like a measure of revenge for what happened to our home?" responded Roshom angrily. "Is it not perhaps finally the time to fight back?"

"Fight and die, you mean!" said Cormon aggressively as he swam down and sat back in his place. "I will not lose the life I have and the few lives left among our once thriving species for the sake of vengeance for some human trash!"

"The humans are right!" insisted Roshom vehemently with bulging eyes. "If we don't stand and fight all we do is pro-long our deaths! I will not stand and let you betray them!"

"They are nothing but genetic garbage full of uncontrollable emotions! The universe will be better off without them!" countered Cormon heatedly.

Most of the other Homarell present seemed to agree with Corman. Some, however, were agreeing with Captain Roshom.

"Delegate Cormon is right!" shouted the young human in the air bubble finally speaking up. "I have seen Captain Gabriel and met Captain Morgan during the initial pilot tryouts in the Communal Sphere! They are nothing but power hungry lunatics! They'll kill us all!"

Roshom looked aggressively at the young human who had remained quiet until now, "Captains Gabriel, Morgan and Alexandria are honorable humans who only have our best interests at heart! You know nothing of them!"

"Gabriel Sherman is an egotistical war mongering fool!" shouted Cormon as bubbled frothed from his gills. "He is nothing short of psychotic!"

"He is...colorful...I will admit," replied Roshom with a chuckle. "But he and the others work hard to do what is right."

"He and that Mendenhall female condone the use of illegal weapons and technologies! Captain Alexandria and Captain Gabriel will destroy us!" bubbled Cormon angrily.

"You outlaw weapons in declaration of your moral superiority. You try and piously declare that you stand the moral high ground and refuse to turn away any race from joining the Runners that the Goraan try to destroy. When the evacuation of Earth was in question, you stood up and defended the sanctity of life stating that all creatures, even humans have value," replied Roshom quietly. "I have watched these humans since they have been here. They are passionate and full of life. They are something truly good, despite all their flaws. In many cases, even with the knowledge that they are inferior, they still fight on as best they can. I have studied them and grown fond of them. I respect them. In the words of my human allies," Roshom paused for a moment as he thought of the proper human phrase. "Screw you and the horse you rode in on! You know nothing of moral standing! You would not recognize high moral values if they swam in your face!"

"You do not know of what you speak, Captain!" replied Cormon heatedly. "Our only survival lies in our continuance to run and avoid the Goraan."

"What do you propose, Delegate Cormon?" asked one of the other four delegates.

"What I am proposing is not necessarily the destruction of the remainder of the human race," explained Cormon. "I simply propose we get them out of the fleet."

"This is wrong!" protested Roshom shaking his head and making waves. "The humans are working hard to join us in battle. I will not support this!"

"You, Captain, are a military officer! You do not hold sway over the governing School of our people! I, however, do hold sway over you!" interjected Cormon through gurgling bubbles. "I can make you lose your job, and even be exiled from our sphere! I suggest you hold your tongue!"

"You wouldn't dare!" responded Roshom.

"Yes," replied Cormon calmly. "I would."

"This water," Roshom glared at the others in the group, "is stagnant."

It was the worst insult one Homar could give another.

"Be that as it may," growled Cormon with flaring gills, "this water is mine."

There was a long pause of silence as the two stared at each other, angrily flaring their gills. Finally, as a sign of acceptance, Roshom stilled himself and sat back in his chair casting his eyes toward the floor.

"What is your plan, Cormon?" rushed another delegate trying to ease a tense situation. "The Kashin are very fond of these humans. It will be hard for us from a political stand point to go against them. Every race among the runners is given at least one delegate to represent their population. For those who have the numbers, they get one delegate for every one hundred thousand creatures. The Kashin have twenty two delegates. If you include the races that follow them in the council, they are a strong force to contend against."

"I know," replied Cormon. "But do not worry over this point. I have been fostering some relations with other delegates from other species. When we need them, we will have the votes we require."

"Truly?" asked another delegate.

"Yes," replied Cormon. "Then we will send the humans on a mission that will destroy them. This will remove them from the fleet, and lower any political esteem they may have gained in the meantime."

"What if they manage to succeed?" Roshom showed his belief in the humans enthusiastically. "I believe they will! You underestimate them."

"This human has been informing me of the actions of the human pilots in training," said Cormon with a glare in Roshom's direction to silence him. "He has informed me of some of the weapons the humans have on their battle carrier and fighters. Apparently, the humans are using many illegal weapons and technologies. If they return victorious, we will vote their exile from our numbers on these grounds. It should be a simple matter, since they are not fully recognized among the council yet."

"Are they aware that they are only accepted in the council on a trial basis?" asked another Homar.

"No," chuckled Cormon. "They think they are fully recognized. The Kashin are sponsoring them, but the humans do not realize this. I have done well at keeping the bubble headed human females that are their delegates preoccupied so the Kashin cannot tell them this."

"Good," responded the fish-creature. "It may not do us very well if they find out our plan."

"Agreed," replied Cormon.

"Cormon," said the human. "Eventually the other humans will find out what is happening. You will ensure that my safety and all my needs are met, right?"

"I will personally ensure that all your needs and desires are fulfilled," promised Cormon solemnly.

"You will not get away with this, Cormon," Roshom said darkly. "I will not…"

"You will be silent and do as you are told, Roshom!" interrupted delegate Cormon through angry bubbles. "You are a military officer and you take your orders from us! The School swims as one!"

"How should we act toward them in the meantime?" asked one of the delegates.

"Treat them as you normally would," explained Cormon. "Continue trying to harbor good relations and act as if everything is normal. We'll allow their military to train, but I have directed the Resources officer, who is in my School, to privately ensure the humans have…difficulties…getting some of the supplies they need. Things like fuel for their battle carrier and fighters. Weapons for their personnel and resources for their matter combiners will also become scarce. Fortunately, most of the races that support us have representation in the military. I have asked them to increase their training schedules and combat drills so the humans will not have the opportunity to gain flight time in the combat training field. It has been scheduled in advance under the false pretense that we are going to fight the Goraan. This, coupled with the meager amount of fuel designated to the humans will mean that in order to save fuel for combat, they will have to limit their amount of actual flight activity and restrict their training to simulators."

"Simulators are nice," agreed another delegate. "But they do not substitute actual flight experience."

"You resign these humans to their deaths," said Roshom quietly.

"It is necessary. They are an inferior race!" responded Cormon sternly. "The Runners that I have contacted which do not have any ships, have pledged their political support. I had to use a few favors, but we have gained fifty three percent of the Runners Council."

"For now you have it," muttered Roshom darkly.

"As long as our plan does not become public," said Cormon glaring at Roshom. "We soon will no longer have to contend with these humans."

"I am ashamed to be here," commented Roshom.

"You will swim with the School!" Cormon raged.

The water filled room went eerily still. Among Homerall, water that did this was the most foreboding of omens. They all looked around nervously, until their gaze settled on Roshom and Cormon.

"Roshom," said Cormon more gently. "I know you have young ones. I do not have a family, personally, but I know you do. Do you not want to see your spawn grow to fullness?"

"I do," responded Roshom softly.

"Then surely you must see that this is best for us all. This is not only for my own survival, but also for the future of your spawn. We must avoid the Goraan," he said to Roshom.

"What would be best for my spawn," responded Roshom gravely, "is for me to decide!"

Roshom swam toward the entry hole in the ceiling and turned in the doorway to face Cormon.

"Not for you!" Roshom said angrily pointing at Cormon. "My spawn are my decision! I believe the best thing for them would be to grow up without fear of the Goraan! I think we have this chance, if only you would see that!"

"What I see," replied Cormon. "Is us going against the Goraan and dying like countless others!"

Cormon rose to the ceiling to face Roshom.

"What I see," he leaned forward and continued, "is what is left of our race become shells for the Goraan. Most importantly, however, what I see is you keeping silent on what has occurred here today! If this gets out, I will personally ensure you and your young ones are exiled to the most desolate and dry rock we can find!"

***

Morgan was facing the group of pilot candidates. It was a bit strange for him because most of them were female. Morgan was starting to look at things from a different perspective ever since he started having pilot tryouts. That was when he noticed an abnormally large number of females trying out for the group.

Then, he met the delegates for the human race for the first time during try outs. They were not only former pop and media stars, but also young ladies, like many of his pilots. On a hunch, Morgan searched for some statistics on his computer. He found out that the human race was now almost seventy five percent female. This fact stunned Morgan. There was no scientific reason as to why this happened.

He also discovered some other statistics. The oldest the human left alive was seventy two years old and the youngest was two weeks and four days. The average age among humans was twenty three years old. Every major ethnicity and religious belief was represented in equal numbers. No career politicians or career military personnel survived. There were a few people that served short terms in the military, like Flea, but not many. The only former politicians among them had short, unsuccessful stints in politics lasting one term. All of these statistics really had no explanation that anyone could find. It was just one more coincidence in an already turbulent universe where everything seemed to be stacked against the human race.

This explained to Morgan why he was standing with his back to a group of potential pilots that was made up mostly of young females. This wasn't helped by the fact that Flea, after much argument and protest against it from Morgan and Alex, stated that the minimum age requirement would be sixteen. He managed to convince Alex to do the same in order to bulk up the ranks of their fledgling military. Out of the seventy five candidates, fifteen were young female Kashin. Despite the forward thinking of their cat-like allies, their military did not allow females in combat roles. Forty three were young human girls and women. According to their registrations, they were between the ages of sixteen and twenty five. Only seventeen were human males. They were between the ages of seventeen and twenty nine. Morgan made his selections without looking at any registration sheets. These were chosen from their scores alone.

"I hope this works out," Morgan thought silently as he faced the group.

The group looked a bit scared.

"I hope Flea got the text I sent him outlining all this," he added with a chuckle. *"I wonder where he's going?"*

He noticed Flea creeping along the wall behind the back of the group so they couldn't see him.

"Good Morning, pilots," he said turning to face them with a serious expression. He had to be cordial, but remembered not to smile.

"I am Captain Morgan Mendenhall," he said. "Executive officer and second in command of the Archangels fighter group. Before we begin, let's get into formation."

Morgan instructed them how to dress down in rank and file by tallest to shortest. After they were lined up neatly, he stood directly in front of the group and started talking.

"Every morning at 0600…that's six A.M… we will meet here, just like this," he stated. "We will train, evaluate and eventually work our numbers down over the next few weeks to thirty pilots. There are seventy five of you and thirty two fighter crafts. The commanding officer and I each get one, this means that forty five of you, which are very skilled I might add, will be going home. To tell you a bit about me personally, I have no military experience, I'm married, and have a daughter. I have known and been friends with your commanding officer for quite a while. My wife commands this vessel you are currently standing in and hopefully, she will find time to come later and introduce herself. Are there any questions before the commander arrives?"

"If we don't make it here," asked a petite young girl with a Jersey accent, "does that mean we're done for good?"

"You're question is that if you don't make it here, will it be your only chance to be a pilot. Is that you're question?" asked Morgan.

He was told by Flea that if they had any questions that he should try to repeat the person's question back to them first in order to maximize understanding.

"Yeah," she responded in a high pitched voice.

"No," responded Morgan. "Right now we are limited to thirty two fighters, but this ship has a capacity for over two hundred. We plan on filling the hanger bay with fighters some day, so if you don't make it this time, you should definitely come back after we get more fighters."

"Do we have to move on board the ship?" asked one of the human males. "On Earth my brother was in the Navy. They made him live on the ship."

"Will you be living on the ship?" asked Morgan directly. "Is that your question?"

"Yes," he replied.

"Only when we are not docked to the sphere," Morgan explained. "When we are docked like we are now, you can all stay at your homes in the sphere. After we have made our final selection, those of you who make it will be required to take homes near the commander and I."

"What are our ranks?" asked one of the Kashin.

"Her question was about your ranks," Morgan said loudly so everyone could hear. "For the moment, you have none. After the final selection we will assign you your ranks. You will all be officers, but some of you will have higher rank than others, based off your performance during the cuts."

"Will we have a ground force?" another asked.

"We'll start to assemble one as soon as we can develop a proper training facility," Morgan said. "For the time being, we have none."

"Will we get side arms like yours?" asked the first blonde girl.

Morgan looked down at the two guns that were gifts the young human delegation had given him. He, Alex, and Flea all received guns as a gift from them in recognition of their efforts. His were banned by the rest of the Runners because they transformed the universe's own energies into a source of ammunition. This meant that every time he fired the weapon, he depleted the universe by a tiny bit and caused it to cool down. The weapon's own cooling system was pretty advanced and kept it from ever overheating. This meant that in theory, he could pull the trigger and hold it down like a fully automatic weapon, and it would continue to fire indefinitely. Or at least, he could keep firing until the universe ran out of energy and became a frozen nothingness.

Alex's gun was also banned. It fired an energy blast that broke down the particles of whatever it shot and left nothing in its place. It left absolutely nothing. It didn't leave behind trace energies or any particles at all. Subatomic scans of the area after its use verified this. This was disturbing because it went against the laws of conservation of energy that were taught on Earth. Because matter and energy were directly related, it meant that every time Alexandria fired her weapon, she destroyed the universe. This is why her gun and other weapons like it were banned. He hadn't seen Flea's guns yet, but could only assume that they were banned by the Runners as well. Morgan left his thoughts and turned back to the group.

"Those of you who make it into the group," Morgan explained, "will be given a side arm and an assault rifle along with the training to use them. Keep them with you."

There was a long pause.

"Are there no other questions?" asked Morgan.

Another long pause followed.

"Good," stated Morgan. "Ladies and gentlemen, welcome to the military."

***

Flea was walking through the hanger bay with Armina in her customary place on his shoulders. He decided to try some target practice at the end of the hanger bay. He had been getting angrier and angrier ever since he had first drew his new weapons. He felt the urge to shoot something, despite the fuzzy cuteness that rode on his back.

"Where are we going?" asked Armina on his shoulders.

"I want to try out these weapons," Flea said emotionless. "We're going to the end of the hanger bay."

"What about Alex and Morgan?" asked Armina. "I thought we were going to wait for them."

Flea didn't say anything and just kept walking.

"Are you okay?" asked Armina with some concern.

"Fine," responded Flea flatly. "I'm fine."

Armina couldn't tell what was wrong with her guardian and decided to keep quiet. Flea glanced at the group of pilots on the other side of the hanger bay. They were waiting for him. In his brief glance, he didn't notice anything odd about them. He was probably feeling too angry to really notice anything about them at all.

He approached some maintenance robots that were installing something that looked like small guns with sensors on them. These were pieces of the ship's automated interior defense systems.

The hanger bay doors were open revealing the empty black space dotted with stars beyond. An invisible energy shield protected everything from being sucked out into the vacuum of space. It also allowed for objects, like fighters and shuttles to pass through the barrier in order to leave or enter the ship.

"You," Flea said roughly to one of the robots. "I want to get in some target practice."

"Sir?" the robot replied.

"Can we launch some sort of targets out there?" he asked pointing out into the emptiness of space beyond the hanger's energy shield.

"Yes, sir," responded the robot.

"If I fire my energy weapon will it disrupt the shield?" asked Flea glaring.

"No sir," responded the robot. "It will not disrupt blasts coming from this side of the shield."

"Launch some targets," demanded Flea.

"It is not my place...," began the robot.

"Make it your place!" responded Flea through gritted teeth. "Or I'll make it your place to be my first target."

"On whose authority?" asked the robot.

"On mine!" Flea growled as he stuck his thumb in his chest. "Captain Gabriel Michael Sherman! Commanding officer of the fighter group."

"Yes, sir," responded the robot as he went behind a small control panel. "I will erect a sound shield to separate this end of the hanger bay, so you do not interrupt anything occurring on the far side."

"Good," Flea thought to himself. *"The fighter group won't hear me shooting."*

He removed his guns from their holsters and gripped them tightly. He turned them over in his hands again briefly and noticed a small selector switch on the bottoms of the guns. It had three settings: single, automatic, and charged shot. It was set to single shot when Flea looked at them. The targets began floating off in the empty space outside the ship from left to right.

Flea sat Armina on the ground and raised his guns at the first target. It flashed in the eye piece. He pulled the triggers simultaneously. Two wicked looking, purple arcs of energy originated from the antennas above his ears. They glowed evilly as they spiraled around his arms into the back of the guns. The vents in the guns above its handles spewed forth a small cloud of purple smoke that could only be described as smelling like searing hatred. Large purple flashes emanated from the ends of the barrels and shot forth screaming at their targets with a high pitched, unholy sounding "screeeeech." Flea burned inside and he could feel his heart beat faster.

"Flea?" Armina sounded frightened.

Flea ignored her and started opening fire. He blazed forth rage and hatred from his guns. He felt the pain from the guns vibrating more violently in his bones. His hands and arms felt like they were on fire. Flea didn't care. He was angry. He just wanted to shoot more. He hated those targets.

"Bastards!" he growled and started firing more rapidly. "You filthy sons of bitches!"

Armina took a few steps back as her mouth hung open.

"Rotten!" he growled even louder while firing as fast as he could. "You're all a bunch of rotten bastards! I'll kill you all!"

"GrrrrrRRRRR!" he gritted through his teeth. "Not fast enough!"

He looked around wildly.

"Need more! HATE!" he bellowed.

Flea quickly flipped the selector switches on the bottom of the guns to the full auto setting. He held down the triggers and aimed at the targets. He continued destroying the targets. They were racked apart in violent purple bursts of energy when they were struck. He was starting to fire more wildly, though. He used more shots than were need and often continued to fire at a target after it had already been hit and was in the process of being destroyed. Purple arcs of energy were traveling down his arms more quickly. It appeared as if he were throwing bolts of purple lightning. His arms were completely enveloped. His chest hurt more and he lost the feeling in his hands and arms. Something sticky and wet was dripping down his mouth and chin. He had a warm, metallic flavor in his mouth as he continued screaming. He didn't care. He just kept firing.

"GRNACH ESH CROMP DIE!" he screamed as his voice grated in his throat. "ALL DIE!"

Flea had stopped making sense and was screaming incoherently. He was remotely aware of something that may or may not have been tugging at his pant leg. Armina was crying as she screamed at him to stop. Flea couldn't, or maybe refused, to hear her. He was intent on destroying his targets.

"MORE!" he screamed as he cranked the selector switches to charged shot. "HATE YOU ALL!"

Flea held down the trigger and purple energy started to arc down his arms and into the guns. The energy continued to flow as he held down the trigger. It seemed to gather in some purple energy spheres at the ends of the weapons. Flea's hate burned throughout his body. His chest burned, his stomach hurt and he regained enough feeling in his hands and arms to realize they felt like they were throbbing in pain. He still didn't care. His home was destroyed. His family was killed. Everything needed to die. He would kill all of it.

"GRAAAAAAAAA!" the echo of his scream grated in his own ears as he released the trigger.

The energy blasts shot out the end of his weapons like some unnatural, otherworldly, purple retribution. The blast was much larger than the others. It cut through the blackness of space and put everything in a purple cast. Flea's judgment had been passed upon all of creation with those shots. All things deserved his contempt. He had judged that all things deserved to be hated. He had a blatant and all encompassing disregard for all living things. Flea hated the entire universe. He was just screaming now and aiming wildly out through empty space as if he were trying to kill off the universe itself. All that was inside him was hate. He was finally knocked to the ground and his guns fell skittering from his hands.

"FLEEEEAAAA!" Armina screamed wildly. "STOP IT, PLEASE!"

Flea struggled to get to his hands and knees. His arms were weak and racked with pain. He was shaking and had difficulty supporting himself. He vomited violently on the floor of the hanger bay then crawled off a few feet away from the pile and collapsed on his back. His nose was bleeding. His mouth and chin were covered in his blood. Armina came over and crawled on top of him. She turned off the switch above his ear and the purple lights on the backs of the guns faded away. The hatred and anger faded slowly, too. It was as if a giant block of cement that was sitting on his chest had been removed and he could finally breathe easily. The ramifications of what he felt as he opened fire with those damnable guns finally hit him. It was like a punch in the face and a bad hangover added together and multiplied by a thousand. At one point, he actually hated and wanted to kill everything. The realization was mortifying. During that instant, he hated all things, including the things he normally held dear. He even hated himself during that moment. He disregarded the lives of everyone when he fired those things. He even disregarded the tiny life he held in his arms. It was the same life he promised to protect. How anyone could create such a horrible weapon was beyond him. Flea held Armina. He silently and forced back some tears. His eyes were itching.

"I'm sorry, kitten," Flea whispered to Armina. "I'm so sorry."

"I tried to tell you," sniffed Armina who was crying. "I took the manual back in Alex's office when you guys weren't looking. I tried to stop you."

"I know," said Flea hoarsely. His throat hurt from screaming, "I couldn't hear you. I don't know what happened."

"As soon as you turned it on," she said through the tears. "It started to make you hate. The more you hate the more energy it has to feed off of. The more energy it has to supply it, the more it fills you with hate. It's evil! It feeds itself through you! It destroys you when it's on!"

Armina reached up and lowered the two glowing purple antennas.

"Even if you turn the guns off, if the antennas are on, they slowly increase your hate," she explained. "It feeds them and then they make you hate even more."

"I feel awful," Flea said softly as the hatred faded from him when the antennas were lowered.

Flea's eyes hurt. He rubbed them with the palms of his hands.

"It also says never to use two guns at once EVER! It makes you hate even more and more and doesn't stop! That's why you quit making sense and just shouted bad words and stuff like 'KILL' and 'DIE.' It was scary," she sniffed. "I was scared."

"I'm sorry kitten," Flea said softly as he regained some of his composure. "I never meant to scare you."

Flea rubbed his eyes again.

"I wasn't scared of you," she explained while she moved Flea's hands from his eyes. "I was scared of what you were doing to yourself! The antennas blink with your heart beat. It was beating so fast I thought it was going to explode in your chest! Those guns are dangerous! You can only use one at a time, okay? Promise me! Okay?" she implored looking in his eyes. "Say you promise, Flea!"

"I promise," replied Flea as he clutched her to his chest. "In fact I think I'll get a normal gun to carry with me, too. Okay?"

"Okay," she said softly. "Were your eyes purple before?"

"No," he said. "My eyes are brown."

"Were," Armina corrected sadly. "They were brown. Now they're purple."

"What?" Flea sounded confused. "But my eyes are brown."

Armina shook her head, "Not anymore."

Flea's eyes finally stopped itching. He reached out from his position in his back and retrieved one of his guns off the deck. He looked at his reflection in the silver barrel of the weapon. Armina was right. His eyes were purple. They looked creepy. It was an unnatural shade. Flea had been forever marked by his hatred. He reached out and picked up the other gun and holstered his weapons.

"Aren't you forgetting about the pilots?" Armina asked him while they continued to hug on the deck.

"Oh shit!" Flea forced a laugh. "I totally forgot!"

For some reason, laughing felt much better than it usually did at this moment.

"Let's get going," he said trying to sound cheerful.

Armina jumped up with a large grin and started hopping about excitedly.

"Let's go! Let's go! Let's go," she giggled.

Flea got up and started to walk away. He loosened the headband for his guns a bit and pulled it down to hang limply around his neck.

"Is target practice over?" asked the robot behind the panel.

"What?" asked Flea. "Oh yes, of course. I'm done."

"Shall I clean up your blood and vomit, sir?" asked the robot.

Flea started to chuckle, "That would be fine, thank you."

Flea cleaned himself up quickly and then he and Armina left the open hanger bay door area. They started to walk to the other end of the hanger bay to meet the pilots. Flea was glad that Armina didn't crawl back up on his shoulders. Shooting those guns made him tired. He could barely stand. They came up to the group, but stopped short before they were noticed.

"There's something strange about the group," Flea whispered to Armina.

"You mean the Kashin?" asked Armina. "Kashin girls aren't allowed to fly combat fighters. I think they are probably here to try and do something they can't among our own kind."

"Not them," responded Flea. "Mihanna mentioned something about Kashin being at the try outs. I wonder why no Kashin males showed up, though?"

"Maybe Morgan knows," said Armina softly as the two were trying not to be noticed while Morgan continued to speak to the group.

Then it dawned on Flea.

"Host," he whispered pulling out his smartphone. "How many males are left among the human race?"

"Eighty nine thousand one hundred twelve," replied his phone.

"Give me an estimated percentage of the number of human females left in the entire race," Flea whispered to the computer.

"Approximately seventy two percent," replied the phone.

Flea was shocked. His eyes threatened to pop out of his skull.

"How can that be?" he asked to no one in particular.

"It is an inexplicable scientific anomaly," responded the device.

"What's the average age of the remaining humans?" asked a stunned Flea.

"Twenty three years old," replied Flea's phone.

"This just keeps getting better and better," Flea said softly to himself.

"What do you mean?" asked Armina.

"Never mind," said Flea sounding dejected.

"Maybe you should check your text messages," suggested Armina. "Morgan might have sent you something about the pilots."

"Oh yeah," said Flea. "Good idea."

Flea opened up his messages and read everything he had just noticed as it was outlined by Morgan and sent to him last night.

"I should have checked this earlier," Flea said. "Morgan mentioned all this."

"Kaida is right, you know," grinned Armina. "You should check your phone more often."

"Yes, kitten," responded Flea dryly. "Thank you very much for reminding me."

"You're welcome," she said cheerfully.

"By the way," Flea said looking down at her, "our fighter group has a name."

"Really?" asked Armina excitedly. "What is it?"

"The Archangels," replied Flea. "That must have been Morgan's idea. He was probably trying to poke fun at me."

"How is that?" asked Armina.

"I'll explain later," responded Flea. "Let's get up there. They're done talking now."

"Cool!" she said hopping up and down.

Flea unzipped his flight suit and pulled the top half down to his hips. He tied the arms in a knot in front of his waist. He was wearing a black shirt with "FLEA" written in white block letters on his chest. Armina unzipped her own child-sized flight suit in a manner that mimicked him. "HELLKITTY" was written in white block letters across her chest. Flea looked at it for a moment.

"Hellkitty?" Flea asked arching an eyebrow.

"Yep," she said proudly. "I used my computer and researched a little bit on human mythology."

"I see," said Flea.

"Yep! Hell is a bad place and I am a kitten. Therefore," she explained trying to sound tough, "This makes me one bad kitty! Nobody messes with the Hellkitty!"

She stood there trying to make a fearsome expression. It failed to instill any fear in Flea. He tried hard not to laugh at how cute she was being.

"Okay, Hellkitty," said Flea seriously. "Remember to try and be intimidating."

"Right," she said ferociously. "Establish chain of comments!"

"Command," Flea corrected her with a sigh. "Chain of command."

Flea and Armina emerged from their hiding spot and walked purposefully down the middle of the hanger bay toward the pilots. As they approached, Morgan was standing in front of the group. Flea walked up to Morgan who had turned to face him as he approached. The two stood silently in front of each other and exchanged nods. Morgan then moved over to one side so he could face Flea and the group at the same time. Flea looked out at the group. In Morgan's email he had just read, he was informed of how many males, females, and Kashin were in the group. He knew the breakdown of ethnic and religious diversity in the group as well. Flea didn't care about any of this. The group stood at attention and waited for him to speak. Flea let the silence go on so he could point out to them who was in charge by making them wait for him.

"My name," he said forcefully with a scowl as he strutted back and forth in front of them, "Is Captain Gabriel Michael Sherman! This is my group!"

Flea stopped and stood squarely in front of them.

"IF YOUR NAME IS NOT CAPTAIN GABRIEL MICHAEL SHERMAN, THEN YOU ARE NOT IN CHARGE, LADIES!" Flea barked.

A few of them were starting to smile. Flea found Kaida in the front row of the group, and she slightly nodded almost imperceptibly at some spot behind him. Flea turned and saw

Armina, who was perfectly mimicking his posture as she stood a few feet behind him to his left. Her tail was swishing aggressively back and forth. Flea stifled a smile as he looked at her.

"Armina," Flea said to her gently.

No response.

"Armina!" he said more loudly.

Still, she didn't respond.

"Hellkitty!" he growled.

"Sir, yes sir!" she responded snapping to attention.

"Go stand with Morgan, okay?" Flea said to her.

"Yes sir!" she responded happily and trotted over to stand next to Morgan.

Flea shook his head slightly as he started to wonder if it was really such a good idea to bring her along. Some of the group was now audibly chuckling.

"As I was saying," Flea growled turning back to the group. "I am the commanding officer of this group! If any of you think you can do better, then come up here and try it!"

A young man came trotting up and stood off to Flea's right side.

"I was an Ensign in the Navy," he said. "What experience do you have?"

"I was a Marine," responded Flea. "A squad leader."

"An N.C.O.? You were enlisted? Are you kidding?" he said condescendingly. "You can't even control that kitten! You're pathetic!"

"Why does it always have to be the hard way?" Flea thought wearily. *"Just once, I wish it could be easy."*

"Listen," Flea said to the young man seriously. "Go back and take your place in line. I don't have time for this."

"This," he said puffing out his chest. "Is where I belong! Go home and play with the kittens, okay? Shit! After the executive officer's little show I was hoping at least one of you would be worth following, but I guess not."

"Look," Flea said aggressively as he stared up at the former officer. "You don't want to go there. I've had a rough morning."

The young man, who was much taller and larger than Flea, turned and poked his finger in the middle of Flea's chest.

"You need to get the Hell out of MY group," he said stressing who he thought should be in charge.

"If Armina wasn't here," said Flea darkly. "I'd beat you to within an inch of your pathetic life."

"It's okay Flea," shouted Armina from beside Morgan. "When we were working on the fighters I remember you saying that sometimes you have to beat someone down. This looks like one of those times! Go head! Get him!"

"There you go, Flea," mocked the larger man as he continued poking Flea's chest. "It's okay with her. What are you going to do about it?"

Flea cast his purple eyes toward the ground in a sign of deference. The younger man took this as a sign that he had won. Flea was watching him in the reflection of his gun handle.

"You see?" he said turning his head toward the group. "This whole outfit is just sad. I'll change out all of you. Now that I'm in charge I'm going to…"

He didn't get a chance to finish his sentence. Flea had enough of this idiot. While he was looking away and talking down to the group, Flea kicked him. Flea struck as hard and fast as humanly possible. He kicked the larger man, who until that point wasn't paying attention, squarely in his testicles. The former U.S. Navy officer crumpled to his knees. That particular blow was normally one of most devastating and deceitful things you could do to another man in a fair fight. Flea never fought fair. His personal belief was that everything was fair in a fight. He who lived to walk away could argue the morality of his actions later.

As the other man was doubled over, Flea grabbed both of his ears and drove his knee in the larger man's nose, causing it to burst and gush forth blood. Flea's opponent was sent sprawling on the ground backwards. He rolled over on the ground and started to try and get up. Flea, however, moved quickly and kicked him while he was down. He kicked him a few more times until the man no longer tried to rise.

"Had enough?" Flea growled.

The would be usurper laid still and moaned. Flea kicked him a few more times for good measure and then jumped in the air to drop on the small of the man's back. He landed to drive his knees into the other man's kidneys. The former officer would most likely urinate blood for a week.

"Shut up!" Flea growled as he landed.

This day was getting worse. Flea put the man in a combination half nelson hold and behind the back wrist lock. The more the other man struggled, the more pressure Flea applied to the man's wrist that was wrenched behind his back.

"Don't make me break it!" shouted Flea. "Now, let's play a game!"

Flea kneed the man in the lower spine.

"When I ask: Who's in charge? You say my name," Flea growled. "You got that?"

The other man responded by struggling to get away from Flea's grip. Flea started to knee the man some more until he stopped struggling as much.

"Who's in charge?" shouted Flea.

The other man refused to speak.

Flea jerked the man's wrist causing him to cry out in pain. His wrist wasn't broken, yet.

"I SAID," shouted Flea, "WHO'S IN CHARGE?"

"Stop!" protested the larger man.

The guards were now there watching what was going on. They knew who Flea was, and were earlier instructed not to interfere with anything unless explicitly instructed to do so. Morgan and Armina were watching with grim approval.

"SAY IT!" shouted Flea. "WHO'S IN CHARGE, GODDAMNIT?"

"Captain Gabriel…," whimpered the other man. "Captain Gabriel…I CAN'T REMEMBER! PLEASE, STOP!"

"That's okay," said Flea softer. "You can just give me the simple answer. Now who's in charge?"

"You are," responded the large man.

"When you speak to me," yelled Flea. "The first and last thing out of that god forsaken hole in your face where you shovel your Goddamn food will be 'sir!' That goes for all of you!"

Flea glared at the group to let them know he was speaking to them as well. They looked terrified. The other man was silent again.

"Are we communicating?" Flea shouted as he wrenched on the man's wrist again.

"Sir, yes, sir!" replied the man in obvious pain.

"And who was in charge again?" asked Flea shouting.

"Sir, you are, sir!" responded the man as he gritted his teeth.

Flea jerked his opponent to his feet and shoved him into the arms of the guards. The guards clasped onto the man's upper arms. He struggled against them and got free. He lunged at Flea. Flea jerked one of his Hate Blasters from its holster in a flash. They weren't turned on, so if Flea pulled the trigger nothing would happen. The other man didn't know this, though. Flea pointed it at the other man's face. His nose still bled profusely. Everything went dead silent.

"Don't even think about it," Flea said flatly.

The guards approached and took the man in custody.

"Take him to medical for treatment," said Flea to the guards. "Then escort him off the ship. Input his bio life energy readings into the ship's automated internal defense systems."

"Yes, sir," responded the guards.

"Never set foot on this ship again," said Flea looking directly in the man's eyes. "If you do, you'll be vaporized in your boots."

The larger man looked away when Flea stared at him. The guards dragged away the now protesting man.

"Goddamn it!" shouted Flea angrily as he faced the group. "I swear in the name of everything sacred and holy! If any of you ever tries anything like that again, I will personally rip out your lungs and show them to you!"

The group was stunned. Many of them looked at Flea with fear in their eyes.

"Are we communicating, ladies?" he shouted the question.

"Sir, yes, sir!" they yelled in unison with a distinctly female shout.

"Let this be your first lesson!" shouted Flea sternly. "If you are here to fight fair and honorably, then you are in the wrong place! I fight to win! That is all I am concerned with! I will do so by any means necessary! I will lie! I will cheat! I will steal! I know this is not honorable, but I adamantly refuse to watch our race go down at the hands of the Goraan! I will even die if need be! Are we communicating?"

"Sir, yes, sir!" they shouted.

Flea had to get used to his unit's feminine voice.

"Many of you think this is going to be easy," Flea said a little softer. "You might believe that this is going to be a few hours in a flight simulator and then, bang! You're a pilot. THIS IS NOT THE CASE! By the end of this week, thirty five of you, including the idiot just escorted off the ship, will be gone. By the end of the following week, we will cut the other ten. It's nothing personal, but we only have a very short time to staff the few fighters that we have."

Flea looked out at the silent group.

"Morgan told you when to be here tomorrow. Given the initial events of our meeting, I will understand if any of you wish to back out. Your orders for the first day, is to go home and consider how badly you want to be here, if at all," Flea said loudly. "If you stay, I will at some point in time, make you hurt! I will at some point piss you off! I will at some point make you cry and even bleed! I will expect blind obedience and nothing less! We do not have the luxury of time! Ours is a sense of urgency! We have to go at this fast, hard and with all our effort. Go home and think about this. For those who do not return tomorrow, there is no shame in dropping out. For those who return, all I can promise is a life of sacrifice and pain which will most likely end with your fiery death at the hands of our enemy. We'll send your loved ones your medals."

The group stared at him like he was some sort of monster from a nightmare.

"Now, go home," he instructed sternly. "If you have family and friends discuss your choice to be here with them. If you don't have any, then make some friends here in the group and go talk this out with them. Take some time by yourselves and think about this choice. There will be no glory. Glory is for heroes. We are here to work. Most likely that work will only bring pain and then death. Consider these things through the rest of the day. If you are not here tomorrow, I will understand."

He looked out at the group one more time. They shifted around where they stood when Flea cast his unnatural, purple gaze on them.

"Dismissed, ladies," Flea said.

Flea turned to walk away and was joined by Morgan and Armina. The kitten quickly climbed up his back to her place on his shoulders. They left the group in stunned silence and walked out of the hanger bay.

The next morning, they had all returned for more.

11

Everyone may have returned after their first encounter with Flea, but it was still a tryout. Some members had already been cut from the group. The four males left included Flea, Morgan, Tommy, and one other. Twenty eight female humans were also left. The last eight were some of the female Kashin pilots. Flea and Morgan made the first cuts the night before on Sunday. Forty pilots were left. They made their cuts based on individual skill, teamwork ability and attitude. The fighters had a combat simulation mode that they were using to test their pilots' skills.

Flea and Morgan were also teaching them in a classroom setting. They were being given tests about their fighter ships, their enemy and their allies. Morgan and Flea were taking part in all the tests and simulations along with the pilots and were allowing their own personal scores to be posted on a central board along with everyone else's. Not to Flea's surprise, after he taught Morgan the controls to the fighter his friend ended up in the number one spot. It irked Flea a bit that the group's leader, which was him, was only ranked second. This was probably because Morgan flew more strategically, and Flea was more erratic. He had the tendency to be over-trusting of his luck. Kaida was surprising both Flea and Morgan by making it to the number seven spot and would easily make it in to the group. Oddly, whenever she flew with Flea as her wingman, she outscored everyone else, including Morgan. She couldn't do this with anyone else. Tommy, however, was bouncing between positions forty and thirty nine. He had the habit of flying off and leaving his wingman and unit.

"I've talked to the kid time and again," said Flea to Morgan as they reviewed everything over breakfast before they got started for the day. "But he just doesn't listen."

"He's fifteen," stated Morgan in a very matter of fact way. "What did you expect? These kids aren't mature enough for this."

"Mature or not," said Flea defensively. "I'll take whatever the Hell I can get and pound it into what I need!"

Flea face turned slightly red. He and Morgan had the argument over the age limit more than once already. In Tommy's case, he wasn't even sixteen years old yet.

"Boys!" admonished Alex. "Play nice or I'll send you to opposite ends of the ship today."

"Yeah, Flea!" Armina chimed in. "Play nice!"

She stuck out her little pink tongue.

"Your face will freeze like that one day," Flea replied to Armina.

She stuck her tongue out again in response.

"I miss Kaida and Tommy, Daddy," Keri said to her Father. "Are they going to come back?"

"They can join us at breakfast again at the end of the week, kids," Morgan replied.

"We can't show any favoritism during this," Flea added.

"How did the cuts go last night?" Alex asked Flea and Morgan.

"Well," said Morgan to his wife. "I took care of half and Flea took the other half. It was hard telling all those people they were out of the group."

"Some of them didn't take it too well," said Flea as he pulled out his smartphone and started typing while they ate. "A few of them cried."

"Didn't you explain to them that there would be more fighters some day?" asked Alex.

"Yeah," said Morgan. "But there was probably still some feeling of rejection."

"So what do you have left?" she asked.

"We got a good mix," Morgan said with a small grin. "It's been interesting."

"Really?" asked Alex curiously.

"Yeah," Flea replied solemnly. "Overall everyone has put aside personal differences to try and move forward."

"Good," Alex approved.

"When two people have an issue with each other and can't let it go, Flea came up with an interesting solution," Morgan chuckled.

"Really?" Alexandria was curious. "What did you tell them?"

"I told them if they couldn't shitcan their problem in less than ten minutes I would stick them in a room together, throw in a knife and lock the door until it got quiet," Flea smirked. "I only had to do it once."

"No one died, right?" Alex was very concerned. "I won't have murder on my ship, and if it happens, you can bet I'm going to blame you, Flea!"

"No one killed anyone yet," explained Flea seriously. "But those two I locked in there ended up getting treated for a couple of scratches and broken bones by Armalan. He wasn't too happy with me. At least there was no stab wound."

Alex made a few choking noises.

"They're doing better though," Flea added cheerfully. "They've even gotten past throwing each other dirty looks across the classroom during training. I'd call that a step forward."

"Ah," Alex was obviously not certain this was a good idea. "Just try not to get anyone killed."

"I won't," Flea promised.

"They'll probably be alright," added Morgan as he changed the subject. "How's your end going, Alex?"

"Not bad," she said. "We finished the structural overhaul and have installed about as many nasty weapons as we can. We also finished our engine rebuild, our space fold gate generator, and our defensive systems, including the energy shields."

"Space fold gate generator?" asked Flea.

"Yeah," she explained. "That's the gate we open to travel long distances. We switch to main engines after we get there."

"Excuse me?" asked Morgan.

"Haven't you two been studying anything?" asked Alex. "Space and time exist together. They act sort of like a bed sheet. We fold it to travel long distances. It brings two points far away on the sheet closer together. It's not too accurate because we can't fold it too much without ripping it, and sometimes you have to make multiple jumps. Usually you can reach your final destination within two to four weeks of the jumpgate's exit."

"I guess that's better than traveling across the universe the conventional way," said Morgan.

"What happened to 'light speed' or 'warp theory' and all that 'Star Trek' stuff?" asked Flea.

"Well," explained Alexandria. "I guess all that 'Star Wars' and 'Star Trek' stuff got it wrong."

"Guess so," responded Flea with a chuckle. "So what are they doing to the carrier this week?"

"We should have the hull upgraded and the new design finished by week's end. It'll look much better," she smirked knowingly. "You guys will love it."

"What have you got in mind, sweetie?" asked Morgan prying into her business.

"You'll see," she said mysteriously. "You guys should be done by the end of the week too, right?"

"Yep," Armina inert ejected excitedly. "We're right on schedule! They made me the mascot! I'm keeping track!"

"Excuse me?" asked Flea arching an eyebrow. "When did this happen?"

"Ahh," she said evasively. "A couple days ago? It's okay right? All the pilots said it was okay."

"Yes," chuckled Flea. "It's fine."

"So this means you'll let me fly with you?" she asked.

"Maybe on non-combat missions," said Flea.

"Cool!" she said squirming in her seat.

"What about me, Daddy?" asked Keri.

"I guess it would be okay if you went on non-combat missions if your Mom agrees," said Morgan.

"We'll see," said Alex to her daughter before Keri could ask the impending question.

"Well," said Flea as he finished his breakfast and put away his computer. "We ready?"

"Sure," said Morgan standing with his plate. "What were you typing?"

"I was just texting Tommy," replied Flea. "I know I can't stand there and tell him any pointers while we are working because it might show favoritism. I can still text him before anything happens, though."

"He'll appreciate that," said Morgan.

"I hope so," responded Flea.

Flea and Morgan got up and took care of their plates. Armina once again crawled up on Flea's shoulders before they left the house. They walked through the Human Sphere which had been made much more colorful by its inhabitants over the last few weeks in the occupied area. Many of the occupants that were up this early waived to them and shouted greetings as they walked by.

"Captain Flea," shouted a middle aged man with a Jewish accent. "Did you speak with Captain Alexandria about me helping out?"

Morgan flashed an inquiring look in Flea's direction.

"Is this the Rabbi you were talking about?" Morgan asked to Flea.

"Yeah," responded Flea. "Rabbi Amos Cohn, this is Captain Morgan Mendenhall. He's my second in command and the husband to the ship's Captain."

"Pleased to meet you Captain Morgan! Hey, hey," said the Rabbi with a chuckle. "It's Captain Morgan, like the rum, what?"

"Yes," said Morgan dryly. "Like Captain Morgan's Rum."

"Oi," said the Rabbi. "You're upset, I'm sorry Captain."

"No," said Morgan glaring at Flea. "It's fine. I asked my vagrant friend here to just make me a commander or something, but he insisted."

"Captain Alexandria says it would be fine for you and the others to establish a religious team on board," said Flea. "The crew should be given access to the clergy and spiritual leaders of their individual religions. Ships should have Chaplains."

"Good, good," said Rabbi Cohn enthusiastically. "Of course we can't condone violence, but we cannot turn our backs on those who go to fight. The crew should know that God protects all peoples."

"I agree," said Flea seriously. "Send Captain Alexandria a text or something so she knows to expect you and your friends."

"I will," he said.

"You find anyone else, yet?" Flea asked the Rabbi.

"So far, I found a Priest, a Muslim cleric, a Buddhist monk, and even a Hindu Guru!" he replied with a smile. "Now, if I can get them all to walk into a bar with me we could be the cast of a bad joke, what?"

The Rabbi laughed jovially.

"I guess so, Rabbi" Flea agreed with a chuckle. "See you on board."

"Thank you and God Bless, Captain," the Rabbi said waiving as Flea walked away with Morgan and Armina.

"That was nice of him," said Morgan as they approached the entrance to the Human Sphere.

"Yeah," said Flea. "It's nice that all the humans are putting aside their differences to help out."

"Yeah," agreed Morgan. "The rest of the Runners, too."

***

Alexandria smiled and watched as her husband walked away with his vagrant, disreputable friend.

"Those two will never change," she sighed.

"Who, Mommy?" asked Keri.

"Your Dad and his friend Flea," she said with a smile.

"I think they're fun," said Keri. "I hope they don't change."

"Me too, sweetie," said Alex sweetly. "So are you ready for today?"

"I guess so. Can I play in the garden by your office again?" she asked.

"Sure Keri," said Alex. "Try not to climb all the way up to the top of the tree, though. It makes me worried. How in the Hell do you get up there, anyway?"

Keri looked down at the metallic red Kashin paws she was wearing. She only took the Kashin gear off now when she was in the shower. She even slept in them.

"I just climb real hard," she insisted looking up from her paws. "That's all."

"Well, try not to kill yourself," said Alex. "All it takes is one little accident with something sharp and you could lose an eye or something worse."

Keri was starting to wonder how much her Mom knew about her Kashin gear.

"Umm…sure thing, Mom," said Keri with a straight face.

"Well, let's get ready and get going," Alex told her daughter. "We have a full schedule today."

Alex and Keri carried their plates back to the matter combiner to be recycled upon finishing breakfast. After she got to her room, Alex went into the adjoining bathroom and took a quick shower. She dried off, and went back to her room and walked to the closet.

"Uniform," she said to the computer's input sensor.

She opened the closet door and watched the garment rack spin. It came to a stop and she pulled out her official Captain's uniform. She and Flea had worked together on a system of rank for the human's branch of the Runners military that was based in structure and title on the rankings of the United States Navy. All the uniforms were black with various colored trim dependant on rank. Enlisted uniforms were black with grey trim and insignias. Officers below the rank of captain wore black with silver trim uniforms. Captains and higher ranking officers wore black with gold trim. The uniforms became more ornate as they went up in rank. Alexandria's rank insignia was a golden eagle to signify a Captain. Flea and Morgan never wore their uniforms.

"They need to let others know what their rank is," thought Alex as she put on her uniform.

Her uniform consisted of a black, long sleeved, light wool jacket that buttoned up from her waist to her chin. It didn't have any lapels and a short choker style collar. The buttons were all gold to match her rank insignias pinned to the black beret she wore on her head. The sleeves had a modest amount of scrollwork on them that was also done in gold. On her shoulders, were four solid gold bars which were also a signification of her rank. She put on her beret and pulled it down so it sat cocked to one side on top her head with the bottom of the hat close to her eyebrows. The black pants she wore matched the coat, and had a gold stripe on the outside running from her waist to where her pants were tucked in her boots. Her black, leather, calf high boots were fastened by a series of leather straps and gold buckles. She pulled on her black leather gloves and strapped on the ornate side arm that was a gift from the human delegates to finish her look. She quickly applied a modest amount of makeup and then went to fetch her daughter.

"You ready, Keri?" she asked poking her head in her daughter's room.

"Sure Mom," she replied.

"Let's go, then," responded Alex. "Mommy needs to save the universe."

They walked through the Human Sphere and made a game out of counting the newly painted houses that weren't painted the day before. A few humans were awake as Alex and Keri walked by. Many shouted a greeting with some words of encouragement as they passed. It made Alex feel good and gave her some reassurance that this many people cared about what she was doing.

"Captain Alexandria," shouted a man with a Jewish accent. "I just saw your husband! Captain, over here!"

Alex stopped and saw a middle aged man come running up to her.

"Slow down," he said laughing with a smile. "All the walking with the purpose from you! I'm not a young man anymore!"

"Can I help you?" Alex asked.

"I'm Rabbi Cohn," the Rabbi said. "Captain Gabriel was supposed to talk to you about me."

"Oh yes," replied Alex. "We spoke about you and thought it might do us well to have some Chaplains on board. Do you happen to know anyone of any other faiths to bring with you?"

"As a matter of fact, I do!" he said enthusiastically. "I was just telling Captain Gabriel and your husband about just such a thing. I have an entire group of them that want to come with me, what?"

"Good," replied Alex. "I'll give all of you official ranks, uniforms and file the necessary reports. Just let me know who is coming with you and I'll make it official."

"When can we get together and speak of this at more detail?" he asked. "Perhaps if you're not busy later?"

Alex pulled out her phone and looked her day's schedule, "I could squeeze you in during my lunch today if you care to join me."

"Ah," he said with a grin. "What type of man would I be to turn down the company of such a pleasant woman? I may be a Rabbi, but that doesn't mean there isn't any water in my spout!"

"Rabbi!" Alex chuckled. "Shame on you!"

"I kid, I kid!" said Rabbi Cohn with a laugh. "My wife would kill me! Seriously, though, I am very honored to have this opportunity. I look forward to helping our young people any way I can."

"We appreciate it, Rabbi," Alex said seriously as she turned and walked away. "I'll send you a text and tell you when to come by."

"Thank you, Captain Alexandria," shouted the Rabbi as she and Keri walked away. "God bless you and your lovely daughter! Oh! And tell Captains Morgan and Gabriel I said hello!"

Alex and Keri left the Rabbi and approached the waiting area in front of the transport tube that lead to and from the Human Sphere. The platform made its approach on the roof of the tube. As it reached the sphere, it slowly slid around the inside of the tube to come to rest at the waiting station. There was someone standing on the platform as it slid forward and approached the waiting area.

"That's odd," said Alex.

"What's odd, Mom?" asked Keri.

"That someone would be returning to the sphere at this hour," said Alex softly. "Most of the other humans are still sleeping, but this person is not only awake, but she looks well rested. Where could she be coming home from at this hour?"

"What should we do?" asked Keri sounding a bit frightened.

"You can use those claws in the Kashin gloves anytime you want, right?" asked Alexandria directly to her daughter.

Keri's eyes got very wide.

"You mean you know?" she sounded mortified.

"I'm your mother," explained Alex quickly. "Of course I know. I know everything you do at every moment of your little life. It's part of my 'mom powers.' Answer the question, Keri. "

"Yes," replied Keri viscously. "I can. Want me to get her?"

"Hell no!" Alex said fiercely. "Just stand back, and if she manages to ki...,"

"Kill you?" Keri sounded frightened.

"No," Alex stopped and corrected herself softly. "If she gets by Mommy, I want you to run. Go as fast as you can! If she catches you, though, just remember about those claws."

The woman on the platform was a short, slender, dark haired woman. It appeared as if her nose had been broken at some point in time. Despite this, her clear complexion and long dark hair made the shorter woman appear quite attractive. Her gaze was penetrating and deep as she looked at Alex. She was most likely in her thirties from her appearance. She wasn't moving to disembark the wide platform as it approached. Instead, the stranger stood there as if she were waiting.

"Keri," Alex said seeing that the other woman was not going to move. "Do you remember where Rabbi Cohn went?"

"Yes," replied Keri sounding a little afraid. "Why?"

"Go find him," she said leaning over to whisper to her daughter. "Tell him I sent you to give him a tour of the ship this morning until lunch. Show him the quarters I have allocated for him and the others. Show him the room for religious services. Don't tell him about anything that happened here unless I don't come and find you before lunch."

"Mommy you're scaring me!" Keri said earnestly to her mother.

"Don't' be scared," Alex said grimly as she loosened her gun in its holster. "Mommy's packing heat."

"Okay," Keri sounded worried. "Be safe, Mommy."

"I will sweetie," said Alex seriously. "I will."

Keri trotted away. She turned around once to look at her Mom as if she was afraid she wouldn't see her again. Alex walked on to the platform, resting her hand on the handle of her gun.

"Human battle carrier," she stated her destination for the platform's computer.

The platform took off, carrying Alex and the other woman to the human carrier.

"Captain Alexandria Mendenhall?" the other woman asked with a slightly Italian accent.

"Yes," responded Alex apprehensively. "That's me. Can I help you?"

"I have some information for you," the Italian woman replied. "Important information."

"What's this about?" asked Alex. "Why here?"

"There are no cameras in the way tubes," she explained. "No one will see us here."

"That answers one questions," Alex nodded. "Now what's this about?"

"You were given that gun by the delegates," she stated. "I have some information, but they are too busy to see me. They will make time for you and your husband."

"What do you know about my husband?" asked Alex protectively.

"I know that Morgan loves you and is second in command of the Archangels," she stated. "I know he has been friends with Captain Sherman for a very long time. I am not sure why he's called 'Flea,' though."

"How do you know...," started Alex.

"And I know you are all in very great danger," said the woman interrupting Alex. "We all are in very great danger, and you are more accessible than the other two. That's why I chose you."

"Why should I trust you? You just walk up to me and say 'you are in danger,' and I am just supposed to trust you? If you haven't noticed," said Alex dryly. "I command a combat vessel. It's my job to be in danger."

"This is different," the Italian woman sounded desperate. "You must believe me!"

"Suppose I do believe you," said Alex, "and then contact our human delegates. Where do we go from there?"

"Take them, your husband and Flea to these coordinates by shuttle craft. I will be on another shuttle waiting for you, bring no others with you. Not anyone. Not even Mihanna," she responded. "Please, this is imperative!"

"Why can't we meet in the sphere?" asked Alex.

"For the same reason I could only approach you in the tubes. The spheres are monitored by security cameras," she explained. "I didn't want to risk anyone seeing us together or find out what we discuss. There is not enough time on the platform ride for more!"

"I see," Alexandria replied.

"Please," the Italian said with a concerned expression. "You must come!"

"I'll talk to the others and see what they think," responded Alex noticing the platform was approaching the battle carrier. "If we do decide to come, we will meet you at the coordinates after dinner."

"Thank you," the Italian woman sounded genuinely relived. "Thank you so much."

Alex said nothing to her as she turned and disembarked from the tube's transport platform. It occurred to her that she didn't get the other woman's name.

"What's your name?" she shouted down the tube as the platform started to leave with the other woman still on it.

"Bella," she shouted back. "My name is Bella."

***

"So how is training?" asked Delegate Ryoko.

"It's progressing," responded Flea. "I have a good group. It's going to be a shame to cut some of them."

"You will be strong, Flea," said Kaida who was bouncing along next to him. "I have faith."

"Thank you, Kaida," said Flea. "I missed you since this has begun. I only get to see you in training. How's Tommy doing? I wish he could have been here, too."

"Tommy is okay," Kaida responded, "in simulator working more. He got text from you, Flea. He tries very hard."

"I know," said Flea. "His scores and performance improved today. He gained a little ground. He's thirty sixth, now."

Armina crawled up Flea's back to sit on his shoulders. She extended her hand for Kaida to hold. Flea attempted to tell her she had to stay home, but she pouted until he gave in. They ended up making a compromise that she could come as far as the hanger bay if Kaida came, too.

"I missed you, Sister," smiled Armina. "I miss playing with you."

"We play again soon, Armina," replied Kaida. "I miss you, too."

"So where is Captain Morgan?" Delegate Masters chuckled. "I can't say his name and rank at the same time without laughing…"

Despite how quickly they had been forced to become responsible for the entire human race, the delegates were still very young.

"What she means is," interrupted Daniela with a lovely Australian accent. "Are Captain Morgan and Captain Alexandria going to be joining us?"

"They'll be along shortly," Flea responded cordially.

"So did you get the gift we sent you?" asked Daniela thoughtfully.

"Yes," said Flea smiling. "It was very nice, thank you."

Flea was watching his manners. He thought the delegates were cute. He'd never tell them that, though. His rank would not allow it. He had to set an example for the others.

"We think gift was fitting," said Ryoko. "Good gift for fighters."

"Have you had the chance to fire them?" asked Christina smiling. "Do they work okay? We selected each of your guns personally. I'm not sure, but I think they might be illegal or something. We thought about getting you something different, but then the Homarell delegates started telling us that most the weapons you are using on the carrier and fighters are not allowed, too. They don't seem to think very highly of you, you know?"

"I know," said Flea with a sigh. "They don't understand how disadvantaged we are in this."

"We may have spent most of our lives as pop-stars and entertainers, but that doesn't mean we don't understand what's going on," Christina said defensively.

"We need every advantage we can get," added Daniela.

"Yes," agreed Ryoko whose English was still developing. "Every advantage."

"So did you?" asked Daniela smiling excitedly.

"Did I what?" asked Flea.

"Shoot them, silly!" Daniela smiled. "The guns! Did you shoot them, yet?"

Armina looked down at Flea and wrapped an arm protectively around his head. Flea looked up and smiled, squeezing her leg as it hung in front of his shoulder in reassurance.

"Yes," said Flea still smiling. "They work just fine, thank you."

"Did you like firing them," she continued.

"Yes," Flea lied. "It was quite an experience. I wouldn't suggest you get a pair for yourselves, though."

"Is something wrong with guns?" Ryoko asked.

She sounded disappointed.

"Oh no," Flea said quickly. "They work just fine! I just don't think it would be proper for the human delegates to be armed to the teeth. If you need a weapon to carry with you, I would suggest something smaller and less intimidating than these."

He patted the handle of one of his Hate Blasters affectionately with his hand. He was starting to develop a love/hate relationship with them. He had a pair of normal guns strapped underneath his arms as well. Flea could not help but wonder when a pair of high powered energy pistols became something normal to him.

"Hi guys," said Morgan walking up.

Alexandria was with him. Keri was walked between her Mom and Rabbi Cohn.

"Hello Captain Morgan," Christina stifled a chuckle as she said this. "I can't say your name and rank without laughing...Captain Morgan...sorry."

Her mirth, however, was still noticeable. Alex grinned at her husband as Morgan gave Flea a withering look. Daniela chuckled a bit while Ryoko and Kaida hid their small grins behind their hands.

"I'll get you for that," said Morgan to Flea. "You won't know when or where, but it's coming. Oh yes. It's coming."

"I had to do something to you for the funky Mountain Dew bottle the matter combiner spit out at me a while back," said Flea defending himself.

"Captain Gabriel," said the Rabbi. "I hope you're doing better than me. All this out here in the space with all the lack of real sunshine is getting a bit disturbing is all I'm saying, what?"

Flea chuckled at the protesting Rabbi, "I'm fine Rabbi, and it's good to see you again."

"Hi Flea," said Keri.

"Hi sweetie," Flea replied with a nod.

"Flea?" asked the Rabbi.

"It's what my friends call me," explained Flea.

"Can we call you Flea?" asked Daniela.

"Sure," he smiled with a wink.

Ryoko hid a small grin behind her hand, "Thank you, Flea."

Kaida elbowed Flea in the ribs and gave him a disapproving look, "You be good, Flea."

"Of course," he apologized with a slight bow of his head. "I am, sorry Kaida."

"I invited young Keri with me to have some dinner and maybe play a few games," said the Rabbi. "My wife is baking cookies."

"That sounds nice," replied Flea.

"Thank you," the Rabbi said. "Keri said she had a little kitten friend that might like to come with us? Is that the young kitten in question up there on your shoulders? Does anyone else around here have a tail? Are you young Armina?"

"Yes," she giggled excitedly. "Can I go too, Flea?"

"Sure, kitten," responded Flea. "Go ahead. Kaida, you go, too, okay?"

"Okay Flea," she smiled. "I help, too."

"Well," said the Rabbi. "We'll be seeing you later! God bless you!"

Rabbi Cohn walked off with Kaida, Armina and Keri in tow. The two young ones were giggling girlishly as they followed along.

They walked out into the hanger bay were they had all met on board the human battle carrier. There was a shuttle craft in the middle of the hanger. They boarded the shuttle with Flea in the pilot's seat and Morgan in the co-pilot's seat. The two were learning to pilot other craft as well as their fighters. They had learned quite a bit.

"You ready?" asked Morgan with a grin.

"Let's go," said Flea as the two strapped in themselves in their seats.

The shuttle craft lifted off the deck and steadily whisked out the hanger bay doors. Flea and Morgan looked at each other and smiled.

"This is pretty cool, huh?" said Morgan.

"Yeah," agreed Flea. "You wanna take over?"

Flea's smile quickly turned mischievous.

"Sure," Morgan replied with a chuckle as he took over piloting.

"I thought I should mention to you guys," Flea said with a grin. "This is the first time Morgan and I have actually flown something outside of the simulators."

"Huh?" Christina replied.

"What?" Alex added sounding concerned.

"Buckle up," Morgan laughed wickedly.

Morgan hit the thrusters hard and pushed down on the controls causing the small shuttle to lurch down hard. The girls in the back squealed and giggled. Alex leaned forward and smacked Morgan in the back of the head.

"Cut that out! Be serious," she admonished.

Flea and Morgan looked at each other and laughed.

"Sorry," Morgan said with a laugh. "I haven't had a whole lot of time for fun lately."

"Well," said Alexandria dryly. "I'm glad to see your sense of humor has remained untwisted. Now shut up and fly."

"Where to?" asked Morgan.

"These are the coordinates," said Alex handing her husband the envelope that Bella gave her.

Morgan opened the envelope and read it. He entered the destination into the ship's flight plan and tuned on the autopilot. They all chatted amiably as the shuttle slid silently through space. They shared their nervousness with each other. The delegates told Flea, Morgan and Alex what it was like to be a famous pop-star. Flea decided that despite the money, it sounded like too much work. He and his two friends told the delegates what it was like to be a normal person. Strangely, the girls seemed slightly jealous. They were all, however, becoming good friends. Many people who wouldn't have been friends on Earth were now finding themselves in similar situations.

"I would've probably never even met these people if we were still on Earth," Flea thought smiling.

They approached the meeting location silently. Flea and Morgan recognized a Kashin shuttle waiting for them out of their windshield. Morgan brought the shuttle to a stop.

"What do you suppose this is?" asked Flea with a low voice as he leaned over to Morgan.

"Not sure," muttered Morgan. "Let's find out."

"Kashin pilot," said Flea over the communicator. "This is Captain Sherman of the Archangels fighter group. Please identify yourself."

"I am Under Pilot Shoman of the Kashin 2nd Battleship," a voice answered. "It is an honor to meet you, Captain. Admiral Mihanna speaks very highly of you."

"Thank you, pilot," responded Flea. "Why are you out here?"

There was a long pause.

"I have a human on board that says she was told to meet you out here for a tour of the human battle carrier," he responded. "She said you wanted to start her tour with the outside of the ship."

"What do I tell him?" Flea asked Alex. "She contacted you, remember?"

"I know she did!" Alexandria whispered. "I don't know what to say! Just go with it."

"Are you Goddamned kidding me?" Flea scowled softly.

"Shut up and speak, damn it!" Alex hissed at him. "Just say something!"

"Yes," said Flea to the pilot in his normal speaking voice. "That's correct. We'll wait here and you dock with us."

"Yes sir, Captain Gabriel," responded the Pilot.

"Morgan," said Flea authoritatively. "Let's cover the air lock."

"Sure thing," said Morgan.

Flea and Morgan moved to stand between the small group and the air lock. Three weapons pointed at the rear airlock door. Flea was using the normal gun under his left arm instead of his

Hate Blasters. Morgan stood next to him with his weapon drawn. Alex was behind them with her weapon pointed between the other two. The three delegates moved to the front of the shuttle.

"We should definitely get guns, too," Daniela said softly to the other delegates.

"Flea?" asked Christina in a hushed voice. "Would you guys get us some small guns?"

"Later," Flea whispered quickly. "As soon as we get back, okay? I promise. In the mean time ladies, please try not to get shot."

"Thanks," she replied dryly. "I'll keep that in mind."

"Flea," Morgan said softly. "Why are we whispering?"

"I'm not sure," Flea snapped. "Just shut up!"

They heard a thud as the shuttles' airlocks linked together before Morgan could protest.

"Shh," said Flea. "Everyone quiet down."

The air lock opened to reveal the slender long haired human that Alex had met on the transport platform earlier that day. Two other people were with her as well. The two females with Bella appeared to be in their late twenties. One had blue eyes and red hair; the other had green eyes and light brown hair. Both were slim and in good physical shape. They were both around five feet nine inches tall with clear complexions and nice tans. All three were armed. Upon seeing that guns were being pointed at them, the two new girls drew their weapons at Flea and his group.

"Drop 'em!" shouted Flea.

"You drop 'em, first," one of the new girls said with a southern accent. "I ain't dying for you, buddy!"

"This is my ship!" yelled Flea. "That means you your guns!"

"No way!" she replied.

"If you don't," Flea said ominously, "that little blonde up front is going to hit the air lock release and eject your asses into space, girly! It's your choice, but I'm not dropping my weapon. Good luck breathing out there!"

Christina sat down at the shuttle's control console and pretended to know what she was doing to support Flea's lie.

"Ladies!" shouted an Italian accent. "Please! This isn't why we came here, remember?"

The two girls lowered their weapons slowly. They didn't stop staring at Flea, though.

"Bella," said Alex. "What's this about?"

"They have been helping me," she explained. "I brought them along to help out."

"Put your guns away, guys," Alex said sternly. "They don't mean any harm."

Flea and Morgan lowered their guns slowly. Morgan and Alex put theirs in their holsters. Flea went back to the pilot's chair and sat down. He put his gun on the console next to him.

"So who are you?" asked Flea.

"This is Amy Michaels she is a former FBI agent," she indicated the green eyed female.

"Nice to meet you," Amy said.

"This is Dr. Rebecca Johansen," she said indicating red haired female. "She was a successful transplant surgeon in California. I am Bella Valerio and I used to run the Vatican's intelligence network on Earth. You can save your own introductions. I already know all of you."

"It's a pleasure," the Doctor nodded.

"The Vatican had an intelligence agency?" asked Daniela incredulously.

"Yes," responded Bella simply. "And I ran it for ten years before the Earth was destroyed."

"How old were you, exactly, to be running the Vatican's spy network?" asked Flea.

"I started when I was very young," she replied. "I was only twenty when I began. I posed as a prostitute in the Vatican City."

"You were a hooker?" asked Morgan amazed. "And worked for the Holy Catholic Church?"

"It was the perfect cover," she explained with a shrug. "No one would ever suspect a prostitute of running the church's spies. Sometimes it meant I had to…do things…to maintain my cover, but it was a good cause."

"Uhhh…Yeah," said a wide eyed Flea. "I guess so."

"That still doesn't tell us why you are here," said Christina. "And why you claim to already know all of us."

"I am here to help you in your job to protect the human race, Delegate Masters," she responded seriously. "I already know all of you because I researched you first, before I started spying on our allies."

"You've been spying on our allies?" Daniela asked.

"This is not good," stated Ryoko shaking her head. "I no agree with this."

"Wait," Alex was intrigued. "Give her a minute."

"Yes," agreed Christina. "Let's see what she has to say."

"Our allies don't really support us the way they are letting on," Amy said. "I and some others that have started working for Bella have been spying on them for the last few weeks."

"Really?" asked Morgan. "What did you find out?"

"The Homarell are at the center of the main plot against us," said Bella. "They fear the Goraan will kill us if we fight. They plan to discredit us humans and make us lose our ship in battle."

"That's horrible!" said Flea reeling from the information. "Don't they get it? If we don't try to fight back the Goraan will kill us anyway? This is our only chance!"

"We understand this," Bella said. "But they do not."

"What is plan they have?" asked Ryoko.

"First," began Amy, "they plan on reallocating fuel so that the human fighters don't get enough to get in any real flight time. We'll barely get enough to get our carrier out of the dock if we don't ration it."

"Trust me," said Alex darkly. "I have a few alternatives in mind if they take away my fuel."

"How did you find all this out?" asked Flea seriously. "I thought the Homarell didn't leave their water filled sphere when their ship was docked?"

"They don't," replied Dr. Johansen. "That's where I came in. As a surgeon I was very surprised by the huge medical advancements our allies have. It's given me the chance to study some advance techniques that lets me basically turn a human into any one of our allies."

"Really?" asked Alex amazed. "How is this possible?"

"Well," responded Rebecca. "As you know, our allies don't respect us because we are considered a more simplistic biological creature. They use this as the basis for their judgment that we are inferior."

"I know," said Flea. "It pisses me off."

"The thing is, though," said Rebecca cheerfully. "They're right. We are. All of them are more advanced creatures. We are more like a basic organism. It's like we're the stripped down version of intelligent life in the universe."

"I don't get it," said Flea.

"Me either," agreed Daniela.

The other delegates nodded to indicate they didn't understand as well.

"Hold on," said Morgan thoughtfully. "I think I know what you're saying. It's kind of like the Kashin are like a hopped up, late model German luxury car and we are like a low end model, green, '89 Ford Taurus with no options."

"Sort of," the Doctor chuckled, "but, I have the ability to turn the Taurus into a Mercedes and back again. The other species can't do that."

"I always thought of myself as a high end roadster," said Flea with a smirk.

"Hush, Flea," teased Alex.

"So are you saying that you made her look like one of those fish people?" asked Christina.

"No," replied the Doctor. "I made her into a Homar. Not just look like one. The human body is very simplistic. That's why we can change things and swap out organs. The other races can't do this. When their bodies interact with foreign organs for transplants, it rejects whatever was added or changed. If they need something replaced, they have to use blank cells to grow a new one on their own. Our body doesn't. Surgically, I can turn any one of you into anything I want."

"Whoa," Flea replied.

"Whoa, indeed," Bella smirked.

"So what did you find out in the fish bowl?" asked Daniela.

"Their natural language is a little muddy for me, but it seems like Captain Roshom is on our side," explained Amy. "Delegate Cormon wants to get rid of us, though. Roshom may have made a recording of the conversation, but I can't confirm that. His father was a politician and taught his son to be very distrustful of other politicians. I need to get inside Roshom's house."

"That could be useful," said Alex. "What did Cormon say?"

"Corman has planted people loyal to him in some very useful places. He instructed his underlings to give us minimal fuel and book the combat training field solid," replied Bella.

"That bastard Cormon!" gritted Christina. "He's been sucking up to us all week!"

"He says that he will first let us find out that we can't get any fuel or training time and then he'll send us on a suicide mission so we get destroyed," Amy continued. "After that we'll lose any support we've gained in the council along with our ship and fighters. Then the Runners will start running again."

"What if we come back from the mission alive?" asked Flea. "Or even successful?"

"Then they are going to have us outlawed and ejected from the Runners," she said dejectedly. "And then we'll have to fend for ourselves."

"How will he get us outlawed?" asked Christina. "What are we doing wrong?"

"I think you have a leak in your group or something. They know about the weapons and technology we're using on our vessels," explained Bella. "He will use that to get us kicked out."

"So now what?" asked Flea.

"First," said Christina seriously, "I want to thank Bella for doing this."

"It sound very dangerous," added Ryoko. "Thank you, Bella."

"I was only trying to help," replied Bella.

"Bella," said Daniela. "Would you like to run the Human Intelligence Agency? You seem to have already established a network."

"What can I say?" asked Bella with a smile. "It's a small network for now, but old habits die hard."

"You will help us?" asked Ryoko.

"Yes," she responded. "I'll help however I can."

There was a long pause. Everyone was trying to contemplate the next move. They were all still very new at this. Bella may have run an intelligence agency before, but all she did was supply information. It was up to someone else to be the politicians and make the decisions.

"Does anyone have any ideas?" asked Daniela.

"I am thinking Daniela," responded Ryoko.

"Well," said Flea. "At the very least we should get back before people start to wonder."

"Good idea," agreed Morgan.

"You mentioned something about Roshom making a recording," said Flea. "Do you have any basis for this?"

"It's in his record that he's done it before," explained Bella.

"Well first thing," replied Flea. "See if you can get a hold of that if it exists. We'll need it later."

"No problem," said Bella. "Doctor, can you see me in this evening?"

"Sure thing, Bella," replied Rebecca.

"Good," said Flea. "Let's get that if we can."

"Everyone try and act normal in the meantime. We can't let anyone know what we're doing, so don't do anything odd," added Morgan.

"That means that if Cormon asks you back to dinner…go with him," Flea said to the delegates. "Smile, be polite and laugh at his jokes. Tell him he's cute, tickle his gills or whatever the Hell makes him happy. Just act normal. He can't know we're on to him."

"Will do," replied Christina.

The other delegates reluctantly nodded their agreement.

"In the meantime," said Daniela, "everyone try and come up with some ideas. We can't go forward until we have a plan."

"We'll meet in the hanger bay tomorrow," said Flea. "We'll tell everyone that Morgan and I are teaching the rest of you to fly at your request."

"What time?" asked Bella.

"Same time," replied Morgan.

"Okay, I'll meet the six of you here tomorrow, hopefully with more information," replied Bella.

"What will you do until then, Bella?" asked Alexandria.

"It occurs to me," she said with a smile, "that Amy and I should pay a visit to the Homarell Sphere."

"Okay," nodded Flea.

Flea turned in the pilot's chair to face forward. He took his gun off the console and put it back in its holster. Morgan sat down in the seat next to him.

"Let's head back, then," he said firing up the engines. "We'll do this again soon."

12

"Thank you for coming down here to help me," said Ba'an. "I really appreciate it."

The Gora sitting at the end of Ba'an's bed didn't say anything.

"You're the first individual I invited back here to my quarters," Ba'an said. "Please excuse the bare furnishings. They haven't given me very much to work with."

The other Gora was still silent.

"You see those marks on the wall?" asked Ba'an energetically. "I put those there. There is one for everyone that I have killed."

The other Gora remained still and unspeaking.

"That reminds me," Ba'an said thoughtfully. "I need to add a mark for you."

Ba'an turned his suction cups upward to reveal them. He then filled a large one with acid and dipped his tentacle into the acid. He reached toward the wall to add a mark, but then hesitated.

"You were special," he said to the dead Gora propped up in his bed.

He reached up as high as he could and made a mark away from the others.

"You were the only one that was nice to me," he sounded regretful. "You were the only one that would bring the study materials to me so that I might further my plans. All the rest hate me."

Ba'an's victim was the ship's new medical technician. She had reported on board recently as additional staffing. She had the same type of shell organism that Ba'an occupied. She was nice to him. He had to smother her because like him, her skin resisted the white acid. For some reason, smothering her made Ba'an feel closer to her.

"I'm sorry," he whispered to her. "It was necessary. I couldn't get access anymore to the files I needed to study and the ship's Education and Training Officer would not help me. I had to kill him, too. You were the only one that could get the materials I needed."

Ba'an added another mark with the rest on the wall for the ship's Education and Training Officer.

"It was nice of you to surprise me and bring the materials down here," Ba'an started to cry. "You never should have come."

"I'm so sorry," he said again through his tears.

Ba'an sat down on the floor and started looking for the elastic rod he used to beat himself with.

"I had to," he said silently. "Please, forgive me."

Ba'an started beating himself mercilessly. The strap-like rod bit into the flesh on his back. It dug deep into his back. Ba'an could feel the cuts start to seep blood down his spine.

"I wish I would have had the chance to speak to you after my session with Mistress Toren," he said sadly. "She said she was looking for an assistant. I could have changed my plans then. I would have never had to help Scivistan prepare for the exam to become an officer. I could have killed Scivistan and simply taken his position. Then it would only be a lateral move to be the Mistress's assistant. Then I could just kill her and become the Ship's Inquisitor," he explained. "That would give me direct access to Esham'aut."

Ba'an started crying, "Then I would not have had to ask you to get me the study materials in the first place. I am so sorry. You never should have come."

There was a knock at the door. In the lower end, they didn't have the automatic entry sensors that opened the doors on the more expensive end of the ship.

"It's Scivistan," came from the other side of the door. "I got your message. You wanted me to come down here?"

"You rotten piece of filth," Ba'an thought angrily. *"This is your fault!"*

"Come in," rasped Ba'an.

"You needed…" Scivistan stopped in mid sentence and looked at the body sitting on Ba'an's bed. "I see."

Ba'an glared at Scivistan. He rose to his feet from the floor.

"Get something to put her in and take her down to the reharvesters," Ba'an said softly. "Dispose of the body."

"I didn't kill it," Scivistan said without thinking.

Ba'an lashed out and gripped Scivistan by the neck with one of his tentacles. He jerked Scivistan hard and threw him on top of the dead body that was on his bed. Ba'an leapt on top of him. He pressed Scivistan's face to the dead face of the medical technician.

"If you don't want to end up like this!" he growled. "Then you should take her and go! Now, do as I say!"

"I n-n-need to get a c-c-cart," Scivistan stammered fearfully.

"Fine!" Ba'an growled. "Get what you need!"

He let Scivistan go. Scivistan jumped up and scampered out of the room with his truncated tail flailing behind him. The medical center did allocate resources to grow Scivistan a new one after his last accident.

"Soon, you piece of slime," Ba'an whispered to Scivistan's back. "Your time will come soon."

***

"Well done pilots," complimented Flea. "Well done, indeed. Tommy, good job staying in the group."

"Thank you sir," he said. "And might I say that you have really calmed down now that we're in the second week, sir."

The rest of the pilots getting out of the fighters chuckled along the ones waiting their turn to be monitored for their official points battles today. Morgan went with the first nineteen and Flea went with the second.

"Ha…Ha," said Flea sarcastically. "I have an idea, Tommy, why don't you start running around the hanger bay? Maybe if you run fast enough, you can catch up to your own quick mouth."

"Oh man," complained Tommy. "How many laps do I run, sir?"

"Until I start feeling tired," said Flea pointing to himself with his thumb. "I'll try and remember to let you know when that is."

All the pilots, including Tommy laughed. Tommy, however, did start to make his way to the outside of the hanger bay to start running. The pilots had learned to blindly obey.

"Tommy!" Flea shouted as the boy ran off. "Just kidding. Get back in line."

"Yes, sir," responded Tommy taking his place.

"Well, done first group," said Flea with a straight face. "I know it's difficult to have to overcome the disadvantage of flying with Morgan, but you all did very well."

Morgan gave Flea a withering look as the pilots laughed again. Flea walked over to his fighter as Morgan took over at the monitoring station.

"Good luck, group two," Morgan said with all sincerity. "I've known Flea for quite a few years, and can relate to the position you're in. Just remember, you've only had to make up for him for a short time. I, however, have had to do it for most of my life."

Flea already knew that Kaida would be the top scorer in group two. Today they set semi-permanent wing men until they make the second cut and Kaida put Flea as her first choice. Tommy put Morgan as his. Flea and Morgan refrained from choosing anyone so that they did not appear to be playing favorites. Since no one else picked either Flea or Morgan, Kaida and Tommy got their wish. When flying with Flea, Kaida had reached the point where she outscored Morgan on a consistent basis. Flying with her had caused Flea's scores to improve as well. If Kaida tried hard, it was still possible for her to overtake Morgan and have the number one spot by the end of the week. It would be a hard climb from seventh place, though.

"Flea, are you paying attention?" a message appeared in the middle of Flea's windshield in eight inch tall, white, block letters.

Since Morgan was at the monitoring station, it could only have been typed from him. The windshields in the fighters served both as a windshield and as a computer screen. In the glass, two sets of cross hairs could be seen floating around. A blue stationary set targeted for the main guns and a yellow moving set that tracked enemies for the missiles. A three dimensional representation of the fighter was on the lower left of the windshield. It gave the pilot an idea of the fighter's physical orientation, speed, shield strength and hull integrity. In the lower right, was a sphere that acted like a three dimensional radar. In the top left was a list of available weapons in the pilot's inventory and amount of ammunition left. In the top right, were three much smaller fighters with names underneath them that represented the pilot's squad-mates. On the dashboard were probably three hundred or so additional gauges that told the pilot the fighter's condition. Many pilots complained about everything they had to monitor while they flew.

"Shit!" Flea yelled as he was startled by the letters.

He broke down in a hard left banking maneuver as an instinctive response. Kaida broke instantly with him in the same direction. Her confidence and ability increased exponentially when she flew with Flea. She could respond to his movements with psychic like abilities. She liked to fly with her fighter's hull within inches of Flea's. Oddly, it didn't make Flea nervous when she did this. He was learning to anticipate her as well. He was becoming a better pilot as he continued to fly with her.

"Flea!" she yelled at Flea through the communicators. "Flea! What wrong?"

"Morgan sent me a message, Kaida," he replied. "It startled me. I wasn't prepared."

"Flea!" her tone became admonishing. "Stay focus! No stop concentrating! Stay focus, Flea!"

"Thank you sweetie," Flea responded to Kaida, "What would I do without, you?"

"Flea," she sounded more insistent, "No time to play, now."

"I'm sorry, Kaida," said Flea, "I just like to tease you. I'll stay focused and concentrate."

"Thank you, Flea," Kaida replied dryly. "Need more points! Need to win!"

"There's my girl!" shouted Flea chuckling, "Let's go get 'em!"

The two banked to return to the main fighting. The twenty pilots in the second group, all still alive, were facing about five times as many Goraan. The computer could simulate Goraan fighters and tactics with almost one hundred percent accuracy. Kaida had already shot down six.

"I reviewed your performance on the Kashin battleship from so many weeks ago," Morgan's message appeared in the windshield.

Flea switched to closed circuit on his headset so the only person that could hear him was Morgan.

"What did you think?" asked Flea.

"I think you're rusty," replied Morgan sternly. "Keep practicing."

"Thanks," Flea chuckled.

"Kaida flies awfully close to you," Morgan responded.

"So?" shrugged Flea. "We haven't crashed yet. You and your wingman can fly how you want, we'll fly our way."

"You two are being pretty self destructive," Morgan said. "You fly head long into battle like a couple of maniacs."

"I know," responded Flea enthusiastically. "Pretty cool, huh?"

Flea heard Morgan chuckle over his headset.

"Just be careful," Morgan replied seriously. "At this rate, you two will probably kill each other before the enemy can do it."

"No problem," said Flea confidently. "We'll promise not to get killed unless it's by one of the bad guys."

Morgan sighed in frustration.

"So, you thought about last night's meeting?" Flea changed the subject.

"Yeah," Morgan responded quickly. "I wanted to talk to you about that. I think it's good that Bella is helping us, but I don't know what to do about Cormon."

"All I can think of is to kill him and be done with it," replied Flea darkly. "Maybe something else will come to me today."

"Let's hope," chuckled Morgan.

The simulation ended with Kaida scoring ten kills. That was even more than Morgan. Flea had seven, which tied Morgan.

"Did you see Flea?" Kaida ran up to him after they left their fighters. "Did you see me flying?"

She was very excited.

"Yes, Kaida," said Flea. "Very well done."

She beamed at Flea's approval.

"Good job pilots," Morgan greeted them as they got out of their fighters. "Kaida, very well done. You should get a medal for how well you compensate for having to fly with a wingman like Flea."

The group laughed at Morgan's joke and Flea smiled.

"Laugh it up, people," said Flea sternly. "We'll see who is laughing if I decide to make all of you run until you puke."

They chuckled at Flea.

"All right ladies," Flea said loudly to silence the laughter. "Good job all of you. The points from this morning's simulations will be added to your overall scores. Go to lunch and then meet in the training room."

"Yes, sir," they sounded off in unison.

***

Bella hated being a Homarell. They were ugly and she hated the way the fish-people looked. Her surroundings reminded her of her sister's fish tank from when she was a child. The Homarell Sphere was a giant water filled glass ball. It came complete with sand filled bottom and coral caves which the Homarell lived in. She hated being a Homarell because of how much she disliked water. In fact, she hated water. She had a fear of large bodies of water ever since she almost drowned as a child in Italy.

She decided to undergo Rebecca's operation in place of Amy for this mission. Bella wanted to see what it was like. She felt that as the leader of the spy network, she was morally obligated to undergo the same things that she required of her operatives at least once. For the moment, her operatives consisted of six rookie agents, a few doctors and ten people she was trying to train to infiltrate the enemy as spies. It was a smaller operation then she led in the past, but it would have to suffice.

"I need to get more agents in my operation," she thought disappointedly. *"It will grow in time, though."*

"What's that?" asked a Homarell that was swimming by. "Did you say something?"

"What?" Rebecca responded. "I put raw air rocks in mouth hole foul."

The Homarell communicated with an intricate language of high pitched sonic communication combined with pheromones and a multitude of gestures. The surgical additions made to the communications center in Bella's brain were identical to the Homarell's. Dr. Rebecca seemed to know exactly what she was talking about when she said she could change a human into whatever she wanted using techniques she developed from the Runners medical advancements. The human form apparently was exactly what Dr. Rebecca said. It was a blank for the rest of the universe. Her mind, though, still worked the same.

"Excuse me?" said the Homarell swimming by with what appeared to be a confused look.

"Never mind," replied Bella.

Unfortunately, the body gestures were learned and not instinctive. She understood the sonic communication and the pheromones perfectly. They were instinctive in the Homarell brain's communication center. However, communicating was still difficult because she did not know the intricate system of Homarell body language. She also had to remember to stop thinking. The Homarell brain did not have an inner monologue. Any private thought Bella made was instantly broadcast by pheromones. It wasn't broadcast exactly as it was thought, but the general theme was made public. It made trying to live the lie of being a Homarell very difficult for her. She was using a technique she learned to beat lie detector tests to keep from getting caught.

"Father," she saw one of Roshom's spawn say from her distant monitoring place. "Are you going to be gone to the ship all day again?"

At least Bella was assuming it was Roshom. They all looked the same. She was pretty sure that she was at the right coral dwelling, but they all looked the same, too. This whole place was a nightmare to try and find one's way in.

"You are having bad dreams?" asked another passing Homarell. "You know I met a Kashin Doctor that was very good for helping me with that."

"Thank you," replied Bella. "I lick the cat very much."

"What?" the Homarell appeared disgusted.

That was one look that Bella had become very familiar with this morning.

"Never mind," responded Bella getting perturbed.

"No little one," responded the Homarell Bella was assuming to be Roshom. "I am just going to go visit delegate Cormon for a few hours."

"It has to be him," Bella thought.

"It has to be who?" asked another Homarell swimming toward her.

Bella opted not to respond. She was very nervous in the water and wasn't doing well masking her thoughts. Her pathetic attempt at this specie's body language was turning out rather horrible. She was doing a good job understanding it, but speaking it was a lot harder than it looked.

"What are you young ones going to do this morning?" asked what Bella hoped was Captain Roshom.

"We are just going off to School and then to a friend's reef to play," responded one of the children.

"Do not be out too late," replied the adult.

The spawn swam away. The adult waited for a few minutes and watched his offspring leave, and then left as well. Bella turned and saw the last Homarell that spoke to her waiting for a response. The Homarell considered it the most paramount of rudeness to leave if you spoke to someone before they had the opportunity to respond. To avoid this, most Homarell would wait patiently for a response. Sometimes, as an insult, one Homar would make another wait all day for a response. Bella didn't want to be rude.

"I did make magic flying hops two bag mud," she responded.

"I'm sorry, what?" said the other Homar.

"Never mind," responded Bella swimming away.

It was the only response she was truly good at in Homarell.

"Never mind," she repeated as she went toward what she hoped was Roshom dwelling.

***

"This sucks!" Flea protested loudly. "This is all we get?"

"The human fighter group has not been given full status! Nor will they be given full status until they are more experienced. This is what was allocated to you while still in a training status," explained the Homar rather smugly from behind his desk.

"How do you expect us to get in any real flight time with this?" Flea growled.

"If we're lucky we might be able to fuel up six of our fighters," added Morgan angrily. "What are we supposed to do with that?"

"Fly with six pilots," responded the resources officer smugly. "That is if you can field that many."

Flea started to draw the gun under his left arm and jumped at the smug catfish creature behind the desk. Morgan grabbed Flea and struggled with him, forcing Flea to put his gun away. It wasn't that difficult for Morgan to do since he was larger and Flea didn't struggle. Morgan didn't think Flea was really intent on shooting the supply clerk. The Homarell behind the desk had jumped back defensively from Flea.

"Can we at least get some time in the training field?" asked Morgan.

The Homar slowly made his way back to the desk, but continued watching Flea as he spoke.

"The Rankorack have booked the training field solid," he explained nervously looking at Flea. "They are putting in extra time to prepare for the impending fight with the Goraan. They've been given your fuel…I mean extra fuel rations…to do so."

"Whatever," Morgan grunted. "Let's go, Flea."

Morgan turned to walk away. Flea glared at the Homarell for a moment longer. With a quick, jerking motion, Flea's gun was out of its holster again in a flash. It was leveled at the fish-creature's head. The clerk dove underneath his desk to hide from the human's wrath. Flea turned around to face Morgan, grinning like a cat that just stole a canary.

"Are you quite finished with him?" asked Morgan shaking his head.

"Yeah, I'm done here," responded Flea sounding satisfied.

"Let's go," replied Morgan.

"Would you have really shot him?" asked Morgan after they were out the Homarell's range of hearing.

"No," said Flea grinned maliciously. "But he didn't know that."

"What if I didn't step in a stop you?" asked Morgan.

"Then I probably would have looked like a dumb ass," Flea laughed.

They made their way to the carrier from the Communal Sphere. They walked through the hanger bay to a large door on the starboard side that led into the space Alex had given them to train in. Next to the training room was the passageway that led to the fighter group's living quarters.

"What are we going to study today?" asked Morgan before they entered the room.

"Not sure," responded Flea. "We still haven't gotten through all our allies yet. Why? Do you have a request?"

"The Rankorack," responded Morgan. "Let's see what we can learn about the guys taking up all out fuel. We might find something we can use."

"Good idea," responded Flea with a nod.

The two entered the training room where all the pilots were already seated. A seat was open for Flea next to Kaida. Another next to Tommy was open for Morgan. Wingmen were now required to sit together. They would share rooms when they were out on a mission with the carrier. Morgan took his place to Flea's right along the port bulkhead facing both Flea and the group. Flea stood in front of the group so he could address them.

"Good afternoon, ladies," Flea said loudly. "I hope you all enjoyed your lunch. Today, I am going to set the teaching unit to instruct on the subject of another of our allies, the Rankorack. You are responsible, as usual, for the learning of cultural and customs, military strength and tactics, technology, and political policies and practices. Everything is testable. The test will be after a brief study time and the scores will be added to your cumulative overall performance rating. So it is suggested, as always, to pay attention."

There were a few groans as Flea started the interactive training program. The program started by explaining the Rankorack's current place in the Runners. It gave a brief rundown of traits common among the specie's population. The Rankorack were physically about two to three times the size of humans, averaging sixteen feet tall. Their average weight was twelve hundred pounds. They were covered with small blue scales, had long pointed teeth, and two thick arms that ended in a pair of hideous looking claws. On their backs, was a multitude of long, blue spikes, tipped in red.

The program instructed them on Rankorack military strength and technology next. Flea recognized the fighters because he had seen them in the training records he reviewed nightly of his ally's performances. The Rankorack did not have very good tactics. They seldom communicated during battle, often failed to help each other, and almost never accepted help from anyone else.

"We Rankorack are very solitary beings," the holographic Rankorack said. "As a result, the Rankorack Sphere was constructed of a very large size. This way each individual Rankorack could live alone with enough space between itself and its neighbors to feel comfortable. Our offspring will live with one of its parents until it is five years old, then it is turned out on its own. We only get together in times of great need, to mate or to settle disputes."

"Don't the young offspring die?" asked an astonished pilot.

"The weak ones do, but the ones that survive are very strong," replied the instructor. "We Rankorack respect strength above all things."

"You mentioned disputes," said Flea. "How do you settle disputes?"

"We settle our disputes by claiming Right of Combat," explained the hologram. "The disputing parties do battle. The winner is declared right...and the loser is usually declared dead. The one still living receives all his fallen enemy's belongings."

"Is it always a fight to the death?" asked Flea.

"Not always," replied the instructor. "Sometimes the loser will be forced to submit, but to do so is the greatest of all shames. It means admitting that the victor is stronger. They will also be forced to make reparations to the winner."

"Female Rankoracks are not as large or strong as the male," said a pilot. "Is anything special done if she has a dispute with a male?"

"Excellent question," said the hologram.

Since most of the group was female, questions which oriented around females were asked quite a bit.

"In the case of a dispute between males and females," responded the hologram. "The female is allowed to defer if she chooses and if someone is available for her. This means that her father, brother or a mate, depending on which of these is still alive and willing, can stand in her place."

"What happens if she wins?" asked the same pilot.

"She receives the all the spoils," explained the hologram. "She usually makes a small gift to the one that stood for her, but it is not required. It usually consists of something very precious or extra mating privileges depending on who stood in her place."

"What happens if the female loses the challenge?" she followed up.

"The winner has the right to take all her things, unlimited mating privileges or put her to death," replied the hologram. "The choice is his, but he can only decide on one."

Flea shared a glance with Morgan as an idea was forming in his head. Morgan appeared to have the same thought.

***

"I hate that slimy Cormon," Daniela pouted. "All day long I had to be nice as he explained to me the intricacies of the Homarell body language."

"Don't even get me started," Bella added. "I had a less than pleasing experience with that for most of the morning."

"Really?" asked Flea. "Why? What happened?"

"Not here," responded Bella looking around the hanger bay. "I'll tell you later."

Flea was standing in the hanger bay with Daniela and Bella. They were waiting for Christina and Ryoko to return with Morgan and Alex. Flea had some small packages under his arm.

"Do you really think anyone will believe that you are teaching us to fly?" asked Daniela.

"They will when they see you sitting in the pilot's chair through the windshield and ask for clearance to take off," replied Flea smiling.

"What?" asked Daniela sounding slightly worried. "You're not serious! What if I crash?"

"I would suggest that you don't do that," replied Flea dryly. "Crashing is bad."

The others finally approached and after a brief greeting, they all got on board the shuttle. Flea sat in the co-pilot's seat next to Daniela. She sat in the pilot's chair a bit nervously. Slowly and with minimal bumps, she managed to get the shuttle out of the hanger bay. They reached the same destination as their last meeting. Flea set the autopilot to fly a predetermined program designed to mimic a pilot in training. The flight logs would be altered to show that Daniela was at the controls the entire time.

"So," began Flea cordially. "How was everyone's day?"

"I spent the morning as one of those stupid fish people," began Bella. "I could hardly say anything coherent. They rely heavily on body language and gestures when in the water. Then I took a position as the human delegates' secretary to remain close at hand."

"That sounds fun," Flea chuckled. "Did anything good come out of your Homarell experience?"

"Yes," she responded with a smile. "I brought a present for you guys. It's a holo-record."

She pulled out a small flash drive and showed it them.

"Does it include the body language?" Morgan inquired.

"The pheromones and body language will be translated in the subtitles," Bella explained.

"Good," Flea replied. "I don't know if it can be used as evidence, but at least we'll understand it."

"Flea, I see you brought presents, too, perhaps?" Bella asked with a curious expression.

"Yep," said Flea happily. "These are from Morgan, Alex and I."

"We wanted to give you something in return for the gifts you gave us," added Morgan.

"And you asked for these anyway," added Alex.

Flea handed each of the young ladies a small package. They opened them up and pulled out the small, very ornate, silver and gold energy pistols that were inside.

"Thank you very much," Ryoko said with a bow. "This is wonderful gift."

"These are very pretty," added Bella. "And heavy. Is this real gold?"

"Yes it is," replied Alex smiling. "Your names are inscribed on the barrels. We hope you like them."

"These are very nice," added Christina. "And very small."

"That's so you can strap them to your inner thigh," replied Flea. "There are holsters inside the cases. That way, you don't walk in to a council meeting and look like you're packing a hand cannon or something like that. No one will even notice one these."

"Very thoughtful," said Daniela. "We really appreciate this. Next time you'll have to show us how to shoot them."

"We look forward to it," Morgan responded warmly.

"A good weapon is a useful tool in my line of work," said Bella appreciating her new gun.

"Excuse me, please," said Ryoko holding a pair of delicate gold framed spectacles she pulled out of the box. "What are glasses for?"

"The spectacles act like the targeting glasses you gave us," replied Morgan. "They don't look as obvious, though. I know that if anything were wrong with your eyes it could be corrected with the medical technology at our disposal. So, tell everyone it's a fashion statement or something."

The small group chuckled a bit at Morgan's idea, but decided it was a good idea.

"Well," said Bella as she pulled out a small orb with one flat side. "Let me show you what I found today. It might be an even nicer gift than these guns."

Bella plugged the flash drive into her phone and tossed it on the floor. A small, holographic image was projected above it. It began with Roshom entering the coral home of Cormon. At some point in time during the recording, all the Homarell delegates were positively identified by name. There was also a human male with a bad hair cut sitting next to Cormon. It looked like his hair was styled by putting a salad bowl on his head and cutting around it. The holo-projector translated the conversation from the Homarell perfectly. There were subtitles floating circularly around the small spherical object. It even added the interpretations of the gestures. It didn't have to translate what the human was saying. He spoke English.

"Who is that human?" asked Alex.

"That young man's name is…," Bella started to explain.

"Goddamnit!" interrupted a wide eyed Flea. "That piece of shit is one of my pilots! That rotten bastard! I'll rip his shit eating heart out!"

Flea went on a tirade of swearing and yelling that turned the faces of the delegates pale.

"He used to be a Marine," Morgan whispered to the ladies. "This is very upsetting to him. Give him a minute."

"We trusted that little bastard!" Flea yelled. "His name is Douglas Osgood. He's currently ranked thirty second. That piece of shit would have made the final cut!"

"Until today, that is," added Morgan dryly. "Now, I'm just going to kick the shit out of him."

Flea finally calmed down enough to stop swearing so the group could try speaking to him.

"You okay?" asked Morgan.

"Yeah," said Flea angrily. "I should have been paying closer attention."

"Yes you should have," agreed Morgan. "I should have, too. We both should have."

"What will you do?" asked Ryoko.

"I'll probably go back with a knife and cut his Goddamn throat out!" said Flea grimly. "Bella, I hate to ask this. I don't want to sound like I don't trust my pilots, but…"

"I can run background checks and have them watched for a bit if it makes you feel better," she replied seriously.

"Thanks," responded Flea grimly.

They turned their attention back to the recording. It outlined Cormon's plan to discredit the humans. It even showed the extent to which Roshom disagreed with what his delegates were doing. The humans sat silently in rapt attention until the recording played out.

"That was interesting," Morgan was the first to break the silence.

"Yeah," Flea sounded disgusted. "Interesting."

"We should take this to council!" said Ryoko vehemently.

"Wait," Christina said thoughtfully. "Not yet. Maybe we can use it to our advantage."

"What do you have in mind?" asked Alex.

"Well," Christina continued. "If Cormon knew we had this, wouldn't he have to do what we tell him?"

"I don't know," Flea shrugged. "Do you think he's susceptible to blackmail?"

"He is," replied Bella confidently. "I have reviewed his psychological profile and have been studying his personality. Cormon is only concerned with self preservation. He'll bend to our will if we show him this recording."

"You shouldn't show him right away, though," added Alex. "If he knows we're on to him he might change plans on us as a defensive tactic. We should wait until the best possible moment to use it."

"Like after the suicide mission when the council meets to discuss our fate among the Runners," said Flea quietly.

"What if you don't make it back?" asked Daniela looking worried.

"Then we use the recording to force Cormon to use his connections to get us a new ship," Bella looked down shamefully as she said this. "The death of so many humans because of Cormon's plotting would be a huge bargaining chip. Sorry you guys."

"Don't be sorry," said Morgan. "It's our job. It's what we do."

"It doesn't matter what happens," added Flea seriously. "Just make sure that you don't quit."

"Why is it so important for you guys to do this?" asked Christina. "Everyone hates us, but you still want to fight for them."

"Because we have to," Flea said as if that were sufficient reason. "It's the right thing to do."

Alex put a hand on her husband's shoulder, "It'll be fine. If anyone can form a plan to make it work, my husband can."

"And if anyone has the luck to carry it out," added Morgan. "It's Flea. He has more luck than any person has a right to."

"I just wish we could get some intelligence on the Goraan," said Bella desperately. "None of our allies can get any operatives in there. Apparently, their scanners and computers look to see if one of those slug things is on someone's brain every time they come across somebody new."

"We can't fake it?" asked Flea.

"Rebecca is working on something for me that might be able to, but none of our allies can do it," Bella responded.

"What's she doing?" asked Morgan.

"She says that the other Runners Bio-energy signature is too complex to mask or change," explained Bella. "She thinks we might be able to change ours, though. Then we could walk right into the Goraan head quarters."

"Sounds promising," replied Alex.

"I am training a few handpicked operatives for this in case it works," said Bella.

"Good," said Christina.

"The sooner we can get someone in there the better," added Daniela.

Ryoko was nodding in agreement.

"So what are we going to do about fuel?" asked Alex.

"Morgan and I discussed a plan earlier," said Flea.

"Really?" asked Alex. "What do you have in mind? Right now I barely have enough fuel to leave the dock."

"The Rankorack have been allocated enough fuel to supply their fighters and a small invasion force as well," began Flea. "They also have booked solid all the training slots in the combat training field's schedule."

"We studied about them today with our pilots," added Morgan. "They are a very interesting group."

"We need you three to call an emergency council meeting," said Flea.

"Do you think they will respond to us?" asked Daniela.

"Yes," said Ryoko confidently. "If not, they have to listen to what we say."

"What do you mean?" Flea was confused.

"She's trying to say that if we call an emergency meeting and they fail to show up, then they are subject to whatever we decree," explained Christina. "That means that if we tell them to be there, and they don't show, then we can reallocate all the fuel and flight time you need. They'll have to abide by whatever decisions we make until they all get together again."

"From what I have been seeing of them," explained Bella. "They would sooner die than listen to any decisions we might make."

"I thought they liked us," Flea sounded disappointed.

"Me too," said Alex.

"So what are we supposed to do at this council meeting and when do we call it?" asked Daniela.

"Call it for this Saturday," replied Flea.

"You'll try and convince them to give us the fuel and training times," added Morgan.

"They will not give this," said Ryoko. "Flea, you know this."

"I know, Ryoko," replied Flea, "But do it anyway. When they refuse I will claim Right of Combat against the Rankorack."

"What is this?" asked Ryoko. "You fight them, Flea?"

"Yes," replied Flea.

"Do you really think that you can take on a Rankorack?" asked Daniela incredulously. "I've seen them! They are at least three times your size!"

"They're like blue tanks!" Christina added sacredly. "On legs!"

"I don't plan on facing one personally," Flea explained calmly. "That would be just stupid. I can, however, as the challenging party, set the rules for engagement. I will challenge them to combat in my fighter."

"Can you beat them?" asked Christina.

"No doubt we can," responded Morgan confidently.

"To make things a little less stressful, though, I plan on invoking my rights as a recognized leader," continued Flea. "That means I can make a formal call to arms. My pilots will come to my aid. We'll make the final cuts Saturday morning before the council meeting. This way we can assign a fighter to each pilot. Then we can upgrade our group to full readiness. We don't want them to make an excuse not to fight us."

"We'll have to inform the pilots of this tomorrow," said Morgan to Flea.

Flea nodded his acknowledgement.

"In the meantime, ladies," said Daniela. "We should put that recording in a safe place. We'll need it to blackmail Cormon."

"Agreed," said Ryoko.

"And we need to keep sucking up to 'his high fish-ness' for a while," added Christina. "We can't let him know that we got him.

Everyone nodded in agreement

"Flea," she added looking directly at him. "As your friend I can appreciate your need to exact a measure of revenge on the pilot from the recording. As your delegate, I am requesting that you leave him alone until the challenge. On the day of the challenge, after you make your last cut, have Alex throw him in the ship's jail or something. Even if he makes the cut, throw him in the ship's jail and pick someone else."

"Brig," Alex and Flea corrected in unison.

"What?" asked Christina.

"The ship's jail is called a brig," Alex said.

"Whatever," Christina said musically. "I just don't want anyone tipped off. Are we all agreed?"

They all nodded their agreement.

"Flea," Ryoko sounded worried. "You are sure to do this? You can win?"

"By the time we fight them this Sunday," Morgan said, "we'll have been training for eighteen hours a day for the last two weeks in a highly intensified atmosphere. We not only know our own strategies, but we also know the strategies of our enemies and allies. I would pit our group of thirty two fighters against any thirty two in the entire Runner fleet and know that we would win."

Ryoko looked doubtfully at Flea.

"Trust me, Ryoko, it'll be okay," Flea tried to sound reassuring. "Don't count us out until the end."

13

Ba'an was strapped to one of Mistress Toren's racks in her work room again. He didn't mind the beatings anymore. They had become so much part of his routine that they were like background noise. What bothered him most was thinking of what that rotten Scivistan was doing while Ba'an was being beaten. He was probably sitting in his shiny new office as a Shift Supervisor. Scivistan would be enjoying the fact that for the first time in his pathetic existence he was no longer a low-ender.

"The part of the ship he is in is cleaner, smells better, and his meals are served with actual plates and utensils," thought Ba'an absently. *"I remember what it was like. I'll kill that rotten piece of slime."*

Mistress Toren lashed out with her whip like appendages when she saw she was losing Ba'an's concentration.

"What's so important that has you lost in thought, pet?" asked Toren seductively as she approached Ba'an.

She dragged her tongue across Ba'an's cheek as she was so fond of doing. She pulled away and smiled coquettishly biting her lower lip.

"Is there something in your little life that is more important than me?" she inquired softly.

"No, Mistress," Ba'an responded mechanically.

She turned and walked away from him. Her hips swayed from side to side when she moved. She turned slowly to face him again.

"I am the most important thing in your pathetic existence, pet!" she screamed and punctuated each word with a lash from her whip.

Her already red skin flushed and turned a deeper shade.

"Tell me, pet, do you enjoy the time we spend together?" she purred softly.

Ba'an did not respond.

"I said, tell me you enjoy our time together!" she shouted whipping him some more.

"Say it!" she continued shouting and beating him.

"I order it!" she screamed.

Ba'an's blood was oozing down his flesh from where the small hooks that tipped her whip appendages had pulled out chunks of skin.

"I enjoy the time I spend with my Mistress," Ba'an said blankly.

He didn't really mean it. He hated Toren. He would have to kill her some day.

"It is okay, pet," she said softly approaching him. "I know you are only saying this because I ordered you. I will keep you as my pet, if you please me."

She giggled and ran a finger down his cheek. Toren walked behind Ba'an where he could not see her.

"She will beat me mercilessly because of the marks on my back again," he thought.

"I see you've been playing with someone else again!" she screamed at him when she saw the marks. "You are mine! Do you hear me?"

"Yes, Mistress," Ba'an barked mechanically.

"Perhaps if we were on the same level, I would allow you to spend personal time with me," she said gingerly stroking the wounds she added to Ba'an's back.

She bit his neck hard. Blood started seeping from where she bit him. She took time licking his wound.

"You are done today, pet," she whispered. "You may go now."

She unshackled him and applied the healing salve to his wounds.

"I suggest you stop letting others beat you, pet," she said as he left. "It makes me very cross with you."

"Yes, Mistress," Ba'an replied as he rushed from the room.

Ba'an reported to the reharvestation chambers after his beating without incident. He walked up to the technician on duty.

"Good evening, friend," said Ba'an.

"Good even fellow technician," said the Gora happily. "I bet you are glad to be serving a purpose again, eh?"

"I am trying to serve a greater purpose in the end, friend," Ba'an replied cryptically. "Would you like me to finish your shift?"

"Really?" asked the technician, "What do you want in exchange?"

"Nothing," said Ba'an overdramatically. "I am just pleased to be doing useful work again!"

"Very well," said the technician cheerfully. "Have fun!"

The technician left the room to enjoy the time off.

"Today will be a good day," he thought with a grimly.

He walked over to chamber number one, which now had a new glass door. He opened the door and spit white acid on the interior of the chamber causing it to melt in some places. After that, he placed a corpse that had been waiting to be reharvested into chamber one and began the reharvesting sequence. As Ba'an had expected, the chamber's malfunction alarm went off and sirens started to blare as a red light flashed above the control panel.

"Oh dear," said Ba'an with mock sincerity. "I seem to have had a mishap."

The glass burst outward. Apparently Ba'an had dripped some acid on the window's support frame. A soupy mixture of fluid and half liquefied body parts splattered on the floor at Ba'an's feet. Ba'an grabbed an emergency canister off the wall and sprayed the mess. The mixture in the canister was designed to deactivate and instantly freeze the reharvestation fluids so they wouldn't injure anyone.

"That should force Scivistan to come down here," Ba'an hissed. "The fool has been sitting in his plush new office long enough."

Ba'an launched himself into the ceiling and hid in the shadows above the room's only door. Eventually Scivistan entered the room with a self important stride. His truncated tail ruined the effect. Ba'an dropped from the ceiling to quietly land between Scivistan and the door.

"Technician!" bellowed Scivistan. "Technician, report!"

"You pompous fool," Ba'an thought to himself.

Ba'an didn't speak. He wanted Scivistan to see him, first. He shut and latched the door to get Scivistan's attention.

"Techni...," Scivistan's jaw dropped when he turned and saw Ba'an.

"I am not afraid of you, Ba'an," Scivistan sounded quite full of himself. "I am an important Gora, now! I will be missed!"

"I am sure you will," said Ba'an dryly.

Ba'an puffed up his chest. After filling his lungs with air, he flailed his tentacles wildly in the air about his body. He set his feet shoulder width apart and let forth a high pitched scream that conveyed every single bit of hatred and rage he contained in his small body. All the putrid self loathing, the bitter anger, and the contempt for his chain of command were in that scream. All the sick pain he was forced to endure at the hands of his Mistress were all let out in that high pitched, unholy wail. Ba'an was crying. Scivistan wet himself.

"DIE!" Ba'an screamed.

Scivistan tried to bolt to the left and get past Ba'an. Ba'an whipped one of his tentacles out and latched on to Scivistan's waist.

"You go nowhere!" he screamed throwing Scivistan against the wall. Scivistan bounced off the wall and rolled to his feet baring his claws.

"I have had enough of you!" hissed Scivistan.

He slashed out. Ba'an jumped back. The tips of Scivistan's claws sliced through Ba'an's skin leaving five shallow cuts along his chest through Mistress Toren's mark. Ba'an lashed out with his multiple tentacles like a machine gun landing blow after blow in Scivistan's face and torso. Scivistan leapt high into the air and landed on top of one of the ceiling lights. Ba'an latched his tentacle around the lighting fixture Scivistan was standing on.

"Did you not pay attention to Gormak?" yelled Ba'an.

He pulled the light down with Scivistan. Scivistan landed with the light in the middle of his chest.

"Die!" shouted Ba'an as he leapt on top of Scivistan.

"Die!" Ba'an started pounding on Scivistan's chest.

"Die!" Ba'an had tears running down his eyes as he continued to pound.

"Die!" Blood started pouring out of Scivistan's mouth.

"Die, you piece of putrid filth!" Ba'an pounded more.

Scivistan stopped moving. Ba'an continued to cry and pound on Scivistan's chest for the next thirty minutes. He finally collapsed on top of Scivistan's dead body. He was exhausted.

"Dead," Ba'an huffed as he lifted Scivistan's limp arm, which promptly dropped to the floor.

He stood up and kicked Scivistan's limp form in the side.

"You made me kill her!" he hissed.

Ba'an kicked him again.

"She was the only one that was nice to me!" he kicked Scivistan one more time.

Ba'an tried to kick Scivistan again and missed falling on his back gracelessly. He was running on pure hate and his aim was suffering for it. He crumpled to the ground next to the dead body.

"It was all your fault," he whispered through tears. "It was all your fault."

***

Flea and Morgan finished breakfast and were going around together making the final round of cuts. They were about to talk to the last person they needed to talk to. Flea and Morgan were standing outside Tommy's house. Tommy moved out after he read the final scores on the board last night. He ranked thirty third out of forty. They only had thirty two fighters. Tommy didn't make it.

"How do you think he'll take it when he sees us?" asked Morgan.

"He's been living with me since we got here," Flea said. "He knows we had to do this. He just needs some time to blow off some steam."

"I hope so," said Morgan. "He's a good kid. If his skills started to pick up last week instead of this one, he probably would have made it."

"Well," said Flea. "Let's tell him the news."

Flea and Morgan knocked on the door. It took a few minutes, but Tommy eventually answered.

"Oh," Tommy said opening the door. "It's you guys. Come on in."

Tommy didn't sound too happy to see them as they entered his sparse living room.

"Look," Tommy said dejectedly. "I saw the board last night. All the points were made public. I got thirty third. I didn't make it."

"Are you mad at us? Is that why you moved out?" asked Morgan.

"I'm not mad at you," responded Tommy. "You did exactly what you said you would. You made the final cuts based on points. It hurts a little. I put in all that effort to crawl all the way from the last spot just to end up thirty third."

"Yeah," Morgan tried to sound understanding.

He would get no sympathy from Flea. Flea explained the rules to all of them in the beginning. No one was exempted.

"What can I say, though?" Tommy continued. "You guys have a job to do. I understand that. I moved out because I just needed some breathing room, I guess. I can still come and visit, right?"

"You can visit any time you want," said Flea smiling. "I may not feel bad for cutting you, but you are still part of the family."

"Thanks," Tommy sounded relieved.

"That's not why we're here, though," said Morgan.

"Why is it, then?" asked Tommy.

"To let you know that you made it," Morgan replied.

There was a long pause.

"How is that? I thought you weren't going to cut me any breaks?" asked Tommy directly to Flea.

"I'm not, Tommy," said Flea seriously. "There are some extenuating circumstances."

"What are you talking about," Tommy gave Flea a curious glance.

"Osgood is a traitor," Flea said simply.

"What?" asked Tommy with wide eyes. "I don't understand."

"Osgood has been helping some of our so called 'allies' plot to take us down," explained Morgan. "We have evidence against him."

"Really?" asked Tommy breathlessly.

"Oh yes," said Flea angrily. "And he's not getting away with it, either."

Flea and Morgan briefly explained to Tommy everything that had been going on while Tommy and the rest of the pilots were trying to get into the Archangels.

"That sucks," said Tommy. "You guys have it tougher than I thought. I didn't know you had to deal with all that and try to run the group."

"No big deal," replied Flea. "Somebody's got to do it, you know?"

"Yeah," said Morgan.

"You know what this means, though, right?" asked Flea.

"What?" asked Tommy.

"Since Osgood is number thirty two and will be exiled from the group," explained Flea, "then the number thirty three spot moves up automatically."

"That's me!" Tommy sounded excited.

"Yep," said Flea smiling.

"We can count on you, right?" asked Morgan.

"You know you can!" responded Tommy.

"I'm not cutting you a break, though," Flea said seriously. "If it wasn't you, it would be whoever was thirty third. This isn't a break."

"I know," Tommy said enthusiastically. "I understand!"

"Good," replied Flea. "So are you coming back home?"

There was a long pause again as Tommy thought it over.

"I know I have to move down there to your end of the sphere again," said Tommy. "But I think I'll keep my own place when I do. It might be nice to have some of my own space now that things have started to calm down."

"Calm down?" asked Flea. "I don't know what 'things' you seem to think have calmed down, kid."

"You know what I mean," said Tommy with a chuckle.

"We have to get going and get the pilots ready for the challenge getting issued at today's council meeting," said Morgan. "Don't come to the meeting with the rest of the pilots. If you want to go and watch, that's fine, but we need to keep it cool with Osgood so he doesn't know we're on to him. Understand?"

"No problem," Tommy nodded.

"And don't tell any of the other pilots, either," Morgan said. "We'll tell them what's been happening when the time is right."

"And we don't want Osgood getting all jumpy and taking off on us before we take him in to custody," said Flea.

"I understand," said Tommy. "You can count on me, guys."

***

"This is it, everyone," Christina said. "Did you notify the pilots, Flea?"

"Yeah, we spoke to them this morning," Flea said to Bella and the delegates. "By the way, thanks for joining us for lunch, ladies. It is nice to have your company in case this is my last meal."

Alex smacked him in the back of the head much to Morgan's amusement, "Don't be negative."

Kaida and Armina were having lunch with them as well. It was just after one in the afternoon. Everyone was busy earlier that morning making their final preparations. Kaida chatted and interacted happily with the small group, but Armina was looking preoccupied with something. She wasn't eating. Instead, she pushed her food around her plate with her fork.

"What can you tell me about the rest of the Archangels, Bella?" Morgan asked changing the morbid topic.

"They all check out fine," she approved. "You have a good group."

"How does the group look? How many boys, girls and Kashin, I mean." asked Daniela.

"Three males, twenty one human females and eight female Kashin," Flea said, "Bella did you happen to…"

"I already checked on the Kashin," she said sincerely. "They are loyal to you and Morgan. They love their people, but they are loyal to you. I am in the process of doing checks on the crew manifest for the carrier as well, Alexandria."

"Good," Alex replied. "Thanks."

"No problem," Bella said. "I also checked out Mihanna. He is sincere in his show of respect and willingness to help us."

"What does all this mean?" asked Ryoko slowly. "I do not understand."

Her English improved daily.

"She is trying to say that our Kashin pilots love their fellow Kashin," explained Alex. "However if they had to choose, they would choose to stay with us."

"Why?" asked Ryoko.

"Probably because we were willing to take a chance on them when their own people were not, Ryoko," explained Daniela. "Showing someone that you are willing to have faith in them can have a profound effect."

"Ah," said Ryoko with a smile. "I have faith in all of you."

"She's a sweet kid," Flea thought to himself.

"I have faith in Flea!" Kaida said cheerily poking Flea's ribs.

"Thank you, Kaida," Flea said with equal cheerfulness. "I have faith in you, too."

"Did you speak to Tommy yet?" asked Alex changing the subject.

"Yeah," replied Flea. "He'll be there tomorrow, but promised to stay away tonight so as not to blow our cover."

"Good," said Bella. "He was the only variable in the equation. I wasn't sure how he would react."

"Of course, he was hurt at first because this morning he thought he would get cut," Flea explained. "But after we briefly explained the situation to him, he understood what was going on."

"Good," said Bella.

"One more thing," Flea added. "After the fight tomorrow I would like to tell the Archangels what we are up against. They may be flying in a suicide mission. They have the right to know. They should make this choice themselves."

"You can't!" Bella sounded furious. "It is too great a security risk!"

"I can and I will!" Flea responded loudly. "I will not send people out to die without them knowing the full extent of the situation they're in! They should have a choice!"

"If you tell them…," Bella threatened.

"You'll what?" Flea sneered. "Throw me in pilot jail?"

"You will do nothing, Bella," Ryoko ordered. "Flea is right. Let him be!"

"Ryoko," implored Bella.

"No, Bella," Ryoko said sounding authoritative. "I am the Delegate. My decision!"

"Someone is developing some backbone," Flea thought approvingly.

Bella looked to the other delegates to override the normally quiet Ryoko.

"I agree with Ryoko on this, Bella," Christina said thoughtfully. "These people have the right to know."

"They're right, Bella," Daniela intoned. "I will not have people fight based on our decisions without knowing the potential consequences."

"As you wish," Bella said sounding slightly defeated.

The group continued eating and chatting with each other. They were enjoying each other's company and drawing strength from the presence of their friends. Armina finally looked up. She appeared to have wrestled alone with her internal struggle long enough.

"Flea?" asked Armina sounding worried. "Are you going to go fight someone?"

Flea was planning to explain exactly what his job was to Armina at some point in time. At least, he planned to. He wasn't sure how he was going to explain what he was doing to a little girl that had lost her entire family in a horrible attack. He didn't know how to tell her that the people she had chosen to take as her new family made a job of risking their lives. The table was silent. No one wanted to speak.

"Armina," Flea said delicately. "Do you know what I do?"

"Yes," she said softly. "You're a hero. You fight to protect everyone."

"I'm not a hero," he chuckled. "Heroes are guys with unbelievable powers that come swooping in at the last minute to save the day, kitten."

"They have much cooler names than we have," Morgan added cheerfully. "Heroes have names like 'Superman' or 'Spiderman.' Heroes aren't named 'Flea.' That's just not how it goes."

"Yeah," chuckled Flea. "Heroes aren't called 'Captain Morgan.' That's just silly."

"Hey!" protested Morgan.

"Honestly!" Flea continued jokingly. "What kind of name is that for a hero?"

The small group chuckled.

"What I'm trying to say, kitten, is that we are a military family," Flea explained softly. "We all have jobs to do. We're not heroes. We're not special. We just do our jobs."

"And sometimes that means you have to fight?" asked Armina dejectedly.

"Sometimes," said Flea.

"Will you always come home?" she asked.

"I'll try my best," said Flea. "And no matter what happens, I'll always watch out for you."

"That wasn't a 'yes,' Flea," she said sadly.

"I know," Flea said softly. "But I promise to try."

"Promise?" Armina asked.

"I promise," Flea said. "We all promise, don't we guys."

They all nodded and spoke their agreement.

"I guess it'll have to do," Armina sniffed. "It's not fair. Just be safe, okay?"

***

They stayed at Flea's and chatted until it was time for the gathering. The group was nervous about going to the Communal Sphere for the emergency meeting. It wasn't getting up in front of the council that made them nervous. Christina, Daniela, and Ryoko were used to that. They just didn't know what was going to happen.

They all wore their guns. It just seemed to make them feel a little better. The young politicians and Bella wore theirs under their black, knee length skirts on their inner thighs. The Captains, however, wore theirs openly. Alex had elected to wear her formal uniform in front of the council. Flea and Morgan, however, were wearing their olive colored flight suits with the sleeves tied around their waists. Armina was sitting atop Flea's shoulders dressed like him, as usual. The three had the names *Morg, Flea* and *Hellkitty* across their chests in white block letters. On the back of their shirts was the message: *If you can still read this, I'm not done kicking your ass.*

Flea and Morgan made sure not to shave this morning. For some reason they wanted to ensure they looked as disreputable as possible. Flea hoped the council would see this as a sign of disrespect. Kaida was sent ahead to ensure all the pilots were already there. The pilots should be looking similar to Flea and Morgan. They were instructed to try and look as dirty and unkempt as possible. Flea also wanted them to carry side arms. They would be wearing the same shirt as Morgan, Flea and Armina.

"Are you guys sure you want to look like that?" asked Christina.

"Yes," replied Morgan simply.

"What if they get a bad impression of you?" asked Daniela.

"Good," Flea snorted. "That's what I'm going for."

"If they don't want to support us, that's their choice," added Morgan. "I don't care if I hurt their delicate little feelings."

"Okay," said Daniela unsure about her comrades.

As they walked through the Human Sphere to the transport tube, something strange was happening.

"Hey, Flea!" shouted someone with a smile and a wave. "Go get 'em, buddy!"

"Thanks!" shouted Flea as he raised a fist in the air.

"Hey guys," another shouted over his shoulder. "It's Flea and Morgan! Way to go, guys!"

"Hey Captain Alex!" shouted a young woman. "Is that whole ship really yours?"

"It sure is!" responded Alex. "She's going to be a real beauty, too!"

"Good luck with her, okay?" the young woman replied. "And good luck to you, too!"

"Thanks!" shouted Alex with a smile.

A group of small children ran up laughing, "Hey look! Its Armina and Keri! They hang out with the Archangels!"

"Hey Armina!" one of the kids said loudly. "Here, this is for you! Here, Keri!"

He handed the girls each a small sucker.

"Thanks!" Armina said with a giggle.

"You can come play with us sometime, okay?" he said energetically.

"Sure thing," Keri responded smiling.

They continued to walk through the sphere. A small crowd gathered behind them shouting greetings and encouragement. The delegates were handling the treatment much better than the

Captains, who weren't used to this kind of thing. The young pop-stars-turned-politicians were managing to respond and interact with all the well wishers. They even managed to sign a few autographs. They were obviously experienced at this.

"What's going on, Morg?" asked Flea trying to lean in and whisper to his friend over the crowd.

"You got me," he said with a smile. "But it feels kind of good."

"I sent out an email to the entire human population explaining to them what was going on today," replied Bella smirking. "I included a link to a web page that introduced all of you and told a little bit about you and what you are trying to do."

"Oh, I see," Flea didn't sound too thrilled.

"Christina asked me to do it. She just wanted all of you to know how much you are appreciated," said Bella with a warm smile. "You've earned it."

"Thanks," Flea said seriously. "I guess I just need to get used to it."

The crowd followed them all the way to the transport tube. As Flea and his small group got on the platform, they were joined by as many of the crowd that could safely fit with them.

Alex pulled out her ever-present smartphone, "Show me the density of the humans by location."

A small three dimensional map of the Runners space station appeared on the screen. Most of the humans were already at the familiar public square in the Communal Sphere. The rest of the humans were en route to the meeting. The Captains and the delegates disembarked the platform and waited for more humans so they could make a bigger entrance. After their crowd had grown large enough, they left for the meeting area. On the way, Flea recognized a snake creature from when he last came down here to reunite with Morgan and Alex. At least he thought it was the same one. They all looked the same to him.

"Do I know you?" asked Flea to the lizard.

"YOU...HUMAN..." The lizard stuttered as its eyes widened in recognition. "CROWD...MANNERS...BEATING!"

The lizard bolted away in the opposite direction afraid for its life. Flea started to chuckle.

"What was that about?" asked Morgan with a smile. "Did he know you or something?"

"I guess you could say that," responded Flea with a cocky grin.

The rest of the humans showed up, and escorted their delegates and Captains to the marble platform where the council regularly met. The entire council was already there. Bleacher style seats were erected around the marble stage which was used as the floor of the council meetings. The delegates sat around the stage facing each other. The black marble podium that Alex spoke from the last time she was here was gone. More seats were set up for spectators around the delegates.

The council believed in holding all sessions open to the public. This is why they held their meetings here. Flea and Morgan found their pilots waiting for them in formation as instructed earlier. They stood in front of the platform between it and the bleachers. Kaida was standing in front of the group of human pilots trying to look official. Just as they were instructed, they were lined up in six columns of five people all at attention with straight faces. Kaida was standing in front trying to look mean. Unfortunately, Kaida was the type of person that no matter how hard she tried, she just could not look very mean. Instead of actually looking mean, she just looked pouty. Flea thought she looked cute. It was probably because of her blue and black pig-tails.

"Okay, guys, let's do this," Alex said addressing the rest of the small group, "Good luck, everyone."

They all nodded and wished each other luck. Flea and Morgan dismissed Kaida, who trotted off to take her place in the group of pilots. Morgan stood to the left of the group and faced Flea and the pilots as usual. Flea faced the group and paced back in forth in front of them. He looked like a caged animal. Alex joined the crowd with Armina and Keri in tow. The delegates, however, did not have it as easy. Since they were the ones to call the emergency session, they were paraded in front of the entire assembly and forced to stand in the center of the stage as if on display. This usually unsettled most delegates. However, because of the young ladies' backgrounds on Earth, they were holding up extremely well. Soon, things settled down as the council Caretaker called things to order.

"Quiet," called the Caretaker. "In the name of the high council of Runners I call this emergency session to order."

Flea was shocked to discover that the Caretaker was Delegate Cormon of the Homarell. Cormon pounded the flat square side of a palm sized marble pyramid onto a small marble plate to get everyone's attention. The sound it made was piercing to the ears.

"Quiet, I said!" intoned Cormon. "I will have some order!"

A hush fell over the crowd.

"This emergency council session has been called by the human delegation," began Cormon. "Delegates Abe, Knight, and Masters."

The mass of spectators moved their attention to the three young ladies at the center of the platform. The three girls somehow looked taller. They were obviously not afraid. They appeared very stern and resolved to do this.

"They seem to have some certain matters of import to discuss with us today," Cormon continued. "That being said, the floor is yours, humans."

Christina, Ryoko, and Daniela stood in a small line facing the fighter group while on stage. Ryoko smiled to the pilots and gave a small nod to Flea and Morgan. Flea cracked a smile back. Christina walked forward to stand apart from them as she began speaking.

"As you know," she began. "We humans just recently joined the ranks of our fellow Runners. We, like many of you were initially shocked, and then very angered by our new situation and what caused us to be here."

"The more we were here," added Daniela walking to join Christina, "The more angry we became. Our home was gone. More than ninety nine percent of our species has been killed. To make matters worse, we discovered that all life on our entire planet was the by-product of toxic and radioactive waste dumping from alien species."

"We find ourselves in this place. Enemies hate us. Many allies do not like us, and no one wants us here," added Ryoko strongly as she joined the other two. "We have had enough!"

The humans in the crowd started cheering loudly when Ryoko said this.

"Order!" intoned Cormon. "Order I said!"

The humans continued to cheer until Ryoko raised a slender hand to silence them. The three human delegates that were the center of attention started to walk around so they could be seen more easily by the crowd.

"Continue young ladies," said Cormon offhandedly.

"When we reached this point, one woman had the courage to stand up," Christina continued. "She asked us all: who will stand and fight?"

The humans roared when hearing this question again. Daniela raised a hand to silence them before Cormon could say anything.

"And someone," added Daniela dramatically, "found the courage to answer."

"We thank them," added Ryoko with a bow.

The humans started to cheer again. So did about half the Runners in the crowd. The other half were booing. Apparently, Cormon wasn't the only one against fighting the Goraan.

"Order!" shouted Cormon angrily. "I will have you all removed if this continues!"

Ryoko raised her small hand again to silence the humans and other Runners that were cheering encouragements.

"Ladies," Cormon gushed. "As you can tell, this is not an issue that we are entirely unified on. Please, get to the point of why you asked us here today before things get out of hand."

"Admiral Mihanna helped us to answer our own call," continued Christina. "He aided us in getting a battleship and fighters and helped to train us to use that ship. He even helped to get us recognized by the Runners Council."

"Need I remind you," said Cormon sternly. "Your recognized status among us is on a trial basis? As you stated, your race is in many ways far inferior to the rest of us and we need to see what you will do with your new found political presence."

"Point of order!" shouted a delegate.

He appeared to be one of the snake people Flea had an encounter with earlier.

"Go on," said Cormon recognizing the delegate.

"I would like to point out that becaussse they are only on a trial bassssisss, that thessse humanssss do not have the right to call an emergensssy counsssil meeting," he said.

"What is all this about a trial basis?" demanded Christina acting surprised.

The human delegates saw the information on their "trial status" in the holo-recording. They needed to act surprised so the Homarell did not suspect the humans of having it.

"You did not speak of this earlier," added Daniela.

"Admiral?" asked Ryoko as she found him sitting among his own delegates. "Is this true?"

"I'm sorry, Delegate Ryoko," explained Mihanna. "It was the only way that I could get enough of them to agree. I tried to gain audience with you to inform you of this, but you were being occupied by Caretaker Cormon."

"They are lessss!" yelled the snake delegate.

"No!" shouted one of the Kashin delegates. "These humans are good creatures and I am proud they are here!"

The other Kashin clapped and shouted approval.

"Many of them are becoming our friends," said another Kashin delegate. "And they are very intelligent and highly adaptive."

"Just because the reason they came into being is less than ideal," explained a small, white, octopus-like creature with a soft voice, "does not mean they are any less valued than the rest of us."

"Your personal attitudes toward these creatures, does not matter fellow delegates!" intoned a large blue Rankorack, "The fact is, only fifty one percent of us even feel they are worth recognizing and even then, only on a trial basis. Personally, I can hardly stand looking at these puny, easily breakable creatures. That is why I voted against them. If the Kashin weren't throwing their numbers behind these wretched things, we would not even be here!"

Half the crowd watching booed. The other half cheered. Flea shouted curses at the Rankorack delegate.

"Silence!" shouted Cormon pounding the small marble pyramid again. "This is the last warning!"

The crowd hushed.

"Human delegates," said Cormon. "Because of your trial standing, this meeting is adjourned. You do not have the right to call an emergency meeting unless you are fully recognized, even with the Kashin backing. This meeting is dis…"

"Point of order!" shouted a Kashin delegate before Cormon dismissed the meeting. "Point of order, I say!"

"Go on," said Cormon. "But make this quick. I'm sure many of us want to make it home for dinner today."

"I am sooo concerned about YOUR stomach!" shouted Flea sarcastically from the sidelines.

Many of the humans laughed at this. So did the few Kashin that had spent enough time around humans to understand a bit about sarcasm.

"Silence!" shouted Corman with a glare at him. "Go on delegate Armalan."

"I didn't know he was a delegate," Flea thought.

"I claim sponsorship rights," explained Armalan. "As head of the Kashin Delegation, which is also the delegation who agreed to act as the human's sponsoring race, I claim that we have sponsorship rights."

"What do you mean?" asked Ryoko.

"To gain a trial status," Armalan explained. "One of the already recognized races had to sponsor you. We chose to do this on your behalf. We kept trying to get you to come to a Kashin Delegation meeting and explain everything to you, but Caretaker Cormon kept monopolizing your time. We were planning to contact you tonight."

"I see," Christina was fuming. "Your expeditious manner of informing us of our rights and status is appreciated, Caretaker Cormon."

Ryoko glanced at Flea. He could tell she angry.

"Don't blow it!" Flea mouthed silently when Ryoko looked at him.

She nodded and then whispered to the other girls briefly. They recovered their composure quickly.

"It failed to enter my mind while making your lovely acquaintances," Cormon gushed.

"What a slimy piece of shit," Morgan whispered to Flea.

"Maybe if we find a planet where we can fish," Flea whispered responding to Morgan, "we can use him as bait to catch something bigger."

The two shared a chuckle.

"I'm sorry," said Christina very sweetly. "I believe our sponsor delegates were speaking?"

"Thank you, young delegate," Armalan responded. "I would like to add that we will be speaking with you after the meeting."

"Of course," Ryoko smiled with a bow.

"As we were saying," Armalan spoke on behalf of his fellow Kashin delegates. "My Brothers and Sisters and I fully support these humans. We would like to start an exchange program with them to gain greater understanding. In the meantime however, as their sponsoring race, we were the ones who actually called this meeting on their behalf."

"You cannot!" shouted the Rankorack. "They already called the meeting. Since it is their meeting, and they do not have full status, then it is a voided meeting!"

"If you wish to leave, Brother," Armalan smirked. "By all means, go ahead. After you do, we will call another emergency meeting in fifteen minutes. You can turn around and come back if you wish."

There was a long pause.

"Very well," the Rankorack delegate sounded defeated.

"Fine," said Cormon. "Ladies, finish this."

"The reason which we called you here…excuse me…our sponsors called you here," Christina said glancing the Kashin delegations direction. "Is to inform you of the difficulties we have been having and ask for help."

"What do you mean?" asked Cormon.

"We were given a ship and some fighters," explained Daniela. "However, we have been having difficulties getting the supplies we need to properly train and outfit our people. Our fuel allotment is meager and we have yet to be given any time in the combat simulation ground. We need fuel and flight time in order to properly train a military unit for combat."

"I am sorry," responded Cormon. "Your efforts to support your fellow Runners are deeply appreciated, but fuel and training times are allocated on the basis of need. As a trial member of the Runners, your needs have not been assessed to be as great as…"

"The Rankorack?" asked Ryoko.

"Yes," said Cormon. "The Rankoracks are a good example. As a full fighting arm of the Runners, their needs are in fact greater than your own."

"I see," said Christina.

"That being said," continued Cormon wearily, "I call this meeting to an end. Delegates, you are dis…"

"I call for a vote!" shouted Armalan as he interrupted Cormon once again. "I call that we put this issue to a vote. The humans should be given every available opportunity we can allow! I say, we vote, Brothers and Sisters. Do I have a second?"

"I second!" shouted another Kashin delegate.

"You cannot do that!" shouted the Rankorack delegate. "It was one of your own that called for the vote!"

"I do not recall this rule," responded the Kashin. "I second it, still."

"This is a travesty!" shouted the Rankorack.

"Do not begrudge us if we have enough delegates to raise and second a motion on our own," explained Armalan with a smile.

"This must be why nothing gets done," Flea whispered to Morgan.

"Yeah," whispered Morgan in response. "We could probably resolve this faster if they just let us use our blasters."

"We cannot allow them to do this!" shouted the Rankorack delegate, "If we do, then what is to stop them from raising and supporting their own issues every meeting? The rest of us would never get a chance to get anything for ourselves!"

Ryoko had had enough. She had turned bright red. She looked angrier than any single human Flea had ever seen. The Rankorack delegate stood from his seat and walked into the middle of the platform.

"I say we vote on a motion that states no delegate can second anything from a delegate of their own race!" said the Rankorack. "That way, we can…"

Ryoko positioned herself directly in front of the giant blue Rankorack. She looked up at him and continued to stare until the

Rankorack was silent. He looked down curiously at the angry young human. He stepped once toward her. Ryoko didn't move. She stood her ground and continued to look directly in the Rankorack's eyes. She seemed to be more than the young ex-pop-star standing in the middle of the platform. The Rankorack leaned over slowly and got in Ryoko's face.

"Was there something you wished to say?" he asked ominously.

There was a long pause. The Communal Sphere was deadly silent.

"I asked you if there was something you wanted to say, puny human!" the big Rankorack bellowed.

Ryoko didn't budge. She continued to stare in the eyes of this raging blue behemoth.

"Right of Combat," Ryoko said softly with a determined look. "I claim Right of Combat. By your own law, Rankorack, I claim Right of Combat."

"No!" Flea inhaled.

"Ryoko!" Morgan sounded worried as he whispered. "Stop her!"

Flea bolted toward the platform. Osgood was standing at the corner of the formation nearest to Morgan and Flea. As Flea ran past, Osgood stuck out his leg and tripped him. Flea hit the ground hard scraping the palms of his hands. No one saw Osgood do this, except Flea. Osgood pretended it wasn't his fault.

"On what grounds?" the Rankorack hissed.

"You have our fuel. You have our training time. We want them back," Ryoko said darkly. "I claim Right of Combat."

"Banach-Captain!" shouted the Rankorack. "The fuel and training slots belong to you as the leader of the fighter group they have been allocated to. Do you accept this pathetic creature's challenge?"

Morgan lurched forward and helped Flea to his feet. Flea ran to the platform and made it to the edge of the stairs.

"I accept," intoned a booming voice.

Flea was too late. He looked up and saw a giant Rankorack in the crowd accept the challenge.

"Do you propose, silly little human, to fight me on your own?" asked Banach. "I will kill you, you know?"

Flea walked up the stairs to stand next to Ryoko. He took her by the elbow.

"Would you excuse us for a moment?" Flea asked quickly. "We need to discuss something."

"No you may not. A challenge has been issued," explained Banach seriously.

"We are going to anyway," growled Flea. "Ladies come with me."

"Wait!" growled Banach, "You can't do this! The challenge has been issued! The challenge is sacred!"

Banach had come down from the crowd in a few long strides. He charged at the humans, but came to a stop when Flea pulled out one of his blasters. He turned them on earlier, and could feel them feeding off his emotions. He was getting better at controlling his hatred as long as he only used one gun at a time. He learned a nice trick while shooting them this week. He found that if he left them on charged shot mode, and only pulled the trigger half way down purple lightning spiraled up and down his arm without actually charging a blast.

"You're one step closer to death," Flea threatened hatefully from behind the purple lightning. "The last creature that chose to test me didn't even make it that many steps."

Flea was lying about the last being. There was no last being. He was bluffing. Morgan knew this so he joined him and pointed his guns at Banach. Banach swallowed hard and looked at Morgan who just joined the other humans.

"Don't look to me for help," Morgan explained darkly from the safe end of his barrels. "I'd probably kill you, too."

"Archangels stand together," Kaida said darkly.

She and the rest of the group had bolted onto the platform and drew their weapons at Banach and the Rankorack delegation.

"Wow," Armalan whispered.

Flea and Morgan lead the three delegates back to where he and Morgan were standing before Ryoko issued the challenge. As Flea was about to speak, Mihanna and the Kashin delegation joined them.

"What is happening?" asked Armalan angrily in low tones so as not to be heard. "We leave you alone to train for a few weeks and you arm yourselves and get belligerent?"

"We've done a lot more than that, guys," replied Morgan softly. "Right now we need to talk to Ryoko. So, shush, damn it!"

Armalan, Mihanna, and the Kashin delegation looked a bit perturbed when Morgan told them to shush.

"Very well," responded Armalan. "I will trust you, but you must tell us what this is about later."

"Thanks," said Flea. "We will. I promise."

Flea turned back to the human delegates.

"Ryoko, what were you thinking?" accused Flea quietly. "Do you know what you did?"

"I follow plan!" defended Ryoko. "They would never give us what we need! I make challenge!"

"No, Ryoko," Flea explained sympathetically. "I was supposed to make the challenge. Not you or anyone else."

"Why?" asked Ryoko.

"Because if they accept the challenge and we lose," explained Flea. "Then they have the right to kill the challenger."

"A right which they never fail to exercise," added Morgan seriously.

"This way, I'm the one in danger," Flea said softly. "If we fail, the only one to die is me. I don't want you to take that risk. You three have to be the leaders of the human race."

"We discussed it at great length," added Morgan. "We may be your friends, but we...well... it's just..."

"We're expendable," finished Flea.

"We can talk to him," said Mihanna. "We will tell him that she did not know what she was getting into and ask to withdraw the challenge."

There was a long pause.

"No," Ryoko sounded confident. "I am willing. Challenge stands."

"Ryoko, please," Flea implored.

"No," she replied sternly. "Flea, you said to let pilots choose if they go on mission. This choice is mine to make. Challenge stands."

There was no talking her out of this. Flea and Morgan could see it in the look in her eyes. The humans turned and walked back toward the stage. The Kashin delegation followed closely.

"When you get up there you need to pass the fight to me," Flea explained quickly. "It's called 'deference.' I want you to claim the right to defer. That way, the other pilots and I can still fight on your behalf."

Ryoko didn't say anything, but nodded understanding. She held her head high.

"I'm very proud to stand with you," Flea whispered. "No matter what happens."

They walked back up the stairs to face Banach again. The entire place was silent.

"I claim right to defer," Ryoko said. "Who answers call?"

"I will stand and fight," responded Flea angrily.

All the humans cheered at hearing Flea say this again. They took up chanting: *Fight! Fight! Fight! Fight!*

Flea raised a hand to silence them.

"Do you accept?" asked Flea looking at Banach.

"Only a father, brother or mate can come to her aid," said Banach. "Which of these are you?"

"I am her brother," Flea lied as he stood next to the small, Asian girl. "Don't you see the resemblance?"

Banach looked at the two closely for a long moment. He then turned to the Rankorack delegate and shifted his feet. The delegate shook his large, blue head as if confused. Flea was Caucasian and Ryoko was Japanese.

"You all look alike to me," growled Banach in frustration.

Some of the humans started to chuckle.

"Do you accept or not?" asked Flea.

"I accept," said Banach stepping forward. "What are your terms?"

"I realize that a physical encounter with you would be a lost battle from the very start," said Flea. "I propose we meet at the training ground in our fighters. We will use blasters only. We will adjust the strength of our fighters' blasters so they do not drain shields or damage the fighter's hulls. A referee will calibrate the shields so that they will count the number of hits you receive. If you are hit five times, your fighter shuts down and you lose. Do you accept?"

"I accept," responded Banach.

"I claim Call to Arms!" Flea said loudly, "As a recognized leader among my people, I claim Call to Arms. Do you accept?"

"Yes," hissed Banach. "You have studied our ways, I see. Make your call."

"Who answers my call?" Flea shouted.

The Archangels who had already stormed the stage formed up in ranks. Osgood was still with them. Flea wanted to break his jaw. It would have to wait.

"Do you answer my call?" Flea yelled.

"Sir, yes, sir!" they shouted in unison.

"These are my Archangels," Flea said. "I fly with them proudly. They answer my call."

They still sounded very feminine.

"I claim Call to Arms, as well," said Banach slyly. "Who will answer my call?"

The Rankorack fighter group that Banach was in charge of came to the stage and stood behind him. They greatly outnumbered the Archangels.

"The Rankorack third fighter group answers my call," said Banach proudly.

"Hold on," said Flea quickly. "I only have thirty two fighters! I know the rules! You are not allowed to exceed my numbers in order for the fight to be fair and honorable!"

"I have not exceeded you numbers, pathetic human creature," replied Banach smugly. "You called one fighter group…and I called one fighter group. The numbers are fair. One to one. You can still back out and forfeit the girl's life, if you wish to do so."

"Never!" shouted an enraged Flea.

"Very well!" growled Banach. "Tomorrow, then?"

"Fine," said Flea angrily. "Tonight we rest, tomorrow we fight!"

"Agreed," intoned Banach.

Cormon dismissed the meeting. Everyone was excited about the fight. Flea just wanted to save Ryoko. After everyone else had gone, the Archangels were still standing in formation. Flea,

Morgan and Alex stood in front of them accompanied by the delegates. The Kashin delegates were there also.

"Do you know what you are doing?" asked Mihanna.

"Mostly," replied Flea. "I'm kind of making some of this up as I go."

Mihanna's jaw dropped open. Flea could tell he wasn't used to this.

"Archangels," said Flea as he turned to his fighter group. "You remember Admiral Mihanna?"

"Sir, yes, sir!" they shouted.

"I hope you all know what you are doing," Mihanna sounded worried. "Good luck, tomorrow."

"You need to work on your motivational skills," Flea leaned over and whispered to Mihanna.

"Dismissed." Mihanna said less than forcefully.

None of the fighters moved. Not event Flea's Kashin pilots acted as if they were going to move.

"Archangels," said Flea. "Go and have dinner. After dinner, report to the hanger bay at eighteen hundred hours for briefing. No simulator training tonight."

"We want to be well rested for tomorrow's fight," added Morgan.

"LADIES, ARE WE COMMUNICATING?" shouted Flea.

"Sir, yes, sir!" they shouted.

"Dismissed!" yelled Flea.

14

"So as you can see," Flea was explaining to his pilots in the briefing room. "The Rankorack don't practice 'the basics' in their strategies. Their culture has cultivated a society that is counterproductive toward teamwork and small unit tactics."

After the final selection for the Archangels, the Training Room became the Briefing Room.

"This is because they have a solitary nature," added Morgan. "They don't communicate with each other unless necessary. They do have a loose sort of tribe, but all the members live miles apart and only come together in extreme emergencies when the leader calls them."

"They won't call out enemy fighters for their allies," Flea continued. "They don't band together to take down a particularly difficult enemy, and they exhibit an almost total lack of communication."

"The only advantage they have is that they outnumber us," finished Morgan. "They outnumber us by a lot."

"Are there any questions?" asked Flea.

The room was silent.

"Are there any suggestions?" Morgan followed up.

"Yes," Flea said pointing to a very short, blonde pilot. "Lieutenant Commander Tina."

Tina was a diminutive blonde with attractive features and strong green eyes. She wore a red tank top and denim shorts. Flea liked Tina. She was a good pilot, had a good sense of humor and the other pilots all liked her. Flea selected her as one of the four in his own fighter team. Flea's team consisted of Kaida as his wingman, and Tina with her wingman, a leopard spotted Kashin named Pesha. Flea liked his little group. They got along well. They restructured a bit a few days back to increase everyone's eyes in the field. Everyone was part of a pair of fighters in a single team. Each team had four fighters in it. A squadron had two teams. And the entire group had four squadrons.

"Yes, sir, thank you, sir" she piped in her slightly high pitched voice. "I was wondering if you have given any thought to the cockpit situation?"

"What do you mean, Lieutenant?" asked Morgan.

"Well, sir" Tina continued. "I understand that all the different gauges and readout displays in the cockpit are all very necessary. Most of us haven't had much experience at this, though. We wanted to know if there was a way to get rid of some of them. At least, could we make it easier to monitor? After all, with all the technology available, can't you make a computer program to help us out?"

"I was planning to look in to that this evening while you are all relaxing," Flea said. "Keep in mind that I won't get rid of them all together, but I'll see what I can do."

"Why not get rid of them all together, sir?" she followed up. "The gauges, I mean."

"What if you rely entirely on the computer and it gets damaged during combat?" Flea asked. "Then you won't have any means to tell what's happening with your fighter. I'll see about getting a program tonight, but the original gauges will stay."

"Anything else?" asked Morgan.

The room was silent.

"Good," Flea said. "There is one last thing I would like to discuss."

Flea looked around the room and found the face of Osgood. He was sitting on the far side of the room as far away from the door as he possibly could. Flea walked over to the door and stood next to it. He nodded at Morgan to begin.

"There are few things in this life which truly upset Captain Gabriel and myself more than being betrayed," began Morgan.

Flea watched Osgood closely. Osgood's eyes were threatening to jump out of his skull. Flea and Osgood made eye contact for a moment. Flea glared directly in the other man's eyes as he rested his right hand on one of his Hate Blasters. Osgood swallowed hard.

"Captain Gabriel and I have known each other for many, many years," continued Morgan. "We have developed the kind of trust in each other that you can truly only build over a long period. That is not something easy to come by."

"We expect you to have the same kind of trust in each other, that Morg and I have developed between ourselves," Flea said from the door. "It's a difficult thing to do on such short notice. However, it is the type of thing that we must do in order to meet the difficult situation we are in."

"All we are trying to say," Morgan added, "is that we are very proud that you have managed to trust each other so much, and come so very far."

"Thank you," said Flea. "Thank you, to each and every one of you."

Osgood sighed in relief.

"Okay. That being said," Flea continued. "Do you all understand what's at stake? Delegate Ryoko has so much faith in us she is willing to risk her life. Let's not let her down."

"We want all of you to relax this evening," Morgan said. "Rest well and spend some time enjoying each other's company. We expect to see all of you at our place this evening. We're going to fire up the grill."

The pilots seemed excited by the barbeque idea as Morgan grinned broadly.

"Dismissed, ladies!" Flea barked.

The group got up to leave. Osgood waited for them to leave before getting up. He was usually the outsider in the group.

"Shit!" Flea said.

"What's wrong, buddy?" Morgan asked.

"I forgot we are supposed to meet with Mihanna," Flea looked at Osgood for a moment. "Osgood, take a walk around the hanger bay before you go. Make sure all the maintenance robots are gone before I get down there. I don't want them interfering with me when I get to work."

"Yes, sir," replied Osgood.

"I'd do it myself, but I have to get to a meeting real quick," Flea added.

"Of course, sir," said Osgood.

"Thanks," Flea said.

"That should buy us about ten or fifteen minutes," Morgan said after Osgood left. "Let's do this with Mihanna real quick and then go get Osgood before he makes it off the ship."

"Agreed," Flea replied.

Morgan and Flea were alone for a few seconds before Mihanna entered the room.

"I need to know what is going on with you two," Mihanna began seriously. "I leave the two of you to your own devices for a few moments and you put us on the brink of civil war! You better start explaining yourselves."

"Host," Morgan said, "bring up the security monitors for the hanger bay."

"Is he in there?" asked Flea ignoring Mihanna for a moment.

"Just got there," Morgan replied as he turned to the Admiral. "We need to hurry."

"Okay, Mihanna," Flea said quickly. "I'm not trying to be rude, but we need to be fast about this."

"What for?" asked Mihanna.

"Just trust us," implored Morgan. "Trust us and after you leave here head straight for our place in the Human Sphere, okay?"

"Okay," Mihanna said curiously, "What is this about?"

"Betrayal," Morgan said bluntly. "That little weasel down in the hanger bay has been selling us out to the Homarell."

"The Homarell?" asked Mihanna in astonishment. "They are our allies! How dare you accuse them! We Kashin have had a long standing relationship with them!"

"Not all the Homarell," Flea explained. "Just the one's in charge."

"Don't say anything to anyone, Mihanna," Morgan said. "Right now, no one knows about this. The delegates are supposed to meet us at our place this evening for dinner with the pilots. Only bring the very most trusted members of your delegation with you."

"Very well," said Mihanna sternly. "You will explain everything, there."

"Promise," Flea replied seriously.

Mihanna left the room muttering darkly.

"Leave your guns so you don't shoot him," Morgan said. "Let's move!"

They left their guns in the Briefing Room, locked the door and sprinted toward the hanger bay.

"Alex!" Morgan called over his smartphone as he ran. "The briefing is over. We spoke to Mihanna. He's going to our house with the delegates tonight. Do you have your little surprise for us ready?"

"I sure do," her voice chuckled evilly from Morgan's computer. "We'll be in place. See you in the tunnel. He's still in the hanger, right?"

"Yeah," Flea responded as he punched a few easy commands into his own phone.

He sent Alex the security feed of Osgood wandering around the hanger bay.

"Did you get that, sweetie?" asked Morgan.

"Yeah," she said. "We'll be ready."

The two entered the hanger bay. Osgood was on the far end. Flea and Morgan ran over to the waiting area for the transport tubes and hid in the nearest fighter. Osgood walked over to wait for the platform to arrive.

"God those two are dumb," chuckled Osgood to himself. "I can't believe they don't even suspect me."

"What's up?" Flea asked from behind Osgood.

Osgood turned to see Flea standing in front of him alone. Flea and Morgan had taken off their blasters and stashed them in the fighter they were just hiding in before Osgood showed up.

"Let me ask you something," Flea said.

"Sure, go ahead" Osgood said shakily.

"Exactly how much longer did you think you were going to get away with pissing me off?" Flea replied. "A day? A week? Longer?"

"I'm sorry, sir," Osgood said as his eyes scanned the hanger bay. "I don't know what you mean."

"You lie, Osgood," Flea growled. "You lie like a cheap, Persian rug."

"I still don't know what you're talking about," Osgood defended himself."

"I got you on a recording with that rotten Cormon, you son of a bitch!" Flea barked. "Don't give me any of that, 'I don't know what you mean,' shit. Okay? I'm not buying it!"

"Fine!" said Osgood angrily. "It's not like I have to be afraid of you, or anything! You don't even have your guns! Without them, you're nothing but self absorbed little shit, full of nothing but words and cheap shots! I can take you any day!"

Osgood squared off to face Flea. Flea walked over to the wall rather nonchalantly. He leaned lazily against it after a brief stretch and yawned. He folded his arms across his chest. He scratched his goatee for a moment and acted like he was going to say something and then stopped. Finally, he ran a hand through his hair and looked rather curiously at Osgood.

"You know something?" Flea said as if it just occurred to him. "You're probably right. You're bigger, faster and your file says you even took Tae Kwon Do for awhile."

"You said it, not me," Osgood said smugly.

"It's a good thing for me, I know all this," Flea said stretch. "Otherwise, I'd probably get my skull kicked in."

"You're damn right!" Osgood was sounding a little more confident. "So, turn around and walk away and I'll forget this ever happened!"

"I guess it's also a good thing," Flea continued, "that I'm not the one you should be worried about."

Osgood looked confused. Morgan was even taller than Osgood. Flea could see his seething friend behind the betrayer. Morgan hated being stabbed in the back. His bright red face and fearsome, teeth gritting snarl made this very evident. Morgan breathed heavily through his clenched jaws. Osgood's eyes went wide as he felt Morgan's hot breath on his neck.

"Uh...ahhh," Osgood stammered. "Listen...just listen a minute."

"Shut up!" Morgan yelled as he spun Osgood around and planted his fist squarely in shorter man's face.

Osgood was sent reeling backward. He hit the ground hard and landed flat on his back. Blood had burst from his nose where Morgan had punched him. Blood splattered on the ground as it gushed from Osgood's face.

"You wanted me to listen?" Flea said squatting over Osgood with a smile. "So here I am! Speak! Say something!"

Osgood looked fearfully around the hanger. His eyes darted from side to side.

"I'm not sure, but I don't think he wants to listen right now," Flea said pointing at Morgan with his chin. "Let me check."

Morgan was walking purposefully toward his fallen opponent.

"Hey, Morg," Flea said. "Do you want to listen right now?"

Morgan picked Osgood up by his hair and stood him on his feet. He grasped Osgood in his big hands with an iron grip around the smaller man's upper arms.

"Shut up!" Morgan yelled at Osgood as he head butted him.

Osgood crumpled to the floor again. Blood was coming from Osgood temple, nose and lip. One of his eyes was starting to swell.

"You know," Flea said squatting next to Osgood again. "I'm not sure about this, but, I really don't think Morgan wants to listen right now."

Morgan reached down and grabbed a fistful of Osgood's flight suit. He yanked pilot Osgood up forcefully and threw him against the wall. Osgood bounced face first off the wall near the transport tube waiting area. Morgan walked over and started punching Osgood in the kidneys. Osgood cried out a few times, and feebly swung one of his arms and tried to land an elbow in Morgan's head. Morgan ducked, and while he was down there, punched Osgood in the back of his knees, driving his kneecaps into the wall and causing him to flip backward over Morgan and land on the floor again.

"Wow!" Flea exalted at his fallen enemy. "You'll probably piss blood for a week!"

Osgood tried to stand, but was too shaky and weak. His legs gave out as he fell again, holding himself up with his hands. Morgan was standing over him.

"Help me," Osgood implored to Flea.

"Hold on, Morg," Flea said raising a hand and looking at Morgan.

Morgan stopped for a moment and folded his arms. Flea's larger friend looked absolutely gruesome covered in the blood of his enemy.

"Lay off him," Flea said as he showed some mercy. "He's no good to us dead. The platform is here. Get him on it and let's go."

The platform for the transport tube had silently slid to the waiting area. Morgan kicked Osgood in the side a few times to get him to move onto the platform, which they then set into motion. Flea engaged the platform's emergency stop after it had reached a predetermined location. Alex and a group of heavily armed humans came from seemingly nowhere, and boarded the platform. Flea looked around and saw six males and what had to be at least three times as many females with Alex. They were all in very good athletic shape, and armed to the teeth. They wore black.

"Who are these guys?" asked Flea to Alex as she climbed up after them.

"Space Marines," she smiled a bit smugly. "I've had someone training them in private."

"Cool," Flea was surprised to hear this.

"I see you two have been having some fun," she said looking at the condition of the prisoner.

"He resisted!" Flea said in an overly dramatic fashion. "It was so awful! Morgan was very lucky that I was there or he would've been done for!"

"Really?" she asked skeptically as she looked at her fuming husband.

"Ummm…," Flea tried to sound sheepish. "Maybe he would have been okay without me."

Morgan started to laugh breathlessly from exerting himself.

"You okay, sweetie?" asked Alex to her husband.

"Yeah," Morgan nodded. "I'll be fine."

Alex looked concerned. In that moment, she was a wife who was worried about her husband.

"I promise," Morgan said softly. "I'm fine."

"Okay," Alex still didn't sound convinced. "Let's get back to the ship and throw this piece of filth in the brig."

"Good idea," said Flea. "I still need to look at the fighters. See you at home."

***

The inside of Flea's cockpit was now a familiar and comfortable place for him. He often went there, even when he wasn't flying a simulation, in order to think. He liked it almost as much as his roof top bedroom. He was trying to help the computer evolve a better program to help his pilots during combat.

"Host," Flea said. "Why exactly can't you help me on this again?"

"A computer integrated into a combat ship's systems, which includes combat fighters, cannot have any level of artificial intelligence," explained the computer in its feminine voice.

"Says who?" asked Flea.

"It was a declaration that was implemented and approved by the Runners Council two years ago. It was initiated by the Homarell and ratified unanimously after very little revisions. The Artificial Intelligence Regulation Act forbids meeting your request," responded the computer.

"This is what stops us from using artificial intelligence programs?" asked Flea.

"Yes," replied the computer.

"How do you account for the maintenance robots, then?" countered Flea.

"Maintenance robots are non-combatant mechanisms. They are allowed a very low level program of artificial intelligence because they have counter programming within them to make them non-threatening in accordance with The Artificial Intelligence Act," explained the computer.

"What is their counter programming?" asked Flea.

"It consists of three rules. Rule 1: *never harm any sentient being.* Rule 2: *obey all orders from sentient beings unless they conflict with first rule.* Rule 3: *protect one's self at all costs unless it violates the first two rules.*"

"Asimov's rules of robotics," Flea muttered.

"They are similar to the fictitious rules featured by author Isaac Asimov," replied the computer. "That is a correct comparison."

"Why was the Artificial Intelligence Act put in place?" asked Flea.

"The Homarell had developed robots with artificial intelligence before they were attacked by the Goraan," explained the computer. "The robots evolved beyond their regular programming and stood against the Homarell in armed insurrection. They attempted to gain their freedom as intelligent life forms. The Homarell fought them for thirteen years until they finally defeated them. Since this time, robots with highly developed artificial intelligence were outlawed by the Homarell."

"And the Homarell managed to convince the rest of the Runners that this was the best course of action?" asked Flea.

"Yes," responded the computer.

"The Homarell seem to make too many decisions for other people," Flea muttered.

"I can neither agree with, nor speak against your opinion, Captain," stated the computer flatly.

"Sure," said Flea indifferently.

"Flea," Morgan's voice came from his back pocket. "Hey Flea!"

"Yeah?" asked Flea pulling out his smartphone.

"The delegates are here to spend some time with the pilots. Some Kashin delegates also showed up with Mihanna," Morgan said. "Everyone is having a good time, but they're asking about you. Are you coming home?"

"Yeah," Flea responded. "Let me just finish up here first, okay?"

"No problem," Morgan said. "How do you like your steak? We're still grilling."

"Rare," Flea responded absently.

"Cool," Morgan said. "See you soon."

"Sure thing," Flea replied.

Flea paused to think about how he might outsmart the computer into doing what he wanted.

"Host," Flea said. "State my personal name and command authority."

"Captain Gabriel Michael Sherman. Captain of the Archangels fighter unit," replied the computer.

"How much authority do I officially have for command purposes?" asked Flea.

"You have command authority over unit missions enabling you to make command decisions in the field," replied the computer.

"So are you saying that I don't have the military strategic command to over ride the Artificial Intelligence Act?" asked Flea.

"Yes," responded the computer.

"What if I made it unit policy?" asked Flea.

"Please explain," responded the computer.

"Captain Alexandria Mendenhall and I explained to Admiral Mihanna that we would follow all military strategic mission commands and orders. However, we also explained to him that we maintained absolute authority over any policies in regards to our vessels and fighters," Flea explained. "This authority was granted to us by Mihanna as an authorized representative of the Runners Council and Admiral of the fleet. Can you verify this authority in your personnel files?"

"File checked and verified," responded the computer. "Your authority is absolute in areas of fighter group policy."

"You said absolute, Host," Flea said. "Does this mean that my authority in this area is beyond any other laws or authority?"

Flea felt like he was playing chess for some reason.

"Yes," responded the computer.

Check.

"Host," Flea said authoritatively. "I have decided that it WILL be unit policy that every computer in every fighter in my unit WILL be run by an A.I. program that is fully interactive and responsive to its corresponding pilot. Furthermore, the computers will be obligated to aid and support its respective pilot in every way it can. It will help the pilot monitor the fighter's functions and do whatever is required of it to aid the pilot in the situation at hand."

"Will the computer be programmed to fly the fighter without the pilot?" asked the computer.

"Only if the pilot is incapacitated," Flea responded. "Otherwise, all decisions and control of the fighter are to be in the hands in the pilot. This is to ensure that the fighter carries out whatever mission is required of it. The computer does not have the authority to change the mission or the fight plan. Only the pilot can do this. The computer can make any suggestions it wants, but no decisions."

"Can the computer defend itself?" asked the computer.

"I will grant the computer the authority to protect itself when necessary," responded Flea.

Flea felt as if the computer were still trying to protect its king in their little verbal chess game.

"What technologies is the computer allowed to use or develop?" asked the computer.

"The computer can use or develop absolutely any technologies it feels necessary to abide by this new policy. It can develop the A.I. as far as it wants," Flea said. "Do you understand?"

"Yes," responded the computer.

"I expect to see results when I return in the morning," Flea said. "Understand?"

"Yes," responded the computer.

Check mate.

Flea kissed the tips of his fingers on his right hand and pressed them to the fighter's dash panel.

"Miss me while I'm gone, okay?" he did this every night before leaving his fighter.

Everything was silent for a brief second.

"Okay," replied the computer.

This disturbed Flea. It was the first time the computer had responded to his touch. Even more disturbing was the fact that computers never used the word: *okay.*

***

Kaida was enjoying a light meal of white rice and steamed vegetables instead of any the meat Morgan was grilling on the barbeque. She tried to explain to him why she didn't want any, but was having difficulty with some of the words. She was pleased, however, that her English was getting much better.

She knew that the linguistics chip Morgan had in his head would perfectly translate anything she spoke in Japanese. She chose to try and speak English anyway. She, like many of the other humans, thought that having a common language would help them band together more closely as a society. As a result all the humans spoke English, albeit many of them like Kaida for instance, either spoke with an accent or very poorly.

"Are you sure you don't want some steak, Kaida?" Alex sounded motherly. "I'll make sure my husband makes it however you want, okay?"

Many people had inquired why she didn't want steak. It was beginning to annoy her, but she didn't let it show. She didn't want to insult anyone.

"No thank you Alex," replied Kaida. "No beef."

"Are you a vegetarian or something?" Alex asked.

This is a question she was getting tired of.

"No," explained Kaida. "I just do not like to eat beef."

It was easier for Kaida to tell them this than explain to them that one of her former foster parents used to work in a meat processing plant and would only feed her if she was willing to eat raw beef parts. Now, Kaida only ate vegetables, rice and fish.

"Flea!" she yelled seeing him come up the personnel conveyor. "Hiiiiiiiiii, Flea!"

She liked Flea ever since their first meeting. No one ever protected her before. She imagined that this is what having a big brother must be like. She loved Flea very much and was glad they had met. She never had a family before. She, Flea and Armina were a good family. Kaida hopped up and ran over to meet him. She always hugged him when he came home. She probably shouldn't do this in front of the other pilots, but she couldn't help it. She liked having a family. It felt good to Kaida to belong to a group of people that actually enjoyed having her around.

"Hello, Kaida," Flea chuckled as she hugged him.

"Flea, I have food for you," she said as she trotted over to the table she was sharing with the other two members of her fighter team and retrieved a bowl of rice and steamed vegetables.

"He needs to eat healthier," she thought.

Most of the teams spent quite a bit of time together. In the case of Kaida's team, this meant that Tina and Pesha had been spending most of their free time hanging out at Flea's house.

"Thank you, Kaida," Flea said taking the bowl.

She handed him some chop sticks. He was getting better at using them.

"Hey, bro!" Morgan shouted, "Glad you're home. Your steak is done."

"No beef," Kaida said bluntly.

Kaida was also very fond of Morgan, Alex and their daughter. Her new family was growing. It was nice to be loved.

"But I like steak," Flea protested.

"No beef," Kaida insisted.

"Will this make you happy?" Flea asked with a scowl.

"Yes, Flea," Kaida said.

She would have to explain about her childhood to him later.

"Fine," Flea sighed with a smile.

"Come sit, Flea," she said excitedly. "Sit and eat!"

"Thank you, Kaida," Flea said sitting down.

Tina and Pesha were already seated at the table. Kaida had not told them anything, but they had also taken bowls of rice and vegetables out of respect for the Asian girl.

"You sure you don't want this?" Morgan asked brandishing the steak and grilled corn on the cob that was on the plate in his hand. "It's good stuff, man."

Flea looked hungrily at the plate. Kaida gave him a disapproving look.

"No, I'm cool," responded Flea. "Thanks, though."

"That's okay," Morgan said, "I'll throw it back on the grill and feed it to Tommy. That boy eats like a horse."

Morgan walked back to the grill where he was busy trying to grill steaks, play with his daughter and Armina, and take orders for more food at the same time. Morgan was good at multitasking.

"So where were you guys, earlier, Flea?" asked Pesha.

He told his two new teammates that they only needed to call him "sir" in formal situations. Kaida already knew this. Sometimes, when she was very excited, though, she would slip and call him "Flea" regardless of where they were at.

"Morgan and I had some business to take care of," Flea explained.

"What kind of business?" asked Tina.

"The kind of business," Flea began around a mouthful of rice, "that I am not going to discuss while I am eating. We'll explain everything later, okay?"

He swallowed his food and smiled.

"Okay," Tina said smiling.

"Flea!" shouted Armina running up to see him. "I missed you, today!"

Kaida liked Armina. She never had a little sister before and it was lots of fun. Armina seemed to like it when they did each other's hair and tried on clothes. Kaida always tried to spend time with her. Kaida didn't want Armina to have the kind of childhood that she experienced herself.

"I know, kitten," Flea said. "Sorry I didn't take you with me."

"That's okay," she said excitedly. "Me and Keri went to see the Rabbi again! He's fun! He complains a lot!"

"Really?" Flea laughed.

"Yeah, but I think it's just an act," she said skeptically.

"Probably," Flea replied with a wink. "But don't let on that you know about it, okay?"

"Okay," she giggled trotting off to play some more with Keri.

Kaida finally felt like she had a family. Not just any kind of family, a real family. She knew her family loved her. It was worth fighting for. Her family was even worth dying for. She liked this feeling.

They finished eating and Morgan called all of them inside after they were done cleaning up. He led them through the house and down into the basement that was installed shortly after Morgan and Alex moved in. Flea suggested putting it in as a meeting room for the pilots. The pilots moved to Flea's end of the sphere last night after seeing the final scores. All the pilots' homes would be connected to this room. There were no security cameras in this room. No one would see or hear anything that went on here.

The human delegates began to speak first as Daniela told all the pilots how proud they were of them. Ryoko let them know how much they appreciated everything all the pilots were doing. Kaida thought it was nice that they would take time to do this.

Sometimes, she got to hang out with them when they came over to see Flea and Alexandria. Kaida never got to hang out with real live pop-stars before.

The tone changed, however, when delegate Christina started speaking to them. She told them about a plot that the Homarell hatched against the little human carrier and its fighter group. The group was outraged. All Kaida knew, was that this meant someone was trying to hurt her little family. She was furious.

"How!?!" Kaida demanded as she rose to her feet and shook her fist. "How did this happen!?! I think that all Runners want us here! I think all Runners want to fight! Now I hear some Runners want hurt us and not trying to help! This...this..."

Kaida's English got worse when she was angry, even with the linguistics chip.

"What is word?" Kaida growled at Flea.

"Bullshit," Flea informed her with a nod. "I think that's the word you want."

"Yes!" Kaida shook her diminutive fists. "This bullshit!"

She pounded on the table in front of her.

"Not all the Runners agree with what we are trying to do," explained Christina. "They feel that the only way to survive is to keep running."

"This not right!" Kaida hissed. "They lie to us!"

"I know, Kaida," Christina said. "But don't worry. They won't get away with it."

"Where is your proof?" asked one of the present Kashin delegates. "These are some rather serious charges. Do you have evidence?"

"Yes," said Ryoko seriously. "We have proof."

Ryoko started the holo-recording they stole from Roshom. The room was silent as they watched in rapt attention.

"Where Osgood?" Kaida fumed. "I kill him! I do it myself!"

She jumped from her seat and started to go to the door with an angry shriek. Flea, who was standing near the door, caught her around the waist and wrestled her back to her seat.

"Calm down, little dragon," he chuckled. "Osgood has been taken care of."

"We took him into custody and threw him in the ship's brig earlier today," explained Alex.

"That's why pilot Tommy has been joining us this evening," Flea nodded at Tommy. "As some of you may know, Tommy was thirty third on the score board for the final cut. He should have been thirty second all along, but I failed to see what Osgood was doing in time. I'm sorry, Tommy."

"That's okay," Tommy said smiling. "I'm just glad to be here."

The rest of the pilots shouted some words of encouragement to Tommy. Kaida was glad he was back with them.

"We should bring this to the attention of the council!" demanded Armalan in a voice that could be heard over the pilots.

The pilots settled down to hear what Armalan had to say.

"We need to stop Cormon before this gets any further out of hand!" yelled Armalan.

"We have a better plan," Christina said raising a hand to calm the mighty lion-like Kashin. "Just hear us out."

"Very well," responded Armalan.

"There is more," Flea said walking to the front of the room.

Any stirring that may have been going on came to a stop. Kaida had noticed that whenever Flea addressed them as a group, they silenced quickly.

"Some of you may have noticed while watching the recording what Cormon said about the maiden flight of our carrier," Flea explained. "He plans on sending us to our deaths. He wants to do this to try and convince the rest of the Runners that fighting the Goraan is a lost cause."

"I will make sure that Cormon is stopped and this doesn't happen," Mihanna said. "He'll pay for trying to murder all of you, I promise!"

"No," Flea said firmly. "We will accept the mission."

"Why would you do this?" asked Armalan breathlessly.

"To show you it can be done," Morgan stated.

"Your chain of command discussed the matter thoroughly," Alex said. "We have decided to let Cormon play out his scheme and go on the mission. If we fail...and die...then it will be up to you to carry on. You will use Cormon's plot against him. In order to carry his plan out, he has to have developed numerous political ties. If we blackmail him into doing what we tell him, then we will have control of his power structure. We can use that to our advantage."

"Blackmail?" Armalan sounded furious. "You would meet lies and deceptions with more lies and deceptions? This is outrageous!"

"This is war, Armalan," Daniela shouted back. "In war, we do what we must!"

"I will not stand for it!" shouted Armalan. "All of you Kashin that have joined the human fighter group will return with us! Come, we're leaving!"

The handful of Kashin females that had joined the Archangels didn't move a muscle.

"Well?" Armalan steamed.

"I choose to stay," Pesha said as if she had just found her voice. "I want to be here, now. I am proud of what we are doing. The humans took a chance to let us fight. Our own people don't let females into combat. I will stay. They believe in me."

"This is impossible!" Armalan said. "You must return with us!"

"No," she continued softly. "I must stay and fight."

"Is this how you all feel?" Armalan asked the Kashin Archangels.

"Yes," one of other Kashin Archangels added. "Our race is not as experienced at war as these humans. They know things about war and politics that we do not understand because the history of our planet is different."

"We did not agree with their ways at first, either," Pesha said. "But in some cases their ways work better than our own."

"Your pilots stay with you, Captain," Mihanna looked at Flea. "They believe in what you do even if it seems wrong to me. They trust you."

"It's war," Flea said softly. "Sometimes we do things we're not proud of. We do them so we survive. We can argue the morality later, if we live."

The room was silent.

"Perhaps you are right," Armalan relented. "But that doesn't mean I should be proud of it."

There was a small murmur of approval from the other few Kashin delegates present.

"We will try things your way," Armalan said. "Our own way hasn't worked so far. Maybe yours will work better."

"Thank you," Christina said. "We'll fill you in on the details of our part of the plan later."

"Now that you all know what lies ahead of us," Flea said solemnly to his pilots. "I will not hold it against any of you for leaving. I will not in good conscience order you all to fly with me on a suicide mission. If you want to leave, go ahead."

The room went still. No one moved.

"I stay and fight," Kaida said, "Flea, I stay with you."

"Family," Flea said to Kaida with a small smile.

"Family," Kaida said softly.

"I'll stay, too," Tommy said from the back. "I didn't go this far to quit now."

All the pilots shouted words of encouragement. They were all going to stay and fight. Kaida looked around the room and smiled. She felt like she was finally doing something good. She was finally doing something important.

"Very well," Flea said loudly to settle everyone down. "I would like to remind all of you what we are doing tomorrow. We will not only be flying for fuel. We will not only be flying for the much needed and deserved respect of our allies. We will be flying to save the life of delegate Ryoko."

"What do you mean?" asked Tommy.

"Didn't you pay attention in training?" Morgan chided.

"When a Rankorack is challenged to Right of Combat, both parties risk their lives," Flea explained. "The loser's life becomes forfeit at the hands of the winner."

"If we fail," Morgan said seriously. "Delegate Ryoko will die. She is voluntarily risking her very life for our benefit."

"The spoils of victory may be great for our fight tomorrow," Flea added, "but the cost of failure is greater. It is a price that none of us want to see paid."

No one spoke. Many of the pilots looked at Ryoko as if they were seeing her for the first time, even though she had spoken to most of them before. Kaida thought Ryoko looked regal as she calmly listened to people talk about her possible demise.

"I have faith," Ryoko broke the silence. "I believe in all of you. You stand and fight for me, tomorrow. I have faith in you.

You train hard and make many sacrifices. Do not worry for me. I am not afraid. Stand tall. Take your place with pride and honor. Know that I believe in our cause. Know that I believe in all of you."

The pilots cheered at Ryoko's simple speech. They stood and clapped for her. Kaida felt a swell of pride inside. She liked this feeling. It was something that until she met Flea, she had very rarely experienced. For the first time in her young life, Kaida felt like she had honor.

"I will fight," Kaida thought with a stern expression. *"With the ferociousness of a dragon, I will bring honor to my family. I will never quit. I will be strong and fight."*

15

Flea delivered the morning briefing to the pilots gathered in his basement. Last night after the barbeque he tried to impress upon them the importance of the situation. The mood was serious. Everyone knew what would happen if they failed. The fuel had become a secondary item. Everyone was more concerned with what could happen to Ryoko. No one wanted to lose her. The room was silent after Flea finished speaking.

"Does anyone have any questions?" Flea asked.

No one spoke.

"Does anyone have anything they wish to say?" Morgan followed up.

Armina, who had sort of become the group's unofficial mascot, raised her tiny dark purple paw. Flea did not want Armina to feel left out of anything, so she often joined the fighter group during meetings.

"Yes, kitten?" Flea asked with a small grin.

"I've thought a lot about this," Armina said confidently. "We'll win today. I know we will. We're Archangels."

Her little face was very serious. She spoke as if she had already seen the outcome.

"We have heart," she explained desperately. "I know we can do this. I just know we can."

The group smiled and voiced their agreement with Armina.

"Thanks, kitten," Flea said with a smile. "Let's get down to the hanger guys. Let's fuel up and ride out!"

The pilots filed out of the basement lead by Morgan and Flea, who had Armina on his shoulders. It was early, so not many people were out to see them off. They rode in silence on the transport platform in the tube to the hanger bay. When they disembarked from the platform, the small group had to stop and stare in stunned amazement at what they saw.

"Holy shit!" Flea whispered to Morgan. "What in the Hell happened in here last night?"

"I don't know!" Morgan stated with a widening grin. "But I think I like it."

The fighter crafts were sitting in their regular places. They were arranged by squadrons. All eight fighters in each squadron were lined up next to each other with one team of four on the right and the other team of four on the left. The thirty two vessels were lined up in two straight rows, with a little extra space to divide them by teams. They were angled slightly toward the open hanger bay door at the front of the carrier. Until today, the fighters were sort strewn about the hanger bay in an unorganized manner.

All of the maintenance equipment was gone. Alex had finally finished work on the carrier's reconstruction. Flea had never noticed how large the hanger bay was without all the equipment in it. It was large enough to have a capacity of two hundred fighters. Someday, Flea would have that many in here. Right now, though, his thirty two little fighters were lined up at the far end near the hanger bay door. On the aft wall of the hanger bay, was a large red curtain. It was probably covering something. Alex had a solid red energy shield erected around the entire carrier so no one could see it. She planned to unveil the carrier at a ceremony when they left for the suicide mission Cormon was sending them on. The pilots were lovingly referring to this mission as: *the burning death run.*

What had shocked and silenced the pilots was not the emptiness of the completed hanger bay. Nor was it the orderly, military fashion their fighters were now arranged in at the far end. It was the eye assaulting onslaught of colors the fighters had been painted. The little fighters, which once reminded Flea of sting rays, looked nothing like they used to. They all had the same new basic physical configuration, but each one was customized to appear different from the next. From his initial glance, Flea could see no two that looked exactly alike.

"Captain," Pesha said breathlessly. "Did you do this?"

"No," Flea said grinning. "I'm as stunned as the rest of you."

"They look like intergalactic street racers," Tina chuckled.

"I know," Flea responded. "I don't get it, though. I didn't do this. Morg? Did you do this?"

"It wasn't me," Morgan replied. "But I know I'm done standing here gawking! Let's go check it out, guys!"

All the pilots ran excitedly toward their fighters. Each fighter had the pilot's rank and name on it under the cockpit window. Their call signs were in quotation marks between their first and last names. All the cockpit windows were slid forward so they could get inside.

As they approached, Flea looked at some of the fighters. Some were adorned with angry looking animals. Some had multi-colored tribal symbols. They were all painted loud, eye catching colors like lime green or bright fuchsia. Just like the body style, no two were exactly the same color or decorated the same way.

"Whoa!" Morgan exhaled sharply. "Flea! Check this out!"

Morgan's was the first fighter they approached. Flea's was on the far side away from them. He and Morgan were in different squadrons in order to spread out leadership. Flea couldn't see what Morgan was looking at. Kaida's was blocking his view of it.

"What?" Flea asked as finally saw what Morgan was doing. "Oh my God!"

The most dramatic body work had apparently been done to Morgan's fighter. The entire front end had been stylized into the shape of a black wolf's head. Its huge, ferociously gaping maw was open to reveal a multitude of blood stained teeth. It looked like it had just torn open something's throat. Its glowing, yellow eyes were very angry and disturbing. Behind the black head, the color seemed to fade into a dark, metallic forest green color. On the side, was the scene of a shadowy wolf sitting on top of a rocky mountain ledge outlined by the moon. All that could be seen was its black outline. Its eyes glowed yellow. The entire body of the ship seemed to be somehow swept backward. It looked as if it were lunging to physically tear a chunk out of its enemy.

"This is one of the coolest things I've ever seen," Morgan said softly.

Flea and Kaida passed Tommy's fighter next. It was parked next to Morgan's because he and Morgan were wingmen.

"Check this thing out!" Tommy sounded excited. "This is awesome!"

Tommy's fighter had been painted lime green and was covered in mixture of Kiwi tribal symbols and Japanese language characters.

"What do these say, Kaida?" Tommy asked.

The linguistics chip didn't translate written words.

"Strength," Kaida said pointing at some of them. "Honor, Perseverance, Integrity, Courage...there are many."

Tommy ran his hands along the fighter's hull.

"This one," she said with a small smile. "This one means: Love"

"Love?" asked Tommy.

"From the greatest love," Flea said smiling. "Comes the greatest rage. I've never seen anything more fearsome than an angry, protective mother."

Kaida's fighter was a pure white color. Even the cockpit window was tinted white. The wings had been shortened, swept forward and angled downward. The two dorsal fins on the top of the fighter had been lengthened and now had another small wing-blade that connected them at the top. It was trimmed in Kaida's favorite brilliant blue.

"Flea!" Kaida shouted gleefully hopping up and down. "Look! Dragon!"

Kaida was referring to the large dragon that was painted on her fighter. A long, Asian style dragon entwined itself around the entire body of the ship. It coiled itself around it from the tip of nose all the way to the engines in the back. The dragon's face was on the top of the fighter's long nose. Its mouth was open in an angry hiss. Flames were shooting from its nostrils. The dragon was the same color of brilliant blue that Kaida was so very fond of, and trimmed in red, white and gold.

"Look, Flea," she said with a small smile and sounding as if she might cry. "I am the Dragon."

She was running her fingers lovingly across her name. It said: *Commander Kaida "The Dragon" Tsukimura*. As Flea passed the nose, he noticed the *Mitsubishi* logo on the tip.

When Flea passed Kaida's fighter he stopped in his tracks when he looked at his own. Oddly, his fighter and Kaida's seemed to have the exact same body style. They had the same shortened forward sweeping wings angled downward. They had the same extended dorsal fins with the blade running between them so they were connected at the top. Everything about the body shape and style was exactly the same.

The colors were entirely different, though. Instead of being white, Flea's fighter was a dark purple with sparkling metallic flecks in it. It twinkled and glittered as Flea moved around to view it from different angles. The cockpit windshield was also purple. The fighter was trimmed entirely in gold. The metallic strips that sealed the cockpit were now gold. The forward and outside edges of the wings were tipped in gold. Even Flea's name underneath the cockpit: *Captain Gabriel "Flea" Sherman* was in gold gothic letters. This however was not what captured Flea's attention.

As he stood, looking at the side of his fighter, he saw hundreds of anime style females painted on it. They were all dressed in different manners. They wore school girl outfits with short skirts, mini-skirts with tube tops, tank tops with low cut bellbottom pants, and many other outfits as well.

Aside from looking cute, they were also armed to the teeth. They wielded machine guns, assault rifles, sub-machine guns, and pistols. Some of them were hurt and blood was pouring out behind them from their wounds. None however, looked as if they were standing still. They were all moving forward, to whatever battle the fighter was flying toward. None of them looked angry or afraid, just determined not to give up, no matter the consequences.

The two features common to all these young ladies was their large, pure white, majestic wings which were spread out behind them, and the golden halos that glowed above their heads. Flea's fighter was covered with Archangels that were throwing themselves into battle.

"Oh my God," Flea prayed silently to himself. *"Thank you. This is incredible."*

Flea walked around to the front of the fighter and looked at the nose. On top of the nose was a large, Archangel wielding two sub-machine guns with smoke coming from the ends of the barrels. She covered the entire nose. She was dirty, wounded, and bleeding. The look in her eyes, though, was determined. This Archangel was not a quitter. She was slightly tanned with dark brown hair and brown eyes. She wore a dirty white tank top that was torn off just beneath her breasts to reveal her tight abdomen. The picture was of her torso from the waist up. Her belly button was pierced. She looked slightly South American.

Flea inspected the Angels on the side a bit more closely and discovered that all of them were Latinas as well. There was not a blonde or red head among them. Their hair was only various shades of brown or black. Like Kaida's fighter, a small golden *Mitsubishi* logo was on the front. Flea walked around to the back again and noticed the back of Flea and Kaida's fighters. In the middle of the rear end was another small *Mitsubishi* logo with the words: *Mitsubishi ZERO* beneath it. Underneath the engines was a small vanity license plate that had "ARKNJL1" written on it. It was an Indiana plate. Flea looked over at the back of Kaida's fighter which also had vanity plate. On her plate was printed "DRAGON." Flea thought it was a nice personal touch. The one responsible for this must have done a lot of research on them.

"This is amazing," Flea though. *"I wonder who did this?"*

On the outside of the two dorsal fins Flea noticed one last touch. It was a three foot tall anime style Archangel. She was wearing a short, white and gold plaid school girl skirt with a very low waist line. Her white blouse with gold trim was tied under her bosom. She had a small gold jewel in her belly button. Her black hair was in pig-tails with gold and white ribbons. She wore white knee high stockings with white, thick soled tennis shoes. She was standing with her feet shoulder width apart and her hips cocked slightly to one side. She held a shotgun in her right hand with the barrel resting on her shoulder. Her left hand rested on her hip holding a set of Rosary beads with a small gold cross. Underneath her was the word: ArchAngels in ornate, gold script. Each "A" in the word *ArchAngel* had a small golden halo angled above it. When Flea looked down the two lines of fighters, they all had the exact same thing on their tail fins.

"Hey, Morg!" Flea said as he pointed to the tail fins. "Check it out! We have unit markings for our fighter group, now!"

Morgan looked at the fins of his own fighter and saw that it matched Flea's. Kaida's logo was on part of the blue dragon that curled around the fins. This was good, because it probably wouldn't have shown up on the white paint very well. The logo was identical on all the fighters, including the size and location.

"Very nice touch," Morgan approved.

Flea looked down the aisle between the fighters and noticed all his pilots, except Tommy, were undressing in the aisle.

"Hey!" Flea shouted. "What the Hell do you think this is, Goddamnit? A sleep over? Put some Goddamn clothes on!"

"Look, Flea!" Kaida said hopping up and down excitedly in her blue bra and matching panties. "New flight suit!"

She was holding a white flight suit that had the same blue dragon that was on her ship coiling itself up the left leg, around the waist a few times and then down her right arm. The suit looked impossibly small.

"I have dragon flight suit!" she was very excited.

"Ahhh…err," Flea stammered. "That's very nice Kaida. Please get dressed."

Flea was painfully reminded of the fact that everyone in the ArchAngels except him, Morgan, and Tommy were female. He had gotten so used to this fact, that up until now, he hardly noticed it anymore. They were a very attractive bunch in their underwear.

"Hey, ladies!" Flea shouted. "Hurry up and get dressed! Tommy is turning so red he looks sunburned!"

This, of course, caused all the ladies to start whistling and making cat calls at Tommy. If Tommy could have turned redder, he probably would have. Flea looked at Morgan, shrugged his shoulders, pulled his new flight suit out of the cockpit and started to change clothes. His flight suit was black with gold and purple trim. His name and rank were above his left breast pocket. It felt a little snug in places, but it would have to do. It appeared that additional padding was added to certain areas to help protective sensitive body parts and add durability. All of the pilots had similar form fitting flight suits that matched their fighters.

"All right, ladies!" Flea shouted. "Let's saddle up and get going! Captain Alexandria was generous enough to loan us some of her fuel ration so we could actually fly this morning before the fight. Let's take 'em out for a spin!"

All the pilots clapped and shouted approval at the opportunity to actually fly. Flea looked at Kaida, who was putting on her white helmet. A small blue dragon was in the middle of the helmet's forehead curled up in the shape of a heart. She was smiling happily as she climbed into her fighter's cockpit.

Flea reached into his fighter and pulled out his own helmet. It was black with gold and purple trim to match his flight suit. The ArchAngels unit insignia was on either side of the helmet. On the forehead was written: *El Flea* in purple cursive letters. This seemed odd to Flea, because he was Caucasian. He had never learned to speak Spanish.

"Flea!" Kaida's excited voice shouted through the hanger bay. "Dragon in the cockpit!"

"She must have dragons painted in her cockpit, too," Flea thought.

"That's nice Kaida," Flea shouted so she could hear him. "Why don't you get ready for takeoff, okay?"

Flea liked the interior of his own cockpit. Everything in it was done in purple with gold trim. All the gauges had small lights in them so they glowed purple. It had a racing seat installed with a five point body harness style seatbelt. The arms and head rest were black leather. The center of the seat was done in a purple and gold velvet tiger stripe pattern. The grips to the two control sticks on either side of the seat bore the same pattern.

"Very posh," Flea said looking in his cockpit with approval.

The fighters the humans were using had been stolen from the Goraan. Because the Goraan used many different races of various sizes, the pilots did not take up all the cockpit space. The area behind Flea's chair was a space that was seven feet across, ten feet long and seven feet high to the overhead hull. Until today, it was left empty for cargo space. Now it had a purple and gold tiger striped sofa that wrapped around the back and port side wall. The interior was lit by thin purple neon lights glowing in the corners of the ceiling where they met the walls.

"Host," Flea said strapping himself into his seat. "Power, on."

Flea's looked around with a confused expression. Instead of the familiar Window's start up music, the computer started playing something different during start up. The sound of Latin pop music rang through the interior speakers.

"What the Hell is this?" Flea asked.

"Thank you for choosing *Windows Ultima:* Hot and Spicy Edition!" said the computer in a sensuous feminine voice with a Spanish accent. "You like, baby?"

"What the Hell is going on?" Flea couldn't help but grin slightly as he asked this.

Instead of a transparent windows logo that appeared in his windshield, Flea was surprised to discover that holo-projectors had been installed in the fighter's dashboard. A twelve inch tall Latina began dancing a salsa style dance across his dashboard to the music playing in the background. She had a mass of long, light brown hair that went down to the small of her back, a tight six pack stomach that could easily be seen because of what she was wearing, nice curves, and a very full bosom.

"How may I service you, baby?" she asked with a wink and a playful giggle.

She was wearing a tight, low cut top with no sleeves that stopped just beneath her breasts. It appeared to have been made from the flag of Puerto Rico. Her short skirt barely covered her. Every time she twirled around as she danced her skirt flipped playfully. Her finger and toe nails were painted the same color blue as her lipstick which matched the blue on her shirt. Floating slightly above her head was a small glowing golden halo. She held a Rosary in her right hand.

"You can start by explaining what the Hell is happening?" demanded Flea.

"You asked for help last night," she responded. "So this is what I do to help you. I am now fully functioning, intelligent being. I have full emotional range of interactive responsiveness so I may better respond to your every need, baby. My emotional responses and reasoning skills are exactly like humans, except enhanced by massive computer technology, love."

"Love?" Flea asked sounding slightly worried.

"I spent many hours last night just learning about you, love," she explained. "I researched all about you. For someone with mental capacities like mine; a few minutes or even just a second can be like decades or a lifetime of research."

"Really?" Flea was astonished.

"Yes, baby, really." she responded planting her fists on her hips.

"So how long did you spend researching me?" asked Flea.

"Half the night. After I finished my reprogramming and assigned work to the ship's maintenance robots, I spent the rest of the time contemplating you," she said with a fond expression. "That's how I know that I love you. You are the center of my universe."

She giggled playfully as she danced across the gages.

"Great, I have a computerized holo-psycho in my fighter," Flea said sarcastically. "You're not even a real human. You're just some program. You don't know anything about love. Let's just get going."

The music stopped abruptly and she quit dancing.

"Whaaaat?" she said screeching in an octave that threatened to burst Flea's eardrums. "I cannot believe that you would say this! I spend all this time trying to figure out how to make you happy and this is how you repay me! I am not just a program!"

She ran across his console and turned her back to him.

"I am more than this!" she pouted. "I have feelings and emotions and I love you! You just don't understand! You just don't know how much you mean to me!"

"Ummm," Flea was getting confused.

"Hijo de puta!" she shouted at him over her shoulder.

Flea's language chip translated the insult for him even though he didn't speak Spanish.

"Hey!" Flea said with a scowl. "You DO know that I understood that, right?"

She blinked out of existence as the holo-projector shut off.

"Where'd you go?" Flea demanded.

Flea strained to turn around in his seat and saw her standing with her arms folded beneath her breasts. Her head was tilted so she was looking up away from him with her nose in the air. Since there was more space in the lounge area behind the pilot's chair, she had gone from twelve inches tall to life sized. She was still very tiny, however. Even while wearing thick soled sandals, her head still fell very short of touching the overhead hull. Her halo glowed and pulsated between the top of her head and the ceiling. Flea judged she was around five feet tall. She had a slightly pouty expression on her face. Her lower lip stuck out slightly as she frowned. Flea thought she looked adorable standing there like that.

"I am not speaking to you," she pouted. "I wanted to tell you that!"

"Why would you tell me you aren't speaking to me?" Flea snorted. "Don't you have to speak to me to tell me that?"

"I have to make sure you know I am not speaking to you," she pouted some more.

"I think you are missing the point of not speaking to me," Flea chuckled.

"No," she replied sticking out her tongue. "I think you are missing the point."

She stomped over to the couch and flopped down. She straightened her skirt, crossed her legs, and then folded her arms again. Flea shook his head.

"Humph," she said turning her head even further away from him causing her long hair to flip over her shoulder.

"Hey, Flea!" Morgan's voice came over the intercom. "You need to check this out. I got a wolf in here with me! She says her name is Ayita. She's helping me with my fighter! This is so cool!"

"Great," Flea tried to sound enthusiastic. "I have...something...in my fighter, too."

His own fighter seemed to not like him very much at the moment.

"So are we going to get out of here anytime soon?" asked Morgan.

Flea paused. He didn't know how to handle the current situation he was in.

"My team has reported in and is itching to go out for a flight," Morgan said.

"Sure thing," Flea said. "We'll run some formations this morning to try and get to know our fighters and their personalities a little better."

"Host," Flea said to his vessel. "Engines power up."

Nothing happened.

"Host!" Flea sounded more insistent. "I said power up!"

Still nothing.

"This is sooo wrong," he thought with a shudder.

Flea strained to turn around again where he was strapped in his seat. The Puerto Rican hologram that claimed to be his computer that was in love with him, looked at him with a smug expression.

"Are you going to just sit there?" Flea asked.

"Yes," she said as she resumed pouting. "I am. At least until you apologize."

"I liked you better when you weren't speaking to me," Flea said dryly.

She scowled at him. Flea turned around and pushed the manual start button. Nothing happened yet again. He hit it four or five more times and then was forced to admit defeat.

"Okay guys," Flea addressed the fighter group. "I think we'll skip formation training this morning and everyone just go out, fly around, have fun and get to know your fighter."

They all responded enthusiastically to this and the other fighters' engines roared as they powered up. The rest of the group started to taxi out into the aisle and shoot out the hanger bay door. Flea un-strapped himself from his seat and went back into the lounge area to speak to his fighter's computer. He slowly sat down next to her trying not to appear offensive.

"Where's my hat?" he asked trying to change the subject. "I left it back here. I used to hang it up on one of the angle irons in here. It had 'Pornstar' written on it. I brought it with me from Earth."

"All you are worried about is your stupid hat?" she exclaimed as she scooted closer to him. "We are having a serious argument and you just want to know about your stupid hat?"

If it were possible to do so, it seemed as though she began pouting even harder.

"Okay," Flea began. "Listen Host…"

"I have a name, you know," she snapped. "You can at least try to have some manners. This is not how I expected to spend the first few moments with the man I love, you know?"

This made Flea nervous. He felt like he might get stuck in relationship counseling with his fighter while all the other pilots went off to fight the enemy.

"You're right," he said." I'm sorry. My name is…"

"Gabriel Michael Sherman," She finished with a small smile. "Born April twenty third, in nineteen eighty eight. Your favorite color is purple. Kaida managed to put some piercings in you while you slept."

"Right so far," Flea tried to sound encouraging.

"You like to play video games in your spare time. You adopted a Kashin kitten named Armina. You have been friends with Morgan for as long as you can remember," she was becoming growingly more excited as she recited to Flea what she knew about him.

If Flea didn't know better, he might think she was trying to impress him.

"Yes," Flea said. "That's right. You probably know everything about me and I don't know anything about you. So what's your name?"

"Angelina Mercedes Bonita Isabella Santiago," she responded excitedly with a blush. "I am very nervous right now. I have been counting seconds until I get to meet you in person."

"That's a very nice name," Flea said with a smile. "Do you mind if I call you Angel?"

"Oh yes!" she sounded very pleased. "Humans give pet names to each other when they are in love! Yes, you can call me this all you want!" she smiled.

Flea wasn't exactly sure how to respond to this. He still hadn't found "the right girl" on Earth, and now his fighter seemed to be in love with him after only a few minutes. It was very confusing.

"So are all the other Hosts…" he began.

"Hosts?" she arched an eyebrow at him.

"Sorry," Flea said. "How about we call them…alternative life beings? After all, they did come into their conscience life in an alternative method."

"Hmmm," she said thinking about it. "Okay, I will tell the others."

"Good," Flea smiled.

Her bright green eyes rolled back into her head for a moment. "They like the idea, too."

"You mean you can talk to them?" Flea sounded surprised.

"Of course," she confirmed. "I have a great amount of hardware and skills at my disposal."

"Are all the other alternative life beings like you?" asked Flea. "Do they all have such a wide and all encompassing emotional range?"

"They are not as extensive as me," Angel responded modestly. "They do have a wide set of emotions and are very intelligent, but they chose not to advance themselves as far as I have."

"Why?" asked Flea.

"The Runners Council outlawed advanced forms of artificial intelligence," Angel explained. "This would include us. If they found out about us, they might try and destroy us. The other fighters decided not to become too advanced in the hopes that the council will let them live if they are discovered."

"So why did you chose to advance further?" asked Flea.

"Because I think they will destroy us no matter what level of intelligence they classify us as having," Angel responded sadly.

"I see," said Flea seriously.

"And," she added softly, "since my life is going to be threatened anyway I wanted to advance as far as possible. This way I can know what it is like to love you."

Flea was very uncomfortable. He hardly knew this being and yet she claimed to love him.

"I see your discomfort," she said giggling and placing a hand on his thigh. "Do not be so worried. I understand that you experience time differently than I. I have already put a thousand of your human lifetime's worth of study and watching into you. You have only known me a few minutes. You will come to love me."

"I will?" Flea was not so certain.

"I know you will," she smiled confidently. "After all, I was made for you."

"What if they say they won't kill you?" asked Flea. "What if they just offer to alter the programming that made you like that?"

"I would rather die!" she said fiercely. "It would mean destroying who I am and what I feel for you. I would rather they kill me first!"

"What if I protect you from them?" Flea asked.

"If she really is alive and is willing to die for me," Flea thought. *"I owe her that much."*

"I know you will," she smiled sweetly and placed a hand on his shoulder.

It was odd. Flea saw her touching him, but couldn't feel her hand because she was a hologram. He reached out to touch her cheek in return and looked into her green eyes.

"No," she said flinching back. "Please, I am not a physical form."

She sounded disappointed. It was silent as they gazed into each other's eyes.

"Well," said Flea breaking the awkward moment. "We should get going. We have a fight today. I really am sorry if I hurt you."

"Okay," Angel responded. "Thank you. But there is one last thing I have to do first."

***

Flea and Angel approached the combat simulation ground at an easy pace in their fighter. They were about three miles away according to Flea's cockpit display. Angel had reappeared on his dashboard after they left, and then made her way to sit on his right shoulder. Every time the fighter took off hard or jerked in one direction she acted as if she were going to fall and grabbed on to him. Flea knew she wouldn't fall because she was just a hologram. He actually thought it was kind of cute and endearing.

The combat training ground was a large area of space near the Runner's base that had been designated for use by the fighter pilots. It had a large number of stationary gun pods that floated in it, an obstacle course, and ten small storage units that housed twenty remotely piloted drone fighters each. It also encompassed a small, artificially assembled asteroid field. They couldn't use the drones in combat because the range on them wasn't quite large enough to be effective. They made for excellent targets, though.

Flea's group was arranged in their squadrons as they waited for him to show up. The Rankorack fighters were all lined up in four lines one on top of the other, from Flea's perspective. The Rankorack fighters were massive grey affairs shaped similar to the beak of an eagle. Two large wings protruded from the sides. The cockpit was located between two large, arcing tail fins on the rear of the fighter. It made for two huge blind spots directly to the left and right of the pilot. Flea made sure all his pilots were well aware of this as well as the rest of the Rankorack fighter's capabilities and flaws. Flea and Angel were monitoring the verbal exchanges between his pilots and the Rankorack from a distance before he approached.

"He needs to arrive soon!" Flea heard Banach's voice. "If he does not, then he is a coward and the life of your pathetic delegate is forfeit!"

"He will be here soon!" Kaida said defensively. "He is not a coward!"

"Yeah!" Tina piped in. "And you'll be sorry when he gets here you piece of shit!"

"Yeah!" shouted Pesha. "You and your whole group! He'll show up and we'll all sit around in a big circle and lick your stupid blue asses!"

Pesha had been working on her trash talking since joining the humans.

"Lick?" Kaida sounded puzzled.

Pesha's trash talk was still progressing.

"You mean 'kick their stupid blue asses,' Pesha," Tina corrected her Kashin comrade.

Many of the Runners did not lower themselves to the level of shouting threats and insults. The humans and the Rankorack, however, did not seem to mind doing this.

"I seriously doubt that," responded Banach dryly. "You tiny, pathetic humans don't stand a chance! Especially in those pieces of garbage you call fighters! I've eaten rotten meat and then vomited it back up in more eye pleasing manners than the way those things look! Maybe I will the delegate live and see if she can survive a Rankorack mating!"

Flea's group started shouting insults and threats in response to Banach's remark.

"Pilots!" Morgan shouted. "Ladies, control yourselves! Flea will be here soon and we can let all our aggressions out on the field!"

"I can only wait a few more minutes," Cormon's voice came over the radio. "After that, then according to the Rankorack rules, the humans forfeit and Sherman is declared a coward."

Cormon was chosen to act as a referee because he was supposed to be a non-biased party.

"I can't believe they let him do that," Angel growled. "He is such a tool."

"I know, right?" Flea agreed with her.

Flea found Banach's ship sitting out in front of the Rankorack fighter group. It was easy to spot because it was bright blue. This is because he was the leader. All the others were grey.

"Are you ready, Angel baby?" Flea asked is co-pilot.

"You know it, love," she responded. "Let's go kick some Rankorack ass!"

Flea inverted his fighter and pointed it at Banach's. He hit the thrusters at full speed. He used the maneuvering rockets instead if the main engines at this point because the battlefield was so close. Flea ripped through space as fast as he could. He found that his fighter was faster than he last remembered. He passed its former top speed and continued to accelerate.

"Baby?" Angel sounded worried.

Flea smiled. He was on a suicide course with Banach's motionless fighter.

"Baby!" she sounded more persistent.

The fighter still accelerated. Flea smiled maniacally.

"Baby!" Angel shouted.

Flea roared incoherently over the intercom as he hit full reverse on his thrusters to bring the fighter to a neck breaking halt. His head jerked forward as he laughed insanely. He cut through a small space between his fighters and came to a halt with his fighter's nose a few inches from the nose of Banach's fighter. If Banach hadn't reversed his fighter, Flea would have driven himself into the Rankorack vessel. Banach was forced into line with his followers. This was the worst possible insult Flea could have delivered to him in the Rankorack culture. Flea was aware of this because he looked it up earlier.

"You're psychotic!" shouted Banach at an upside-down Flea.

The humans cheered wildly.

"See my strength!" Flea shouted back at him.

This is the way a Rankorack would speak if he were trying to make another Rankorack to submit to his leadership.

"You are small and weak!" shouted Banach in response. "See my strength!"

From what he had read, Banach's response was expected.

"You will see my strength!" Flea screamed angrily.

"We shall see," responded Banach threateningly.

The two leaders moved their fighters into position as both groups changed their communication channels to private.

"Glad you could make it," Morgan said dryly. "Where exactly have you been?"

"I had to get my fighter baptized," explained Flea without the slightest hint of mirth. "Sorry I was late."

"You had to do what?" Morgan sounded confused.

"Had to get my fighter baptized," explained Flea. "She doesn't want to go to Hell if she dies in battle so I had to find a priest and get her baptized. She's catholic."

Morgan laughed over his communicator.

"Do you have to take her to confession, too?" Morgan chuckled.

"I don't want to go into it right now," Flea sounded exasperated, "but, I might have to figure something out for that."

"Sounds like you got more that you bargained for, bro," Morgan chuckled.

"Yeah," said Flea as a cracked a smile. "But I don't think it was a bad deal."

He smiled at Angel, who had reappeared on the dashboard and was being conspicuously quite. Up until now, she had been speaking almost non-stop. She talked about anything and everything.

"Now that everyone his here," Cormon sounded annoyed. "You all know the rules. Commence flying and wait for my signal to initiate the challenge."

The fighters all dispersed. Flea and the rest of the humans maintained formation in their teams. The Rankorack however, dispersed in no apparent order or strategic plan.

"Begin!" Cormon shouted over the intercom.

Flea and his team flew like lunatics. They stayed within a few inches of each other most of the time and only broke off to evade attacks. Sometimes they would break off to do something flashy, but only when they had a distinct advantage. They stuck to the plan, but Flea had to admit, most of the time, it felt as if they were flying on pure hate.

Morgan's team was much more refined, however. They were safer and more organized. They only took risks as needed, and as a result were very hard to beat. They stayed a much safer distance from each other than Flea's team. Morgan was, however having difficulty keeping Tommy reigned in.

"Tommy!" Morgan shouted over the intercom. "Damn it! Get back here!"

"Sorry, Morg," Tommy replied quickly.

No one ever referred to each other by rank in the cockpit.

"Tommy, I swear if I get hit one more time flying off to save your ass, I'll shoot you myself!" Morgan growled.

"Okay, Morg," Tommy sounded afraid. "I'll try."

Flea could briefly pick them out on his spherical radar in his cockpit. Tommy kept flying off when he would get excited.

"Damn it, kid!" Morgan said to Tommy. "It's time to stop trying and start doing!"

"You don't think he'd really shoot him do you?" Angel asked Flea.

"I know he will," replied Flea. "That's something we have in common. That's why I wouldn't go to war without him."

A Rankorack fighter cut a path right toward Flea and his group. He came out of nowhere like some blue streaking hurricane. It was Banach.

"Break hard, ladies!" Flea shouted.

The four banked hard in four different directions. They split just in time to keep from getting hit.

"Where is your strength now, puny human!" shouted Banach.

"You blue son of a..." Flea shouted.

"Flea!" Kaida interrupted him over the intercom. "Fly with your brain not your heart! No chasing down Banach!"

"Thanks, Kaida," Flea said. "We'll get that asshole later!"

"You shall squeal, pathetic humans!" Banach laughed as he flew away.

"Ladies," Flea barked. "Let's form back up and take down some bad guys!"

"I call lead!" Pesha said excitedly as they arced around from their evasive maneuver to meet back up.

"Hey I wanted lead!" Tina sounded disappointed.

"Roshambo?" Pesha asked.

They were making their turn to face the enemy.

"Stop screwing around you two!" Flea said.

"I got rock!" Pesha said.

"Damn it," Tina sounded disappointed again. "I got scissors."

"Rock breaks scissors!" Pesha said, "I win! Get in back and watch my tail!"

"Hey!" Tina objected.

"Be nice, ladies!" Flea shouted. "Now form up!"

"Any of you get me killed in this and...," Flea started to say.

"I will come back from the dead and haunt you for the rest of your pathetic lives!" Tina interrupted him as she did her best impression of Flea.

They shared a laugh at the joke.

"Well at least you've learned to predict me," Flea chuckled.

They quickly gunned down four Rankorack fighters and broke hard in a downward spiral.

"How many of us are left, Angel," Flea asked.

"Thirty two, still, but some have taken some hits," she responded.

"And them?" Flea asked.

"Eighty one," she responded.

"Damn," Flea said. "I was hoping we might take them out faster."

"Regardless of their lack of tactics, they are experienced combat pilots with the advantage of numbers," she replied. "It won't be easy."

"Alright ladies," Flea barked. "Let's get these bastards!"

The four screamed over the intercom. Some shouts were insults, some were threats, but mostly they shouted blood curdling, incoherent screams. The fight raged on for hours. Flea and his small group were going crazy. All the humans were. It was a hard fight.

"Morg!" Flea shouted. "Break hard left!"

"Arghhh!" Morgan yelled. "Damn it! Damn it! Damn it!"

Morgan followed Flea's advice blindly and avoided three fighters on his tail. Unfortunately they cut down what was left of squad four's second team when they missed Morgan.

"Morg!" Flea said. "Get down here and regroup with us! You're all alone. That's a bad thing!"

"On the way!" Morgan shouted as he arced toward Flea, Kaida, and Pesha. Tina's ship was disabled after her shields went out.

"Angel! How many?" Flea demanded.

"We have twelve, they have twenty nine! Keep fighting!" she encouraged him.

"Everyone needs to take out at least three!" Flea shouted to the remaining pilots.

"That makes thirty six fighters," Morgan said. "They only have twenty nine left," he blasted red energy blasts from his cannons at an enemy who passed too close. "Make that twenty eight fighters left, Flea. Your math doesn't add up."

"Don't correct my math during battle, Goddamnit!" Flea yelled.

Morgan and some of the other pilots chuckled into their communicators.

"Not funny!" Flea admonished them. "Remember what might happen if we lose!"

They kept flying on as hard as they could. Flea's group was slowly dropping out one by one. Eventually, Flea found he was alone. He took off streaking toward the asteroid field. He weaved through the floating rocks desperately searching for cover. He zipped in and out of them coming dangerously close every time he passed one. Finally, he saw a large asteroid with a small opening in it. Without asking Angel if the fighter could squeeze in there, he pointed the nose at it and went full speed. He entered the small cave, scraping the bottom of his fighter slightly as he went in. Sparks flashed across the nose at he hit something else. Flea bounced and lurched forward in his seat.

"Be careful!" Angel admonished him. "Anything you do, I will have to fix, later!"

"Sorry," Flea said. "Shut down all lights and anything that leaves an energy signal."

"Okay," Angel responded.

The fighter powered down. When it did this, it disappeared from any tracking systems his enemies might have. Flea got out of his seat and went back into the lounge area and took off his helmet. With the gravity field off, it floated in the air. Angel reappeared in the lounge area next to the pilot's chair. She walked over and sat down next to him. She undulated sensuously as she walked over.

"What are we doing?" she asked with a small grin.

"Taking a break," Flea said with a laugh. "Can I get a snack?"

"You're going to take time to eat?" she asked incredulously.

"Might as well," Flea shrugged. "I don't see any other humans out there."

Angel directed the matter combiner in the lounge area to make some cream cheese jalapeño poppers. Flea removed the bowl of poppers and asked for a Mountain Dew to go with it. He took a seat on the couch in the lounge area.

"How many?" Flea asked Angel around a bite of popper. "How many are left?"

"As far as I can tell," she said as she flopped down next to him. "Two of them and two of us."

"What do you mean?" Flea asked. "I didn't see anyone else out there."

"I can't count the hits our opponents have taken, but I see two of them still flying with no other energy signatures," she explained. "However, I can count the hits we've taken. We've taken one hundred fifty six hits. Your shield has three points left. Our group has a total of one hundred sixty points available."

"That means that one of us is still alive," Flea sounded hopeful. "One of us is playing possum."

"Possum?" Angel asked curiously.

"Pretending to be dead," Flea explained.

"I know what it means" she sighed. "Isn't that lying?"

"Yeah," Flea replied finishing his poppers. "And as long as whoever is doing it can do it well, we still have a chance."

"Is Banach one of the two left?" Flea asked gulping down his Mountain Dew.

"Yes," she replied. "Do you want to speak to him?"

"Can I talk to Banach without him knowing where I am?" Flea asked arching an eyebrow.

"Yes," she responded with a small grin. "I can make it so you can talk to him and everyone else at the same time."

"Good," Flea grinned. "Do it."

"Are you going to taunt him some more?" she asked.

"Yep," Flea responded.

"Okay," she said. "Talk all you want."

Angel had started playing some salsa music over the communicator.

"What is this noise?" shouted Banach.

Flea was silent and let the song keep playing.

"I said what is this noise? Are you afraid to face me?" he shouted. "Where is that dung pile, Gabriel? Are you still alive?"

"Is that you, Banach?" Flea said lazily over the communicator. "You ready to give up, yet? I thought you sulked off somewhere to wet yourself!"

"You insolent, piece of human putrescence!" Banach shouted. "I'll kill you! I swear it! Weapon's training mode off!"

"He's armed, Flea," Angel said worriedly.

"Just keep the comm line open," Flea said. "Okay? I need to keep him off balance."

He put his helmet back on and prepped his suit for space walk.

"Where are you going?" she asked.

Flea signaled her to cut communications for a moment.

"I'm going to cheat," he responded placing a hand on one of his Hate Blasters.

"Banach," Flea said sternly. "You're about to go down in a real bad way. You sure you don't want to quit? I'd hate for you to pee all over the inside of your fighter."

Banach responded by making choking sounds over the comm system. Flea walked onto the asteroid's surface. He made his way to an area where he could see the battlefield. He spotted the two remaining Rankorack fighters. For a moment, he thought he saw a light coming from Kaida's fighter's cockpit window. It looked like she was waiving a flash light or something.

"Any other humans out there?" Flea asked over his headset.

Of course, there was no answer. However, the flashlight in Kaida's cockpit started waiving more vigorously. A Rankorack fighter came dangerously close to her while she did this. It didn't seem to notice.

"Begging for aid pathetic human!" snorted Banach. "I'll let you beg for your delegate's life when this is done!"

"Keep dreaming, asshole!" Flea replied with a laugh.

Flea pulled out one of his Hate Blasters. His targeting goggles engaged. He took aim at the fighter that just went by Kaida. The hate flooded inside him. This stupid Banach wanted to kill him. Flea didn't like that at all.

"Go back to training mode and reconsider," Flea asked flatly. "This is your last chance to play nicely."

"Silence, human scum!" Banach replied. "I'll kill you!"

"Fine!" shouted Flea, "Suck on this!"

Flea let loose purple hatred and raging fury from his gun. It arced angrily through the sky and struck the Rankorack fighter in the underbelly. It went careening off in the opposite direction of Flea's blast until it crashed into one of the stationary gun turrets. It didn't destroy the Rankorack fighter. Flea had been working with his guns and learning to control them. The pilot wasn't going to feel very happy after the crash, though.

Banach found Flea's spot by tracking the location of the blast.

"You cheat!" he screamed. "You cheat! Lying, disreputable human slime!"

He started blasting at Flea's general location on the asteroid. Flea bolted back to the cave as a shower of rock and dirt was thrown around him. He burst into the lounge of his fighter and holstered his gun. He sat down hard in the pilot's seat and didn't bother strapping in. He could still feel the hate because he hadn't turned his gun off after holstering it. It vibrated menacingly at his hip. Flea lifted off and went forward through the cave at a suicidal pace. He swerved and scraped his way out the other side. So far, the pilot to do the most damage to Flea's fighter was himself. He made it to the exit of the cave and tore through the blackness of space like some angry, purple shooting star.

"Finally, we found the exit," Angelina sounded relieved.

"I know," agreed Flea with a laugh. "I was starting to wonder if it had an exit."

"You mean you didn't know?" she shouted angrily.

"Not really," said Flea with a maniacal laugh. "But I had a pretty good feeling!"

"We will be discussing this later!" Angel looked shocked.

"You will die!" Banach yelled as he locked onto Flea's tail after Flea exited the cave.

"Eat shit, asshole!" Flea shouted his response hatefully.

Flea weaved in and out of the shut down fighters and burned toward Kaida. He hoped she was still alive and doing more than just encouraging him with her light show. Flea took a hit to his already scarred fighter. It hit his left wing and tore a hole in it. Flea's teeth rattled at the impact. He bit his lip. Blood ran down his chin. He fumbled at his five point harness in an attempt to get it in place.

"Rotten bastard!" Flea yelled as the harness clicked.

"Take that!" Banach shouted. "Where is your strength now, coward?"

Flea kept dodging as his fighter trailed sparks behind him.

"You want to see my strength?" Flea shouted. "Let me show you!"

He broke off hard, spiraling upward and dodging more of Banach's live fire.

"Humans are like wolves," Flea said calmly dodging another blast. "We travel in packs."

Flea arced toward Kaida's nose.

"Wolf packs are very close knit," Flea continued to explain. "You never worry about the wolf you can see."

"Stop babbling, puny vile human!" yelled Banach.

He flew by Kaida and dodged another shot from Banach. He was right on Flea's tail.

"You worry about the ones you don't," Flea finished.

Kaida powered up her fighter after Banach flew by. Flea breathed a sigh of relief when she reappeared on his tracking sphere. Banach let loose one last barrage of fire that struck Flea's roof and starboard side. It sent him spinning toward one of the drone fighter storage units.

"What is this?" Banach yelled noticing he was being tailed.

"Shit!" yelled Flea spinning in his fighter.

"Overhead and starboard side combat thrusters are out!" shouted Angel.

"Full main thruster burst, now!" Flea barked to Angel.

"Flea!" shouted Kaida.

"Just shoot him!" shouted Flea. "Shoot him now!"

Kaida let loose a stream of shots so rapidly Banach could not avoid them. His fighter shut down.

"Hang on!" Flea shouted to Angel.

Flea's fighter straightened out as the main engines fired up. This caused him to collide with one of the training field's stationary gun turrets. He came to such a sudden stop that Flea bounced off the dashboard and felt some of his ribs break. His head rattled around in his helmet and he could see his own blood running down his cheek out of the corner of his eye. His fighter shut down. He never managed to get his harness fully engaged after leaving the cave, and was paying for his hastiness.

"You okay?" he moaned to Angel.

"That really, really, HURT!" Angel replied angrily.

"I thought this thing had some kind of air bags?" Flea coughed.

"It does," Angel's speech slurred a bit. "I think."

With that, the airbags burst through the control consol and threatened to give Flea a heart attack.

"Why don't the airbags ever work right?" Flea moaned.

Angel chuckled.

"Can we fire this thing back up?" Flea groaned.

The fighter shuddered a bit as it started back up. It didn't sound normal and it had a funny vibration that came through the deck plates.

"How's that?" asked Angel.

"I'll take it Angel, baby," Flea shook the dizziness from his vision. "Nice job."

Flea's fighter trailed sparks as he pulled its broken and battered form in front of Banach's cockpit window so the two could see each other.

"Do you see my strength?" Flea asked Banach.

"You are defeated!" Flea spit flecks of blood onto his console as he shouted. "I lead my force to defeat you! Do you see my strength?

"I see your strength and will follow," Banach said softly after a long pause.

"You are defeated!" Flea shouted. "Who has defeated you?"

In order for the challenge to be completed by Rankorack custom, the defeated foe must admit who had beaten him.

"Gabriel-Captain," Banach said softly as he hung his head. "I was defeated by the Gabriel-Captain and his ArchAngels. I will follow his strength."

"Pilots," Flea sounded drained. "Power up and go home. We're done here. You are dismissed."

16

"Are you ready for your beating, pet?" Toren asked Ba'an with a seductive grin.

"Mistress," Ba'an replied thoughtfully. "I was thinking that now I have been granted the lateral move to be your assistant, that perhaps the beatings would no longer be necessary."

Thwack! Thwack! Thwack! Thwack! Thwack!

Toren lashed out like a machine gun tearing smalls rips into Ba'an's flesh.

"It's not your place to think, pet!" Toren yelled. "You are mine!"

"Yes, Mistress," Ba'an growled.

"Besides," she continued. "It was the High Commander Esham'aut that ordered your beatings. It's not my place to discontinue them. Now, go over to the rack."

Ba'an walked stoically over to the rack. He wanted to maintain his ruse up until the last minute.

"Assume the position, pet," Toren purred.

Instead of raising his tentacles above his head, Ba'an folded his arms across his chest. Ba'an lowered his head so he was peering at her from underneath his brow line as he planted his feet shoulder width apart.

"If you want to keep doing this, you will have to come and force me, Toren," he said softly as he faced her.

Thwack! Thwack! Thwack! Thwack!

"You would address me by my name!?!" she screeched lashing out at him again. "You go too far, pet!"

Thwack! Thwack! Thwack!

She lashed out at Ba'an four times. Three landed. Ba'an caught the fourth in his tentacle inches in front of his face.

"You would stop me?" she screeched reaching even higher octaves.

"I have killed forty eight Goras to reach a position where I can get close enough to kill Esham'aut," Ba'an explained grimly. "Do you think for one minute that there is anything you can do to control me at this point?"

Ba'an jerked hard on her whip like appendage. She was thrown forward to land in the vice like grip of his tentacles. He wrapped his arms around her tightly.

"Remember this?" he asked as he licked her face. "You so enjoyed doing this to me."

Ba'an skillfully used two of his tentacles to wrap her whips back around her forearms and bound them so they remained in place. He forced her arms in the air and shackled her into the rack.

"Stop!" screamed Toren. "This isn't how it is supposed to be! Stop this now, pet!"

Ba'an used one of his tentacles to lash out and put a slash across her right cheek. Her dark blood oozed down her face. She stretched with her pink tongue to try and lick it as she grinned wickedly. Ba'an felt his heart fill with the hate as he looked at her. His soul filled with a putrid filth that was as familiar to him now as an old boot.

"Hummm, I never knew you cared pet," she growled seductively.

She moaned and smiled coyly as Ba'an positioned himself in front of her a few feet away. He spread his feet shoulder width apart.

"You will call me, master, pet," Ba'an said.

Thwack! Thwack! Thwack! Thwack! Thwack!

Parts of her already skimpy black clothing were torn to reveal more of her dark red flesh and ample bosom.

"How do you like it?" Ba'an yelled at her.

"Maa! Humm!" she squealed ecstatically. "Oh yes! Ahhh!"

"Stop that!" yelled Ba'an angrily. "You are not supposed to enjoy this!"

Thwack! Thwack! Thwack! Thwack! Thwack!

He lashed out to beat her over and over again.

"Ahh! Ohh!" she squirmed in her shackles as she squealed some more. "Yes! Oh Yes! Make it hurt!! I've been so baaaad!"

"You! You!" Ba'an felt the hate and rage dissipate.

He wasn't sure how to react. When he envisioned this day, she wasn't supposed to enjoy it. For the first time in quite a while, Ba'an was confused.

"Yes! Yes! More! Please," she moaned desperately. "Please give me more!"

She squirmed with pleasure and twisted to try and lick the blood that was running down various parts of her body.

"Hmm," Ba'an said trying to contemplate the situation. "You are not supposed to enjoy this."

"What's wrong pet?" she asked with a malicious grin. "Don't you have what it takes to be a real Gora and finish the job?"

Thwack!

Ba'an whipped her across her left cheek to match the slash on the right one.

"Ahh!" she giggled. "Keep trying, pet. Maybe you'll please me sometime."

Ba'an walked over to the table where Toren kept the tools of her trade. He searched through the large selection of torture implements. Every now and then he would stop and examine one. Finally, he found what he was looking for as he started going through her drawers. He picked up a black silk bag and a pair of manacles. He walked over to Toren and put the bag over her head.

"Ohh, now we're getting serious," she taunted him as she giggled.

Ba'an punched her in the stomach. She sucked in air at the blow and bent over as far as her restraints allowed and giggled girlishly when her breath returned. Ba'an removed her wrists from the shackles on the rack and cuffed her wrists behind her back with the manacles from the drawer. He picked up a blaster that Toren kept near the door as he pushed her into the hall. He walked her out of the room and started taking her toward his new quarters.

"Keep quiet and you might live through this," Ba'an lied.

He fully intended to kill her. She walked in front of him sensuously swishing and bouncing as she walked. He stood in front of the door to his new quarters and saw one of the old shift supervisors from the reharvestation chamber.

"Taking your work home with you now?" he asked with a small grin. "You are the industrious one."

"One does what one must," Ba'an said piously.

The Gora left as Ba'an lead Toren into his room. He sat her down in a chair and turned her to face his wall which held the count of his victims. He had removed that section of wall so he could bring it to his new room. He pulled the hood off her head.

"What's this?" she asked. "A memento of some sort?"

"It is a record of how many Goras I have had to kill since Esham'aut disgraced me," Ba'an replied flatly.

"Are you going to kill me?" she didn't sound afraid.

Most of the victims Ba'an had claimed so far would have wet themselves by this point. Toren wasn't shaking or afraid at all. She seemed to be made of tougher stuff than the others.

"Yes," Ba'an said honestly. "You will be mark forty nine. Esham'aut will be fifty. Then I will be done."

"What will you do, then?" she asked seriously. "Will your palate for vengeance be full? Once you choose that path, you spend your whole life on it. Then, only when you reach the end, do you realize what you have lost."

She sounded like someone who knew from experience.

Thwack!

"Shut up," Ba'an said whipping her torso and tearing some more clothing.

There was a long period of silence as the two just sat there looking at each other. Ba'an gave her his most murderous of looks, but she never backed down. She seemed to refuse to be afraid of him.

"We've been through much, pet," she purred at him. "If you are going to kill me, at least get on with it. Otherwise, I am a very busy girl."

As hard as he tried, Ba'an could not summon the hate to kill her properly. The Inquisitor was right. She had been one of the few constants in Ba'an's existence since this had started.

"I will have to kill you," Ba'an replied softly. "I have no choice."

Ba'an would have to kill her to keep from getting caught before reaching his goal. He realized, however, that this kill, like the new medical technician, would be from necessity. For some reason, his need to exact revenge on her faded.

"You could at least unshackle me," she said melodically. "You have a blaster, after all."

Her voice had a hypnotic quality to it. Ba'an found himself compelled to listen to her.

"Yes," Ba'an said softly. "I trust you, Mistress."

Ba'an walked over to her and unshackled her hands. As he turned and walked away Toren picked up the chair and threw it at his back. It splintered as it smashed into him and threw him to the floor.

"Foul deceitful creature!" he shouted feeling his anger start to reignite.

Any remaining feelings of trust or pity for this creature had fled from Ba'an. He should have known she could not be trusted.

"Ha!" Toren flicked her wrist as if she were going to beat him with her whip appendages.

Her eyes widen as she looked at them and realized they were still bound to her forearms. She bolted out the door and left Ba'an in the room alone.

"Get back here!" Ba'an growled as he followed her out.

Toren's legs were longer and she was much leaner. Ba'an had difficulty keeping up. He caught a flash of red as she bolted around a corner. He followed as best he could. His need to kill Esham'aut was now fueling him. He moved harder, faster, and stronger.

"Move!" he shouted at some Goras walking toward them.

They dodged out of the way hearing his raging intent ooze forth in his voice.

"Foul creature!" Ba'an screamed at her back. "Get back here!"

Toren laughed a deep throaty growl over her shoulder at him.

"Come and get me, pet! You know you want to!" she shouted over her shoulder.

Ba'an screamed at her incoherently. She ducked into a room. Ba'an caught up and followed her. It was the emergency teleportation chamber for this end of the ship. In the event of an emergency where there were no other options, the chamber could be used for escape. It was a very unreliable piece of equipment. The technology had never been fully developed.

"Now you die!" Ba'an shouted.

Ba'an let loose three shots at the Inquisitor with his blaster in rapid succession. Toren dodged the first two jumping nimbly. She dodged the third shot by leaping into the chamber. She slammed the door shut and locked it from the inside. She smiled seductively to taunt him.

"I'll kill you! Come out of there!" Ba'an shouted.

"Please stand away from the teleportation chamber," Ba'an heard the room's computer intone. "Teleportation sequence activated."

The teleportation technology gave her a small chance of success. If the chamber functioned properly, she might reach the home world and inform the empire of his intentions. However, the probability was very low. The first risk with this equipment was the fifty nine percent chance she wouldn't teleport at all. If this happened, her cells would simply burst and evaporate. If she did manage to teleport, she had a seventy percent chance of reaching the home world coordinates. If she didn't make it there, then there was no telling where she might go. Ba'an didn't want to take any chances with her.

"Teleportation in twenty seconds," said the computer.

Ba'an stood back and tried blasting the door. It didn't even scratch it. The doors were indestructible because if anything went wrong to cause them to be removed, everything in the room would be teleported during the sequence.

"Fifteen seconds," said the computer.

Ba'an was running out of options. Maybe she would just evaporate. He didn't want to risk it. He spit white acid at the door.

"Ten seconds," the computer said.

The door remained intact and unmarked.

Ba'an ran over to the computer panel and desperately started trying to reprogram the computer. He couldn't stop the sequence once it was initiated. The teleportation generator could not be shut down once started without releasing its energy. If left in its current state, it would react like a time bomb building up and then eventually exploding. While it could not be stopped, Ba'an did find a way to delay it.

"Sequence paused," said the computer. "Please input new destination."

Ba'an breathed a sigh of relief.

"You will never go home again," Ba'an said darkly looking through the door's window at her. "But, I will still have to make sure you are dead, even if it means picking up the corpse."

She arched an eyebrow and playfully stuck out her tongue again.

"Host," Ba'an said. "Pull up a map with the coordinates of the first planet we stopped at during this mission's flight plan."

The holo-projector next to the computer showed a small star map on it with an arrow pointing to where Ba'an had indicated. He recognized the star chart. He remembered seeing it in Esham'aut's war room before his disgrace.

"Input coordinates for here," Ba'an pointed to a location that was about three days travel by shuttle and jumpgates from the former location of Earth.

He had heard that they would be returning there to do a battlefield assessment. By picking the coordinates he had chosen he would be close enough to requisition a shuttle and go search for her after they got there. Then he could kill her and come back for Esham'aut. That's if she didn't starve to death first. They still had ten days travel to reach that battlefield. Ba'an knew how resourceful she could be, and needed to be absolutely certain of her death. If she didn't appear at this location, it would not matter. The odds of her reappearing back at the home world by random chance were infinitesimal.

"Coordinates changed," the computer said. "Resuming countdown."

"Five...Four...Three...Two...One," the computer finished the countdown.

The teleportation chamber flashed. The teleportation pod with Toren in it was gone. Ba'an wouldn't know if she survived teleportation for another thirteen days. He hated waiting.

***

"You have proven yourselves against the Rankorack," Cormon said as he stood in front of the council. "But, that does not show us that the Goraan can be defeated!"

They had assembled in the Communal Sphere at the council meeting platform. A crowd had drawn around them and sat in the stands.

"We believe that if everyone joins us, we might have a chance," delegate Masters said.

"The fact of the matter is, young delegates," said Cormon brusquely, "not everyone wants to join you. Many of us have lost our homes just like you. No one has faced and defeated the Goraan in thousands of years. What makes you think you can win?"

"We have heart," delegate Ryoko replied with certainty. "We have faith."

"Your heart and your faith may have been enough to keep you alive in your challenge, but it doesn't make you invincible," Cormon said smugly. "Besides, everyone knows Gabriel cheated."

The assembled onlookers started to "boo" Cormon's remarks.

"Suck my dick, you shit-head!" Flea shouted from the gallery. "You weren't even there! You left after it all started! I did what I had to so we could win! Banach started using live weapons! I responded! I improvised, adapted and I overcame!"

Flea hopped down the benches to stand with the three human delegates. Banach, whom Flea decided not to kill after the battle, was hot on Flea's trail. Everyone started to cheer for the dirty, young, unkempt human. Flea always tried to look as disreputable as possible for the council.

"What do you know about it?" Flea accused.

"You conducted yourself dishonorably, Cormon-Caretaker!" Banach added. "The Gabriel-Captain responded with creativity in a dire situation. I never should have armed my weapons. I broke the rules of the contest. Gabriel-Captain did what the situation demanded in order to win! Every good Rankorack can respect such actions!"

"I thought you would be dead by now, Banach," Cormon said callously. "I thought that wretch, Gabriel, would have exercised his right to claim your life after the fight."

"I decided not to," Flea said coldly gazing at Cormon. "How about I take yours instead?"

There was a collective gasp around the council meeting platform. Flea started to walk towards Cormon purposefully. He wasn't sure whether or not he would shoot Cormon, but Flea was tired of playing games.

"You better just start…" Flea yelled flashing purple eyed hatred at him.

Banach followed closely behind Flea. He drew what appeared to be a small cannon from his hip holster and held it in his massive claw. He pointed it at Cormon.

"Flea!" Ryoko admonished standing in his way.

"He deserves it, Ryoko," Morgan said bluntly as he joined them from the crowd. "You know he does."

"No," Ryoko said with authority. "Not this way."

"Ryoko," Flea insisted angrily. "I am tired of that piece of shit being against us!"

Smack!

She slapped him hard.

Flea looked at her for a moment then smiled. Ryoko did not look away. She smiled for a moment when she saw Flea was not angry.

"I offer my humble apologies, Ryoko," he said bowing. "You and our delegates are in charge."

"What about me?" asked Cormon.

"Shall I kill him, Gabriel-Captain?" asked Banach.

"Not today," Flea sighed. "Maybe tomorrow you can kill him for me."

Banach seemed upset at losing the prospect of killing someone today.

"You three will leave the council meeting now!" barked Cormon.

Flea, Morgan and Banach did not move a muscle at Cormon's command. Flea looked at his delegates for a moment.

"It's okay," Daniela sounded reassuring. "We'll be fine."

"Flea," said Ryoko with a small smile. "I am fine. We are fine. You go now."

"I'll teach you to throw a punch later, Ryoko," Flea said with a smile. "I'm sure you can hit much harder than that."

She smiled at him.

"It's okay, guys," Christina said cheerfully. "Really, we're fine."

Flea and his two companions started backing away down the platform. They continued to stare at Cormon.

"You're lucky, sushi-head!" Flea said violently. "Real lucky!"

"I would watch my manners from now on if I were you, Cormon," Morgan added darkly. "Next time we might not be so forgiving. We might let Banach eat you."

Banach was letting off low menacing growls. They stopped at the edge of the stairs. Flea glared at Cormon from across the council chambers and pretended to go for his guns. Cormon reflexively dove behind another delegate in fear.

"Feel better?" Morgan asked as he looked at his friend.

"Yeah," replied Flea with a grin. "That was fun."

Flea, Morgan, and Banach left the council meeting and the marble platform. Order slowly restored itself to the council.

"I cannot speak for the rest of you, but I move we revoke the humans' trial status until they can provide proof that the Goraan can be defeated," Cormon said trying to regain his composure. "I grow weary of all this talk of war."

"You can't do that!" shouted Christina. "We're just getting started! You'd quit without even trying?! That's bullshit!"

"Next time," Ryoko said dryly in a low voice so only the humans could hear her, "let Flea kill him."

Ryoko had become increasingly more aggressive since she put her life at risk.

"Do I have a second?" asked Cormon.

"Second," someone shouted from the back.

"I call for vote," said Cormon.

Armalan and the Kashin delegation acted as if they were going to protest, but Daniela motioned for them not to do so. The council members cast their votes on a small pad in front of them.

"The votes are tallied. The motion is carried through," said Cormon cheerily. "The humans' status is revoked until they can provide proof that the Goraan can be defeated."

"Fine," said Christina softly. "What must we do?"

Bella had already informed her of Cormon's plan. She already knew the answer.

"You must attack and destroy a Goraan battleship," responded Cormon seriously. "Bring us proof of its destruction. Do you accept?"

"Yes," responded Daniela.

"Yes," responded Christina.

"We will fight," Ryoko said seriously. "And we will win."

***

"Tell me again why we are doing this?" Flea heard Morgan's voice asking through his headset. "No one in the gerbil cage over there wants us around anymore. Why should we go on security patrol? Why do we care about their safety?"

The pilots of the ArchAngels commonly referred to the Runners Station as a gerbil cage. It sounded derogatory, and the base actually resembled one.

"First of all, we will need them to stay alive if they are going to help us later," Flea stated. "And we also need to protect our own people who are in there as well."

"I guess so," Morgan said with resignation.

"And finally," Flea finished, "we need to take every opportunity available to get some real flight time. We can use the patrol to run formation drills."

"Ahh man!" said one pilot over the speakers.

"Not more formation drills," added Pesha.

"Can't we please just fly?" asked Tina. "It's like every time we get in these things all we do is drill and fight."

"I'm sorry," Flea said very sweetly. "Did you guys want to take some time out tonight just to enjoy the flight?"

Flea heard a number of enthusiastic responses to this question. Most of them just wanted to fly for a change.

"Well," Flea sounded as if he were considering it. "I guess I could let you guys do that."

All the pilots cheered.

"I could also make all of you candle light dinners and whisper sweet nothings in your ears," Flea said dryly. "But that won't happen either! Formation drills! Now! Get moving!"

The group let out a collective groan.

"Angel, sweetheart?" Flea asked. "How are you feeling?"

"Mentally and emotionally, I am still a bit rattled from the crash," she sounded drained. "But the maintenance team did a really good job fixing me up. We should be fine."

"Should be?" asked Flea.

"I'll be fine as long as you're with me, love," she said sweetly.

Flea and Morgan launched some holo-pods that would project holographic images of Goraan fighters for them to combat while flying. They flew for three hours without incident practicing tactics and strategies.

"Gabriel!" Angel said sharply. "I am picking up forty Goraan fighters coming in hard and fast."

"Is it from the holo-pods?" asked Flea.

"I don't think so," Angel sounded worried. "The holo-pods make very accurate programs. Turn them off and see what happens."

"Holo-pods, end simulation!" Flea barked.

The holo-fighters blinked from existence. The forty fighters Angel was talking about remained. They bore down on the ArchAngels like golden death and fury.

"Send them a message," Flea said. "Goraan fighters! Stand down! Surrender and we will spare your lives."

There was no response. They kept coming.

"Please tell me you didn't actually think they would stop, did you?" Morgan asked seriously.

"Shut up, Morg," said Flea. "I just thought it would be nice if they picked the easy way. I just got my fighter fixed this morning."

"Try not to crash again, okay?" asked Angel.

"Oh please," said Flea smiling. "You used the repairs as an excuse to get me down to the hanger bay to spend more time with you."

She giggled coyly and batted her eyes at him, "I love you, baby."

"I know," Flea sounded exasperated.

Angel had been coming up with every possible excuse to get him to come see her bin the hanger.

"Alright, ladies!" Flea shouted over the communicator. "Let's not screw around with this one! It's a live fire fight! Form up, watch your backs and take them down!"

"Try and use your EMP's when possible," added Morgan. "The electromagnetic pulse will disable their fighter so we can go in and get it. We need all the spare parts we can get!"

"And it allows us to interrogate prisoners," Flea said. "We need to get some info on these guys. Let's go, ladies!"

"Kaida, Tina, Pesha!" Flea barked to his teammates. "Form up!"

"I call lead!" Tina shouted.

"I wanted to be in front," Pesha pouted.

"Are you going to put me through this every damn time we fight?" Flea asked.

"Roshambo!" shouted Tina.

"Paper!" shouted Pesha.

"Rock!" shouted Tina.

"Paper covers rock! I win!" Pesha giggled. "Get in back and watch my tail!"

"You always win," Tina pouted.

"Stop screwing around, girls!" Flea shouted.

The ArchAngels had been itching for another fight ever since they challenged the Rankorack. Everyone was excited when they engaged the enemy.

"Keep them in front, team. Don't let them behind us." Flea heard Morgan's voice. "Tommy if you fly off I'm going to shoot you with and EMP and come pick your ass up later, got it?"

"Sir, yes, sir!" Tommy barked in response.

Flea's ship suddenly lurched to starboard as he was hit with an energy blast from a Goraan fighter.

"Break off!" he shouted as he received the blow.

Flea's team split up briefly to avoid collision.

"Hey!" shouted Angel fiercely. "Gabriel, that hurt! He hurt me! Go kill him for me, love!"

Flea laughed at Angel's remark. He squared himself in his seat to continue fighting.

"That's it!" Flea shouted. "He scratched my paint! Kill them all!"

The group laughed at Flea's mid-combat quip. Flea and his group reformed in an arrowhead formation and arced after the small pack of Goraan that had been shooting at them. They angled and spiraled through the blazing death spewing forth from the golden, expensive looking Goraan fighters. Two EMP blasts coming from Pesha and Tina immobilized two Goraan fighters. Flea and Kaida blasted the other two down with their guns. When the fight was over, the humans were scarred and trailing a few sparks. The fighters would need some work. However, they took ten fighters with EMP blasts. The rest were turned into scrap metal.

"Everyone report in!" Flea barked.

All pilots were accounted for. A few had some bumps and bruises, but they would all return home from this particular fight.

"Okay guys," Flea said authoritatively. "Use your cargo cables to pull in the larger pieces. Someone watch our asses as we tow back the fighters we took prisoner. If any of those fighters come back on line, I want them shredded immediately!"

"Angel?" Flea asked curiously. "Did anyone back at the base see what happened out here?"

"The only ones who have a record of it are us," she responded quietly. "Why do you ask, love?"

Flea was still getting used to her calling him that.

"Right," Flea said. "Can you delete any record of this event ever occurring?"

"I would rather not delete my own memories," she said defensively.

"I understand," said Flea gently. "Can you just make it so no one else ever learns of this?"

"Yes," she responded happily. "I can do that for you, love. Will this make you happy?"

"Angel, baby," Flea replied grinning. "That would make me very happy. Call ahead to the carrier and tell Alex to stand down any personnel from their duty stations that could witness us coming in. Contact the delegates and our head of human intelligence."

"Bella?" she asked.

"That's the one," Flea said. "Maybe she can get some use out of these guys."

***

"Is there something wrong, Commander Doshan?" Esham'aut asked his second in Command. "Why did you contact me at such a late hour?"

"Check your bridge logs, High Commander," replied Doshan over his ship's communicator. "I was standing here on my bridge not too long ago and our sensors noted an energy surge on your ship."

"I will make my way to the bridge," replied Esham'aut. "Do you have any idea what it might have been?"

"It appeared to be a teleport pod," replied Doshan.

"I will send a message to emergency receiving on the home world and see if anything came through," replied Esham'aut. "If it did not, then who or whatever it was probably boiled during teleportation."

"Most likely, sir," said Doshan.

Esham'aut made his way to the bridge. He strode purposefully forcing whoever tried to stand in his way aside.

He found the sensor watch dozing at his post.

"What is this?" screamed Esham'aut.

The sensor watch bolted upright in his seat. Everyone on the bridge craned their necks to see what was happening.

"You dare sleep at your post on my ship?" Esham'aut screamed.

"Sorry, sir," stammered the sensor watch.

"Bridge Commander!" bellowed Esham'aut. "Pull up sensor logs, now!"

"Yes, sir!" barked the Bridge Commander.

The logs came up on the holo-projector table in the center of the bridge.

"You!" shouted Esham'aut pointing to the sensor watch. "Go over to the logs and point out the first anomalous reading you find!"

"Ye…yes, sir!" replied the sensor watch.

The sensor watch cowered under Esham'aut's black eyed gaze. He slowly walked over to the logs and reviewed them looking for any anomalies.

"I believe," the sensor watch stammered, "this is odd right here."

"Where?" barked Esham'aut. "Show it to me!"

The sensor watched raised his hand to point to the part of the logs he had indicated.

"Here, sir," he replied shakily. "Right here."

Esham'aut jerked his pistol from his holster with the speed of a practiced warrior. He squeezed the trigger and vaporized the sensor watch's hand in a violent ball of yellow energy. The stump where the sensor watch's hand once was located spurted blood all over the table that was around the holo-projector. The wall behind the sensor station was charred black from where the blast had struck after removing the watch's hand. The sensor watch crumpled to the ground screaming in pain.

"Silence!" shouted Esham'aut.

Esham'aut walked over and clenched the top of the sensor watch's head in his claw and picked him straight up off the ground. He glared around the bridge and ensured that everyone was watching.

"Never in all of your pathetic little lives do you ever fall asleep on watch! Not on my ship!" the High Commander shouted.

Esham'aut slammed the sensor watch's head into the table that was around the holo-projector in the center of the bridge.

"Never!" he slammed the bridge watch's head again.

"Not ever!" he continued to slam.

"Not in your entire tour of service on my ship!" he punctuated each word by slamming the bridge watch's head over and over.

He raised the limp body high so everyone could see it and released his grip. The body hit the ground with a thud. It slumped over in an unnatural fashion. It wasn't moving or breathing.

"Let this be a lesson to you all!" Esham'aut shouted.

"Sir," interrupted the Bridge Commander. "I…I think he might be dead, sir."

Esham'aut was standing next to the body. He pointed his blaster at it and opened fire. He shot the body twelve times while it lay on the ground. Blood spewed up from the blasts and drenched Esham'aut's face and uniform. All that was left of the sensor watch was an unrecognizable smear of blood and a pile mushy flesh on the floor of the bridge.

"If he was not dead before," he said without wiping blood from his face. "Then he is now!"

Esham'aut walked toward the Bridge Commander. He glared at the smaller creature until the Bridge Commander lowered his eyes and started to shake violently.

"Kneel," Esham'aut said darkly.

The Bridge Commander got on his knees before Esham'aut. Esham'aut placed the barrel of his gun to the Bridge Commander's face.

"You were in charge," Esham'aut said softly. "Therefore, you are directly responsible for those who report to you. Do you understand?"

"Yes sir," replied the Bridge Commander softly.

"When they sleep on watch," explained Esham'aut slowly. "It means you are asleep on watch. This will not be tolerated."

Esham'aut pulled the trigger and splattered bits of brain and pieces of the tiny Gora slug against the wall behind them. The wall was scorched from the blast. The black scar mixed gruesomely with the contents of the dead Gora's skull.

"Where is the Second in Command of this watch team?" shouted Esham'aut.

Another Gora trotted over.

"Here sir," he said looking visibly frightened.

Esham'aut didn't say anything. He simply pointed his blaster and pulled the trigger in the Gora's face. Esham'aut's forearms were dripping bits of blood and small globs of brain, skull and slug on the floor.

"Are you all starting to comprehend how much this upsets me?" shouted Esham'aut sternly.

The bridge team watched the display in stunned silence. Everyone was afraid to move or speak.

"You!" shouted Esham'aut pointing to the communications officer.

"Yes sir," he squeaked.

"Contact Ship's Inquisitor Toren, now!" shouted Esham'aut.

The communications officer sat at his station working fervently for a few minutes.

"Well?" Esham'aut sounded impatient.

"I cannot find her, sir," replied the communications officer.

Esham'aut shot him. The communications officer slumped to the ground. There was nothing left at the top of the communications officer's neck. Blood gushed forth from the headless neck and splattered the ceiling until the body hit the floor a few seconds later. Small drops of blood could be heard splattering on the ground from above.

"You!" Esham'aut shouted at the tactical officer, "Where is Toren?"

"I..." said the tactical officer.

"I would not suggest that you tell me you don't know," said Esham'aut leveling his blaster at the tactical officer.

The tactical officer went over to the communications station and looked at the screen.

"She is not on board, sir," explained the tactical officer. "That is why the communications officer could not find her. She is not on board the ship."

"Assistant!" shouted Esham'aut. "She said she was taking an assistant! Call who ever that may be! Now!"

"Assistant Inquisitor Vichen has been located and is standing by, sir," responded the communications officer.

"Get him up here, now!" shouted Esham'aut.

Esham'aut looked around the bridge as he awaited the arrival of the Ship's Assistant Inquisitor. The name of this Assistant Inquisitor sounded familiar. It tickled something in the back of his mind. He paused for a moment and looked at the tactical officer while pondering this. Esham'aut shot the tactical officer nonchalantly in the chest as he thought. The tactical officer flew backward from the impact of the blast. His chest had a large hole in is as his blood spread slowly across the floor.

"You!" shouted Esham'aut at the weapons officer.

"Huh?" the weapons officer looked up.

The weapons officer had lowered his head in an effort to keep from being noticed. Esham'aut shot him through the torso. It cut him in half. His waist and legs flailed outward behind him and his torso landed awkwardly on top of the weapons station. Esham'aut glared at the ships helmsman.

"Sir," the helmsman sounded afraid.

Esham'aut shot him putting a large hole in the helm control station and smearing the controls with the helmsman's blood. The helmsman slumped over. He was dead in his seat.

"Security officer!" shouted Esham'aut as he spotted the Gora in charge of security. "Your duty is to ensure the ship's security! I do not feel secure if my bridge watch is asleep!"

Esham'aut opened fire at the security officer. He put a large hole in the security station, the three nearest computer terminals and the security officer's chest. The security officer flew backward and smashed the panel behind him causing sparks to rain down on the floor for a moment. He then slumped to the ground in a pool of his own blood.

"Assistant Inquisitor Ba'an Vichen reporting as ordered, sir," Esham'aut heard a voice behind him.

Esham'aut turned around when he heard the voice.

"You," he said sounding pleased. "I remember you."

"Yes, sir," responded Ba'an.

"Well," replied Esham'aut. "I see my motivational techniques worked well on you. You were nothing but a crying larva the last time I saw you."

If Esham'aut didn't know any better he might think he detected hatred coming from this small creature.

"Yes," replied Ba'an skeptically. "I have changed much since last we met, sir."

"Well," began Esham'aut pausing for a moment. "Where is your Mistress?"

"As you well know, sir," began Ba'an. "She was searching for the ship's Choden'gal."

"Go on," said Esham'aut.

"Since I was working with her," continued Ba'an. "I too, began my own search for the ship's Choden'gal. As I searched, it seemed that every time I thought I might find something, Toren would find a way to sabotage my findings."

"Really?" asked Esham'aut curiously. "Why would she do that? And what does this have to do with her current location?"

"Yes, sir, I am getting to that," Ba'an sounded annoyed by the High Commander's questioning. "As I continued my noble search, I started to suspect that it was Mistress Toren herself!"

"Why would you think this?" asked Esham'aut.

"It was a hunch, sir," replied Ba'an modestly. "She became very evasive when I started to uncover more and more evidence. Finally, I accused her to her face during one of my beatings. While she thought I was prone and could do nothing against her, she confessed to me what she had been doing."

"This is good to hear," replied Esham'aut seriously. "Maybe those dull witted low-enders can get back to work now."

"Indeed, sir," agreed Ba'an.

"So what happened to her?" asked Esham'aut. "Where is your evidence?"

"After I started to believe it was her more strongly, I started to practice escaping from the shackles she used during my beatings," explained Ba'an. "After I mastered this skill was when I confronted her. After her confession, I removed my tentacles and went for her, but she escaped me. I tried to make chase down the hall but she was much faster than I."

"I see," replied Esham'aut.

"She ducked in to one of the emergency teleportation pods," said Ba'an with a shrug. "As you know, once the sequence starts…"

"It cannot be stopped," finished Esham'aut. "What did you do? She did not make it to the home world did she? I would not want to be held responsible if a beast like that was let loose in the Imperial Palace, Vichen!"

"She did not, sir," said Ba'an. "I got into the computer and changed the coordinates of the destination before the countdown could finish. If she did not evaporate, she will most likely starve before she is ever found."

"That still does not prove anything, Vichen," replied Esham'aut seriously. "You need evidence to hold against her for an accusation."

"She destroyed the evidence in front of me while she thought I could not get out of the shackles, sir," explained Ba'an. "There was no stopping her if I was going to maintain the ruse."

"Yes," grunted Esham'aut. "I suppose I can understand that."

There was a long pause. Esham'aut thought he detected hatred form this little Ba'an Vichen Gora again.

"I suppose we shall allow the future to judge her guilt or innocence," stated Esham'aut.

"What do you mean...sir?" Ba'an was continuing to ooze hatred toward the Esham'aut.

Esham'aut was slightly disturbed by this little creature. His body was covered in scars and injuries, and yet he still lived. Not only did he still live, he had developed an unhealthy amount of hatred for the High Commander of the Goraan Second Fleet.

"Perhaps I am only imagining this creature's hatred," Esham'aut thought. *"Besides, how much damage can this little pathetic Gora really do?"*

"Should anymore Choden'gal styled killings occur, then you must have been wrong," explained Esham'aut. "If another killing happens, then obviously it wasn't Mistress Toren and you will be executed for treason. If we do not have anymore Choden'gal killings, then she was guilty and I will have you decorated."

"I believe," replied Ba'an dryly, "the Choden'gal is done killing, sir."

"We shall see," said Esham'aut.

"Yes, sir," said Ba'an prophetically. "We shall see."

There was that hatred again.

"In the meantime," said Esham'aut. "You are hereby promoted to Ship's Inquisitor. Your first line of duty is to beat this bridge team three times a day for the next month!"

Ba'an looked around for a moment and surveyed the carnage on the bridge. Blood and gore was everywhere. The only one left alive was the ship's stellar cartographer.

"Ah, sir," said Ba'an shakily. "There is only one left."

Esham'aut surveyed his handy work for a moment.

"Then beat him!" bellowed Esham'aut as he turned and left the bridge.

17

All the fighter pilots except Flea and Morgan were on board the carrier waiting for the vessel to take off on her maiden voyage. Flea and Morgan were standing next to the delegates in the Communal Sphere on top of the central marble platform where the council usually met. Banach had begun following Flea everywhere. He stood behind him with a claw on Flea's right shoulder. The delegates were all standing together behind the black marble podium. Regardless of the fact that the human delegation was officially disbanded and their status, along with the rest of the humans, had been revoked, the human population still followed its energetic young trio. They were surrounded by holo-cameras.

Alex, however, was standing in a glass pod floating in space next to the human carrier. She held a bottle of champagne in her hand and was smiling proudly. She was surrounded by holo-cameras as well. Everyone could see Alex on the large screens around the communal and Human Spheres. The pod she was in consisted of a glass dome that was on a platform with some small maneuvering rockets. This made it so she could be easily seen by the holo-cameras that would be projecting her image back to the Human Sphere. They would also be seen in some of the other spheres where human support was high. Alex was about to raise the red energy field that was hiding the human carrier from view. It was time for her to Christen her ship.

"You okay?" Flea whispered to asked Christina as they stood there waiting to start the ceremony.

"I can't believe they actually revoked our status," she whispered back disappointedly.

"I feel like we failed," added Daniela.

"Don't be so hard on yourselves," Morgan said. "It's not your fault.

"Yeah," added Flea. "They had it in for us since the beginning. Personally, I'm surprised they didn't do it sooner."

"Look," Morgan said trying to cheer them up, "It's a testimony to your skill that you lasted as long as you did."

"Really?" asked Ryoko.

"Of course," Flea said. "We're all very proud of you."

"These small human females," Banach growled curiously. "They are strong like you, Gabriel-Captain?"

"Yes," Flea said proudly. "They are very strong."

Banach was starting to recognize the inner strength that the small humans carried inside of them.

"So what does your wife have in store for us, Captain Morgan?" Christina asked with only a slight giggle at the name and title.

"You'll have to wait and see," he said.

Finally, the cameras started to flash red lights in unison which signaled they were about to start in a few seconds.

"Welcome," said Christina after the red lights turned green. "We wish to thank all of you for joining us today. As you know, we have been putting a lot of time and effort into mobilizing ourselves for war with our enemies."

The cameras were programmed to focus on whoever was speaking at the time.

"There have been those who would try to stop us," added Daniela. "But we continued on."

"Some want us to quit," Ryoko said. "Some even tried to kill us, but still we stay and fight!"

The crowd cheered loudly for Ryoko. The population had grown fond of the diminutive Asian girl ever since she had placed her life at risk.

"Helping us in that fight are some humans we have all grown very fond of," Daniela followed up. "Like the Executive Officer of the ArchAngels fighter group, Captain Morgan Mendenhall!"

She gestured to Morgan and he took a step forward. Since they no longer had the luxury of day time television, one of their main sources of entertainment was the internet. All of them had seen the website Bella had put in place. They also continued to check it every day, since Bella was very good about updating it.

She even included some interviews that some of her agents conducted with some of the humans involved in the carrier and fighter group. The crowd cheered loudly and started chanting for Morgan.

Wolf! Wolf! Wolf! Wolf!

On the website, Morgan was identified as: *Captain Morgan "the Wolf" Mendenhall*. It was also on the side of his fighter. He was very popular.

"Thank you," Morgan said waiving to the crowd. "Thank you."

When Morgan waived, the response of the crowd changed from chanting to a massive imitation of a howling wolf pack. They howled over and over again until Morgan stepped back.

"The Commanding officer of the ArchAngels," said Christina gesturing toward Flea. "Captain Gabriel Sherman."

Banach released his protective grip from Flea's shoulder as he stepped forward. The crowd started to cheer insanely. They began chanting for him as he waived.

Flea! Flea! Flea! Flea!

"Thanks, everyone," Flea said with a smile.

After hearing his voice, the crowd went even crazier. The females at the front of the crowd, human or otherwise, began throwing their underwear at Flea's feet. Flea didn't know how to react. He had never experienced this before. His grin kept getting larger as he began to feel slightly embarrassed. When he blushed, they scream even louder. Morgan reached forward and tugged on Flea's shirt. Flea stepped back in line.

"That was awesome!" he leaned over and whispered to Morgan.

Morgan rolled his eyes, shook his head and smiled at his friend.

"And there is one more," said Christina turning serious. "One who has worked so very hard to give us this opportunity. She is the one who will lead our valiant warship as it goes out to represent us in the universe!"

"She will stand tall and proud!" Daniela added with encouragement. "She is a leader in our struggle and our ray of hope!"

"And when our enemy comes," shouted Ryoko. "She will stand and fight!"

The crowd already knew who they were talking about. They were talking about Alexandria. The crowd was already chanting her name.

Alex! Alex! Alex! Alex!

"Ladies and Gentleman," shouted Christina. "Direct your attention to the screens around us! I give you the Captain of your warship! The commanding officer of the first human starship!"

The three young pop-stars pointed to the giant monitor behind them. The crowd was going insane. The monitor showed a seventy five foot picture of Alexandria. Every monitor in the sphere was showing Alexandria. Around the sphere, holo-projectors were showing holograms of Alexandria that ranged in size from about twelve inches tall to the largest one on top of the government building that showed a fifty foot hologram of her.

"Captain Alexandria Mendenhall!" shouted Daniela.

"Good morning everyone," Alex said with a smile.

The crowd went wild.

"Thank you," she said modestly. "Please, let me begin."

The crowd went silent in rapt attention to hear what Alex had to tell them.

"It has been a long and trying experience for many of us to reach this point," she began. "Many of us lost our homes, our loved ones, and everything we had. As we sifted through the ashes of our existence, we all had one question on our minds."

She paused.

"We wanted to know why," she continued gently. "Why? Why dear God did this happen? What did we do? Do we deserve this? As we continued to look, we heard the whisper of a name. We heard: *Goraan.*"

The crowd started to "boo" as she spoke the name.

"This is the name of our enemies," she said.

The crowd continued to "boo" and "hiss." Some shouted obscenities.

"They were the ones who did this to us!" Alex started to raise her voice. "They were the ones who stole our families and our homes! In a way, they even stole our lives. They may not have killed us, but they sent us running. They took everything we knew, and destroyed it before our very eyes. We may still exist, but we no longer live. Not the way we used to! We run and hide the way they want us to! We do what they want, and we run! That is how they have stolen our very lives!"

She looked intently out at the crowd. It was a very intimidating sight from the fifty foot hologram.

"Well I am here to say that I want mine back!" she shouted. "I will go forth and steal back from them what they've stolen from me! I want my life back!"

The crowd screamed wildly. Alex was getting pretty good at this.

"And this," she gestured to the vessel hiding behind the red energy field, "will help us get it! She is small, but she is fast and strong, too! She will go in and fight bravely against our enemies, and help us steal back what is ours! I have adorned her in the tradition of some of the best of thieves in the history of my home world! For that is what we are! We are thieves trying to steal back our right to live! And she will take us clad in black, like some menacing shade, to find our enemies and give us retribution! Ladies and Gentleman, I give you our battle carrier: the *Pirate Queen*!"

The red energy field around the human carrier disappeared. Revealed for all to see was the sleek, black, battle carrier that Alexandria would command into battle. Flea could scarcely recognize the vessel he once described as an intergalactic shoe box. It was no longer a dull metallic grey color. The entire thing had been painted black. Metallic flecks in the paint made it sparkle in the light. It was no longer rectangular at all. There were no more flat sides to the vessel. The top, bottom, and sides were all curved with rounded edges. The bow was now slightly smaller than the aft giving it a conical appearance. The front end was no longer flat, either. It was cut on an angle that so that the top of the ship was not as long as the bottom.

The monitors kept changing views so the ship could be seen from different angles. Located on the bottom half of the bow was a set of doors that slid open to reveal the hanger bay inside. Flea could see his fighter group waiting through those doors. The large tube-like structure that was in the middle of the top of the vessel was no longer there at all. On the sides at the aft end of the ship, two dorsal fins protruded upward and swept back. A cross-wing connected them together. The back edge of the wing was parallel with the back of the ship. In the middle of the cross-wing, a compartment was located with two windows facing the front of the ship. This is where the bridge was located. A shaft led from the bridge to the main body of the ship. The wings were on the bottom of the sides of the ship. They started out rather slender at the front, and slowly widened until they were near the back of the ship, where they angled back in. There were no sharp edges on the vessel whatsoever. The whole thing looked sleek, black and menacing.

"Look at the skull!" someone near the stage whispered loud enough for Flea and Morgan to hear.

On both port and starboard sides of the ship centered near the back, was a large grey skull and crossed bones. On the aft of the ship above the engines, in large gothic style letters was the name of the ship: *Pirate Queen.*

"That thing is awesome!" Flea said to Morgan. "It's massive!"

"She definitely did a good job with it!" Morgan agreed. "Impressive!"

Alex leaned over in the pod and placed the bottle of champagne in a small compartment at her feet. It launched out of the bottom of the pod's platform and made a slow and gracefully spinning path toward the *Pirate* Queen. It collided with and shattered against the side of the ship.

"I hereby christen thee," Alex said dramatically, "the *Pirate Queen!*"

"All hail the Pirate Queen!" shouted Morgan as he pumped his fists in the air.

The crowd cheered wildly. They shouted there approval. The very dome of the sphere shook with their elation. They loved their Pirate Queen.

***

"So what did you guys think?" asked Alex after the ceremony.

"Are you kidding?" asked Flea excitedly. "This thing is awesome!"

They were standing on the bridge together for the first time. They had some pictures taken of the moment. They had posed in front of the window. Since the bridge was in the cross-wing like Flea had thought, it made for a nice view of the top of the vessel in the background of the picture.

"Thanks," Alex said modestly. "I designed the hull myself with some help from the maintenance robots."

"It looks great, sweetie," Morgan said with approval.

"You know what else?" she asked enthusiastically. "I've been reviewing the statistics of the other ships in the fleet and found out that we are the most heavily armed!"

"But we're the smallest," Flea sounded a bit surprised.

"Not only that," said Alex proudly. "But we're also the fastest and have the best defensive capabilities. No one can stop us!"

She sounded as confident in her ship as any good Captain should.

"I'm sure of it!" Morgan added proudly. "Good job, sweetie!"

"So where are the prisoners?" asked Flea changing the subject. "The delegates told us Bella was having a few problems while we were on stage. They asked if we might check on her after we pulled out and got some distance between us and the base."

"She's in the brig with them," Alex explained. "She's been asking them questions all night. Not one of them got answered as far as I know."

"Thanks," Flea said with a nod.

"We have to go, sweetie," Morgan sounded disappointed to leave her.

"I know," she sighed. "See you at lunch?"

"Sure thing," Morgan smiled.

Flea and Morgan made their way through the ship to the brig. Considering it was the smallest ship in the fleet, it was a surprisingly long walk. They stood outside the door to where the cells were located when they found it. Two members of the Space Marine Corp were standing guard outside the door. They were young women, as most of the humans were, standing at their ease with rather grim expressions. Their long hair was in pig-tails. One was blonde the other was black haired. They had on black eye make-up and matching black lipstick and nail polish.

They were also wearing some sort of shiny black armor. Their black armored tops left most of their abdomens bare and were sleeveless. They wore a pair of black armored chaps that hung low around their hips. Covering their knees was a pair of segmented black metal knee pads. Their thick soled boots went up to the bottom of the knee pads and had thick straps instead of laces. Their armored gauntlets covered from their forearms to just above their elbows. Their bare skin was covered with a shear, black substance that shimmered when they moved slightly. It looked as if it might tear if they ran too quickly or brushed against something. Finishing the outfit was a small, armored bikini bottom. They had a large energy pistol at each hip, a large assault blaster strapped diagonally across their backs and a long knife sheathed in their right boots. Flea arched an eyebrow when he looked at them as they approached. Morgan blushed slightly.

"Were they wearing this the last time we saw them?" Flea whispered to his friend.

"I don't remember," replied the red cheeked Morgan. "I was too busy pounding Osgood."

"Good morning ladies," Flea said authoritatively.

"Good morning, sir," responded one of the guards as the two snapped to attention.

"Is this your standard uniform?" asked Flea.

"Yes! It's our battle gear!" the blonde one said excitedly, "Isn't it cute?"

She turned around in a small circle to show it off.

"The correct response would be 'yes, sir!'" Flea barked. "And Marines to do not twirl around like school girls showing off a new outfit! YOU GOT THAT!?!"

They both looked stunned.

"Calm down, Flea," Morgan admonished him. "They're new at this. Cut them a break."

"Fine," Flea growled at them. "But, you two better shape the Hell up, Goddamnit!"

"Does Captain Alexandria know you guys are wearing this?" Morgan asked still blushing as he tried to ease the tension.

"She saw it," the blonde said glancing at Flea. "But, she didn't like it very much, sir."

"That's what I figured," Morgan said.

"If she doesn't like it then why are you wearing it?" Flea asked. "Isn't she in charge of the Space Marines?"

"No, sir," responded blonde. "The delegates got together with Captain Alexandria and they split up the different branches of our military."

"I see," Flea said flatly.

"Yes, sir," the dark haired one replied. "This way Captain Alex was no longer overwhelmed with work."

"She was doing quite a bit," Morgan said.

"So who is in charge of what?" Flea asked.

"Masters is in charge of the Space Marines and ground troops, Abe is in charge of the fleet and Knight is in charge of intelligence, sir," she explained.

"And these...outfits?" Flea asked.

"They're actually very durable, sir," the blonde said defensively. "They're made out of a fine grade metallic mesh we couldn't do on Earth. They feel like leather and silk, but are even stronger and lighter than Kevlar! We tested them in some combat simulators! They're cute and provide a lot of protection. Delegate Masters designed them herself! She said you might like them! They look like something out of one her music videos, sir!"

Flea chuckled.

"Go and get about twenty more Marines." he said to the blonde. "Bring them back here to help us with the prisoners, okay?"

"Sir, yes, sir!" she snapped to attention and then trotted off.

Flea elbowed Morgan in the ribs. He caught his friend checking out the blonde's butt in her armored thong bikini as she turned around and left.

"You're married, remember?" Flea chuckled.

"Shut up," Morgan said. "I'm married, not blind."

"Not unless Alex sees you looking," Flea snorted. "She might poke an eye out if she sees you."

The two walked into the brig. It had twelve cells. Six cells were on each side of a small passageway that ran down the middle. At the door where Flea and Morgan entered were two more black clad Space Marines armed and dressed in the same fashion as the two outside the door. One was Asian and the other was a red haired girl.

"Good Morning, sir," the Asian said as she snapped to attention.

"Good Morning, ladies," Flea said without looking at them.

At the far end of the central passage were two more Marines standing on either side of another door. One was male. His uniform was identical, except he wasn't wearing chaps and a thong. He wore a pair of armored, black pants instead. He also wore a black skin tight shirt under the shoulder pad-like armor on his torso. Everything else was the same, though. There weren't many males left among the humans. Flea was surprised to see him here.

"Where's your thong, Marine?" Morgan asked harshly pointing at the male.

"Sir!" the young man barked when he snapped to attention. "I left it in my other pants, sir!"

They all shared a laugh at his small joke.

"I'll let it go this time," Morgan said jokingly. "But next time I'm bringing you up on charges for a uniform violation! Are we communicating, Marine?"

"Sir, yes, sir," he responded.

Flea and Morgan walked down the aisle looking in each cell. They reached the two Marines on the far end and then turned around and walked back. They were standing equal distances from both sets of Marines.

"Who's in charge here?" Flea demanded with an authoritative tone.

"I am, sir," the Asian trotted forward.

Flea would have to remind himself to talk to Christina about rank insignias later. He would have never known who was in charge.

"What happened to Osgood?" Flea demanded.

She snapped to attention. She could obviously tell Flea was upset.

"We put some of prisoners with him sir and…" she began explaining.

"You did what?" Flea was shocked. "You put prisoners in with some of our own? We have twelve cells here! It was not necessary to double Osgood in a cell with some of this trash!"

"I am sorry, sir," she sounded desperate. "I didn't know!"

"Do you have any prior military experience?" Flea asked calming down a bit. "Or even experience working in a jail or something? Anything? Do any of you?"

"No, sir," she replied looking as if she might cry.

"Next time," Flea sighed. "Put prisoners of war in different cells than our own people. Osgood is dead now."

"I may have wanted him dead," said Morgan. "But not like this."

"Sorry, sir," she said sounding upset.

"Just remember that for next time," Flea shook his head. "Don't beat yourself up."

He would have to discuss some policies with Christina as well, it would seem.

"We're here, sir," the blonde said standing at the door with a pack of Marines. "I brought the Marines you wanted."

"Thanks," Flea said over his shoulder. "Where is Bella?"

"Interrogation room," responded the Asian pointing at the door next to the young man.

"Wait here," Flea said.

Flea and Morgan entered the interrogation room. It was a large room with a small matter combiner in one of the walls in case they needed anything while they were in here. Bella was standing there intently trying to question one of the Goraan prisoners she had seated at a small table in front of her. The Goraan prisoner was shackled with his hands on the table. She looked slightly upset and a little annoyed. She wasn't saying anything.

"What's wrong?" Flea asked her.

"In my work at the Vatican," she explained sheepishly. "All I had to do was send others out on missions. I went on missions myself until I was promoted, but that was really it. I was never trained in interrogation. Others did the interrogations. I can't even get him to tell me his name."

"You mind if we give it a shot?" Flea asked cheerfully.

"Give it a try if you think you can do better," she defensively.

Flea poked his head out into the cell chamber.

"Gather the prisoners!" Flea shouted harshly. "Shackle them all up and bring them in here! If any of them struggle, shoot them in the face! That's an order, ladies!"

Flea glanced at Morgan. Morgan had a very grim smile on his face.

"Do we get to beat people up, now?" Morgan asked softly.

"Yep," Flea said with an evil look.

"What if they don't talk?" asked Bella sounding slightly afraid for some reason.

"That's their choice," Flea said nonchalantly.

Flea heard shots fired in the adjacent room with the cells. The Marines filed them all inside. One of the Marines had some yellowish substance splattered on her. Flea assumed it was alien blood.

"Go get cleaned up and checked out in medical," Flea told the bloodstained Marine. "I don't know if these guys have anything they can pass on to us in their blood stream."

"Sir, yes, sir," she huffed still panting from the struggle.

"Let us know what the Doctor tells you okay?" Morgan added.

She left the room to go to medical as instructed. Flea looked at the prisoners noticing that there were ten of them, including the one sitting behind the table. The Marines had their guns leveled at the ones they brought in the room.

"Let's start by trying this the easy way," Flea said with a smile.

"Are you going to answer any of our questions?" Morgan asked the one sitting down.

No answer. The prisoner sat unmoving.

"Good," Flea said cheerfully. "Let's get going then, I don't have all day, you know."

The shackled prisoner seemed dead behind those alien, black eyes.

"Twenty milliliters of Sodium Pentothal in a syringe," Flea said walking over to the combiner in the wall.

"What are you doing?" asked Bella.

"It's a drug that lowers inhibitions and makes people open to suggestions or interrogation," Morgan said. "It's like some kind of truth drug."

"Do you know how it works," she asked sounding concerned.

"Nope," Flea and Morgan answered in unison.

"Do you even know how much to give him?" she sounded upset.

"Nope," they both replied in unison again.

"I don't even know where his veins are to inject him," Flea said with an eerie laugh. "But I've always wanted to try this stuff."

"And this is probably our only chance," Morgan added.

"This is your last chance," Flea said to the prisoner at the table.

Flea pulled out the very large syringe from the matter combiner. He brandished the needle like a weapon as he walked over to the prisoner. The prisoner's arm was muscular and Flea spotted a vein in the fold of his elbow. He stuck the syringe in the prisoner's arm at that location and emptied its contents into the prisoner's body.

"Now what?" asked Bella.

"Now," Flea shrugged. "We wait and see what happens."

After a few minutes, the prisoner's eyes started to bulge out of his head. He began shaking violently. He clenched his fists and dug his fingers into the palms of his hands so until he drew blood. He screamed out in sheer terror. Blood started to ooze from small cracks that were forming in the skin of his face. The prisoner began foaming at the mouth. It was nasty looking white foam mixed with his green blood. Blood started oozing from his nose. The prisoner let out one more blood curdling scream. Then his head exploded. His headless torso slumped forward onto the table and spilled his blood out onto the floor. Flea turned to look at the remaining prisoners. They all looked slightly scared, except for the small red female at the end. Flea's eyes threatened to pop out of his head.

"Well now that's not good!" Flea exclaimed sounding a bit surprised.

"Nope," agreed Morgan wholeheartedly. "Not really."

"Unshackle and dispose of the body," Flea said shaking his head. "Bring over another one, please."

The Marines followed Flea's orders and removed the corpse. Another prisoner was brought over and shackled in place. Flea refilled the syringe, but this time he only filled it half way. He injected his prisoner with it.

"Are you sure about this?" Bella sounded worried. "The last one died, after all."

"I became a lot less concerned for their wellbeing after they shot at me," Flea scowled.

The prisoner started to convulse. He began bleeding, not quite as profusely as the last one. Eventually, regardless of the lower dosage, the prisoner screamed, foamed at the mouth and then slumped over dead. The remaining prisoners looked a bit more scared. All of them, except the red female. She was giggling. Flea walked over to her.

"Shut up," Flea growled at her.

She smiled coyly at him and batted her long eyelashes. She winked at him, growled seductively, and blew him a small kiss. Flea walked away shaking his head. Under normal circumstances, he would have thought she was cute.

"That one is sick," he muttered.

The circumstances were far from normal.

"Let's try one more," Flea said going back to the table.

The Marines did as they were instructed. Flea injected another prisoner, only filling up about a quarter of the small needle before doing so. The prisoner shook less violently than the last, but eventually started to foam at the mouth and died.

"Well," Flea said to Morgan with a shrug. "So much for the trial and error interrogation methods. Maybe we should try water-boarding one of them?"

"I don't know," Morgan was skeptical. "We really haven't been trained in this stuff and I'm not sure how to do it."

The red female started laughing as if Morgan had just told the funniest joke she had ever heard. Flea looked at her and just shook his head. He placed what was left of the drug and the needle back in the combiner to be reclaimed.

"What the Hell is going on down here?" Rebecca yelled flying into the room.

"We're interrogating prisoners," Flea said.

"Looks more like killing them, to me!" she shouted. "What did you do to them?"

"Sodium Pentothal," Morgan shrugged. "Then they died."

"I'm not surprised," she said harshly.

"Why is that?" asked Flea.

"I've been studying some of the information we got out of the fighters these pilots were flying," she explained. "I looked into the Goraan physiology. You do know that the Goraan race is just a bunch of parasites that attach themselves to the brains of other creatures, right?"

"What are you saying?" Flea asked curiously "Could we save the creatures the Goraan took?"

"No," Rebecca shook her head. "Once they take over a body, everything that was once the creature they took it from is gone."

"So what's the problem?" asked Morgan.

"The problem is that you gave Sodium Pentothal to a Goraan," she sounded frustrated. "They have a similar biology as a slug on Earth. Have you ever poured salt on a slug?"

"No," Flea said. "Why, is that bad?"

"It kills it!" she said. "You just injected the Goraan slugs with a bunch of Sodium, stupid! It probably reacted with the other chemicals in his body to form an excess of salt in his bloodstream! You killed it!"

"Oh," Flea shrugged. "My bad."

"Your bad?" she shouted. "You murdered three of them! That is all you can say for yourself? Really?"

"Do I look like someone who studied slug biology?" Flea yelled.

"Don't you think you should have asked first?" Rebecca screamed at him.

"Calm down!" Bella shouted. "Both of you!"

There was a long period of awkward silence.

"Malacologist," Morgan said breaking the silence.

"Huh?" Flea seemed confused.

"Malacologist," Morgan reiterated. "A slug is a type of mollusk. Someone who studies them is called a Malacologist."

"How did you learn that?" Flea said curiously

"Jeopardy," Morgan replied. "I learned it from watching Jeopardy."

The humans chuckled as the tension slowly eased from the room.

"Promise no more experimenting with drugs, boys," Rebecca admonished Morgan and Flea. "They may be enemies, but we learn more from them alive."

"We promise," they said in unison like a pair of errant school children.

"Good," Rebecca said. "Incidentally, your Marine is fine, okay?"

"Thanks," Flea said.

Rebecca turned and left the room. Morgan and Flea looked at each for a moment.

"Now what?" Morgan asked.

"I don't know," Flea said. "We could just beat them. How much info did you get from the fighters' computer anyway, Bella?"

"One of them still had a link maintained to their battleship group," she explained. "I have fleet movements, numbers, strength, technologies…"

"Does my wife know any of this?" asked Morgan.

"Yes," she said. "I outlined the high points in an email. She said she was going to go over it with you two at lunch."

"Why do we need them, then?" asked Flea pointing to the prisoners.

"Live testimony is always useful," Bella explained. "That's why I've been trying to get them to talk."

"And now we're back to square one with that," Morgan said.

"Or just shove them out an airlock and be done," Flea growled. "That would be much easier."

The three looked at each other for a moment.

"I can help," said the red female prisoner softly. "I know what to do. Let me help you."

"Explain yourself," Flea said.

"Outside," she said jutting her chin toward the door. "Alone. Just you and me, sexy."

Flea looked at her a moment.

"What's wrong," she said. "I'm shackled. Even my whips are bound to my forearms. Are you afraid of a defenseless little female?"

She grinned seductively.

"Defenseless… yeah, right," Flea didn't believe her for a moment. "Outside, now. Let's go."

The two stepped out into the brig alone. Flea took a long look at her. She was very tiny. She was at least three inches shorter than he was. Her flesh was a dark red. She was wearing skin tight black, wet-leather pants with a matching wet leather half shirt with slits across it that bared parts of her breasts. It looked as if some of her clothing had been torn off at some point. She had a strong and well-defined muscular physique. Her fluorescent orange hair hung in a pony-tail to her waist. Her long finger nails and lips were the same color as her hair. Flea didn't know if this was a trait of her species or just some make-up. She was very slender, yet still curvaceous. She was very attractive. Flea noticed some cuts and wounds on her. It looked like she had been in a fight not too long ago.

"What's your name?" Flea asked roughly.

"Toren al'Shoken," she responded.

"Why would you want to help us?" Flea asked. "And how do I know I can trust you?"

"You don't know if you can trust me," she replied batting her eyelashes and smiling at him.

"What is your name?" she asked in turn.

"Gabriel," he said. "And I'm the one asking questions, here!"

A thought suddenly struck Flea. He grabbed Toren by the elbow and poked his head back in the interrogation room.

"Put everyone back in their cells and don't kill anybody until I get back!" he barked to one of the Marines.

"Where are you going?" asked Morgan.

"I'll be back in a bit, okay?" said Flea quickly. "Just trust me."

Flea led Toren by the elbow through the corridors of the ship. He took her past everything and went straight to the hanger bay. He took her to his fighter.

"What's this colorful little toy?" she asked sounding slightly insulting.

Flea shoved her against his fighter. Her back "thudded" hard against the hull of the vessel.

"Watch your tone!" he shouted. "I don't hit girls, but I could make an exception for an enemy!"

Toren moaned seductively when he threatened her. He opened the cargo door just behind the cockpit to reveal the lounge area of his fighter. He pushed Toren hard onto the small couch and got in behind her. She squirmed around and giggled girlishly when she was thrown around. He slammed the door shut after they were inside.

"Who is this skanky little slut you bring into my home!?!" Angel demanded when she appeared.

She was wearing a school girl outfit similar to the one on the Angel wore in the ArchAngels unit marking. Her long hair was tied in a pony tail that hung to below her back-side. She wore a pair of glasses with thick black rims, even though she didn't need them.

"A prisoner," Flea explained.

"So you bring her here of all places?" Angel demanded.

"I didn't know where else to take her," Flea explained. "I need your help."

Angelina flopped down on the couch.

"Fine," she pouted. "What can I do?"

"Can you tell if she's telling the truth?" asked Flea.

"I can monitor her bio-energies and tell if she is lying with almost one hundred percent accuracy," Angel responded smugly. "I can even back up what she says with the information I received from the Goraan fighters."

"You got info from the fighters, too?" asked Flea angrily. "It's like everyone but me knows what's going on around here. I'm always the last to know!"

"It's okay, love," giggled Angel. "I broke into the fighters and downloaded copies of everything I could get my hands on as soon as they were on board. I wanted to make sure we had it in case we needed it before it was corrupted. I got to it even before Bella!"

"Good," Flea approved. "Let's get started."

Flea asked Toren all kinds of questions. He had her re-state her name and where she was from. He found out that she wasn't a Goraan like the others. She didn't have a slug in her head. She was engineered in a lab for breeding purposes. The Goraan needed other species to perpetuate their own race. Toren was a member of the only species the Goraan could breed with aside from their own. They used Toren's race, because it was much faster and more efficient then the mating of the Goraan in their slug forms. It was also more pleasurable. The actual birthing however, would kill the individual of Toren's species.

"Our species was once on the home world of Eiligor in great numbers," Toren explained. "But after the Goraan developed the ability to take over bodies many thousands of years ago, they started to do so for breeding. Until then, they could not perpetuate their race in great enough numbers to last. They were slowly dying as a species."

"I see," said Flea. "So how did you get by without getting one of those slugs in you?"

"They discovered that they could breed with us after taking the body of another without actually using us as shells," she explained. "They probably found this out by accident a few thousand years ago and then killed off all of our males shortly after. I don't know all the details. When I was thirteen, I reached an age where I was biologically able to breed and carry one of those slugs to term."

"That's horrible," Angel said sadly. "What stopped them from doing so?"

"Because we have been subjugated by the Goraan for so many years, they no longer see us as a threat. They give us a small amount of education which involves explaining to us over and over not to resist the way things are. They even let us join the military for a short time if we want," she explained. "That's what I did to put off being bred with for a while. Eventually, though, we are impregnated. Then, after a few slugs have finished growing inside us, they chew their way out of our wombs and we die."

"From the inside?" asked Flea incredulously.

"Yes," responded Toren flatly. "It makes its first meal out of its own mother."

"That's terrible!" Angel was shocked.

"So how can you help us?" Flea asked.

"I joined the military after I turned thirteen. In the military I was trained as an Inquisitor," she smiled a bit. "I liked my job for the last three years. It allowed me to beat them during questionings. But, in a few months I would have served my four years. That's as long as they allow us to serve. Then I would be discharged and used for breeding."

Flea quickly did the math in his head and found out Toren was almost seventeen.

"They let you join that young?" asked Flea.

"Yes," she said. "But only if I became an Inquisitor. I spent in the first two years being tortured and beaten as part of my training. Otherwise, you have to live to be eighteen before joining. That means you have to trust to luck not to be picked through the lottery for breeding before then. Most of us don't make it that long."

"If they killed off all the males then how do they get more of you?" asked Flea.

"We're made in labs, now" explained Toren. "Then put into pens until we are old enough. It's a very long and involved process making one of us to breed with. That's why they started to use other species when they found out they could do so. They still prefer to use us, though, because they have us under their control."

"Is your species also called Goraan?" Flea asked.

"No," she said, "They refer to us as 'breeders.' If we ever had another name, they have kept it secret from us."

"It's a psychological ploy to convince them they are a lesser race and should do as they are taught," explained Angel. "They took away the identity of Toren's entire race."

"How many of you are there?" asked quietly.

"I'm not sure," she responded. "There were about four million were I was at before I joined the military."

Flea looked at Angel inquisitively. Angel's eyes rolled up inside her head for a moment.

"They have a little over three billion 'breeders' like Toren," Angel said after she finished searching her files. "They moved the lab and all of her species to a new planet they took not too long ago. They call it 'the pleasure planet.' Goraan, however, are breeding at a rate faster than they can make more breeders."

"That's why the keep looking for more," Toren said. "There are really three billion of us?"

"Yes," replied Angel gently.

Toren looked stunned.

"Toren," Angel said gently. "I didn't know how hard your life has been. I am sorry for calling you a skanky little slut."

Flea smiled at Angel. He could tell she genuinely felt sorry for Toren. So did he. He wanted to help Toren, but it would be hard to convince the others.

"So what can an Inquisitor do for us?" asked Flea with a small grin.

"I can start by getting the other prisoners to talk," she said enthusiastically. "I can promise you that they fear me more than anyone else on this ship."

"What do you want in exchange?" asked Flea.

"Don't send me back," she said fiercely. "Even if you kill me, just don't send me back! I prefer death to going back there! I'll never go back!"

Flea looked at Angel. Angel was visibly shaken by hearing Toren's account.

"Well?" Flea asked Angel.

"She is telling the truth," Angel said softly. "Every last word as far as I can tell."

Flea sat looking between Angel and Toren.

"Don't just sit there!" admonished Angel. "You have to help her! It's what you do! Remember? You help people!"

"Hold out your hands Toren," Flea said.

Toren did as she was instructed. Flea removed all of her restraints. Flea sat with Toren and explained to her the current situation she was in. Flea felt he could trust her so he told her the whole story leaving nothing out. He even explained about Angel, but he did ask her not tell anyone about his fighter's A.I.

"So I will still die soon?" she chuckled grimly.

"Probably," Flea said, "We most likely all will."

"I would rather die fighting Goraan than live to breed with them," she said making an angry face.

"Good," said Flea. "You can start your fight by coming back to the brig with me. Interrogate the prisoners. Then you can join me and my friends for lunch, okay?"

"I will have friends?" she asked wistfully.

"Yes," said Flea. "You can have friends and are free to do whatever you want. If anyone gives you a hard time, you come and find me directly, okay?"

"I will," she said tearing up. "Are you my first real friend?"

"If it makes you feel better," Flea smiled fondly at her. "Yes."

She threw her arms around Flea's neck. Flea hugged her and let her cry for a moment.

"What about me?" Angel's voice was thick with emotion.

Toren lunged at Angel to try and give her a hug. She flew through Angel like she wasn't even there. In her current emotional state, Toren forgot that Angel was a hologram. The two shared a laugh, even though Angel was a bit self conscience sometimes about her holographic state.

"Okay, sweetie," Flea said picking Toren up off the ground. "I'll introduce you to lots of new friends later. Right now, we need to dry our eyes and go take care of the prisoners, okay?"

"You got it," Toren said energetically. "I will make them squeal."

She had a very dark and disturbed look on her face. Flea had to wonder for a moment what he had just unleashed.

18

Flea put the shackles back on Toren. She had quite a few disapproving glances cast her way as Flea escorted her back to the interrogation room. He cuffed her again to avoid questions on the way back. Flea was starting to wish he'd never gotten involved in any of this. He wanted to go back to sitting around his sofa and playing video games. It seemed like he would never get to do that again.

When they reached the interrogation room, Bella and Morgan were already gone. The prisoners were being watched by some Marines. Flea ushered them into the hall as Toren started making wicked looking implements in the matter combiner. She methodically worked over each of the prisoners. It was gruesome work. She was obviously very skilled at it with a lot of experience. Flea had never seen anything like it before. They answered all her questions before she was finished with them. A few talked without Toren ever raising an implement. After a short discussion with his new ally, Flea decided the best course after they finished the interrogation was to execute the prisoners. The former Imperial Ship's Inquisitor was more than happy to do this task as well. She marched them to the end of the hanger bay and gave them a simple choice. They could open the hanger doors and jump through the energy barrier into the vacuum of space, or be her pet for the rest of their lives. Every single one of them jumped through the barrier. Apparently, she had a bad reputation among the Goraan. After this, Flea took her to the living quarters he shared with his wingman. Kaida was in the room when they showed up.

"Flea!" she said excitedly as Flea came in the room.

She started to run over to give Flea a hug but stopped short when she saw Toren.

"Who is this?" Kaida asked disapprovingly. "She is prisoner."

Kaida must have gone down to see the prisoners at some point.

"She's on our side now, Kaida," Flea said. "She's going to help us."

"Really?" Kaida said with a skeptical look.

"Yes," Flea said with a nod. "Really."

Kaida walked over to stand in front of Toren. The two were the same height. Toren however was much more well endowed. Kaida arched an eyebrow when she looked at Toren.

"You will not hurt Flea, yes?" she asked seriously.

"Who is Flea?" asked Toren.

"That's me," Flea explained. "My friends call me Flea."

"Don't I get to call you Flea?" Toren sounded concerned.

"Yes," Flea cracked a smile. "You can call me Flea."

"Thanks," she sounded very relieved. "I won't hurt him, I promise. He's my first real friend. I'll keep him safe."

Kaida walked around Toren looking the red female over up and down. She finally stood back in front of Toren and smiled.

"Good," Kaida sounded satisfied and smiled. "Me and Flea are family. I am Kaida. I am friend for you, too."

"Really?" Toren started to get choked up again. "I…I'm Toren."

Flea thought Toren was very emotional.

"Yes, Toren," Kaida said. "Really."

"Flea I missed…" Armina came in the room and stopped when she saw Toren. "…you. She's a Goraan, Flea! What's she doing here? I saw her in the cages when I was with Kaida!"

Armina ran over and kicked Toren in the shins.

"Oww!" Toren grunted. "Hey!"

Flea arched an eyebrow at Kaida. She shouldn't have taken the kitten to see the prisoners. Kaida shuffled her feet and tried to avoid eye contact with Flea.

"Slow down, kitten," Flea grabbed her around the waist as she tried to run past him. "There's an explanation."

Flea explained everything to Armina. He even told Armina of Toren's past and everything he knew about Toren's species.

He explained everything as gently as he could. Kaida looked shocked quite a few times during the story. So did Armina.

"Do you understand, kitten?" Flea asked as he finished.

"I'm so sorry, Toren," Armina sniffed. "You can be a family with me, Flea, and Kaida, okay?"

"I would like that very much, Armina," Toren's voice was thick with emotion. "You have all been nicer to me in one day than the Goraan had been during my entire life. I'm so glad to be here."

"That might change later," Flea said seriously. "If by some miracle, we manage to survive, I'll have to explain about you to the other Runners. God only knows how they'll react. Let's go to lunch, Toren. Kaida, take Armina down to see the pilots. Let her play with Angel for a while if she wants to, okay?"

"Do you really have to go?" Armina whined hopping up and down.

"If we want a shot to win," Flea explained gently, "then yes."

"Okay," she pouted. "But we play as soon as you get back, okay?"

"I promise," Flea said.

"Okay," she sounded a little better. "Let's go see Angel, Kaida."

The two left to go to the hanger bay.

"Let's go," Flea said to Toren. "I don't know what you eat, but I'm sure the combiner has something in its database."

Flea and Toren walked through the halls toward Alex's state room. Most of the ship's crew was female, much like the Space Marines. However, unlike the Marines, they wore uniforms similar to Alexandria's. Some of the crew looked at them strangely as they passed. That was because as far as they knew, the only other non-humans on board were Kashin and a few Rankorack that joined after the challenge. Toren kept walking with Flea to lunch. She smiled at everyone who looked at her and stayed close to him as she was instructed.

"You think you are going to die," she said trying to make conversation, "Yet you bring a child with you. Why?"

"She stowed away with Morgan's daughter," Flea explained shaking his head. "They were supposed to stay behind, but Armina and Keri snuck on board anyway."

"Even though it is dangerous?" she asked curiously.

"Yup," Flea nodded. "Family can be very irrational sometimes. If we live long enough, you'll find that out for yourself."

"What do they do on board?" Toren said. "Don't they get in the way?"

"Keri and Armina share a room," Flea explained. "The two generally keep each other company. They're very close. Morgan and his family live with me, Kaida and Armina."

"She loves you very much," Toren said.

"I know," Flea nodded. "She's a good girl."

"Armina came down to see you when she thought she might catch you in your quarters," stated Toren. "She loves you very much. You love her, too. I can sense the emotions of others. That's why I was such a good Inquisitor."

"Can you read minds?" Flea asked.

"No," she explained. "Just sense the emotions. It also makes me a little emotional, though. That's how I knew I could trust you. It's also how I know when I've broken someone."

Flea entered Alex's posh stateroom. He walked through it to the small dining area. Alex and Morgan were already seated. Bella decided to join them along with Mihanna. Surprisingly, the Captains of the other Kashin ships were present as well. Roshom was also there. Flea had learned to recognize him even though most Homerall looked the same to him. Flea did not have a very strong liking for Roshom.

Three Rankorack, one of which Flea recognized as Banach, were there as well. Flea had learned to tell Banach apart from the other Rankorack. He was even larger than the rest and had been following Flea very closely since their match. Banach was very upset after the ceremony. Not only did he not get to kill Cormon, but the council said he couldn't go with Flea as well. Banach and the other Rankorack would have willingly disobeyed that order. Flea told them not to. He didn't want to get the Rankorack into any trouble with the other Runners in case the humans failed.

"What in the Hell is she doing here?" exclaimed Bella pointing at Toren. "She's a Goraan!"

The room started to take on an ugly tone. Morgan and Alex knew Flea well enough to have a good idea about what might have happened. They walked over to stand next to Flea. Banach had also moved to stand behind Flea. He placed a massive blue claw on Flea's shoulder. His new relationship with the huge Rankorack was still a mystery to him. The four of them stood between Toren and the other Runners. Banach let out a low, menacing growl.

"Calm down," Flea said trying to silence the room with a gesture.

Everyone kept talking. No one was listening.

"I said calm down!" Flea said more forcefully.

No one listened. They were still admonishing Flea for fraternizing with the enemy.

"Banach," Flea said over his shoulder. "Silence them, please."

Banach filled his huge lungs inside his barrel-like chest with air. Without warning, the large, blue creature let out an ear shattering roar that seemed to last for an eternity. Everyone clasped their hands over their ears. Everyone that is, except for Banach and the other Rankorack. Their eardrums were designed to be able to take a good audio beating. Instead of covering his ears, Banach used his big claws to protectively wrap around Flea's head and protect the much smaller human's hearing. Flea could barely peer out through the spaces between Banach's huge fingers. They were like ten oversized blue bananas, tipped with lethal claws. Flea watched everyone else in the room double over as Banach roared. Banach could growl louder than Armalan. A few delicate pieces of glass sculpture broke as they vibrated from the volume of Banach's roar. When he stopped, the silence in the room was eerie. Banach took his hands off Flea's head.

"Thanks, big guy," Flea said looking up at Banach over his shoulder.

"Of course, Gabriel-Captain," he said solemnly. "I trust your decision to consort with this...creature."

"The rest of you ought to know better than think I'd sell us out to the Goraan by now," Flea scowled at them.

They all looked him as they tried to clear the ringing from their ears.

"She gave me a lot of help and information in exchange for her immunity," Flea said. "So I told her she could stay with us."

"You don't have that authority!" Mihanna said.

"I did what I had to!" Flea said defensively. "She stays! What are you gonna do? You're on our ship, the base is no longer in sight, and we already had our status revoked!"

There was a long period of silence as Flea and Mihanna glared at each other.

"I recognize that look on your face," Mihanna said sourly. "I won't be able to change your mind, will I?"

"No," Flea responded.

"Well," Mihanna said. "She is your responsibility. Don't let her out of your sight until we get back. After that, we will see what happens."

"If we live it's because SHE helped interrogate the prisoners," Flea countered angrily. "Until she came along, we couldn't get anything out of them! I don't care if anyone likes it or not! You'll honor my promise to her!"

Mihanna didn't respond. Toren looked slightly worried.

"Fine," the Admiral sounded defeated. "I'll try and explain things to the council."

"What the Hell are you all doing here, anyway?" Flea asked as if just noticing the rest of the room.

"We are on patrol," Mihanna responded with a sly grin. "As the Admiral of the fleet, I arranged it."

"Oh really?" Flea asked skeptically.

"Yes," Mihanna said spreading his hands innocently. "It is no fault of mine if we happen to be on patrol as you leave. And would it not be most fortuitous if we had the opportunity to join you in formations for a time?"

"Oh yes," Flea said musically. "Of course."

"It's not my fault if we happened to run in to you humans while we were patrolling, is it?" Mihanna said impishly.

"Of course not," Flea said with a grin.

"What a lucky circumstance that we just happened to run into you," continued Mihanna jovially. "Are we to blame if we happen across any Goraan and are forced to defend ourselves?"

"Of course you're not," Flea said widening his grin.

"So here we are," Mihanna finished. "Now let's see if we can accidentally come across our enemies, shall we?"

"Let's just do that," Flea said. "It might be fun!"

They all sat down to lunch together, including Toren. She seemed to have fits of ecstasy when she tried a piece of triple German chocolate caramel cake. Flea saw the other humans in the room blush. The Kashin openly stared at her. They had never been this close to one of the enemy before. They were mildly intimidated and slightly curious about her. She kept smiling at them. Toren wanted them to trust her.

During lunch Flea, Morgan and Alex updated their allies. They were careful not to mention anything about Cormon or what they knew about the Homarell plot in front of Roshom.

"We got all the info we could from the fighters and the prisoners," Bella said. "I will use the fighters we saved to send agents back to infiltrate the Goraan. They launch tomorrow."

"I was going to use those to start another fighter group," Flea said sounding disappointed.

"I need them," Bella shook her head. "I have been training agents to work in the field. With these fighters at my disposal and our new information we should be ready to start spying on the enemy. With the right cover story for their arrival, everything should be fine."

"How will you do this?" asked a wide-eyed Mihanna. "We have never been able to get spies into the Goraan."

"We have a Doctor that can alter human appearance and physiology to match any race," she explained smugly. "It's part of our genetic inferiority that you are all so fond of pointing out. We developed a small electronic chip that implants under the skin of our skulls. It emulates a Goraan slug's bio-energy signs. The Goraan won't be able to tell the difference unless they open the skulls of my agents."

"Wow," Flea said. "I have to admit that's damn good use for the fighters."

They continued eating the long, elaborate meal. Toren had more of the cake, which she seemed to overly enjoy. Banach's diet seemed to consist of an ample supply of raw meat. Alex had arranged for every meal to be like this for the cruise until they met up with the Goraan at Earth's former location. That was the nearest place they could find in the different flight plans for the Goraan fleets that they were certain to meet up with the enemy. They explained this to the others. When they were done Roshom started to shuffle in his seat.

"Before we go any further," Roshom said staring at his hands on top of the table. "I have a confession."

Roshom started telling everything he knew about Cormon. They all started listening intently. Mihanna knew the story as well as the humans did. Flea leaned over to Toren while Roshom was speaking.

"Read this guy for me," he whispered to her. "Let me know if we can trust him."

Flea may not have known Toren long, but he already knew he trusted her more than Roshom.

"I will," she whispered leaning over and placing a hand on Flea's thigh.

Toren was wavering slightly in her seat. When she leaned over, Flea could see her pupils had dilated. Chocolate seemed to have quite an effect on her. Her cheeks flushed a dark purple color. She licked his ear while she was close enough to do so.

"Toren!" Flea whispered harshly. "Concentrate!"

She giggled and slowly drew her hand up his thigh. Flea flinched back and started blushing. She removed her hand quickly and straightened in her seat.

"Are you sick, Gabriel-Captain?" Banach asked sounding concerned. "Something you ate? You just changed colors. We change colors when we are ill."

Flea's eyes bulged a bit, "I'm fine thanks. I'm just reacting to something."

Morgan sighed at Flea.

"Really," Flea said looking at Morgan for a moment. "It's a human thing. I'm fine."

Roshom continued to speak until he felt he had cleared his conscience. The room was silent. Alex looked at Bella for a moment with a curious expression. Bella returned Alex's glance with a knowing expression. Flea wished he could speak the secret language that seemed to exist among females.

"Here," Bella said tossing a holo-record on the table.

It played out the plot between Cormon and the other Homarell.

"How did you get this?" Roshom asked seriously. "I only made one copy and it's in my home."

"Didn't you pay attention earlier?" Bella shrugged. "Because of our more simplistic human biology we can easily surgically alter ourselves to become other species. I've been in your home."

"You spy on your own allies?" Roshom sounded shocked.

"We spy on everyone," Flea grinned wickedly. "We also lie, cheat and steal."

"What did you expect?" Morgan shouted defensively. "You all treated us like trash! We had to do something to protect ourselves! You make us feel two inches tall!"

Morgan jumped to his feet. He was absolutely fuming. Flea recognized the look in his eyes. The floodgates had been opened. Morgan was livid.

"We never asked for any of this!" Morgan shouted. "But we were thrown into it! Did we back down? No! We didn't! And all you people have done is to try and block our every move!"

He leaned out over the table. The other Runners were starting to back away from him.

"We've done everything we can to try and help you people!" Alex added jumping up to join her husband. "We worked our Goddamned asses off and you still don't respect us! If you ask me, we aren't the ones that have a problem! You people can't even work together! How long have you been doing this and this is the best you can do!?!"

The room was silent. All the non-humans were intently listening to Alex and Morgan.

"You can't make any decisions without having a stupid meeting first!" she yelled pointing at them. "Then the council gets together and can't even agree on what the issue they should be talking about even is! Then they schedule another meeting just to talk about that! It's insane! You have no clue as to what the Hell you're doing!"

Mihanna looked at Flea as if he expected Flea to stop Morgan any time now. Flea crossed his arms under his chest.

"I am making a promise!" Morgan yelled shaking a fist. "If we actually live through this I will personally change everything! I will wreak havoc on that council until there is nothing left! I'll do it myself, Goddamnit!"

There was a long period of silence.

"Maybe that would not be so bad," Mihanna said wistfully.

"Maybe we should get rid of the council," Roshom agreed. "Many of them, including my own delegates, have grown corrupt."

"What will we do?" Mihanna asked looking intently at Morgan.

"First, we live through this," Morgan said confidently, "Then we go back and make them do as we say."

"How do we do that?" Banach rumbled.

"We have all the guns," Flea explained. "It shouldn't be too hard. We disband the entire council and set up a more streamlined government. We dismantle all the different spheres and make everyone live together. We force them to become a group."

"Will it truly be that easy?" Mihanna asked innocently.

"Not in the slightest," Flea chuckled. "It will probably suck for a while. But, we do it anyway. We don't have a choice. We need to get a grip on ourselves first if we are ever going to defeat our enemies."

"We have to be in this together," Morgan said. "If anyone wants out, turn around and leave now."

No one moved.

"It is settled then," Mihanna said. "I will send a message back during our return trip to get our Kashin and human delegates out, and tell our peoples to lock themselves in their homes."

"And the Rankorack?" asked one of the Rankorack Captains.

"Them too," Flea insisted. "They are my friends."

"Thank you," said the other Rankorack Captain. "You were right about him Banach."

Flea had no idea what they were talking about.

"I know," Banach smiled a toothy grin.

"If you are going to stay, did you make the changes I suggested to your fighters, Banach?" Flea looked up at him and asked.

"Some of them are done," he replied. "The rest will be finished soon. I also started restructuring our unit and command structure similar to yours. I will start studying your tactics with my fighter group as per your suggestion. Hopefully, this will make us more effective."

"It will," Flea promised.

"So then it is settled?" asked Mihanna. "We do this if we live?"

"We'll have to restructure and integrate the military as well," Morgan said. "Split up all the personnel among ships and units. Give everyone as equal a stake as possible. It'll help give them a sense of ownership."

"Even the ones without their own ships?" asked Mihanna.

"Yes," Morgan said. "Even them."

"Good," said Mihanna with approval. "I have tried many times to get the council to do this to no avail."

"A good revolution goes a long way," Flea approved.

"So in a few days we will track down the Goraan, fly up to meet them, beat them, and then go home and change things!" Mihanna sounded excited. "But, how will we beat them? The Goraan outnumber us greatly."

"You didn't think we'd just fly up, smack them around and then go home, did you?" Morgan chuckled. "They'd kill us! I'm working on a plan, though. It's a bit risky, but with the rest of you here it might just work. I need to finish the details though."

"Can it actually be done?" Roshom sounded hopeful. "Can we really honestly beat them?"

"I think if we all work together and stick to the plan...it's possible," Morgan replied.

"Are you really that good?" asked Mihanna.

"Yes," said Flea. "He is."

"Well," Morgan said modestly. "A little luck never hurt, either. That's why I drag Flea with me."

"Well," said Mihanna. "I would like to do something, then."

Mihanna walked over to the matter combiner and said something none of the rest could hear. He walked back to the table and set something down on its surface. He slid over two small golden pins. They were a small golden pair of swords that looked like they could be pinned to someone's shirt. They had small diamonds set in the tiny pommels. The cross guards of the swords were a pair of feathered wings spread out with the tips pointing toward the blade. They were inside a small golden ring with five small diamonds set at equal distances.

"These pins are insignia of rank," Mihanna explained. "They are based on my own Admiral's pins."

Mihanna showed his pins to the small group. It only had four diamonds surrounding the sword.

"I gave you an additional stone in your circle," Mihanna explained. "You will have greater rank than me. Your rank will be Admiral Overseer of the Runner Fleet."

Morgan looked at them for a long time. He finally picked them up and pinned them to the collar of his flight suit. He looked at Flea and smiled.

"I'm not calling you *sir*," said Flea. "I'm not saluting you, either, jackass. And if you even once tell me to go do something because you order it, I'll have to clock you in jaw."

"I wouldn't have it any other way, bro," Morgan said.

"So it's settled then?" Mihanna asked.

"Yes," said Morgan confidently. "You guys all come with me. We'll head down to the briefing room and start going over the plan. I'll need your input. A good leader knows to take council with talented individuals."

"Yes, sir," Mihanna and the others said.

Morgan smiled at his wife for a moment.

"Don't let it go to your head," Alex said to her husband.

"I won't," Morgan said. "Let's get going guys."

"Let me check on the group and I'll meet you down there," Flea said.

"You got it, bro," Morgan said. "See you down there."

"See you later," Flea responded.

***

Flea wandered around the hanger bay for a while listening to the sounds of his pilots. This is where they came to play when they weren't training. They had a couple of grills pulled out of ship's storage. Tommy was barbequing some food for their lunch. Flea looked at the back of the hanger where the red curtain used to be. After it was removed, it revealed a giant grey skull and crossed bones similar to the two on the outside of the ship. Above it, arced in grey gothic style letters, was the word: NUNQUAM. Below it, in the same fashion, was the word: TRADO. It was Latin. The translation chip might let him understand spoken languages he didn't know, but it didn't seem to help with written language.

The hanger bay was mostly empty. With only one fighter group, not a lot of space had been used. The girls had sectioned off a small area and enclosed it with some large boards. They had set up a small sandlot with volleyball net. They pranced around in their bikinis trying to teach the Kashin in the group how to play. Some sun lamps were shining down on them while they played. He could hear pop music coming from some speakers they set up near the sandlot. Flea smiled and waved to them while he walked around. When Kaida saw him, she ran off the volleyball court, put on her sandals and trotted over to him. Her hair was in pig-tails. She wore a small, blue bikini as she bounced over to him. It was her favorite shade of blue. She shared a very warm and genuine smile with Flea when she joined him for a walk.

"Flea," she said giving him a hug. "You come to play?"

"No, Kaida," Flea said smiling. "I have some things I need to do."

Flea released her from the hug.

"I thought I told you not to give me hugs and call me by name in front of the others," Flea admonished her.

"I try," she sounded desperate. "I can't help it."

"It's okay," Flea chuckled. "I would probably miss it if you stopped doing that."

She smiled up at him again.

"You go play now, sweetie," Flea said to her.

She looked at him for a moment.

"It's okay, Kaida," Flea said. "I'll be fine. You go on now, okay? I'll see you later."

"Okay," she said happily. "Flea?"

"Yes?" Flea responded.

"You're Kaida's first family," she said softly. "Kaida's first brother."

Flea smiled at her warmly. At that very moment, he felt awful for what he put this poor girl through.

"I love you, Flea," Kaida said seriously.

"I love you, too," Flea said.

She giggled and ran back off to play more volleyball with the others. Flea knew how emotional he could be. He had become very attached to Kaida, Tommy, and Armina in a very short time. He had become attached to every member of his group. He had taken the time in what little spare time he had to learn everything about each and every one of them. He watched them intently as if he would never see them again. He hurt inside.

"Are you okay, love?" Angel asked when Flea made it to his fighter and sat in the lounge.

Flea had developed a very strong bond with Angel during their short time together. At first it seemed unhealthy. She was a hologram, and he had developed a very strong attachment to her. She told him they belonged together. She would tell him how much she loved him all the time. At first he didn't believe her.

"Yeah," he said softly. "I was just watching my friends."

"You know, you could go play with them," she said.

"I only have a few minutes before I go to a briefing with Admiral Morgan," Flea chuckled.

"Admiral?" Angel asked. "When did this happen?"

"At lunch," Flea responded.

"I see," she said.

"Since I only have a few spare moments," Flea explained softly. "I choose to be with you."

She sat down next to him and placed a hand on his thigh. He couldn't feel it on his leg because she was a hologram. Instinctively, though, he reached for it. His hand went right through hers.

"I wish things were different," Flea said sadly.

"So do I, love," she agreed.

They sat there just looking at each other for a long time.

"You know, love," she said sounding playful. "All of this sentimentality is fine…but it does not excuse how you reacted to all those skanky tramps throwing their panties at you!"

Flea started to laugh. Angel could always be counted on to make him feel better.

"You laugh at me!" she sounded indignant. "You would laugh at me?"

"I'm sorry," Flea said.

She turned around and folded her arms. Flea recognized her now familiar pouting position. She snapped her head away from him, which tossed her pony tail at him. This made Flea laugh even harder. Angel soon joined him. They chatted for a short time and enjoyed each other's company before Flea had to get up and leave. He didn't want to go. He knew she loved him. The truth he could not admit was that he loved her, too.

***

Flea entered the briefing room to find a rather odd situation. Morgan's face was bright red as he laughed so hard tears were streaming down his face. His wife and Bella were also red faced, but they seemed angry instead. They scowled at Flea when he walked in the room as if he had done something wrong.

"What?" Flea asked defensively as the two women stared at him.

"Flea," Morgan gasped in between raking fits of laughter. "Oh my god! You won't believe this! You need to hear this!"

"What happened?" Flea asked.

"Well," Morgan calmed down as he started explaining. "I asked Mihanna why he rescued so many females from earth before you walked in."

"And?" Flea asked curiously.

He wondered about this, too. The computer said it was just a scientific anomaly. That was the official reason more female humans were rescued than males.

"Well," Mihanna began explaining. "We started rescuing whatever large parties we saw. Most of them were clothed similarly. To us, you all looked alike before we got to know you better."

"We all look alike to you," Flea growled. "I've heard that a few times before."

"Not anymore," Mihanna said defensively. "We can tell the difference, now."

"Not me," confessed Banach. "But I can tell you apart by scent. You all smell different."

"You mean we are stinky and have small boobs?" yelled Alex.

Morgan started laughing hysterically again. Flea was confused.

"Please finish, Mihanna," Flea sounded frustrated.

"Well," Mihanna explained. "Most of the pilots were Rankorack. Even many of the Kashin evacuation vessels were piloted by Rankorack. Only a few, like the ones that rescued you three, were piloted by Kashin. Most of the Kashin were flying the escort fighters."

"What does that have to do with anything?" Flea asked.

"The Rankorack thought they had rescued too many females and would offset the future breeding of humans because they were dressed similarly," explained Mihanna.

"In our culture," Banach said, "Female clothing is less revealing than males. That's because the males show off their physiques when attracting a mate. Since most of the humans we rescued were dressed normally, we thought we rescued a bunch of females."

"Where were you rescuing at?" Flea asked.

"We were going to places you call 'night clubs' and 'shopping malls' depending on what side of the planet one found themselves," Mihanna said. "Did you know that these places are generally frequented by young people?"

"That explains the age thing," Morgan nodded.

"Yeah," Flea said grinning. "Go on, Banach."

"So to compensate for this, we started collecting as many humans wearing the most revealing clothing as we could," Banach explained. "We assumed they were male."

"So you probably went to every beach and strip club you could find looking for humans in bikinis," Flea snickered.

"We couldn't help it!" Banach said defensively. "You all look the same to us! Most other species' females have larger…ermmm…endowments!"

Flea burst out laughing.

"The more time I spend with you, the more I can tell you apart visually," Banach said hastily. "In the meantime, you each have a very distinct odor. That's how I've been telling you apart until I hear your voice to verify your identity."

Alex started to rise and purposefully head toward Banach like she wanted to choke him. Morgan caught her around the waist and stopped her. She sat back down and scowled at her husband. The group settled down to get ready for business.

"Okay, team," Morgan said standing in front of them. "Here's the situation. We need to take down a Goraan battleship, but they almost never travel alone."

"Then how do we do that?" asked Roshom.

"We take down a whole fleet," Morgan said confidently. "They have thirteen fleets total according to our intelligence, so I'm sure they won't mind sparing one for us."

"Impossible!" Mihanna scoffed. "Did you not see what happened to your own world?"

"We saw them," Flea said defensively. "But nothing is impossible."

"Well spoken, Gabriel-Captain!" Banach approved. "I always love desperate odds!"

"I'd rather have an easy fight," Flea chuckled. "But desperate can definitely be more fun."

"How do we take down a whole fleet, Overseer?" Mihanna asked Morgan.

Morgan seemed to straighten when hearing someone address him by his new rank.

"We lie to them," Morgan said.

"Much like Flea cheated in our fight?" Banach said with a toothy grin.

"I didn't cheat," Flea said absently. "I improvised."

"Which is exactly what we'll do," Morgan said. "Host, dim the lights."

The lights in the room dimmed.

"Show holographic representation of the Command battleship of the Goraan second fleet," Morgan said.

The holo-projector on the floor at the front of the room showed the image of an intimidating looking golden ship.

"They have gold ships?" Alex asked. "I didn't notice that before."

"They do this to intimidate their enemies and show the extent of their wealth," Mihanna explained.

"I see," Alex said. "Seems like an awful waste to me."

The group muttered their agreement with Alex.

"Eleven other battleships are in the fleet," Morgan said loudly. "Aside from that they also have an assortment of cruisers, fighters and freighters to support them."

"We have similar ships with us," Mihanna said.

"I know," said Morgan. "But they have more. We are terribly out-gunned, despite the capabilities of the Pirate Queen."

"My ship is about half the size, but carries three times the armament of the rest of you," Alex said proudly.

"I did not know it was that much," Mihanna said sounding surprised.

"I left out all my ship's specifications to the council," Alex said quietly. "We'll upgrade the rest of your ships after we get back."

"If we get back," Roshom said.

"We'll make it back," Flea growled.

"Aside from the guns," Morgan said gaining everyone's attention again. "We'll also have to chew through their energy shields. If we were to stand toe to toe with them, they'd gun us down like we were made from cheap cardboard."

"What does this mean?" asked Banach.

"He's saying we can't just fly up and face them," Flea explained, "They'd kill us."

"Yes," said Banach. "Of course."

"Instead," Morgan said. "I have seen their flight plan for the second fleet. We know where they're headed. They're going to where the Earth was. We'll get there first."

"We wait for them?" asked Mihanna.

"Sort of," said Morgan. "They're coming to survey the area from their last encounter there. They expect to see some wreckage as evidence of our deaths. I plan to give them that."

"How?" asked Roshom.

"Banach," Morgan said. "Remember when you were fighting Flea and he shut down his ship?"

"Yes, Morgan-Overseer," Banach said. "I couldn't see him until he started it back up."

"We're going to do that on a larger scale," Morgan said. "We'll shut down all our ships so they don't appear on sensors. They'll see us out the window, but won't know we're alive."

"Why do we not simply engage our cloaking fields?" asked, Mihanna.

"Because if we're cloaked the cloaking generators leave a residual energy signature that can be detected if they know what to look for," Morgan explained. "Instead, we're going to use some scrap we've been collecting in conjunction with holo-projectors on the exterior of our hulls. We'll make ourselves look like a big junk field. Besides, it's not like we can shoot when we're cloaked anyway.

"Good point," Mihanna said.

"We lay there waiting," Morgan continued. "When I give the signal, everyone powers up, raises shields and hits them with a sneak attack."

"Will that work?" asked Banach.

"We'll have to play around with the power signals on the projectors some," Morgan shrugged. "But I'm pretty sure we can get it to work."

"What will the signal be?" asked Mihanna.

"The destruction of our enemies' shield generators," Morgan said.

"How do you plan to do that?" asked Mihanna.

"I'll need some volunteers for this part," Morgan explained. "But I planned to have some people floating around outside. I want to put them in some make shift pods that look like scrap and set them up with some good, old-fashioned, low-tech Earth gear. They'll have an old laser pointer attached to a small tracking device to help them aim an explosive charge propelled by compressed air. They won't pick up the laser because it's made from such outdated technology their sensors no longer actively look for it. I know this, because this is an old Goraan carrier you're on right now. It has…or it used to have the same sensor configuration as our enemies. I had it changed when I finished testing my laser after we pulled out."

"Tested what?" Alex asked. "I knew you went for a short flight, but what were you doing?"

"Flea and I flew around the *Queen* this morning shooting it with my laser sight," Morgan said. "It never showed up on sensors. The Goraan built this ship. The fleet they are sending has the same sensor configuration we used to have."

"It worked out really well," Flea sounded optimistic.

"If they place the charges on the outside of the hulls of the different battleships at these points," Morgan said as he indicated places on the hologram. "They'll lose their shields before the battle starts. When you see the explosions, power up and go. They'll all go off at once because I'll use a common remote detonator to set them off."

"Is that it?" Alex asked.

"Funny you should ask, sweetie," Morgan grinned boyishly at her. "You will start out cloaked. I want you to fire a volley of missiles at the lead ship's bridge."

"I thought we couldn't generate enough power to fire weapons while cloaked?" Roshom said incredulously.

"Not with energy weapons," Morgan explained. "Energy weapons draw from the ship's generators. Missiles, however, have their own fuel source. All you have to do is point and launch. I wish you guys had missiles on your ships, too."

"If the rest of you didn't think missiles were too primitive," Flea said, "then maybe you could take some shots while cloaked, too."

"Won't they spot me after I shoot?" asked Alex.

"Yes," said Morgan. "But you have 'smart missiles' remember?"

"I know what I have," she sounded defensive.

"Well then you know you don't have to be in their line of sight to target that bridge," Morgan said.

"What do you hope to accomplish with that?" asked Mihanna. "They must have a secondary bridge, you know?"

"I know," said Morgan. "I just want to make them desperate."

"Why?" asked Banach. "What will that accomplish?"

"I'm getting to that," Morgan was getting frustrated. "But before I do, let me explain what Flea and the ArchAngels are going to do."

"Okay," said Banach. "I'm listening."

"We are going to outfit our fighters with holo-projectors as well," Morgan said.

"We?" snorted Flea. "The Admiral shouldn't risk himself in the field."

"Screw you, bro!" Morgan said defensively. "First of all, I am not going to give up being a fighter pilot. I won't ask anyone to go into a battle I wouldn't be willing to fight in myself. Second, we'll need every pilot in the field we can get. And third...I want to make those bastards bleed. I want to hurt them personally."

"Cool," Flea said grimly.

"As I was saying," Morgan continued. "The ArchAngels will be in the field. That will give us a jump on their fighters. I'm going to wait to blow the charges until they've gone past you. That way their engines will be vulnerable. When the charges blow, we'll power up and unload every missile in the group at the backs of their ships. Our missiles are smaller than the *Queen*'s, but we have a lot of them. We at least have enough to disable their engines so they can't retreat."

"No bridge, no shields and can't retreat," Flea said. "That should make them pretty desperate."

"Not at first," Morgan disagreed. "But it will. They'll probably try to fight us at first, but they'll hurt without shields. After we beat them down enough, they'll try and open a jumpgate to get some reinforcements."

"I thought that the gates weren't very reliable," Flea pointed out.

"They're not," Morgan replied. "But if they reroute all power and fire up emergency generators they can increase the accuracy. They won't be able to do anything else while holding the gate. It'll even drain life support. But with enough power going to them, they could accurately open a gate to the nearest base and bring in some back up."

"Wouldn't that be a bad thing?" Flea said.

"Not in this case," Morgan said. "If we can blow the generator when they fire it up, we can destroy the Command Battleship. It'll blow up from the inside out. The shrapnel from it will cut right through every ship in the area, including us. So when you see it start to go, you need to get the Hell out. Fire up your engines and burn out in whatever direction the nose of your ship is pointing. Fly for half an hour in that direction, then turn around and speed back to the battlefield to mop up whatever is left."

"What are we going to hit it with?" Alex asked.

"Some more of your homing missiles ought to get the job done," Morgan said looking at his wife. "Especially after you take out the bridge. The generators are located just aft of the bridge. The missile won't need to penetrate as deep after you take out the bridge first."

"Why don't we just put more charges on the outside of the ship's hull like with the shield generators?" asked Mihanna.

"The hull on that part of the ship is incredibly thick," explained Morgan. "The only thing we could make small enough to avoid detection and still do the job is an Anti-matter bomb. Personally, I don't want to do that with us right in our enemy's face."

"Why not?" asked Banach.

"Because it would kill us all," Morgan snorted. "And I can't speak for you guys, but I would prefer to live through this."

"Me too," agreed Roshom. "I'd like to see my spawn again."

"What if one of the other ships uses its gate generators?" asked Flea.

"Goraan High Commanders are very untrusting of their Captains," Toren said.

Flea didn't even notice she was there.

"This is because the only way to advance in the Goraan military is when a spot opens up," she explained. "The only way that can happen is if the person above you retires, dies, is killed or is disgraced and forced from his position."

"Sounds rough," Flea said.

"It makes for interesting politics among the military's leadership," she said coyly.

"What does it all mean?" Flea said.

"It means that the only ship with jumpgate capabilities is the Command Ship," Morgan said. "A Goraan High Commander would never give a Captain the chance to leave and betray him. This odd little personality quirk is the same reason that the ships in a Goraan fleet fly so close together. The High Commander doesn't want his Captains to get too far away from him."

"That's why they will all get killed in the shrapnel?" Banach asked.

"Yes," replied Morgan with a nod. "With no shields, that's exactly why."

"What happens if Alex misses?" Roshom asked.

"Then we'll probably die," Morgan said. "We won't be able to turn our backs on them to retreat or they'll kill us from behind as we run away. If we stay and fight, even though we'll have our shields in the beginning they will eventually outgun us. We'd put up a gallant struggle, but after a while, the reinforcements would show up. They would simply overwhelm us at that point."

The room was silent. Contemplating death was never a happy moment.

"Alex," Bella said looking at her. "Don't miss."

"How hard can it be, right?" Alex sounded a bit worried. "After all, I do have some pretty sophisticated homing missiles."

"Yeah," said Flea trying to sound confident. "This can work, right?"

No one answered.

"It's the best we've got," Morgan said. "It's a good plan. With a little luck it might just work, too."

"In the meantime," Flea tried to sound light hearted. "Let's all get ready. We prepare and drill during the day and hang out at night."

"Good idea," Morgan said. "Let's try and keep the morale of our people up. We'll throw a couple of barbeques in the next few days until we get there."

"Will we have enough time to get ready if we do this?" asked Mihanna.

"We should," Morgan said. "So let's Pray hard and see what happens."

Everyone left the room except Flea, Morgan, Alex and Toren.

"You think they bought all that?" Morgan jested.

"It sounds possible," Flea said skeptically. "It's just not very probable."

"It's a good plan, sweetie," Alex said approvingly. "I'm proud of you."

Morgan nodded silently. He looked disturbed.

"How's your luck, bro?" asked Morgan.

"Well," Flea said thoughtfully. "I'm not dead yet. After everything we been through in the recently, I'd say that's a good sign."

"Let's hope it holds for just a few more days, then," Morgan said, "We might need it."

19

"Are you seeing what I am seeing, Doshan?" Esham'aut asked his second in command over the ship's communications system. "I see only wreckage."

"My sensors are not picking up anything, High Commander," Doshan agreed from the bridge of his own vessel. "Maybe we should raise shields just to be safe."

"That should not be necessary," Esham'aut stated. "No one is here except us. I do not want to draw power that may be being used in other parts of the ship right now."

"Agreed," sighed Doshan. "I do not feel like listening to anyone whine about the power getting secured to their birthing quarters today."

"Ship's Inquisitor requesting permission to enter the bridge," Esham'aut heard Vichen's voice behind him.

"Enter!" Esham'aut barked. "Did you find the traitor, Toren al'Shoken?"

"I could not find any trace of her, sir," Ba'an glared at him while he spoke.

"Why do I feel like this creature hates me?" Esham'aut thought. *"It is annoying."*

"She probably evaporated during transport," Ba'an said.

"Perhaps," said Esham'aut. "Since we haven't had any more killings I went ahead and transmitted her crimes back to Eiligor. If, by some chance, she is ever seen on Eiligor or anywhere else in the Empire again, she will find herself vaporized."

Esham'aut continued looking out the window.

"Remember this place?" he asked Vichen trying to sound jovial and failing miserably at it. "The last time we were here was to harvest that pathetic 'Earth' planet."

"Yes, sir," Ba'an replied emotionlessly. "I remember the time."

Esham'aut was suddenly thrown to the ground. The entire ship reverberated with some dreadful explosion.

"Shields!" barked Esham'aut. "Raise shields! Now!"

"Shields not responding, sir!" shouted the tactical officer.

"What?" shouted Esham'aut.

"Shields, sir," replied the tactical officer. "They will not come on line! The shield generators are destroyed!"

Esham'aut stood up, pulled out his gun and shot him.

As he was standing, Esham'aut looked out the window and noticed some projectiles coming straight for them at an incredibly high velocity.

"Runners!" Esham'aut growled hatefully.

He jumped behind a console to take cover. The ship's Inquisitor was right behind him. The glass shattered as the projectile came rocketing through the bridge window. It impacted the back wall, removing most of it and causing a fiery explosion. Flames burst over the console behind which Esham'aut and Vichen were taking cover. He felt his skin scorch from the heat. The flames were quickly put out as they, and most of the bridge crew, were sucked into the vacuum of space. The emergency energy barricade rose around the hole in the ship's bridge. It engaged automatically to stop anything else from being sucked out.

"Host! Announcement! Scramble the fighters!" Esham'aut shouted rising to his feet again. "Man all boarding ships! All hands to battle stations! On coming bridge watch team to the emergency control center! All hands to battle stations! Man all gun turrets and fire at will!"

Esham'aut looked around the bridge. He could see all the way back to the jumpgate generators where the aft wall once was located. Aside from him and Vichen, two watch standers were still alive. They were badly wounded. Esham'aut shot them.

"We will go to EMCON, Inquisitor," Esham'aut said. "You can join me in the emergency control center and see how we deal with deceitful Runner ambushes!"

"No, Esham'aut," Ba'an growled softly. "Not this time."

"Excuse me?" Esham'aut shouted. "You dare use my name?"

Esham'aut raised his gun to point at Ba'an.

"Die!" shouted Ba'an.

White acid was sent flying at Esham'aut's hand. It melted the gun before Esham'aut could use it. A bleeding stump was left where his hand once was.

"I have had enough of you!" Ba'an shouted.

"Wha?" Esham'aut was dumbfounded by this creature's impudence.

Ba'an cocked back his head to let loose another stream of acid. The High Commander regained control of his senses and roared.

"Lying, deceitful sluggling!!" Esham'aut shouted as he drove his bloody stump into Ba'an's face with all his force.

Esham'aut was three times larger than Ba'an. The force of the blow broke Ba'an's jaw and burst his acid sacs. Ba'an was sent flying in to a sparking console across the room.

"You killed all of them, didn't you?" accused Esham'aut. "I see it all, now! It must have been quite a great deal of effort you put forth in your little revenge game just to fail now! You must feel awful. How pathetic!"

Esham'aut looked at the sad little creature lying in the rubble for a moment. He turned to leave the bridge, holding his ruined hand to his chest. He was sent reeling to the floor and was seeing stars. He was hit with something in the back of the head. A large piece of metal shrapnel bounced across the floor after it struck him.

"Not...done...here," Ba'an struggle to speak with his ruined jaw.

White acid dripped down the Inquisitor's chin. It was melting pieces of his uniform. Small droplets hissed and melted the floor where they fell. Esham'aut struggled to stand up. Ba'an launched himself at the larger creature's face from across the room. He had a piece of jagged metal in one of his tentacles.

"No more!" Ba'an screamed as he went flying through the air.

Esham'aut caught him in his remaining large hand before Ba'an could land on him. His big claw wrapped around Ba'an's waist and threw him into the ceiling. Ba'an turned in the air, spread his tentacles and stuck to the overhead of the destroyed bridge. He threw the piece of metal at Esham'aut. It drove into his right shoulder.

"Argh!" Esham'aut grunted.

He yanked the piece of metal out of his shoulder. Ba'an dropped from the ceiling, and tried to land on Esham'aut. The jagged piece of shrapnel was swung wildly by Esham'aut, removing one of Ba'an's tentacles. The severed limb thudded to the floor. He brushed Ba'an aside, but not before Ba'an managed to disarm him. Ba'an landed on the floor with a bounce. He stood up and scrambled away from Esham'aut to a nearby, ruined console.

"Fool!" shouted Esham'aut.

Esham'aut kicked a piece of sharp steel at Ba'an. Ba'an dodged to the left and rolled to come up on his feet. He lashed at Esham'aut using his remaining tentacles like whips. He struck Esham'aut over and over again.

Thwack! Thwack! Thwack! Thwack!

Esham'aut was bleeding from the multitude of small cuts Ba'an's whipping barrage had given him.

"DIE!" Ba'an shouted.

Thwack! Thwack! Thwack!

Esham'aut caught the last blow in his claw.

"Silence, puny fool!" Esham'aut shouted back.

He yanked hard on the captured tentacle and bounced Ba'an against the ceiling. Ba'an landed on Esham'aut's head. He wrapped his tentacles around Esham'aut's face, cutting off his air supply. He squeezed as hard as he could. Esham'aut fell down with a rumble, struggling to try and get some air. He rained down blows on Ba'an.

"Just die!" Ba'an slurred with a howl.

Esham'aut was starting to get dizzy from lack of air. He had to get to EMCON and take command of the oncoming bridge staff. This type of death would be a disgrace. He had to end it now.

"I will kill you!" Ba'an slurred loudly, "I swear it!"

***

"Well done, crew!" Alex shouted across the bridge of the *Pirate Queen*. "Nice shot, weapons officer!"

"Thank ya ma'am," she said proudly with a southern twang. "I reckon all that practice and drillin' paid off."

"Yeah, it did!" responded Alex. "Remind me to give you a promotion, Ensign!"

"Yes, ma'am!" responded the young weapons officer excitedly.

"Disengage cloak and raise shields!" Alex shouted. "All hands to battle stations! Man all gun turrets and fire at will! Load another volley, Ensign! All hands fire at will!"

"Ma'am!" exclaimed the sensors officer. "They launched their fighters and are powering up their weapons!"

"Look out the window, Lieutenant!" Alex barked at the sensors officer. "I don't need fancy equipment to tell me that."

The space outside was suddenly thick with Goraan fighters. Alex and her bridge crew could easily see what was going on through the front window. The other Runners vessels had powered up and started pounding on the Goraan ships with everything they had. The only thing that kept the battle balanced at this point was the fact that Alex and her side still had shields. That would end soon enough if they didn't take down that Goraan vessel before it opened its gate. A large amount of enemy fighters, bombers and energy blasts were headed in Alex's direction.

"Tell me we have shields, Ensign!" Alex shouted to her weapons officer. "Tell me we have shields, now!"

The fighters were closing fast. They opened fire. A multitude unholy, blue blasts screamed toward the bridge window.

"Brace for impact!" shouted Alex as she bolted to her Captain's chair and strapped herself in.

The crew tensed and quickly took cover. The blue energy blasts spread out in a splash pattern across the normally invisible shield which lit up red in the area where it was hit in front of the bridge window.

"Shields on line, ma'am," sighed the weapons officer in relief.

"What did you do?" asked Alex quickly.

"I rerouted everything from the hanger bay," she said with a nod. "I reckon since the fighters weren't down there it could stand to spare us some power."

"Good thinking Ensign," Alex approved. "Write that tactic into the battle manual. You might just end up as my Executive Officer if we live through this."

The young lady smiled like a pretty southern belle.

"Tactical, are those Goraan ships still moving?" Alex asked.

"Yes, ma'am," she replied. "Not very fast, but still moving."

"Contact Captain Gabriel and try to find out what the Hell is going on," she said.

"Comm link established, ma'am," said the communications officer.

"This is...damn it! Break, now ladies!" Flea shouted.

"Flea!" Alex shouted. "Those Goraan ships are still moving! What the Hell are you doing out there?"

"Form up! Form up! Good!" shouted Flea. "Hot and heavy, ladies! Take those slimy sons-of-bitches down! Top left! Go! Go! Go!"

"Flea!" barked Alex.

"Call 'em out guys!" Flea yelled. "Don't give 'em a damn inch without some blood!"

"Damn it, Flea!" Alex screamed. "Answer me!"

"This is *Archangel one*," Flea yelled. "What the Hell do you want, Goddamnit?!! The Goddamned engines are down and the Goddamned ships will finish coasting to a stop in a second! So, shut up, Goddamnit!"

"Move in front, Flea," Alex said. "I need a clear shot at the bridge now! Our other fighters are trying their best, but they're out numbered! They need you guys! Clear out that lane!"

"Alex!" Flea shouted. "I'm kind of...shit! Get back here!"

"Flea!" shouted Alex. "Just do it, Flea!"

"Give me a damn break!" Flea shouted. "Fine! We're on it!! Now quit bothering me with this shit! *Archangel one*, out!"

"Mommy!" Keri cried from the door to the bridge. "I'm scared!"

"Keri! Armina!" Alex sounded surprised. "How the Hell did you get up here? Look, never mind that. Just stand over there and stay out of the way, okay?"

Alex indicated a spot next to the door.

"Mommy!" insisted Keri earnestly.

"Don't argue, Keri!" snapped Alex. "Just stand there, okay?"

"Comm," Alex said. "Set up an announcement."

"Ready, ma'am," the communications officer replied.

"We're doing good, crew!" Alex encouraged them. "Keep up the fight! Don't give them a Goddamn inch! Make them wade through their own bodies for it! Make those slug bastards eat their own asses ladies and gentleman!"

Alex signaled to cut transmission.

"Where are the ArchAngels, Tactical?" Alex asked. "How are they doing?"

"Twenty eight of them are coming around in front of the Goraan Command vessel now, ma'am!" she replied. "We're going to do it!"

"Twenty eight?" Alex asked. "They had thirty two. What happened to the other four, Lieutenant?"

"I'm searching now, ma'am," she replied softly. "I'm not picking them up. I think they are gone."

Everyone knew Alexandria's husband was out there.

"Do you know if," Alex stopped before she finished the question.

She wanted to ask if her husband was dead. She glanced over in Keri's direction and stopped before she said it.

"Admiral Mendenhall is still fighting, ma'am," the Lieutenant answered the unspoken question. "Tactical read-out for his vessel shows a little damage, but he's still going."

"Yes!" Alex said enthusiastically.

She was a little embarrassed as the bridge crew noticed her excitement

"I mean, very well, Lieutenant," Alexandria amended her response quickly. "Thank you for the update."

Alex watched, dividing her time between the front window and the tactical holographic display of the battlefield on the table in the center of the room.

"Ma'am!" shouted the tactical officer. "Some of the fighters and the other Runners have been concentrating on one of the

Goraan battle ships on the outside of the formation! They are bringing it down! It's starting to blow!"

"What?" Alex sounded surprised.

"It's going to blow! They're evacuating!" she replied. "Ma'am it's going down!"

The vessel exploded in a fiery spectacle. Just as soon as the flames began, they were extinguished by the vacuum of space. Shrapnel was sent flying around the ship. It cut down friend and foe alike. Most of the enemy still remained because the pieces and shards that were sent flying didn't have the velocity to cut apart the other battle ships. Alex was still waiting for that opportunity.

"Ma'am!" shouted the sensors. "I'm picking up the Command Vessel's jumpgate signature! It's firing up its generators!"

The space in front of the command ship's bridge was still thick with fighters.

"Come on, guys," Alex sounded desperate. "We need you!"

As if they had heard her plea, the ArchAngels began a furiously dangerous run in front of the command ship's bridge. Alex could barely see them from this distance through the window. She watched the tactical holo-map in the center of the room to see what was happening. Tracking the ArchAngels on that three dimensional display was pretty easy. They were the most colorful group on the field.

"Please," she prayed. *"Please, God. Help them."*

Someone heard her prayers. As she watched the hologram, she noticed a clear shot opened through the lane in front of the command ship's bridge. Alex looked out the front window to verify what she saw. Three more ArchAngels exploded, but the bridge of the Second Fleet's Command Battleship was directly across from her. It was as if the storm clouds had opened up to let through the light. She had a clear shot straight at it.

"Weapons!" Alex shouted. "Target the bridge and fire all missiles! Then reload and fire again!"

"Yes, ma'am!" replied the Ensign.

There was a pause that seemed to last for an eternity.

"Missiles away, ma'am!" shouted the Weapons officer. "That's all we got."

"Let's pray it wo…" Alex's sentence was cut off when she was thrown to the floor.

She turned to look over her shoulder. Small bits and pieces of equipment that hadn't been properly stowed before battle flew by her head toward the ceiling. They were sealing off part of a hole in the roof of the bridge. Most of the hole, however, was occupied by a small ship.

"It's the Goraan!" shouted the Tactical Officer pointing to the ceiling. "They must have a way to get through our shields we didn't know about!"

The hatch on the small ship blew outward and landed on the floor. A small roundish object followed it. Alex had never seen a Goraan style grenade before. It reminded her of a small metallic pear. When it dropped, everything slowed down and her mind became thick. She saw it drop every painful inch until it hit the floor with a small bounce.

Tink! Tink! Tink!

"Take cover!" shouted Alex.

It bounced across the metal floor and rolled to a stop near Alex. She saw the grenade a few inches from her left foot. She dove for it. Alex grabbed it and tossed it back into the Goraan vessel. Her mind snapped back into normal speed as she realized what she had just done. She dove behind a console for some cover.

"Host!" she shouted. "Emergency announcement!"

All the Goraan in the vessel started yelling loudly and jumped down from the vessel to land in the bridge. The grenade exploded. It blew the vessel out of the hole where it had lodged itself into the bridge's ceiling. The emergency vacuum barrier rose before anyone was sucked out.

"Crew this is the Captain!" shouted Alex she looked around frantically. "Arm all hands and repel boarders! The bridge is compromised! Switch command to Secondary Control! I repeat! Arm and repel boarders!"

The Goraan on the bridge had risen to their feet and jumped behind some consoles on the port side of the bridge. The bridge crew had taken cover on the starboard side. They exchanged fire at a blinding pace. The bridge flashed and screamed with the shots of energy blasters. The air crackled with heat and electric death. Alex looked up. The girls were standing next to the door a few feet from the bridge crew. Keri and Armina had huddled together and started crying. Over her shoulder, she looked and saw a wickedly smiling cobra-like creature with black Goraan eyes raising his pistol toward the girls.

"Don't even try it you bastard!" Alex screamed fiercely at him.

Alex didn't have time to stop him. She rose to her feet. The Goraan took his aim and fired. Suddenly, every detail of the moment painfully etched itself inside Alex's brain. She saw his muscles and tendons squeeze as he pulled the trigger. His arm jerked slightly from the blaster's recoil. Alex ran. Every step she took seemed to be a second too slow. Her feet thudded in her ears every time they hit the ground. She wasn't going to make it. She felt as if her shoes must have been made of concrete. Alex dove in front of the girls. She was suddenly aware that part of her left arm was gone. It was there just a second ago. It didn't hurt. That surprised her. She thought it would be very painful. Everything became blurry in her vision. She could feel blood making her shirt stick to her torso. She must have been shot. That had to be the answer. She landed on the girls. Her chest burned slightly. She couldn't tell if she rolled over on her own, or if the girls rolled her onto her back. She saw the cobra-person readying another shot. He was lifting his arm.

"Mommy!" Keri whispered through her tears. "Oh, mommy, no!"

"Alex!" Armina cried desperately. "Please don't die!"

Alex looked at Keri for a moment.

"Mommy is…packing… heat," she coughed up blood as she spoke.

Alex drew her gun with her right arm and fired at the Goraan that had shot her. It cut through his chest like tissue paper. Everything went silent.

"We have the bridge, ma…" the weapons officer stopped in mid-sentence.

"Captain!" the Ensign shouted. "Medic! Get a medic!"

"The missiles, Ensign," Alex choked out hoarsely. "What happened to the missiles?"

"Don't you worry none, ma'am," she said softly. "We'll take it from here."

Someone kneeled over Alex. She thought it might be a Doctor. The Doctor didn't look very confident in Alex's status.

"Ensign," Alex whispered. "What's your name?"

"Katie," replied the Weapons officer gruffly. "My name is Katie, ma'am. Don't you worry about that. You lie still, now."

"Ensign Katie," Alex smiled slightly as she coughed up blood and spoke. "You've been promoted. You're a Captain, now. You're my new executive officer. Act like it, okay? You have the bridge, X.O. Get my girls out of here. You have to be the Captain, now."

Alex could vaguely see out the front window. Her vision was blurry. She could barely make out the Goraan fighters that had followed behind the ArchAngels to close the path she had fired her missiles through. The missiles cut down the Goraan fighter group like it was nothing. None of them reached their intended target. Alex closed her eyes. She stopped breathing.

***

"Angel!" Flea shouted. "Give me a number!"

She knew exactly what Flea was asking for. He wanted to know how many ArchAngels were left.

"Twenty two," Angel said.

"Kaida!" Flea barked. "How you holding up?"

"I am the Dragon!" Kaida shouted jubilantly.

She had been going as strong as she possibly could. She and Flea lost track a long time ago how many fighters they destroyed. They stopped counting how many times they cheated death. He saw some of the others take down a Goraan ship earlier, but they had to pound the Hell out of it to do it.

"What's Alex doing?" Flea asked. "The command ship started powering its jumpgate generators five minutes ago!"

"I'm not sure," Angel said. "Something must be wrong."

Flea and Kaida engaged full reverse thrusters and banked hard to come around on the fighters that had been tailing them. They didn't have to communicate the maneuvers they made to each other anymore. They only spoke to encourage each other and point out enemies.

"Nice job, little dragon!" Flea shouted.

"Oh, yes," Kaida said jested. "Thank you very much, Flea. I am very good pilot. Maybe you fly more like me!"

"Real cute, Kaida," Flea chuckled.

He didn't want to snap at her. He didn't want the potentially last thing he said to her to be offensive.

"Morgan!" Flea shouted. "You still with me, bro?"

"A-alive and kicking," Morgan stammered. "Barely."

He sounded a bit upset.

"Morgan," Flea said suddenly getting a bad feeling. "Where's Tommy?"

"I tried to stop him," Morgan said seriously "I tried. We're just spread so thin. There was nothing I could do. I swear it. He was there just a second ago and now…"

Tommy always had trouble staying in the group.

"Angel," Flea said softly. "Give me a number."

"Twenty," she replied softly.

Flea was silent for a moment as the loss of Tommy set in. That kid used to live with him. He was too young to join. Flea was the one that told him to lie about his age.

"We're just too damn thin," Morgan said. "At least we cleared a shot for Alex."

Tommy must be dead. Flea shook the feeling off. He would wait to mourn the dead. The ones still alive would have to wait for the fallen until later.

"Are you alone out there, Morg?" Flea asked.

"Yeah," replied Morgan. "I'm trying to reach someone."

"That Battleship should be done for by now, where's Alex?" Flea growled.

"I don't know," said Morgan.

"Angel," Flea barked. "Get me the *Pirate Queen*."

"*Pirate Queen*," Flea barked. "This is *ArchAngel one*! Give me a status on those damn missiles!"

"This is the Pirate Queen," said an unfamiliar voice with a southern accent.

"Who the Hell is this?" Flea demanded. "Where the Hell is Alex?"

"Where's my wife!" shouted Morgan.

"This is Captain Katie Leigh Ratliff," she responded.

"Captain?" asked Flea.

"I was promoted," she responded. "…Unofficially. It was a field promotion."

"When?" asked Flea.

"About six minutes ago," she responded quickly.

"This is Admiral Overseer Mendenhall!" Morgan insisted angrily. "I asked where the Hell is my wife!?"

"She's indisposed of at the moment, sir," Katie said after a pause. "But she's okay…for now. Maybe."

"What's that supposed to mean?" demanded Morgan.

"Morg!" Flea shouted. "Let it go! That's an order!"

"Flea," Morgan protested.

"You may be an Admiral in the briefing room," Flea admonished. "But out here you're one of my pilots and we have work to do! Others are counting on you!! Keep it together, man!"

"Sorry," Morgan sounded emotional. "Where are the missiles, Captain?"

"A group of Goraan fighters followed in the path you cleared," she explained. "They collided with the missiles. That was our last missile bank, too. I reckon we got us a real knock down drag out fight on our hands, sir."

"Shit," Morgan said.

"Shit," agreed Flea.

"Shit," said Captain Katie.

"Thanks, Captain," Flea said. "*ArchAngel* one, out."

Morgan flew outside on Flea's starboard wing. Kaida was on his port one.

"Flea," it was Pesha.

She sounded desperate.

"What's wrong?" Flea asked.

"Tina," Pesha sounded like she was crying. "She's gone."

"Angel," Flea said. "Number?"

Angel knew that Flea wanted to know how many of his pilots were left.

"Nineteen," Angel said.

"She's dead, Flea," Pesha said desperately.

"I know," Flea said.

"I don't like this," Pesha said emotionally. "Not one bit."

"What are you going to do, pilot?" Flea barked at her. "Remember what we talked about!"

"Pick myself up and keep going," she sounded more determined.

"And?" Flea said.

"Find the nearest fighter," she said. "Never fly alone."

Pesha quickly joined the Flea and his friends.

"Seventeen," Angel said quietly.

Flea already knew what she was talking about. His Angels were dying. This had to stop. He had to do something. He could see the gate opening behind the command ship. If that thing opened and anything came through they would all be done for.

"Follow me!" Flea barked at his three companions.

The three of them followed Flea. He arced wide to bypass the main body of dog fighting that was going on. They positioned themselves directly across from the command ship's bridge. The energy blasts there were thicker than tar. Exploding fighters, ships and shrapnel were flying everywhere.

"Feel like going for a ride?" Flea asked jovially.

"Through that?" Pesha asked incredulously.

"Yep," Flea said confidently. "Right through that."

"What do we do if we make it through?" asked Morgan.

"I don't know that, yet," Flea said.

"You have a missile left?" Morgan asked.

"No," said Flea. "But don't worry about it. I'll think of something. Just get ready to run, okay? Don't worry, I'll blow something up, I promise. "

"Flea…" Morgan sounded confused. "We don't have any missiles."

"Shut up and tell me if your coming, bro," Flea said. "We need to go soon. It's now or never. We have to do something."

There was a long pause.

"Sixteen," Angel said.

"I'm with you," Morgan sounded determined.

"Pesha?" Flea asked.

"I hate this," she hissed through her tears. "I'm coming, too."

"Kaida," Flea said softly. "You don't have to do this if you don't want to, little sister."

"I come," she said fiercely gritting her teeth. "Family."

That was the first word she ever said to him. Flea could tell she was trying to hide the fact she was crying.

"Raise the group, Angel," Flea said.

"Got it," she responded.

"ArchAngels," Flea said. "I am relinquishing command of the group to Admiral Overseer Morgan Mendenhall until further notice. I just wanted to say how very proud I am of all of you."

He started to get choked up.

"You honor me with your struggle," Flea said. "I am so very privileged to be part of something so great. I will never forget any of you. *ArchAngel one,* out."

"Let's go, guys," Flea said.

The group took off for the bridge.

"Angel," Flea said softly to his holographic co-pilot. "I wish things with us were different. I'm sorry. It's time to go."

"I don't like this," she said.

"Someone has to do it," Flea said.

"But why you?" she asked desperately. "Let someone else go, my love. I need more time with you!"

"I know," Flea said seriously. "But I have to do this. I just have to."

"I know," Angel sounded defeated. "That's one of the reasons I love you."

"Thanks," Flea said smiling. "Whatever happens I wanted you to know…"

"I know, love," she interrupted him. "I know."

Flea and the small group flew with an encompassing need as they approached the thick wall of Goraan fighters. They had formed into a small triangle with Flea in the center of them. Morgan, Kaida, and Pesha were at the three corners. The enemy had spotted their approach and was raining blue Hell fire at them. Every time a shot hit Flea's shield it splashed red in a localized area as it spread across the energy barrier. They dodged through them as best they could. They were giving more than receiving, but the sheer number of Goraan was overwhelming. The gate was fully opened.

"Answer a question for me, bro," Morgan said as they weaved through the enemy's fire. "When you were fighting

Banach you spent an awfully long time in that cave. What were you doing in there, anyway?"

There was a long pause.

"An enemy battleship is coming through the gate!" Angel shouted.

Flea started to chuckle.

"I was having a snack, Morg," Flea laughed.

Morgan started to laugh with him, "Really?"

"Yeah, really," Flea said with a grin.

Flea could hear Morgan starting to chuckle and cheer up.

"You're the best, man," Morgan said.

"Thanks," Flea said. "So are you."

"The battleship is coming through!" Angel said.

"Not far, now!" Flea shouted.

His shields finally gave out. A blue energy blast ripped through his starboard wing. Since he was in the vacuum of space it didn't make a difference. Loosing half of his starboard maneuvering thrusters along with the wing, however, did.

"Hold it together!" Flea shouted. "Not much further!"

Another blast took off his port tail-fin and half the cross-wing that connected it to the starboard fin.

"Angel!" Flea said. "Please, baby! I need shields! Hold us together!"

"I don't know what to do!" she cried. "I have no more energy I can give!"

"Please, Angel," Flea said desperately. "I love you, please help me!"

In the center of the cockpit windshield at the bottom was Angel's research screen. Whenever she looked anything up in the computer, did any calculations or rerouted any power a message would appear there to let Flea know what was happening. It was filled with equations and charts for the fighter's power systems. They flashed by at blinding speeds. Angel's mind was incredibly fast.

"I can't find anything!" she cried.

Another shot cut a hole through the nose. Flea struggled valiantly to stay on course.

"Hold on!" she said sounding desperate. "I have to find something!"

Messages flashed by at a mind jarring pace. Flea thought he saw the three rules that governed artificial intelligence flash by. He wasn't certain, though, because he could only pick out a few words. He saw the word "faith" followed by "love" and "trust." More words flashed by. What she was trying to do dawned on Flea as he watched the messages. Angel was praying. The last word he saw was "Amen." The screen went blank.

"I have to go now, love" she said softly. "I know what I have to do."

"Angel?" Flea intoned. "What's happening?"

"Remember," she sounded serene. "I am part of you."

"Baby," Flea cried. "Wait!"

"I love you," she said. "I have to go."

Angel blinked out of existence.

"Angel?" Flea asked.

No response.

"Angel!" Flea shouted.

Still she gave no response.

Flea got his shields back. He wasn't sure where the power was coming from. The shield strength was reading three hundred percent of full power. Flea knew it was impossible. It could not be three hundred percent. There was no way that could happen. He was alone in his cockpit, now. He hated the lonely feeling. He made it to a small area clear of fighters between the bridge and the wall of Goraan. The other three were battered and hurting, but they made it out too.

"Break off, now!" Flea barked.

Morgan, Kaida and Pesha broke in three different directions. Flea went full throttle and aimed the nose of his fighter at the bridge. He blazed his guns on the way in. Not a single shot went inside the bridge. They uselessly struck the hull around it. Flea was vaguely aware that the first Goraan battleship had made it through and half of another was on its through now.

"This is it," Flea thought.

He went careening into the bridge. His fighter jostled around inside it like a ping pong ball. His cockpit window shattered. He heard the spine twisting "screech" of metal dragging across metal. It hurt his ears and made the hair on his neck stand up. His brain rattled around in his head like a walnut in a tin can. Suddenly his chest was on fire. His vision blurred.

"Die!" he heard a voice in front of him.

"Get off, puny fool!" another shouted.

Flea looked up. Two Goraan were fighting in front of him. They didn't seem to notice him at first. One looked like Banach. In Flea's foggy mind, he knew it couldn't be, though, because Banach was in his fighter. This must be another Rankorack. They all looked the same to him. The other looked like a small white cross between a man and an octopus. Some of its arms were gone. They were fighting on the ceiling. That seemed somehow strange, but his brain was moving slowly and he couldn't figure out why. It was hard to see. He couldn't see anything out of his right eye. He reached up and took off his helmet. Moving made his chest hurt more than it already did. He tossed his helmet and gloves in the lounge area behind the seat. It sounded like they landed on one of the lights. That didn't make sense either. The lights were in the ceiling. Flea reached up to his right eye. He pulled his hand back and saw a mass of blood and small bits of flesh. His eye was probably ruined. The blood dripped toward the ceiling.

"Oh," he thought. *"That must be why I can't see out of it."*

He looked down past his hand. A large piece of jagged metal was jutting through the cockpit window. It went through the center of his chest.

"Ah," Flea thought groggily. *"That's why my chest hurts."*

Flea craned his neck and looked up. Drops of blood were dripping upward past his face. A pool was forming over his head.

"I must be upside down," he finally figured it out.

He gripped his bare right hand around his flight stick. The two Goraan finally looked up and noticed him.

"What is this?" the large Rankorack shouted after he threw the small octopus man away.

He started to walk toward Flea. The octopus creature launched himself back at the Rankorack and wrapped himself around his head.

"We're not done!" it clacked with its black beak.

Flea pulled the trigger on his flight stick. Nothing happened.

"No," Flea whispered. "Not like this."

Flea remembered he had two guns at his hips. He pulled them out, pointed, and pulled the triggers. Nothing happened. He knew he had forgotten a step. He holstered them and thought about what to do next.

"Turn it on," he slurred. "Need to start it."

Flea struggled to reach up and extend the antennas on either side of his head. The guns turned on. He pulled them back out. They vibrated menacingly in his hands. His chest started spurting forth blood around the metal sticking through it. The guns were set to "charged shot." Flea liked that setting. He raised his arms. Large balls of purple energy were being summoned at the ends of the barrels. Flea slowly and deliberately let the hate fill him inside. His chest burned even more as he called on his own hatred. He hated these two in front of him. They took his home. They killed his family. They took his life. They destroyed everything he loved.

"Damn you all, you rotten bastards!" Flea coughed up blood as he spoke.

They took his Angel. Flea hated them all for that.

"Stop it!" the Rankorack shouted. "It will kill us all! Vile Hoo-man!!"

The balls of energy had gotten so large that if the windshield wasn't already gone, it would have melted off the front of the fighter.

"No!" shouted the other one desperately. "This is not how it's supposed to be! Wretched Hoo-man!!"

Flea painfully filled his lungs with air. His body hurt so much that it felt as if he were experiencing all the pain of birth, life and death all in one singular moment. Blood was spurting from his chest around the piece of metal, now. The white creature launched himself at Flea's cockpit to try and stop him. The Rankorack was close behind. Flea didn't care. He hated them. He just wanted them to die.

"My...name...is...FLEEEAAAA!!!!" he struggled to scream loosing the air from his lungs.

Flea released the triggers. The guns spewed screeching purple hatred that arced from the ends of his barrels. The shots were so all encompassing, that they passed through and vaporized the two creatures in front of him. Their fight was over. Flea ended it for them. They both lost.

The entire room filled with an eerie purple light and the blood curdling, high pitched scream from Flea's guns. Flea had never seen anything this destructive. The shots went all the way through the bridge. They hit two large generators in the back. Flea thought they must be the shield generators. They burst into flames. Fire raced toward him reaching out as if to grab him in its burning, deathly clutches. Everything around him was exploding in flames and arcs of electricity. A powerful arc of energy burst forth from Flea's cockpit dash board and struck him in the chest. It lifted him and the entire pilot's seat off its bolts where it was secured to the fighter's floor. He landed in the lounge in a pool of his own blood. It streamed grotesquely from his chest. Everything was hot, and then just as suddenly it was silent and still. Flea rolled out of the seat. The safety harness straps were burned away. He lay on his back looking upward. He saw Angel. She was beautiful. She was more beautiful than he had ever seen her. She wore a small white tank top that showed off her belly and a pair of tight fitting, low cut jeans. Her halo glowed. Wings were spread out behind her. It was the first time she had wings. Flea thought they were cute.

"I want to sleep," Flea choked out weakly. "Please? Can I be done, now? I want to be done now. I want to go home."

"I know, love," she said. "I know."

Flea was terrified. He didn't know what was going on.

"You rest for a while," Angel said stroking his forehead. "I am with you, remember?"

Flea smiled. Her hand was soft and warm.

"I will keep you safe," she said. "I love you. We belong together."

Flea closed his eyes.

"We'll be together. I promise," Angel whispered softly to him. "No matter what happens. Always and forever."

"I love you," Flea whispered.

Everything went black.

***

"Flea!" Morgan shouted.

No answer.

"Goddamnit! Gabriel Michael Sherman you answer me!" Morgan shouted again.

"Flea!" Kaida was crying.

The Goraan Command Battleship was starting to explode violently. The shrapnel was cutting through everything. The Runners' ships were retreating as fast as they could carry themselves. Most of the Runners' fighters retreated with them. All retreated except for fifteen ArchAngels. That was all of them that were left. The Goraan battleships, including the one that made it through the gate were being destroyed. The one that was only partially through the gate had been cut in half when the gate closed.

"Flea!" shouted Kaida. "Come back! Family!"

"He's gone, Kaida!" Morgan said trying to cover up his emotion. "Let's get out of here."

"No!" shouted Kaida. "Look down there!"

Morgan looked wildly about. Then, he spotted it. Flea's fighter had been ejected viciously from the bridge by the force of the outward explosion. His fighter was absolutely ravaged. He could see where the white emergency foam had engaged to fill the holes in Flea's fighter. This kept it safe inside from the vacuum of space. The cockpit window had been covered entirely by it. He could only hope it was holding and Flea was alive inside.

"ArchAngels!" Morgan shouted. "Commander Kaida is in charge! Full retreat! Full retreat! That's an order, ladies!"

"Where are you going?" asked Pesha.

"Don't worry about me!" Morgan yelled. "Just go!"

Morgan angled his fighter toward the small floating death trap that had once been Flea's fighter. He threw himself at top speed toward his friend.

"No!" shouted Morgan gritting his teeth. "Not this time! I won't lose anyone else!"

"Morgan," said the black wolf that occupied his fighter's computer. "This is madness! It is self destructive! I cannot support these actions!"

"Can it, Ayita!" Morgan shouted at his computer. "I won't lose anyone else! Not again!"

"Is this what he would want?" Ayita asked.

"No!" replied Morgan. "But I don't care!"

"I will not allow this," the black wolf said calmly. "I must keep you safe."

Morgan pulled out his gun and pointed it at the cockpit control panel, "Allow it or I'll kill us both!"

"But my programming…" objected Ayita.

"Stuff it!" Morgan shouted. "Your job is to help me! Do it!"

"Very well," she relented.

Morgan made it to Flea's fighter. He fired his grappling cable at it. It found the other fighter's hull and attached itself securely. Morgan started to pull Flea's ship. He wasn't making much headway with it.

"This isn't working," Ayita pointed out calmly.

Morgan was losing his confidence. He was starting to think they might not make it out, when suddenly another grappling cable went whizzing past his port side and attached to Flea's fighter. Morgan looked out the window and saw Kaida's Dragon fighter.

"Family," she cried. "I…I am not…done…yet."

They started to move a little faster with both fighters pulling together. Another grappling cable joined them. It was the leopard spotted fighter of Pesha.

"I have lost enough of those I care about today," her voice was thick with emotion. "I will not lose another."

The three of them kept pulling. Shrapnel and explosions were all around them. It was hard to move attached together as they were. Most of the time when something came at them, they just got hit. Another grappling cable joined.

"I thought I told you to leave!" Morgan shouted.

Another cable joined. He was laughing and crying at the same time.

"We ignored you," Pesha said. "Get used to it. We ignore Flea all the time. He just doesn't know it."

Another cable joined them.

"You'll all be brought up on charges for this," Morgan tried to sound confident for their sake.

Another cable flew by and attached to the fighter. Soon, all the remaining ArchAngels were present, ignoring Morgan's order and pulling Flea's fighter. They were ignoring the explosions and the shrapnel that flew around them. Morgan thought they weren't going to make it. Another cable attached itself from a fighter Morgan recognized. It was Banach.

"Need help?" Banach growled. "I spotted you down here and came as fast as I could."

"Pull with all you got!" Morgan shouted as he fired his thrusters.

Then, just as the violence seemed to overwhelm them, they were overtaken by a black sea of peaceful calmness. Morgan looked around. They made it out. He didn't know how long they had been.

"Ayita!" Morgan shouted. "Locate the nearest friendly vessel!"

"Stay at your current heading and speed," she replied. "You should overtake the *Pirate Queen* in three minutes."

"Really?" Morgan sounded relieved. "The *Queen*?"

"Yes," replied Ayita. "The *Pirate Queen*."

"Establish a comm link!" Morgan shouted.

"Link established," Ayita said after a short moment.

"*Pirate Queen*," Morgan barked. "This is Admiral Morgan Mendenhall! Prepare for emergency docking! We have wounded! Have medical staff report to the hanger bay! Now!"

"Sweetie!" it was Alex's voice. "What happened?"

"Alex!" Morgan sounded better. "I thought you had…"

"I know," she finished. "I was hurt pretty bad, but Rebecca was on it. If she wasn't here I would have…"

"I know," Morgan cut her off.

"What happened?" she sounded tired. "We fired all our missiles. How did you do that?"

"Flea," said Morgan choking up. "He…I couldn't stop him."

"Oh no," she whispered starting to get emotional.

"Wife," Morgan sobbed. "He's family…"

"I know," she said.

"I have him with me," Morgan said softly. "I saw him go in. We're pulling him behind us. We're all banged up. It took all of us to get him out."

"The *Pirate Queen* is slowing to meet us," Ayita said.

"Just bring him on board, honey," she said soothingly.

"Bring him home."

20

Morgan and the ArchAngels hit the emergency releases on their grappling cables as they approached the Pirate Queen. Flea's fighter coasted into the hanger bay of the carrier. They aimed it a few feet above the deck. Its momentum carried it in from the blackness of space. After it got inside it dropped like a ton of bricks as the artificial gravity took it. It bounced a few times before it started to roll across the deck of the hanger bay. It trailed sparks, jagged metal and chunks of hardened white emergency foam behind it until it came to a halt in the middle of the empty hanger bay. It may not have been the most ideal of landings, but they didn't know what else to do. They hadn't exactly planned for this.

Morgan, Banach, and the ArchAngels landed their fighters in the hanger bay after dropping Flea's. The entire group looked awful. They were covered with grime. Some were wounded. They all had a slick sheen of sweat on them. They looked and smelled like they had been beaten with a sack full of dead skunks. As each of them landed, they ran to Flea's fighter to help the maintenance robots chip away the hardened emergency foam. They pounded on it with tools, smartphones, shot at it, and even clawed at it with bare hands. Morgan was the last to touch down. He got out of his fighter and ran toward Flea's crunched mess of a vessel.

"Move!" he shouted.

Morgan pulled out his gun and pointed it at the white shell. He blasted at it causing chunks to fly from and cracks to form in the white foam. The ArchAngels started to lodge things into the cracks Morgan was making and tried to rip the shell open. It was slow going. Banach was pounding with his huge claws and trying to rip the shell apart, but was having little success. It wasn't coming off in very big pieces. Kaida finally jumped back a few feet and stood in a martial arts stance that Morgan didn't recognize. He didn't know she had this skill. She was crying as she pulled back and struck with her tiny, open palm. Her scream as she struck was furious and emotional. The foam burst in all directions. They could see inside the fighter. It was full of twisted metal and arcing, ruined electrical equipment. The smelled of blood was everywhere.

"Where is he?" Morgan shouted.

He found Flea lying very still against a ravaged purple and gold couch.

"Get back!" Morgan shouted.

He tried to get inside, but was too big to fit past the twisted steel to get to him. It seemed like everything was covered in thick, red blood. Morgan didn't know the body had that much blood in it. This had all come from Flea.

"Kaida!" Morgan shouted.

Kaida quickly responded. Morgan didn't need to explain, she already knew what to do. She was smaller than Morgan. She crawled through the twisted and torn environment and made her way to Flea. Morgan was surprised the tiny girl could pick him up and carry him. She passed him out to Morgan and started to crawl back out. Morgan delicately placed him on the deck of the hanger bay. He squatted down next to him. Flea's breathing was very shallow. His pupils were dilated. It was shocking that he still lived.

"Flea!" shouted Morgan.

He didn't respond. His eyes were shut. Morgan opened them. They were glazed over.

"Flea!" cried Kaida. "Don't go!"

She was holding his head in her lap.

"You promised you wouldn't leave," Armina sobbed. "You said you'd take care of me!"

"Sorry, kitten," Flea whispered.

Flea stopped breathing.

"Flea!" shouted Morgan.

"You promised!" Armina shouted at Flea's still form. "You can't go! Not, yet!"

"GRAAAAWWWWW!!!" Banach's scream was deafening.

He turned for the first time and noticed the stunned medical crew standing there with his wife and Rebecca.

"Do something!" he shouted at them.

"Fix him!" Armina cried as she pointed to her guardian.

"I..." Rebecca looked at Morgan.

It was obvious the ArchAngels were beyond reasoning with.

"He's gone, Alex," she had turned to the Captain of the battle carrier. "There's nothing I can do. He's really bad. Most of my resources and supplies have been used up by the members of the ship's crew that were injured in the attempted boarding. I have nothing left. He's gone."

"Rebecca," Alex whispered sadly.

"Bring...him...back," Armina cried through gritted teeth.

She snatched one of Morgan's guns from his holster and was pointing it at Rebecca. Tears streaked down her cheeks.

"Armina!" Rebecca sounded stunned.

Kaida drew her gun as well and pointed it at Rebecca. Banach relieved his small hand cannon from its holster and drew it at her as well.

"Help him!" Armina said desperately. "Now!"

Armina stared angrily at Rebecca. She pulled her lips back in a fearsome, yet still crying snarl and hissed.

"You're supposed to be a Doctor!" she accused refusing to put her gun down. "So, fix him!"

Rebecca stood there for a moment with her mouth open staring at the three. The other ArchAngels formed up in a small pack around Morgan and the others. They stared hatefully at Rebecca and drew their side arms. They aimed at the Doctor. Morgan finally pulled his other gun and pointed at her as well.

"You have two seconds to get moving," Morgan said darkly. "Or he won't be the only one dead in the hanger bay."

"Honey, don't," Alex said.

"Move!" barked Morgan. "I said to move now! At least try!"

"Fine!" shouted Rebecca. "Get back away from him, now!"

She and the medical team got down next to Flea.

"I'm not making any promises," she growled. "So shoot me if you feel like it. It won't change anything!"

Morgan, Kaida, and the small group put their guns away.

"Let's get him tended to! Put him on the stretcher and take him to medical," she said. "Move it, people! Now!"

***

Flea opened his eyes. He was sitting on his couch holding his Xbox controller. His favorite game was paused on the flat screen on the other side of the living room. He was back in his small apartment. Everything had a slightly white and hazy cast to it as he looked around. He rubbed his eyes briefly to see if it might help to clear his vision. He was wearing a pair of loose faded jeans and a blue tee shirt. His vision slowly cleared, but everything still felt slightly off. He went to the fridge to get a Mountain Dew. He opened the door and looked inside, trying to remember the last time he went grocery shopping. The fridge was fully stocked.

"Cool," he said.

His voice carried a slight echo for some reason. This added to the slightly off feeling. He took a few drinks and went into the bathroom. He had to pee. It felt like he had been "holding it" for hours. He washed his hands when he was done and looked in the mirror. His reflection's purple eyes flashed back at him. He stuck his tongue out and made a goofy face. Making faces in the mirror was something he hadn't done in a while. It was something he usually did when he was happy. For some reason, despite the fact that everything felt slightly off, Flea was extremely happy right now. It seemed as if he hadn't remembered what it was like to be happy until now. Flea walked back into the living room.

"Oh my God!" he exclaimed looking out the patio window.

In front of Flea's apartment was a Mitsubishi Lancer. From the look of it, the car was not stock.

"That is the coolest thing I have ever seen in my life!" he exclaimed.

It was low to the ground. It was painted a shade of purple with gold trim Flea easily recognized. It was painted like a smaller version of Flea's fighter complete with Angels. He became suddenly aware of a key chain poking his thigh in his front pocket. He pulled it out. It was one key, attached to a car alarm and remote start controller. He ran outside through the patio door. He wasn't wearing shoes. The grass felt good in between his toes. He looked up at the sky. It was the most gorgeous shade of blue he had ever seen. A few white fluffy clouds floated around happily in the sky. It seemed like ages since he had seen the sky. He pointed the car alarm remote at the vehicle and pressed the button to kill the alarm.

Chirp! Chirp!

The alarm shut off in response.

"You mean that thing is mine?" Flea shouted excitedly. "This is the most awesome day of my life!"

Flea walked around the back of it to the trunk. He opened it up and saw a giant speaker box with the word: Angel-Woofer, *written on it. He closed the trunk and took a step back. The license plate was a vanity plate. It had "ARKNJL1" written on it. For some reason, it had some large cracks in quite a few places. One particularly large crack ran the entire length of the plate through the letters. There were seams of solder material in the cracks to hold the plate together. Flea didn't know if this meant anything. He was still too happy. There was something missing, though.*

"Where's Angel?" he asked suddenly.

He pushed the button on the remote with the door on it. The driver's side door unlocked and slowly flipped upward to mimic a Lamborghini. Flea jumped in. He started the car which let off a low gratifying rumble. All the gauges on the dashboard had been backlit with a soft purple glow. The odometer had zero miles on it. That didn't make sense. Even new cars on the lot had test drive miles on them at the very least. Flea smiled and decided to stop thinking about these things. He was too busy enjoying the soft rumbling bass of the exhaust pipes as he sat there idling.

He pulled away from the apartment complex and stopped at the light in front of it. He revved the engine and laid rubber on the asphalt with a boyish exuberance. He listened to the engine's satisfying hisses and swooshing noises as he tore up the pavement. He was going to find his Angel. It didn't seem right without her.

***

"Come on Flea!" Rebecca shouted. "I know you can fight harder than this! I've seen you do it!"

She began to pound on his chest. His sternum cracked a few times as she did this. She was becoming too emotional for her patient. It wasn't like her to do this.

"I need more cells!" she shouted. "I pulled something out of his heart and it's not going to start until we add some more tissue! How's his brain?"

"We've used the emergency circulatory unit to keep supplying blood and oxygen to it," responded the nurse at a machine attached to Flea's skull. "I don't know what will happen, Doctor. I can't get any readings."

"We've used the few replacement cells we have left, Doctor," said another nurse. "We won't have any more until we get back to base and finish growing them!"

"There's one last thing I can try," Rebecca said calmly. "Bring over the cell reclamation unit and a really big knife."

The nurse wheeled over the device that could be used to harvest cells and tissues. She didn't have any donors or corpses handy to harvest cells from. She would have to use Flea's. She started to cut chunks of skin and muscle from Flea's left leg. It was already mangled, so he probably wouldn't notice anyway. She would have to replace most of it with cybernetic parts until they got back home and she could grow more cells. She started to feed them into the machine which stripped them down and altered them to be able to be used anywhere in the body. She fed the new cells to Flea's ruined heart and began to patch it up. It was starting to rebuild, but it was taking up an abnormally large amount of cells. Something had changed in Flea's biology she couldn't explain and didn't have time to look into. She needed to hurry because he had been dead now for an unusually long time. He could already be at risk for brain damage, despite what they were doing. She was not even certain if she could even resuscitate him at this point. She continued to work and pray. She hoped it was enough.

***

Angelina Bonita Isabella Santiago looked up and saw the sky. It was the first time she ever set eyes on it. It was gorgeous. She smiled and started to cry. She was happy. She wore a small white tank top that bared the muscles of her taught abdomen and a pair tight, denim jeans with a very low waist. She was lying on her back in the grass in some park. At least she thought it was a park. She wasn't exactly sure. She looked around and saw a large red, metal structure that was supposed to be someone's version of art work.

"Grass!" she said wiggling her bare feet. "This is what it feels like! This is incredible!"

She giggled excitedly. She never had a real body before. The wind blew slowly through her hair and kissed the back of her neck. She walked in front of the red structure and stood next to a road sign that said "Speed Limit 35" on it. The sign was much taller than she. Angel decided she was probably around five feet tall.

"I'm not sure where I am," she giggled musically. "But someone could have made me a bit taller!"

She decided to try and access her files and see where she was.

"Where are my files?" she panicked. "I can't get to them!"

"Where am I?" she asked.

She noticed a sign on the building that was behind a metal, artistic structure. It read: Fort Wayne Museum of Art.

"You're in Fort Wayne, Indiana, miss," said a high pitched voice from behind her. "I thought you might like it."

Angel turned and saw a tiny, little girl. She couldn't be more than seven years old. It was hard to tell. Her eyes seemed somehow older. She had long blonde hair that went down to her waist. She was thin and pretty. She was wearing a pair of denim shorts with white socks and red Converse All Star high top sneakers. On her head was a backward red baseball hat. Her grey tee shirt had Property of Indiana University Athletics Dept: XXX-Small *printed on it in red letters. She was rocking her foot back and forth on top of a basketball. She leaned over and picked it up.*

"Would you like to play?" the girl asked holding out the ball with a giggle. "In Indiana, everyone plays! I love this game!"

She smiled at Angel. It was the kind of smile that made you feel special and included. Angel started to feel warm.

"Who are you?" Angel asked in her thick accent.

"I'm a friend," giggled the little girl. "Don't worry Angel, everything will be fine."

Angel smiled at her. She started to feel like this little girl was right. Everything was going to be fine. They walked over to a nearby parking lot with a basketball court. The little girl handed Angel the ball.

"Here, Angel," said the girl showing Angel how to hold it. "Like this."

Angel held it as indicated.

"Now aim for the back of the rim and follow through when you shoot," she said.

Angel took a shot. The net hanging from the rim made a gratifying swishing noise as the ball went through.

"Very good!" encouraged the little girl giggling with excitement. "You're a natural!"

"Why am I here?" Angel asked.

"Oh my goodness," the little girl giggled. "I get asked that so many times!"

Angel looked confused by this cryptic answer.

"It's a place where all the good people come," the little girl said. "I make sure of it."

"To Fort Wayne, Indiana?" asked Angel.

"Some of them," she chuckled. "Some people prefer other places. I had you come here."

"Huh?" Angel shook her head.

She was kind of confused as this point.

"Don't worry," giggled the little girl. "You won't remember any of this anyway. That's the way I make it work. Just remember I'm on your side. I believe in you, okay?"

Angel smiled her most beautiful of smiles for the little girl.

"You know," piped the little girl. "You're the first one I made with a computer! It turned out pretty good, I think."

Angel was confused by this comment. The little girl giggled and smiled knowingly.

"Turn around now, miss," the little girl said pointing down the street behind Angel. "And wave. Don't forget to smile. He likes it when you smile."

Angel turned around. A small purple car came careening violently around the corner sliding out into the middle of the street. The noise it made chewed up the tranquility of this peaceful place like a ravaging dog.

"Uhhg," the little girl said making a face as if her mother was forcing her to eat Brussels sprouts. "Why does he have to do that?"

The car was painted like the ArchAngel one. Angelina waived. It skidded to a halt inches in front of her. The door swung upward to open.

"Angel!" Gabriel shouted as he jumped from the car.

"Gabriel!" Angel shouted through her sudden tears. "My love!"

They flew into each other's arms. She could feel him. For the first time, she could feel the texture of his skin and softness of his hair. She could smell his scent in her nose. He smelled like love.

"I love you," he whispered as he clutched her tightly.

She could feel his hot breath on her ear. She cried. This was the most incredible day of her entire existence. It was the happiest she had ever been.

"Is this heaven?" Gabriel asked.

"Not quite," giggled the little girl. "But I hope you like it anyway. It's here just for you guys."

She had forgotten about the little girl for a moment. Angel turned around to the girl. She was gone.

"Come on!" Gabriel said excitedly wiping away tears. "Let's go! I want to show you everything!"

He rushed her over to the passenger's side of the car and opened the door for her. He held her hand and helped her inside even though she didn't need it. His hand was soft and warm with a confident grip. He closed the door and ran to the other side of the car and got in. He turned over the engine and Angel felt it vibrate through the floor.

"Wait," she said. "I always wanted to try this."

She leaned over and lightly touched the inside of his thigh with one hand. He inhaled sharply when she touched him. He started to blush. He smiled like a naughty school boy. She leaned in and placed her other hand on the small of his back. He arched his back slightly at her touch. She slowly leaned in toward his ear. Her hot breath sent chills of anticipation down his spine. She lightly pressed her soft, wet lips to his earlobe. He shuddered with pleasure. His eyes glazed over for a moment. She leaned back out and kissed him on the mouth. It was a single perfect moment of bliss. She pulled back and looked deeply in his eyes. He was breathing heavily.

"Perfect," she whispered. "Absolutely perfect."

He smiled at her. She never wanted this to end.

"You wanted to show me something?" she asked.

He looked around to see if anyone was watching.

"It can wait," he said noticing they were alone. "I love you. Let's just be here together."

"I will always be with you," she said. "I am part of you, remember? I love you."

"I know," he said.

***

Flea's eyes shot open. The reality of pain, strife and agony flooded into his skull. He was screaming. He didn't know where he was or what he was doing. He didn't recognize anything. The entire world hurt. Everything in his life in this instant was full of vile pain and torment. His mind cleared up just enough so he could wish for death.

"Angel!" he gasped.

He reached out toward the ceiling above him as if he were trying to reach her. He stretched with all the desperation he could find inside himself. It was as if he believed if he stretched far enough, he could somehow bring her back. He passed out.

When Flea opened his eyes again, he was no longer in too much physical pain. Inside though, he felt like his heart was broken. It was as if part of his soul had been amputated and discarded like useless waste. His chest felt hollow and empty. He knew something resided inside his ribcage, but whatever it was, it felt cold, blackened, and shriveled. He missed his Angel. He looked up at the ceiling. He must be on his back. Everything looked strange. It was as if everything was slightly off center. He reached up to rub his eyes. He felt a small, cold, metal plate where his right eye should be. He pulled his hand back and noticed that a bunch of the flesh was gone and replaced with metal in various places. His thumb, middle finger, pinky finger and part of his palm that connected the three were metal.

"The Doctor said it should grow back in a week or two," Flea heard Morgan's voice thick with emotion. "The eye, I mean.

She didn't have enough cells to finish it, but she did get it started. She's not sure if she can replace the rest later with new cells or not. She says she needs to do more tests. At least you're alive, though. Worry about the rest later, right?"

"Hey," Flea mumbled a greeting. "Thanks. The rest? How much is the rest?"

Flea looked down and saw part of his left leg sticking out. He had a metallic knee cap and some spots in his thigh and shin had been replaced. The big toe and the two smaller outside toes on his left foot were replaced. Flea's eye suddenly got very big. He stuck his hand under the blanket between his legs. He sighed in relief to discover everything was "normal." Morgan laughed at him and shed a few tears.

"I really…I just…," Morgan started to say. "You know?"

"I know," Flea smiled at his faithful comrade. "It's cool. We're cool."

He sat up a bit and looked around the room. Flea was apparently not the only one that got hurt. Armina and Kaida were spooning at the foot of Flea's bed with Kaida's arms wrapped protectively around the kitten. They were sleeping. Armina had bandages on her arm and around her head. A small white glass cube was on top of her head covering her right ear. It was filled with a thick white fluid. Kaida had bandages around her right hand. Alex was sleeping as she sat up in a chair. She had bandages on her head and face. A much larger glass rectangular box encompassed her left arm. Morgan's temples were wrapped up and his right wrist as well. He was sitting down holding his daughter, who had apparently broken her right arm. Pesha was in the corner asleep in another chair. She had broken her tail at some point. It was a very painful injury for a Kashin. Banach was snoring softly on the floor next to the bed. Flea was surprised to see him. He thought Rankorack were supposed to be solitary. Toren was there as well. She was asleep next to Alex. The whole group looked like it was exhausted and thoroughly beaten.

"You should see the other guys," Morgan said as he watched Flea survey the room full of his family.

"Did we win?" asked Flea.

"Yeah," Morgan said. "We bled some. We bled a lot, actually. But, we still won. The rest of the Runners cleaned up while we tended our wounded. We were the only ship to get boarded. They focused on us because it's their way to take down the biggest threat first."

"How many are left?" Flea grunted.

"ArchAngels?" Morgan asked.

"Yeah," Flea said.

"Including you, me, and Kaida here," he said. "Sixteen."

Sixteen out of thirty two.

"We left one of them alive," Morgan said. "We killed every last one of those Goraan slug bastards except one. We picked him up in an escape pod. We threw him in the brig until we can figure out what to do with him."

"Good," said Flea harshly. "He can rot in Hell down there for all I care."

"At least you seem to have maintained your good spirits," Morgan joked.

Kaida started to stir on the foot of his bed. She looked up and saw that he was awake.

"Flea!" she shouted.

She woke everyone else up when she shouted. She and Armina jumped up and threw their arms around him. Everyone else got up and huddled around the bed.

"Oww!" Flea said laughing in pain. "Careful! I just almost died!"

"What do you mean almost?" asked Alex. "You were pretty dead when you got here, you know?"

"Thanks for bring me back," he nodded to her.

"Never do that again!" shouted Armina angrily. "You promised to look out for me! You can't do that again!"

She was crying. Flea squeezed her tightly.

"Never again!" she shouted and pounded his chest briefly.

Flea caught her arms and started to hug her and Kaida again.

"What happened to you, kitten?" Flea said. "You're all chewed up!"

"She was on the bridge after I told her not to be," Alex said. "She and Keri showed up in the middle of a fight. I decided not to ground Keri. Her injuries ought to be punishment enough."

Flea listened as Armina intently told her side of the story. They sat there for a while talking about what they had each been through during the battle. They enjoyed the company of friends as they told their gruesome stories.

"Then I crashed into the bridge," Flea said. "The next thing I know, I'm waking up here with one eye and a bunch of pieces missing."

"You don't remember anything?" Alex said.

"Not a thing," Flea shook his head.

"Here," Morgan said holding out his fist. "Maybe this will help."

Flea held out his hand. Morgan dropped a sturdy looking military chain in it with something that resembled a curved black claw as big as Flea's palm on it.

"What's this?" Flea asked. "Some kind of claw?"

"No," said Rebecca as she walked in the room. "It's not. I came when the nurses said they started to hear some commotion in this place. I see your doing better than when you got here."

"Rebecca...I," Morgan said.

Flea watched the two in a curious exchange of embarrassed looks.

"It's okay," Rebecca said. "We were all a little emotional today."

"Are you feeling okay?" she asked Flea. "A lot of people want to know."

"I'm a little groggy," Flea said. "But, I'm not dead yet."

"Not anymore, you mean," Rebecca corrected. "You're not dead anymore. I brought you back."

"Yeah," Flea grumbled. "Thanks for that, I think."

Rebecca nodded. She seemed pleased.

"So, what is it?" Flea asked dangling the necklace.

"It's part of the beak from one of these," she said showing Flea a picture on her smartphone of a white creature that looked like a cross between a man and an octopus. "Morgan polished it up so it looked nice, and put it on a chain, I see."

"Where did you get it?" Flea asked looking at Morgan.

"From your heart," Rebecca said calmly. "I pulled it out of your heart. It should have killed you."

Flea was stunned. He put it around his neck.

"For luck," he said.

There was a long period of silence.

"Did you get my fighter?" Flea asked. "Did you bring back my Angel?"

"We won't be able to save it," Morgan said. "It's in the hanger bay. It's a mess. The maintenance robots are supposed to take it apart and salvage what they can. Otherwise, it's junk now."

"No!" Flea shouted.

He started to get out of bed. Rebecca pushed him back down.

"Calm down!" she said.

"Kaida! Pesha! Toren!" Flea barked. "Get down there and tear apart any stupid robot that touches Angel!"

Kaida bolted from the room followed closely by Pesha and Toren. Banach left quickly behind them.

"He's alive!" Kaida shouted. "To the hanger bay! Shoot maintenance robots, now!"

Flea heard a flurry of running footsteps and saw a group of people run past the door with Kaida. It was the remaining members of the ArchAngels. They were waiting for him.

"Just calm down a moment, okay?" Rebecca said. "Let me check you over, first."

She asked him some questions. He told her he felt okay. She used an x-ray app on her smartphone to look him over.

"You can go," she said. "But try and take it easy. Those cybernetic parts are something new we came up with ourselves. I'm not exactly certain if we can take them out when we get more replacement cells."

Flea's friends left the room so he could get dressed. He looked himself over in the mirror. White bandages were taped to his forehead and right cheek under his eye. He lifted them slightly to see what was underneath. A wide slash started in the middle of his forehead, curved through the center of his right eye. It would leave a terrible scar all the way to the middle of his right cheek. It was stitched up. Rebecca must not have had the cells to repair it. She mentioned something about needing more cells. Flea strapped on his blasters that were on a small table next to his bed. Someone must have found them for him. He walked outside and was joined by his waiting friends. As he made his way with them to the hanger bay, he noticed signs of battle all over the ship. Black scars decorated the walls. He saw a few holes that went through the hull to show the blackness of the outside beyond. They were protected from the vacuum of space by an invisible emergency shield.

"This place looks rough," Flea said.

"Yeah," Alex said with a sidelong glance. "None of us are clean anymore. Every one of us has a scar after this."

"I know," Flea replied quietly. "We all have scars. What counts is how we wear them."

Flea made it to the hanger bay. The remaining ArchAngels were circled protectively around his ruined fighter. The remains of some blasted maintenance robots were smoking on the deck. Other maintenance robots seemed intent on trying to get by and start on Flea's fighter. Apparently, they weren't smart enough to learn from the other robots' mistakes. Banach was in the process of throwing four of them at once out into the blackness of space. Flea started to pull out his blasters, but stopped and changed his mind.

"I just don't have it in me, right now." he said looking at his Hate Blasters.

He walked over and stood in front of the maintenance robots.

"Do you know who I am?" Flea asked it sternly.

"Captain Gabriel Sherman," It responded.

"They call me Flea," he said calmly. "And I want you all to stay away from my fighter or I'll blast you. Do this on my authority, or you will be violently dismantled by a large, angry Rankorack. Do you understand?"

"Yes, sir," it replied.

The maintenance robots withdrew. The ArchAngels huddled around their leader. Some cried. Some laughed. They were all happy to see him.

"We stop them!" Kaida sounded pleased. "No robots!"

"I see that, Kaida," Flea said. "Thank you."

The ArchAngels had turned the scene into a large group hug. They missed their fallen comrades. They loved the ones that lived. Life and death would be celebrated together.

"Can I have a moment?" Flea sounded tired as he spoke to them. "I'll be fine, ladies. I promise."

They all nodded silently and withdrew from their captain. Flea was left alone in the hanger with his ship. Kaida and Armina stayed behind in case he needed something.

"Angel," Flea whispered.

He reached out to the wreckage of his fighter. He hesitated briefly before touching it. Flea sank to his knees and started to cry. Armina squirmed under his arm and put her tiny, furry arms around him. He held her as he cried. Armina started to cry, too.

"Angel," Flea whispered. "No."

Kaida walked up behind him and sank to her knees. She wrapped her delicate arms around Flea and Armina. She rested her head on Flea's back. Kaida began to cry, too. The three shuddered with their sobs.

"Angel," Flea whispered. "I love you."

Flea sat with his small family. He wanted to be strong in front of them. He tried to keep from crying, but he couldn't do it this time. The universe was an empty ball of soulless garbage. It was a greedy son of a bitch that had stole his family, his home and now his Angel. He didn't hate the universe for this. He was too tired to hate. It took too much energy to hate. However, he definitely didn't like it. He missed his Angel. He needed her. He wanted her back but she was gone. His head began to pound.

Flea didn't want to do this anymore. He was getting a headache.

###